THE COURTS
OF
ILLUSION

THE COURTS
OF ILLUSION

Rosemary Hawley Jarman

LITTLE, BROWN AND COMPANY · BOSTON · TORONTO

In memory of Sarah Hawley,
who gave me the words

LIBRARY OF CONGRESS CATALOG CARD NO. 83-80792

FIRST AMERICAN EDITION

MV

PRINTED IN THE UNITED STATES OF AMERICA

Part I

1490

'I am thy evil genius, Brutus,
and thou shalt see me at Philippi.'

Plutarch: *Lives*

I even remember the weather, that morning when my bad angel asked me to go to Bart's Fair with him. A May sun through the glass window, sparkling clean after a night of rain. Edmund had opened the shutters before he left the house, and the sun washed my pillow and face, drying tears shed in the last dream before dawn.

Rolling my head away from the brilliance I lay still. Faintly I heard St Paul's bell strike seven. In the calm morning its great voice reached as far as our house in Watling Street. I had slept late again. The bed's other half was empty; my brother, as always, had risen before the sun. A mug of ale and the heel of a loaf had been left for me by a servant. This sounds grand and lordly, only the bread was stale, the ale first cousin to water, and the servant one of the mere handful supported by a pittance in my mother's household.

I had been dreaming of Bedesman, and I wondered for a moment whether it was shameful for a grown man to weep over a horse. But, with the dream's bitterness lingering, I saw no dishonour in crying for a beloved friend. Even Christ mourned for the sparrows. Bedesman had been my father's Saint's Day gift. I had broken him myself to the jewelled bridle and saddle. In the dream he had had full dimension: the feel of his hide like oiled damask and of a colour I had never seen in any other horse, so light a chestnut it was more like butter against the black mane and tail. And the little black hoofs like shells, and even his hot fragrance of grass and sweet sweat. It had been Bedesman, with his dark full dreaming eyes who had listened, my true Bedesman into whose velvet muzzle I had wept, the night of my father's execution. His hide had been perfect, without a mark, and his soft mouth could have carried an egg. He had borne me bravely to Leicester, five years earlier, to watch my father die. Was Bedesman's hide perfect now?

I could still see the arrogant face of the young lord who had bought him, haggling over the price but finally conceding his great worth, for he came of a line of Barbary Arabs and could sire equine princes. He had never known the spur. The lordling—a

9

nephew of Sir William Stanley—had mounted him. I had seen the spurs go deep. Bedesman reared and whinnied, and turned his eyes to me. I could not speak his tongue, to explain that it was evil necessity that was parting us. So I turned and walked away from the dumb creature I loved best of all.

I wiped the last of the dream away from my eyes, sat up and drank some ale. The birds were calling in the little walled garden outside. They were nesting, near the rose trees. White roses, of course. My mother would not grow the red rose of Lancaster within a league of her demesne. I came from bed and went to the window. I could see my mullioned reflection, wavering, but true enough to show, even after a bad haunted night, that I still had form and being. Tall, tow-headed Nicholas Archer, eldest child of a ruined family, all under heavy attainder. Bereft of inheritance, fame, almost of name. All because my father, at Bosworth Field, had fought on the wrong side. The loser loses all, but still I couldn't understand, even after five years, why all those men, the Household knights and esquires who rode with King Richard, should be punished together with their families as traitors, merely for upholding the man whose servants they were. Unless, perhaps, because King Henry Tudor had, with Celtic foresight, pre-dated his reign from the day before the battle. . . . if only. Then we should not now be a headless family. I should not be awakening on this rapturous May morning, sad for Bedesman. I would have starved to keep him. But I had been powerless to object; the first of the hard times was on us then, before we succumbed to charity and moved to London.

I often wished my father had fought for Henry Tudor and not for the Plantagenet cause, already lost on the battle-eve, when the secret allegiances had been made, the warning note pinned to Richard's tent, the cup poisoned with tales of infanticide, the main chance spotted by Richard's enemies—the Stanleys and Northumberland—the outcome already decided in campfire whispers. I knew better than to speak so, though. Never was I so afraid as when, at fourteen, I was unwise enough to voice my opinion, and saw my mother's giant rage—the fury of Margetta de Hauleigh. I even had to watch my thoughts on this score, for often I felt she could read me, with her grey eyes and her slim pale face and her edged tongue ready to whip my heresy. That makes her sound unkind, which isn't so. But she loved my father beyond life, and doubtless had thoughts which might have surprised my younger brother and sister and me. I think she would gladly have ridden in that suicide charge beside Sir Mark d'Archier, her husband, and Kendall and Ratcliffe and King Richard, and would with honour and grace have shared my father's scaffold. Her family motto was *Suivez moi*, and men would have followed her in ancient times. In her solar she kept King Richard's emblem and his raison of *Loyaulte me lie*. She would sit before it, her long black white-skeined hair loose, her brilliant eyes glaring, willing the embroidered words to leap from the cloth in justice, bringing back Sir Mark d'Archier and King Richard to topple the Tudor, if only as vengeful ghosts.

We all had grey eyes. I had my father's yellow hair and his height and yet it was Edmund, smaller and very dark, who people said favoured him most. That hurt me once. I recovered when they began calling me the handsome one, though I couldn't see much difference in us. The trouble was, Edmund never smiled. He had stopped smiling when he was ten years old, in Leicester market place, and it was just as if he had sold or sent the smile away, like an outgrown frippery. Last year he had closed his school books, bidden farewell to the old monk who tutored us, and gone out and apprenticed himself to a fletcher in Budge Row. My mother had been angry then, too.

'And you a knight's son!' she had cried. 'Dear Jesus! What shame!'

'An attainted knight's son,' Edmund had answered gently, and gone his own way. He called himself plain Master Archer, as, after a time, so did I. She couldn't stop him. The only proviso was that he should sleep at home, and the fletcher, noting with a sad satisfaction the White Rose in our garden, had agreed. Still malcontent, Edmund had made himself useful to a bowyer and learned that trade too in his spare time. Thereafter he set about making himself longbows of yew and elm, with unsmiling haste, as if he fancied time were his especial enemy; and he practised at the butts in Moorfields with the common people.

That was why I was alone in the bed. He would be at his trade now—or at the shooting. Eyes faultlessly trained on the target, body stressed for perfection. He had my father's eyes all right.

11

They could see over nearly half a league. We'd tested them; he could read banners, quarterings, symbols, as a hawk on a mountain marks grounded prey. They called my father 'The Man of Keen Sight'. He had spied out the enemy for Richard at Bosworth.

I opened the window to the scent of the knot garden. My sister Josina was there, the sunlight on her bare head. She looked as if she wore a shawl of gold cloth. I whistled to her softly. She was busy, bending gracefully to some puny plant, then stretching up to tie back a spray of wall germander that bordered the beds. Tall plants, with whorls of pink blossom. Her long blue sleeve fell back over her forearm revealing the white facing and the whiter flesh. She was so tiny and slender, like a fairy. The colours of her hair merged with the silver-gold leaves and flowers of the steepled agrimony. She bent again to tend a small field of flax. She was nurturing this for spinning, although what garment she could make from that little plot I couldn't imagine. Near the flax grew her wound herbs—the sphagnum moss (not thriving, the ground was too dry), the knight's pondweed with its swordshaped leaves by a little stream, the Madonna lily. A few paces away a medlar stood, with its hard round fruit that always seemed to rot before it ripened. I gazed at Josina again. Her dress clung, too tight, it was shameless with innocence. She should have been married, but she was dowerless. Yet she must marry one day. I thought: please God, let that day be far off. I whistled again. She looked up at last.

'Slug!'

'I overslept.'

'Come down. Come and help me.' A clear honey voice. I thought: if her husband, whoever he shall be, mistreats her, I will have his liver on my knife. I promise. By the tears I shed for Bedesman, this I swear.

I dressed. My linen shirt was beginning to go under the arms, my doublet patched, my hose shrunken and faded. My good leather boots were the best part of my ensemble, but unfashionable with their pointed toes. Although decent, I looked somewhat beggarly, and I cared. Unlike Edmund, who would have gone off to work in rags, concealed by his prentice's apron.

A stone wall in which gillies grew separated the garden from the street, where people were out and about. We were cut off from the worst of the noise, the iron cartwheels, the clatter of hoofs, the shouting. In Watling Street, we dwelt between other houses, most of them larger and grander. Once we had acres, deer parks and forests, with fortified towers for our security. In winter we had seen no one for months. All our estates were gone, forfeit to the Crown. The manors in Worcestershire and Kent, the farm near Middleham in the north with its noisy flowing river of sheep, a gift from King Richard. My mother's splendid litters and horses were gone, and nearly all her jewels. A hundred servants had had to go, and not all had managed to find other employment; some had taken to the roads, pushed from town to village, beaten and pilloried.

Towards the end of my childhood and of Richard's reign, when my father was in constant attendance as a knight of the bedchamber, I had lived at Westminster. His eyes were very keen those days; death and disgrace were creeping inexorably towards us all, he looked overborne and bewildered. My brother Richard was born the year before the battle. He died before he was two. My mother saw omens in it—he had been named for the king. The debts began to mount; her pride was constantly lowered in anger and shame. She had written to the Pastons at Caister and Hellesden, for they had been friends of my father since Young John Paston was seventeen, but they declined to help us. They had managed to avoid involvement in the wars and now, with their precarious fortunes finally stabilized and after years of land disputes with greedy lords, they were wary. We were pitch; they could not afford defilement. So, in despair, my mother flung herself on charity.

Josina was bending over a clump of sage, a patch of thyme; she moved as I approached, to a row of St John's Herb, growing untidily in a hairy lilac crowd. All the tall flowers and plants seemed to lean towards her like idiot children round their mother. Like Witless Walter, who spent his days on Paul's Cross among the preachers, begging passers-by with his purple, drooling mouth to answer his gibberish, and cuffed black for his efforts.

Charity had come with Sir James, my mother's great-uncle whom she hated, but he was widowed and heirless and must have had a sense of duty. 'Get you good lordship and friendship at any cost, for on this depends all the law and the prophets,' had been one of the Pastons' favourite sayings. Sir James had managed to retain his good lordships, and now had the new king's favour. He was, like many others (like my father should have been, I thought in secret), a time-server. My mother was bitterly ashamed of him. But it was either accepting his protection, or the open road, or a convent. And her grieving heart was too fierce to be cooled in a cloister.

Sir James had come to the lodging-house at Leicester where we had stayed for some months until the weeping died. He was very dignified and admonitory, although I discovered later that his ancestors were far from stainless, one being a notorious pirate. He wagged his head at my mother.

'An unlucky business, niece.'

'These are Mark's sons,' she told him. She pushed Edmund and me forward. It was some time after the battle, but still Edmund could not speak. It was weeks before he could. I bowed, and muttered.

'Yes. Unfortunate, Margetta.' He might have been talking of a lamed horse, rather than the collapse of a reign, a dynasty and fifteen hundred families. He peered at the letter she had written him.

'Your husband. He was knighted by King Richard?'

'By King Edward.' Her face was pale as the dead. 'Years ago, when first we were wed.'

This seemed to relieve Sir James. 'Hmm. Possible, given time, to petition his Majesty for a pardon . . . Richard was his mortal enemy, not King Edward.'

'Never.' Her soft voice held a scream. He clicked his tongue. Finally he agreed to lease to her the house in Watling Street, to provide her with a small income, and at some future date, a dowry for Josina. So far the latter promise remained unfulfilled. (Josina was not with us that day, nor on the day of death, for which I never ceased to thank God. She had a fever and had stayed with the monks at the Abbey of St Mary, east of Leicester.) I suppose Sir James was kind—or was it a salve for his conscience; he had suffered no tragedy. At any event, we were out of debt (although indebted) and the whole transaction was like a running sore in my mother's pride.

The mansion in Watling Street was small but fair. It boasted windows of glass, not horn, an ornately carved frontage with gables and pentices, and Sir James's arms carved above the front door. It had an oak staircase and a pretty solar, gable-rooms for the servants, an east-facing bedchamber for Edmund and me, while Josina and her old nurse, Dame Philip, shared the room next to ours. There were stables and a bakehouse at the back. But no good horses, for charity can only stretch so far. And no Bedesman, to whom I had said farewell at Leicester so that we could eat.

Josina stood under the rose arbour, an angel in the margin of a manuscript. I kissed her hand, stroked her hair, fine and soft with its silvery glitter. Anyone watching would have thought us lovers.

'Slug!' she said again.

'Where are they all?' The house had been very quiet, with no sound from my mother's solar, and only the faint snores of Dame Philip, who succumbed to sleep at the most unlikely hours, such as five minutes after rising.

'Mother went out. Look!' She held out a small network of leaves. 'This is the one. It cured Jankin's pain. The charm worked.

'As Christ healed the issue of blood,
'Do thou cut what thou cuttest for good.'

'Buckshorn.'

'Robin Hood's hatband.'

'*Griffe de Loup*.' I was showing off.

'Fox claw.'

'It healed Jankin.' She was skilled, like Edmund. What was I? I couldn't distil herbs or shoot straight. My eyes were ordinary. And I had wept for a horse.

'She went out early,' I said.

'A letter came, before Prime. She left a message for you.'

'Why didn't she take me with her?' Black, fierce handwriting on a little parchment directed me to Bucklersbury. Spices, wax tapers, honey, a small amount of liquorice. I would have to ask for credit. What was I? My mother's steward. My function as household head; unpaid, for stewards were costly.

'She's taken Jankin, and John.' That meant walking. There were four spavined horses, and the cob, when last I saw him, had a sore hoof, from lack of proper shoeing.

'Who sent her the letter?'

'I don't know.' Josina moved away, by the small stream, threading through the pond lilies. Pollen dusted her upraised hand. 'She was very stirred up. She said we were to have dinner without her.'

A summons from his Majesty? An invitation to petition King's Bench and have the attainder lifted? A longed-for impossibility, after all her rebel oaths. She would never bow to Henry, nor would I be able to buy back Bedesman. Josina's hand reached back and drew me on. The stream led into a round pond where a willow grew. We looked down into the water.

'Tristan!' she said.

'Up in the tree, spying out his betrayers.'

'The wicked dwarf, Frocin.'

For years I had always been Tristan. Edmund was King Mark of Cornwall. One of the little serving maids we had then took the part of faithful Brangien and later of White-Hands, whom Tristan married and who lied to him when Iseult came to fetch him away in her ship. We hadn't played it lately. We'd lost King Mark—Edmund was done with games. I had always missed out the bit where Iseult is led to the stake, then thrown to the lepers, for even in play something checked me from hurting Josina.

'What would have happened? If White-Hands hadn't lied?'

If. If only my father had fought on Tudor's side.

'They'd have sailed away, in glory.'

'I wonder what the sea's like?'

'Big,' I answered at once. 'Grey. Cliffs of water. Frightening.' The sea had once been part of my life, although none of us had ever been near the sea. My soul knew it, and not from tales or ballads. Josina still held my hand. She looked in my eyes and said: 'You're tired, Nicholas. You slept badly.'

'I dreamed.' She reached up and kissed my unshaven cheek and I held her softness. It bred a strange, unfitting memory: my one and only sight of a woman's naked breasts. Mistress Shore, doing penance through the City, crying and carrying her lighted taper at the orders of King Richard. My mother had been gleeful, for she had always hated the harlot Shore, for her treason. She said that Shore was a criminal, carrying messages to the Queen-

16

Dowager, Elizabeth Woodville, in Sanctuary, contributing with others to the ultimate downfall of my parents' lord, Richard. Later, she had been treated leniently, and did it matter? What mattered, now?

Elizabeth Woodville, the present Queen's mother, had not escaped so lightly. She now lay in the Abbey of St Saviour, Bermondsey, stripped like us of possessions and mortally ill. Through her own fault—she had upheld the pretender Lambert Simnel, acknowledging him as one of her vanished sons, a claimant of the throne. How could anyone be so foolish? We had a new king, who seemed to rule with great sadness and wisdom. There were no more battles. Why seek to change the unchangeable?

'Don't be sad,' said Josina, watching me. 'Sweet Nicholas. Such a fair morning.'

So it was, and on it I had to run errands like a slave. But suddenly, I wanted to walk, to shake this malaise. And I wanted to see someone; I needed that person at this time, even more than I needed Josina, whose sympathy fed my sadness. I wanted barbs, and laughter. Since last Christmas, I had known where to find them.

I straightened my doublet, and stepped through the door in the garden wall. Reeking London opened to swallow my soul.

There's a dark side to the City. Like the black vein of melancholy that ran in me that morning, it was there, an echo of my own malaise. After nearly five years I knew London enough to keep my purse safely hidden, when I had any money, and a stout staff to hand. I knew which streets to avoid. I followed my mother's edicts; how I should comport myself as her eldest son, her steward, and, although I could never think of myself thus, head of the household. I was fourteen, younger than Edmund was now, when she had first defined my way.

'You represent our good name. Act as your father would have wished. A gentleman of high degree. We may be landless, but we are noble, Nicholas.'

Hers were such fierce, grieving eyes. Calm, they were like a cold north sea, brilliant with sadness. And when stirred by her will, they blackened, the sea held storm. The sea again—familiar yet unknown. The tempestuous eyes were not to be challenged. I did not think I was afraid of her. I thought only—she maps out

17

my path because she cares for me. As much as for the ruined glory of our name.

Most of the houses in Watling Street belonged to the Drapers' Guild. To the east they became larger and finer, with courtyards enclosed by gilded gates from which leaned oak flowers and angels like the devices on the ship of which I sometimes dreamed. Parallel with Watling Street to the north was Chepeside, with even lovelier houses, their ground-floor windows displaying the wares of the Goldsmiths' and Silversmiths' Guilds. Jewelled mazers and rings, collars such as my father once wore; house after house, becoming a glittering river that extended up Guthran Lane to the hall owned by the Guild Mystery. In one display I had seen the gold salt-cellar set with beryls that we once used at table in the Kentish manor. Soon afterwards I noticed it had been sold.

Near St Mary-le-Bow south of Chepeside, between Bread Street and Friday Street, they were raising a great number of houses at least four storeys high. The goldsmith, Sheriff Thomas Woode, had commissioned them. The main dwelling was almost complete and a great effigy of a woodman mounted on a gilt beast was being winched up over the front door. The workmen on the scaffolding hammered and sawed and sang. They were skilled. They made me dizzy. Further east was Budge Row, where fur-sellers traded and where Edmund, in the fletcher's tiny shop, would be stripping and shaping his quills, binding them with goose-feathers or parchment or peacock's plumage, silent and unsmiling. The fletcher, an enfranchised craftsman, had paid thirteen pence to the Guild for Edmund's apprenticeship. When my mother discovered his charity she reimbursed him, proud and furious. Edmund was becoming skilled and worthy. Black with melancholy, I walked on.

First, my errands, and then, to lose my black thread in the darker side of London. My mother need not know. I had promised myself a certain lightening of the heart; I knew where to find it. At the foot of my mother's little parchment roll was a flying note: *Bring me all the news.*

So I went, not eastwards through Budge Row or north-west up the curving strip to the spiceries of Bucklersbury Lane, but west towards Ludgate Hill and St Paul's churchyard. As always it was full of people, transacting business, gossiping. Velvets rubbed against lousy rags. Monks wandered in and out of the church

18

door and lawyers in their striped gowns conferred with clients near the north cloister. In the north-east corner of the churchyard a sermon was just finishing. The preacher was a clerk of Dr John Colet, and I caught the end of the sermon, something from Dionysius: 'Do not confuse yourself with philosophers, they're the companions of devils. In the table of the Holy Scripture alone lies truth.' He came down the stone steps from his block, and there was a chorus of perfunctory amens.

A town herald took his place. Someone was about to be named by King Henry for treason. This fact sang through his preliminary: Hear Ye! More interesting than last week, when we were given an account of the royal army's campaign against the French in so garbled a manner that no one was clear who was winning. My mother had sneered through peachlike lips: 'It must be difficult for His Majesty. To avoid offending France's new ally, Brittany!' Brittany had sheltered Henry before the invasion, and Bretons had struck down Richard and the others at Bosworth. The herald was flanked by two Yeomen Warders, elegant in their tabards on which the devices of the White and Red roses merged.

It seemed that the Abbot of Abingdon was again in disgrace. This same Abbot Sante had upheld the pretender Lambert Simnel three years earlier. He had sheltered the rebel Stafford brothers and Sir Francis Lovell and the Earl of Lincoln whom King Richard had named as his heir and who had died at the battle of Stoke. Lambert Simnel now worked as a potman in the royal kitchens. The whole business had been mysterious. First, Simnel was supposed to be the younger of King Richard's nephews, the Duke of York, come to claim his inheritance from Tudor. Then he was said to be a bastard son of King Richard, and lastly, the young earl of Warwick, son of George of Clarence. The King made short work of this masquerade. He had brought the boy Warwick out of the Tower, showing him to the people. Simnel may have been only the son of an organ-maker, as was later disclosed, but the Earl of Warwick looked far from regal, his eyes were as blank as those of the town idiot. Men said prison had stolen his sanity. It all seemed to me a senseless, sad affair.

The King had imposed a fine of two thousand marks on Abbot Sante, waiving the balance after eight hundred had been paid. But now, the herald informed us, Sante was under attainder, his goods

19

being forfeit. With others, he had vainly attempted to release Warwick from the Tower, yet again. I thought it madness. We were in the same straits as the Abbot. My father was dead and we mourned him (oh yes, I mourned him!) but it was over and done.

Next, the herald gave us a new law; Gascon wine was henceforth to be carried only in English ships . . . the heavy vein in me fed on boredom and I turned and walked quickly away. The boom of the Jesus bells followed me from their squat stone tower. I took a drink of water from the Great Conduit before turning up into Bucklersbury where I discovered I had lost my little list. Salt? Spices? I breathed their aroma, the astringent Gum Benjamin, myrrh (for Dame Philip's sore mouth), Sweet Gale (for beer-making), nutmeg, saffron we couldn't afford. Cloves and cubebs. Liquorice. Something else, forgotten.

The grocer sighed when I asked for credit.

'You're a good lad, Master Nicholas. But I pray, remember my taxes.'

King Henry's new import tax was to finance the French wars. Even indulgences sold by the priests were put to use too, to pay for a planned crusade. I was reminded that I hadn't heard Mass that day. Neither had Josina. We no longer had our house chaplain, but I knew that somehow, somewhere, my mother would have been at prayer, even in her morning haste with her mysterious letter.

I left the little sack of provisions behind the counter for later collection. I had no wish to lug it eastward through the City.

'Now I suppose you're off to pleasure yourself,' said the grocer.

The spice-smell drifted off on a west breeze as I entered Eastchepe. The way narrowed abruptly. At one place I had to hug the wall to avoid a surge of rubbish and slops overflowing from the central gutter. I held my breath, then the stench passed and I smelled only the cookshops and eating-houses that lined the street. Good roast beef, the tang of new bread, the salt of oysters, boiled fowl with herbs, eel pies with fruit, oven-hot. I tightened my belt against the ache of appetite. The pies were displayed on a laid-down shutter and their baker, an old woman, sat in her doorway. A tear lay in the furrows of her face like a murky dewdrop. When she saw me she scrubbed it away with her apron. Some weeks ago she had given me a broken pie as I passed, saying

20

how thin I was. My mother would have swooned with rage had she known.

'God's greeting, Mistress Seward,' I said awkwardly.

She gulped, rose and went to the back of her counter. I had an idea why she wept. Since Christmas I had learned something of London's dark side. A counter smashed, little vicious fires blazing. I'd seen two men come laughing from that shop, tossing up a chinking bag. I hadn't looked too closely; danger marked their faces, but I would know them again.

Four doors down, I forgot Mistress Seward entirely.

This cookshop was the largest in the street. Years ago it had also been fired, by extortionists, among them Dan Fray, a man so hated in Eastchepe that when he was found with his throat cut no one was ever charged with the crime. Now new windows and a new top storey had been added. The black beams glittered with paint. I pushed open the door. Although I dared not come too often, I knew this front room well, could have mapped it from memory. The oak table, the smouldering fireplace with its gilded overmantel and the old man's chair pulled up in the inglenook. The chair was vacant, but I hadn't come to see the old man. Squinting over his pile of manuscripts at the table was Piers. It wasn't Piers I'd come to see either.

He rose and pulled out a bench for me, saying quickly:

'Yes, I know who you want. But I've found out more about your name-saint. I'd like to tell you.'

He rummaged among manuscripts copied in his clerkly hand. He was no older than Edmund, but he was very clever; far too clever for such a place as Eastchepe.

'I had such luck,' he said. 'All through Master John.'

I had heard much of Master John. Piers had been befriended by a priest at the Greyfriars on Newgate. John was Piers's mentor and idol, and Piers drank up learning like a thirsty horse. He was still shuffling papers, swearing mildly because he couldn't find what he wanted, while, impatiently, I looked towards the door which divided parlour from kitchens.

'Is he in?' I asked, in a lost-journey voice.

'Yes. He's not up yet. Now, let me tell you . . .'

He took off his small round spectacles. They kept sliding down his nose, when he would tighten the rivet to secure them. He had

21

a long jaw, mouse-coloured hair. He looked young, but he always seemed old, like his father, who usually occupied the hearth. Patch, the royal jester, whose shop this had been in the beginning.

'Master John,' he said, hushed, 'has obtained my access to the Whittington library. The one behind the cloister—Nicholas, it's treasure beyond belief. Four hundred books. Twenty-eight desks and eight double-setters. All the great philosophers . . .'

'The companions of evil,' I quoted the preacher in Paul's churchyard. Piers smiled sadly.

'I admire Dionysius, but never mind.'

'Well, my congratulations,' I said. 'What does your father say?'

'I think he's pleased, but he's so much in the old days . . . now, about St Nicholas . . .'

'Will it take long?'

'You can go up in a minute. Now, Nicholas was most holy (this is Iacobus de Voragine, the Golden Legend)—he saved three dowerless daughters from losing their virtue by throwing gold, in secret, to their father by night. They were to go on the streets, you see. Also he went with fishermen and stilled the tempest (he'll always answer mariners), then to Alexandria where he brought down the evil pagan Diana by setting the sea on fire, and the people forsook her and recognized Nicholas as the holy one who had saved them . . .'

I rose. 'I've a great name to live up to. My thanks, Piers.'

He was so clever. I wasn't clever. I couldn't see for leagues, or hit a cat at ten paces. I couldn't heal with herbs, or build houses. There was a black vein in me. I lived by default.

'He brought back to life an infant strangled by the Devil disguised as a pilgrim who came to dinner. This was on the feast of St Nicholas, when he entertained many holy men.'

He tightened the rivet on his spectacles again and smiled. He was exceedingly old for his age. But at least he smiled, unlike Edmund.

'You know your way up.' I went toward the kitchen door, past another parlour where the table was set with silver for a party. There were elegant rooms above, leading from this parlour, where men diced or did whatever men do. The only part of the house I hated was the kitchen.

'He also converted a Jew to Jesus Christ!' Piers shouted after me as I passed through. By one of the great wall ovens the master cook lay, dead drunk as was customary. It was always a mystery how eatable victuals came from those premises. I avoided looking at the floor, except when I had to skirt a cauldron full of steaming grease. Apart from the vermin, there were noisome things. One of the cookboys had suppurating sores all over his face, and hands laden with warts. (Josina could have taken his warts in a week. She'd buried mine in the garden in moonlight some time ago.) As I passed, the turnspit spat accurately into a saucepan. Picking his nose, he said: 'Master Hugh's aloft,' and giggled.

'Nicholas! Nichol-arse!' A voice, and a chuckle, rich enough to dispel all my gloom, came wafting downstairs. I ran up; the stairs were fat-slick and narrow. I pushed open the bedroom door. There, laughing, languid among damask sheets, lay Hugh Finch, my beloved bad angel.

'Ho, Nicholay! Ho, Nichol-arse!'

I picked up a discarded bolster and threw it at him. He caught it and tucked it behind his black head. Ever since I'd accidentally sat down on a hot gridiron in the kitchen he'd called me Nichol-arse. He'd laughed so lustily I thought he would be sick, carolling out 'The Miller's Tale':

'And Nicholas is branded on the bum,
And sweet Christ send us all to kingdom come.'

'Those stairs are plaguey slippery,' I said. I thought: To be with Josina is like larkrise. To be with Edmund is like cockshut, he's so dour. But to be with Hugh Finch is like drowning in red wine.

'I greased them for the old dad,' said Finch. 'Hoping he'd break his poxy neck.'

I laughed. He didn't mean it. We looked at one another in silence, his curly mouth holding its smile. I loved beauty. One reason why I loved Bedesman and Josina so. And Hugh Finch was the most beautiful person I had ever seen. His hair was black and shining as the new timbers outside, a curling fall on his shoulders. His blue eyes were almost violet, with smoky lashes. He had long hands, and wore a small ruby ring. He'd flung the sheet back and the creases of muscle on his dark belly were lighter lines of gold.

23

'I thought I was lazy,' I said. 'It must be nearly dinner-time.' I threw the lattice wide, letting in street-noises and sun.

He yawned shatteringly, showing his flawless teeth.

'I was very late last night, Nicholas,' he said contentedly. 'Very late indeed.'

'And who brought you home?' I asked. I was terrified that one night he'd be murdered. For I remembered the way we had met. As it was Christmas, my mother had ordered us the luxury of some wine. She had sent me, with the cob and a cart, to the ordinary, the Eagle, between Butcher's Row and Soper Lane. It was growing dark and beginning to snow. I went to the side entrance and bought the flagons, and was just loading my cart when I saw Hugh Finch, lying in the main doorway. People were stepping over him. He was so drunk I thought he was dead. He stank like a vat, and the snow was falling over his beautiful clothes and face and lodging in his hair like melting diamonds. I hauled him up, while a tiny voice deep within me said *Let him lie*, over and over, and he opened his eyes and vomited all over my best boots. Though it was a strange remedy, I uncorked a flagon and gave him some of our wine, which seemed to revive him in an extraordinary fashion. I took him home to the cookshop, leaving with an open invitation for whenever I wished. I had never seen anyone so drunk before. I never recall my father drunk; when he and my mother took wine it only made them laugh and kiss more. But I took Finch home, and met the studious Piers, and the ancient Patch, who had entertained King Edward and King Richard and now King Henry, and who lived almost entirely in the past. Patch was the father of Piers, but not of Hugh.

'Is the old dad in?' Hugh asked. I shook my head.

'Then he's off to Westminster. I wonder why the King keeps him. He forgets his jests, can't dance for the rheumatics, and never could sing. I reckon the King has a soft spot for old fools.'

'Why does he go?' I asked. 'He has his comforts here, surely.'

'He's in love with the Queen,' said Hugh with a leer. 'His little Bessy. Ever since she was a babe, when her father was alive. If you want to taste his ginger, talk about queens. But if you'd really see him howl and hop, talk about nuns.'

'I saw a mad nun once,' I said. 'Quite mad.'

It was a terrible memory, damped-down like a sick fire, jarring

24

through the bright forenoon. It was something to say. I always tried to find something to divert Hugh, and sometimes I said things that would have shocked my sister and mother and which even shamed me a little after I left the cookshop.

'Did you see the priest?' He meant Piers. Whereas Piers was Patch's son, Hugh was the son of Patch's dead wife, Grace, by her first husband, Jack Finch. 'She rather sprang me on the old dad,' he had told me, grinning. 'I was fostered until I was two. He didn't even know she had a son.' Grace had died five years ago, of the new plague, the sweating sickness that had carried off the Mayor and six aldermen and had been brought from Brittany by Henry's mercenaries at Bosworth.

'She led the old dad a life, though,' he said. 'She was a bitch.' He laughed. Most of his humour was malicious but his looks and laughter took the sting away. 'Poor old Patch. Poor old devil!'

'The cook's drunk,' I told him. 'Shouldn't you be seeing to the customers?' I could hear people downstairs, and St Swithin had just struck the hour.

'The priest can do that. Get him away from his books.' He looked sharply at me. 'You're hungry, aren't you?' He slapped his flat belly. 'So am I!' Bounding stark naked out of bed. 'You'll dine with me, Nicholas. Devil damn me, so you will.' He was always naming the Devil, as if he were a personal friend.

'Not here, Hugh,' I said hastily, 'No offence, but . . .'

He burst out laughing. 'I wouldn't eat here myself.' He stood there, slender, all of him erect. His was bigger than mine. He was two years older . . . did it make any difference?

'What are you gaping at?' he demanded. Still laughing, he looked down at himself. 'That rooster,' he said pridefully, 'has seen more service, Nicholas, than there are rings on the Queen's Oak.' He plunged his head in a pail of water, stropped his knife and shaved quickly, still naked. 'No time to bathe,' he said with regret.

'I know the kitchen's a piggery'—hunting for his clothes—'the knaves are filthy. I'll take you somewhere better than this.'

'But it pays,' I said. His shirt was black silk faced with white, with gold thread at wrists and neck.

'Oh yes.' He drew on his hose, palest fawn silk, and tied the points at his waist. He wore a codpiece in the new Italian fashion,

25

which certainly drew attention to the rooster. 'We've some wealthy customers.'

'Do the mayor's deputies ever come here?' for there were penalties for such filthy kitchens. His tight saffron doublet reached only to his belt. It was slit diagonally across the chest so his lovely shirt could be seen. He put on a short loose murrey gown faced with green silk, and sat down to draw on long hide boots. I helped him. The toes were round, not silly old-fashioned pikes like mine.

'Even mayor's deputies can be . . .' He twitched fingers over palm, then cuffed my ear, a light caress. Passing through the kitchen, I saw the cookboys cringe before he spoke.

'Devil in Hell, Nicholas! It's worse than ever. It's disgusting.' He smacked the head of the warty boy with such sudden violence I felt the blow in my own skull.

'Clean that floor, you poxy knave. Turn that spit, you scum. I suppose you thought you wouldn't see me today.' He kicked over the cauldron of grease; a slow sludgy river joined the other abominations on the floor.

'Clean it up. Or I'll kill you,' he said. The boys seized cloths and brushes and dived, becoming a row of bobbing backs. We went through to where Piers was ushering some gentlemen into the side parlour.

'I'm off now, priest,' said Hugh. 'Mind you don't sprout wings and fly up to heaven while I'm gone. See they have all they need.' He gestured towards the parlour. Piers, silver flagon in hand, nodded, said nothing.

The roar of Eastchepe met us. It was the first time I had been out with him, and I must have looked like his servant. He knew I couldn't afford to pay my way. No bad thoughts, now, I told myself, no black streak. Only the joy of being with him in the sunshine. He took my arm, walking a little unsteadily and I pulled him out of a wagon's path. Some goats were nibbling at a vegetable stall. A skein of prentices went jeering by. Deafeningly a fishmonger yelled his wares. The offal of melwell and mackerel mounted, a bloody pile beneath the stall, where skeletal cats congregated. Hugh began to sing.

'Back and side go bare, go bare,
Hand and foot go cold,
But belly, God send thee good ale enough,
Whether it's new or old!'

The Greyhound's windowpanes were amber in sunlight, and
the bush over the door threaded with flowers. A party of
noblemen followed by priests and pages was emerging.

'Morton's pack,' said Hugh. 'The great man does himself, and
his followers, well. If I chose,' he said thoughtfully, 'I might
attach myself . . . perhaps. But one priestly knave in our family's
enough.'

The very name of Cardinal Morton was anathema in our
house. Cardinal Archbishop, King Henry's Chancellor; even his
pages smart and fed and gleaming. Cardinal Morton had betrayed
King Richard, had brought us death and defilement and penury.
All for our loyalty.

'This is the place,' said Hugh. I had never been in the
Greyhound. It was for lords. I would have been a lord save for
that misplaced loyalty.

I said, 'No, Hugh. I'll be too much in your debt.'

He leaned against the doorframe to let a woman come out. She
was rosily past youth, escorted by two yeomen with staffs. Hugh
inclined his head to her. A sudden startled hunger burst in her
eyes.

'They're all whores,' he said softly. 'You see?'

'Hugh,' I said, 'this place is too costly.'

'Hold your tongue,' he said. 'Get in.' He gave me a painful dig
in the ribs. 'I love you, Nicholarse. You skinny devil.'

We sat opposite one another. The bench was slick from trade, I
kept sliding about. Wine was brought to the table, red Bordeaux,
heavy as blood, spiced with grains of Paradise.

'Drink to me,' he said,
'And I to thee,
And let the cup go round.'

I hadn't tasted wine since Christmas. I thought of the woman
who had looked at Hugh with such lust. She had been about the
same age as my mother. I wondered what my mother would say

27

to find me here. Such ill-fortune was extremely unlikely, and I said so, to Hugh.

'Oh, how is your lady mother?' He was always interested in my family. More than once I had thought of inviting him home but something stopped me. My mother would not approve of Hugh Finch, fair and kind though he was. The first course was set before us. Whole fowls, roasted with sage and galingale and a sauce of little pippins. Pastry coffins of leeks. I wished my mother could have shared this feast. Likewise my darling Josina.

'My mother's well, but so sad.'

With hands and teeth he ripped his fowl apart. Sauce ran down his chin.

'And your brother Edward?'

'Edmund.' I shrugged. 'Even sadder.' At this moment he would be eating his bit of bread and cheese in the fletcher's back room. Even for that he wouldn't stop, sharpening his barbs, binding his shafts, trimming his quills. He was so tired and sour at night it was like having a mute for a bedmate.

'So all's much the same, at home?'

I nodded, chewing on the delicious bird. It was so good I felt faint. I realized I had never mentioned Josina to Hugh. My sister was my one treasure, whose beauty was something to boast about.

'The leeks are excellent. More wine!' he shouted, and the tapster's boy came running. My belly was tight, my head and face wine-warmed. Even my clothes looked less miserable. The wine went down, fire and silk, the crusty loaf we tore at was warm and white—lord's bread. I had to stop eating at last, but I drank deep. Hugh's smooth voice sounded from the tankard's depths, talking about my family's attainder, in between remarking that he fancied a change of wine, some Gascony, sharper.

'Can't you persuade your mother to petition King's Bench? I don't know all that much of the court, but the old dad says that Henry loves to show magnanimity, and it *is* five years . . . I'm sure he'd lift the attainder. He's done it for other folk, greater than your father.'

'She'd never. Even Sir James has given up trying to bend her, and he has the King's ear.'

He poured the fresh wine.

'It's outrageous that you should have to suffer.'

And so he tore the black vein straight from my soul and it hung in the air between us, full of rancour and poison. He said, with a strange smile, bright between his lashes:

'Does it pleasure you, Nicholas, to be living like a lord again?'

I looked into my tankard. My reflection wavered redly: Tristan, spying out his enemies; Tristan, cheated at the last moment of his heart's desire.

'More than you know,' I said bleakly. 'Hugh, what would you have done in that battle? Whom would you have fought for?'

'Tudor, of course. What fool would not? Stanley paid lip service to Richard's cause, but he was Tudor's stepfather after all—only logical that he should turn his coat in the end. And even the people had lost faith in Richard—as soon as King Edward's sons disappeared from the Tower.'

Slightly diffused by all the wine I had drunk came a bad, sad memory of one night in our apartments at Westminster, towards the end.

'Richard should have fled the country,' said Finch. 'He could always have come back with a new army, instead of getting himself killed and fifteen hundred along with him.'

'Perhaps he wanted to die,' I said slowly.

'A whit unkind to those who rode with him!' Unsmiling, he was looking at me. 'Nicholas. I wish you'd dress better.'

Shame crucified me. His voice was gentle.

'You've looks, you could cut a good figure. Appearance is all.' I felt his hand brush my sleeve. When I looked, a couple of gold angels lay on the board.

'No, Hugh. I can't borrow.'

His purse lay open, crammed with gold.

'Some of this is to sweeten the mayor's deputies, I told you. And I'm not lending you anything. "Seldom comes a loan, Laughing home."'

He said: 'It's a little payment. For rescuing a small bird from a big one.'

'What?'

'Me. At Christmas! A finch in the mouth of an Eagle!'

I laughed with him, looking at the money. I would be able to

29

pay off the grocer on my way home. My mother would be mystified. So be it.

'Thank you,' I said.

'Now. Fruit? Cheese? A cup of ypocras—good for the digestion?' He looked for the tapster's boy again.

'No more. I'll burst my skin. And no more wine, or I'll be drunk.'

'I don't often get drunk' he said reflectively. 'Last Christmas, yes.'

'Did they throw you out of the Eagle?'

He looked wounded. 'Certainly not. I tripped, going out for a piss. The Fray brothers would never throw me out. They're kinsmen, in a roundabout way—by marriage—the old dad's mother was Dan Fray's cousin.'

That was nothing to boast about, I thought, but said nothing. He settled the reckoning, sprinkling small coin among the serving boys. I thought: Now it ends, today is ending. Alas. He got up, steadier than I on his feet, his eyes brilliant.

'Let's go and see them at the Eagle. But first, let's see who's in the cage. It'll be sport.'

We went up Mincing Lane and turned west into Cornhill where the petty felons were taking their punishment. A red-faced wife hung in the pillory with her dishes of stinking butter suspended under her nose. Next to her, a cutpurse had had his ear nailed to a cartwheel. He held a knife in his trembling hand. A group of interested spectators were laying bets. 'Take heart, man!' one roared. 'A slash'll do it! Free yourself!' 'Hold on, Will!' cried another. 'Two marks that he endures till sundown.' In the stocks sat a butcher charged with giving short weight, and next to him, blue-lipped and babbling, was Witless Walter. In the cage on top of a pole several people crouched painfully, being pelted with rotten food. A handsome strumpet in the cage was lustily returning the fire.

'Ho, Maggie!' Finch guffawed. 'I told you to stay in Southwark!'

I couldn't ever remember being in Southwark over the river, near the Clink, which was out of the Mayor's jurisdiction. Most of Southwark was the province of the Bishop of Winchester, who built churches from the proceeds of the stews and brothels there.

Hugh said: 'I met Maggie at Bart's Fair. I warned her not to whore in the City. I wish I'd met you then. Wasn't it the best Bart's Fair you ever remember?'

'I didn't go,' I said. 'I've never been.'

'Let's go to the Eagle,' he said.

He took my arm as we crossed the corner of Fish Street and said quietly:

'When will your mother stop mourning?'

I looked into his sympathetic eyes. There was a shadow there like a cowled presence, its intent hidden. I wondered how he knew so much of me. My mother even eschewed the great double festivals of St John's Eve and Peter and Paul, the Marching Watch and the Standing Watch in the City, and none of us would have thought of going without her. As for St Bartholomew's Fair . . . I had only mentioned it to her once, having heard of its delights from a prentice friend of Edmund. In her eyes I had seen mares' tails of anger, a look of storm.

'Do you know what day that falls on?' she'd said coldly.

I did. August 23. The day after King Richard's death. My father's Month-Mind. The week in which we had waited at Leicester to see him die. No week for sport.

'We could pleasure ourselves right well,' said Hugh. 'Will you come with me, Nicholas? Bring your brother. There's an archery contest. And your mother too, I'll escort her.'

Inside the Eagle noise struck us, worse than in the street. A large oak-panelled room, beer-soaked rushes on the floor. Men shouting, singing, arm-wrestling, rattling dice. Girls hurried about with armfuls of tankards. In one corner two terriers fought, and men laid odds on them. A girl hastened up to us. She flung her arms about Hugh and kissed him. From her ragged gown, her blue-veined breasts looked ready to burst forth. 'Four weeks!' she screamed above the din.

'*Du vin grec!*' he said in an execrable accent, and slapped her bottom. She rushed away.

'I've ordered wine,' he said. 'Don't drink the ale here, Nicholas. It's too new.'

The girl returned at speed. A different wine this time, resinous and warm. A cat and a pup began fighting in my belly. My vision

31

blurred and my hearing seemed faulty, but I was aware that Hugh and the girl were quarrelling.

'Not a word, not a sign. Four weeks! Don't you want to see him, you false nigget?'

He was laughing, but cross. 'Ah, be still, woman. What more do you want?'

'Your company,' Tears. 'A little comfort.'

'You've had both. Don't say you lack food in this place?'

'No. But *he* . . .'

'You've plenty to nourish him,' said Hugh Finch. With arrow speed, he whipped open the neck of her gown revealing her great breasts. He squeezed their tips, hard. Two jets of mother's milk soared straight into the tankard of a dozing ancient at the next bench. The girl shrieked and swung at Finch. He weaved his head away, laughing so loudly that even the terriers stopped their fight. It was the most outrageous thing I had ever seen. Yet I, starved of such wanton joy, started to laugh even louder. The girl flounced off, dragging her dress together.

'Sweet Jesu,' I said. 'Oh, Hugh.'

'She's just borne my son', he spluttered, wiping his eyes. 'Shall we drink to him? Poor little bastard. I'll name him for you, Nicholas, if you like. Devil damn!'

I recovered to realize that two men had joined us. They were laughing too, which set me off again until my marrow ached.

'Now you've properly overset her,' said one. 'If she quits, you can come and work in her place.'

'Satan have you, Robin,' Finch said. 'I'll die in a ditch before I work.' He had thrown his money on the table again. The two men were pushing it into three piles, they slid Finch's portion across and he put it away.

'I must introduce my friend,' he said. 'Master Archer. May I present Masters Robin and Simon Fray. My kinsmen by marriage.'

Even while I grasped their forearms in greeting I knew them as the two I had seen coming out of Mistress Seward's pie shop. They had been laughing and handling money then. I knew them, and their evil manner of life, yet I smiled and gave them my friendship, because they were part of Hugh Finch, part of his power.

32

I am not seeking excuses, I am telling what was so. Today it is like a bad bitter old dream, but I remember how the twin brothers Fray rose, after a few pleasantries, and left us in our warmth and wine and the residue of laughter. I remember Hugh Finch—his blue eyes bright between his lashes, his slender dangerous hands folded round his cup, his smile, binding and bending me.

'You'll come to Bart's Fair with me, won't you, Nicholas?'

I looked, and I loved him. The taste of his words was like grains of Paradise.

'Yes, Hugh.'

I'd go, if it were my last act. He nodded gently, and said: 'Good.'

At times I still see his face, changed, by my own hand, as last I saw it. Even though I must have known that his life of pleasure was made possible only by the basest crimes, I shut off the knowledge, as easily as I closed the polished parlour door upon those reeking kitchens. I was snared by a vicious enchantment.

There were gaps in my memory that day wherein the wine rushed in little red tides. We stayed together all afternoon, and every time I wished to leave he pulled me down again and started on another of an inexhaustible fund of jests. I told him he should be entertaining at Westminster, instead of the old dad. Arms linked, we moved from tavern to tavern.

'We'll not go back to the Eagle today, Nicholas,' he said. The girl had annoyed him. 'One good swiving or two, and they reckon they own you.' I remember a very grand tavern on the corner of Candlewick Street, crammed with feasting lords, and there he tempered his behaviour and passed for one of the lordliest, cold and haughty as he gave his order, then warmly winking as he looked at me. He got out his dice-box—blue enamel with finches carved into the lid—and I won half an angel from him and lost it again, and he tossed it back saying I could buy my mother a present. I remember that we pissed in the gutter in the Drapery and hazily thinking: This is strictly unlawful, and he told me how the Watch had chased him one night for that very thing, but that those constables who couldn't be bribed were so stupid a child could outwit them. We met a pretty young woman drawing water from the Great Conduit (he came with me as far as Bucklersbury) and he paid her a few outrageous compliments before making a grab at her so that she ran screaming up the lane to her house. He leaned against the wall laughing even when her menfolk came out and swore at him—laughing his enchanted life away, while I stood plaiting my feet and wondering what time it was.

'I really must go home now, Hugh.'

'Don't leave it too long,' he said, 'or I'll come looking for you. Which is your house, did you say?'

I hadn't said, and the thought of my mother warned me not to.

'I'll come to you,' I said. 'Very soon.'

He punched my chin lightly. 'Farewell, then. I'll go and beat the devil out of those cookboys.' I saw his eyes harden as if he weren't joking. Then he smiled, turned and walked off towards Eastchepe.

I settled our account at the grocer's. I had nearly two pounds in my purse. Edmund, if he became an archer, would earn sixpence a day. The grocer had some little caskets of sweets, tied with pink ribbon. I bought one for Josina. At least there was something to go home for, in that awful moment when the wine sours and you feel alone in your own head, yet in bad company.

She was in her herb garden just as I had left her, crouching to gather the tips of the purplish bugle-flower in a flat basket. Half the skip was filled with yellow honey-wort which she used for dyeing and treating the cuts on Edmund's fingers. About her the branched long-leafed pennyroyal grew prostrate, its flowers like hairy lilac tubes.

I'd had enough wits left to chew some cloves on the way home; just as well, for she ran to kiss me. She was always kissing me, the only one who did. My mother seldom kissed any of us and when she did it was Edmund. Last week I'd seen her holding him, their faces grey and sad. Josina's hair was now in two plaits, covering her ears in fine gold wings and falling over the outgrown gown that stretched over the small breasts like medlar-fruit. I wished I could buy her a new dress. I put my hands round her waist; my thumbs and little fingers met.

'I was lonely without you at dinner,' she said. 'Dame Philip's been asleep nearly all day!'

'She's old.' I gave Josina the comfits, and watched her bewildered delight.

34

'Don't tell Mother.'

'She came back only half an hour ago. She brought Edmund with her.' That was odd; Edmund home early.

'You've enjoyed yourself today,' she said. I picked up her basket, tangled in the spreading fronds of pennyroyal. An evil herb, I'd once heard Dame Philip remark. Brings women on before their time. Women's talk.

'I have.' She put the little ribboned box in her basket, drawing some sprays of honey-wort over it. She didn't ask questions, as my mother would: where have you been, why weren't you overseeing the household. The small pale face between the shining braids said: 'I'm so glad, Nicholas.'

I picked her up in my arms. She was so light and small, hard to believe she was ripe for a husband, and babes. 'My sweeting,' I said. 'My dove.'

The sun was dying brightly, the sundial marked a lovely day of waste and wine. I carried my sister into the house, she pressed her lips to my cheek, and her black kitten came twining about my legs.

'You didn't shave today.'

'Does it show?' Suddenly wine-sour, I wished she were not my sister. I envied her future husband, whoever he might be. Rot his hide.

'No, you're so fair. Put me down, Nicholas.'

The two menservants, Jankin and John, were seeing to the horses. The thin nags were snatching ravenously at hay, and the men looked worn. I asked them where they'd been with my mother. Devil of a way, Master Nicholas; and at that I grew curious. Josina told me my mother was in the solar, so I went up, still weaving a little unsteadily, but thinking, why worry? I was a man, head of the household. I could surely drink with my friends. I heard voices inside the solar. The door was locked. Dame Philip came tottering upstairs, and yawned at me. Feeble old woman! Josina should have a bright young maidservant, two or three . . . I remembered my mother's maids at Westminster, shortly before the shattering of our lives. Tib, so acute and comely, and Jane, who 'tired my mother's hair until it was black satin under a pearl diadem and the tall hennin long gone out of fashion . . . I heard my mother's voice, and Edmund's. Only one or two words were

35

audible, yet genuine excitement sneaked through the oak to my little pig's ear.

'It's certain, then.' Edmund's voice was gruff for his age, deeper than mine.

'So said the letter. I trust John Taylor. He's York through and through . . . Rouen.'

'. . . seen him?'

'His agent . . . today. Oh, Edmund!'

Then I heard her begin joyously to cry.

'This is the answer.'

'. . . the cause. My son!'

Then I heard my own name. 'I'm ill-pleased. He doesn't know what or who he is. He knows nothing . . . shall we drink? Edmund?'

The dull sound of tankards made me feel thirsty again.

'The cause. Loyalty.'

'Ay, loyalty.'

'He knows nothing of loyalty.'

I had never felt so excluded in my life. Except perhaps one night at Westminster. Then, as now, I had my ear to the door, crying because they were crying, and kind Tib had her arm round me, saying Hush. My father had been to the Tower to see the Constable, Sir Robert Brackenbury. He was trying to get Edmund employment as a donzel at Barnard Castle, where King Richard's wards were. A cold March night. I think I was eleven or twelve and my father had come shivering into the apartments looking as if he had seen a demon. Tib had rushed to him with possets and he had put her gently aside. I was struggling with my Latin; he didn't answer my greeting, as I sat at my lesson books. I can see him now, not as I saw him last, but whole and handsome, tall and straight, with his broom-yellow hair under the velvet cap sleeked down to his shoulders, and his firm kind mouth thinned with despair, and his unforgettable eyes, so like Edmund's, brilliant grey with the thin circle of white round the pupil. Far-sighted eyes that looked blind until you realized that they could see things of this world and the next . . . but then they were desperate, with no glance for an ink-stained little boy.

He had been in the Mermaid tavern. He had King Richard's White Boar blazoned on his tunic, and he looked haunted. Long

36

afterwards I discovered that he had been hearing the whispers implanted by Morton and his paid tongues, that Richard had had the young princes done to death. But at that moment I was only hurt that he didn't notice me. He went into the heart of our apartments and locked the door so that he could be alone with his wife Margetta and the small Josina and the baby Richard who later died.

With Tib comforting me, I had heard my mother cry out loud.

'Oh God! Did any labour to harm *my* children, I would haunt him with a curse, unto my last breath. I would find blackest poison to sweat the bowels from him who touched my babes . . . I would give my body to be burned . . .' Terrible, sibylline words.

Josina cried, and the baby began to bawl. I heard my father hushing them brokenly, as Tib soothed me, although I was weeping not from danger and slander and evil as they did behind that door, but because I was locked out. I don't know where Edmund was that day, but I remember that eventually he did go to Barnard Castle as a page in King Richard's private northern establishment. He was there for only a short while, returning close-mouthed yet excited by whom he had shot with at the butts—the royal bastards, no less. Again I didn't know this until long after the battle and the final defeat and my father's death. Edmund talked only of a girl he had met there. Even at eight or nine one can fall in love. She was Katherine Plantagenet, an older girl with nut-brown hair, a natural daughter of King Richard. She was betrothed to the Earl of Huntingdon, but Edmund still wrote poems to her. He smiled a lot those days. Now his smile is dead, and so is Katherine Plantagenet.

'Did any labour to harm *my* children . . .' my mother had cried, and why couldn't I be in there, sharing, instead of grizzling in a servant's arms? Only later was the hurt expunged a little, and then the end was almost upon us. Later was when the King was taken ill and my father spent the night wakeful with him. King Richard's little son had recently died at Middleham, and Queen Anne was mortally ill. When we saw my father in the morning we almost thought the bell would be tolling for another corpse, he looked so sick. Yet there was exultation and a weary relief in his haggard eyes. He called us all together, and our servants. We stood in line, but my mother stayed behind the chair where he sat with black shadowed face and a trembling smile.

'There is only one thing I wish to say to you all,' he'd said. 'Never hearken to rumour. Especially concerning the King's Grace. I can say no more, but when the Tudor invasion is over and the enemy is vanquished, and Richard reigns unharassed, all will be plain. Rumour is a viper's tongue. Rumour is the devil's iron. Never heed it. Do you all understand?'

Mystified, we had bowed, then he dismissed the servants and put his arm about my mother, his weary exultation dimmed a little.

'Ah, Margetta, sweetheart. I've been such a fool. I met Brereton—Stanley's slippery esquire, you know. I told him . . . at least, he had it from me before I thought . . . I was so tired. I told him that the King slept badly.'

'So, my love?' My mother had stroked his head.

'He will say that conscience troubles his Grace. Christ preserve me from bringing him any hurt. I'd die for Dickon.'

Well, die for Dickon he did, and much good it did any of us. I tried the door again. By now I was so wine-acid I thumped the oak, crying: 'It's Nicholas. Are you all right in there?'

There was quiet. Then the key turned and Edmund looked up at me. Except for the black hair it could have been my father come back, shorter, smaller, and so thin. He looked at me steadily.

My mother had a tankard in her hand. It looked ill-fitting, that white hand was made for a jewelled mazer. Her eyes were more black than grey today, the sea was passionate. Her dark-grey dress matched their colour. Her funnel sleeves were faced with fur rubbed bald. Her hair was scraped back under a purple hood. Her lips were pink, as if she'd bitten them in excitement. I went forward boldly and kissed her. She turned her cool cheeks this way and that, as if greeting a stranger.

'Did you have your dinner?' she asked me.

Edmund answered. 'Yes. He had dinner,' and I knew without doubt he'd seen me, God knew where, in the City. I wondered if he'd tell, or if he'd told.

'I have been to Windsor,' my mother said. 'Sir James is there.'

I could hardly believe it. Windsor was the King's new demesne to which he was making sumptuous additions, as at Winchester.

Hope leaped; could she be weakening? Was she also tired of disgrace and penury? As if she read me, she shook her head.

'His Majesty' (with contempt) 'is at Westminster. Your brother has some good news.'

Edmund's stern face weighed me in the balance and found me wanting. He said: 'I have gained a permit to shoot on Bachelor's Acre.'

Bachelor's Acre, on the tract of Windsor land known as the . Worth, east of Peascod Street, was kept as a practice area for archers who were either knights bachelor or novices following knights at arms. There stood the best butts for miles. Edmund would be shooting cheek by jowl with Tudor's young donzels. The King's crack force. Hopeful news indeed.

'We need Edmund to shoot true,' said my mother. 'Sir James has arranged it. Good archers are useful.'

'He is a good archer already.' I smiled at him. He gazed back at me with his fated falcon's look.

'But he must be the best.' Her eyes met Edmund's and I was again locked out, and knew that there was more between them than the doubtful honour of shooting on the enemy patch . . . I felt the scourge of jealousy. Evening was falling. John tapped, entered to light the candles. My mother and Edmund stood plainly awaiting my departure. I toyed with asking them outright: Who was your letter from? Who is Taylor? Why Rouen? And why am I not trusted? My mother's beauty hollowed and glowed and Edmund's young-old face grew gaunt as John carried the candles to the table; I thought of Piers, also old-faced but courteous in his learning, and then I thought of Hugh. I wondered if he'd gone out again, to meet the Frays. Was he chasing a girl? I wished I were with him. I thought: Is this the time to ask? Devil damn! why not?

I said: 'Madame my mother. I wish us this year to go to the Fair of St Bartholomew. There are good prizes for archery . . . I think we could all benefit from a holiday.'

John blew out his taper and left the room.

I said, less firm, more fiercely: 'I'm right spoiled from having no sport. It would do Edmund good, likewise yourself, Mother. And Josina.' She would love it, the dancing, and music, and jugglers. Why didn't they speak? They looked at one another like

39

judges about to pass sentence. My mother said slowly:
'You know my mind, Nicholas.'

'And I,' said Edmund, 'may not be here.'

My mother slapped her tankard down on the table as if to stamp out his words. I thought: Where's he going? Why in God's name don't they trust me? Am I so treacherous to whatever passes? Let me share, or I don't know what I'll do, except that it won't be to your liking. It couldn't be because of today. I wondered where Edmund had seen me. Coming out of an inn, pissing in the Drapery? Sweet God, I thought.

'I beg you to let us go,' I said. 'Edmund . . .'

'If I'm still here,' he said unexpectedly, 'I should like to go, Mother. Nicholas is right, the finest compete at Bart's.'

Her face changed. He was the judge now, she his clerk waiting to pen the verdict.

'And Josina,' I said.

There was silence. Evening wind blew at the candles through a cracked pane.

'Edmund may go,' she said. 'And Josina. She will be your charge, Nicholas.'

I went across and kissed her icy regretful cheek.

'You'll come?' I said. The bells of St Anthony began to ring Vespers in Watling Street. Anthony, patron of boars and children, was the dead King's especial saint.

'I'll be at prayer; ah, Nicholas. Remember your father. Remember.'

If you only knew, I thought. But the chasm between us had widened during the kiss.

'Thank you for letting me go to Bart's Fair,' I said.

At the door, she looked hard at me. In her eyes the sea-storm raged in candlelight. Ship-lanterns, swinging in a gale . . . remembered by me, somehow, somewhere. . . .

'You, Nicholas, can do as you please.' She went out.

Edmund stood, arms folded. 'I saw you,' he said tightly. 'Staggering home. I told no one. Sweet Mary Virgin! you reek of drink!'

The cloves hadn't worked for him. I went to find Josina, for she, at least, thought my breath sweet enough for kissing.

During the following days and weeks my mother and Edmund

40

remained close and secret, bound by looks and silences, he contriving to ignore my presence. I wondered what in the world they were brewing together, and then, for a time, I ceased to care.

My father had a scar on the back of his hand, shaped like an arrow-head. Before I was born, Dickon had held my father's hand over a flame in some kind of blood-pact to do with loyalty. The incident had taken place one night at an inn, when they were exiled abroad. Richard was Duke of Gloucester then, very young like my father, and it was strange to think of them drinking, laughing, doing foolish things together such as Finch and I did more frequently as weeks passed. Now I was in exile myself, cast out by the whispers of my mother and Edmund.

There was something else about that night in the foreign inn, concerning a woman. My mother's love was the most jealous in the world. I'd seen her beating my father with her white hands just for teasing her about other women, until he had carried her raging into their bedchamber. They had stayed there for hours. If he were unwary enough to remark on Shore's beauty the little rageful hands started beating again, and he would laugh and kiss, and she would weep and be sorry. She was so merry and passionate, now so changed. Believe this or not, Edmund was born with an identical arrow head scar on his hand. I often saw my mother's eyes, doting upon it.

'You, Nicholas,' (how cold her voice) 'can do as you please.' So I started to slide down, and by the Eve of St John in late June, the night of the Marching Watch, I had done things which appal me now . . . but then, it didn't matter; nor even that I stopped hearing Mass, and forsook my confession. I felt only that I saved many a priest from thunderous shock.

Piers went to confession, and not just to please Master John. He had just returned from the Greyfriars that June evening when I entered the cookshop. In the hearth, still as a windless bush, sat the old man, Patch. He was wearing, over each eye, a poultice of green leaves and chewed bread. He was still in his fool's costume. Little sleeve-bells hung silent over his hands. His jester's staff with its sun-moon face was propped against his chair, and he was wandering among the May-meadows of youth.

'You got Hugh's note,' said Piers.

41

'It's a wonder I could make it out,' I said. A boy had come with a message addressed only to Watling Street. I was surprised it had found me, what with the execrable writing and vague address. But they say that more folk know Tom Fool than Tom Fool knows. Edmund had been at home. Before leaving, some impulse had made me taunt him.

'Are you off to Bachelor's Acre? I guess you're planning to assassinate the King!' and he had looked at me with utter contempt in those white-ringed eyes. 'No wonder they call you Witless Nick,' he'd said.

Hugh's note had accused me of neglecting him. But it had been less than a week, in fact. He hadn't signed the note. For his mark he had drawn an elegant little finch on a spray of berries.

'What are you reading now?' I asked Piers. He was illuminating his manuscripts, capitals in rose and dark blue.

'Dante Alighieri.' His eyes went somewhere into bliss. 'I'd like you to read it too. Will you, some day?'

My learning was not half as great as his. He was so clever. So, in youth, had been his father.

'Will you?'

'I promise, Piers—when I learn Italian.'

He sighed. 'My life is changed,' he said. Mine too, I thought. And who has profited the most?

'Well,' I said. 'Where is he then?'

'Out. You're to wait.' I wondered whether to greet the old man, but he looked so enclosed behind his covered eyes.

'How quiet it is,' I said. 'No customers?'

'Not today, fortunately,' Piers replied. 'They'll all be at the Marching Watch. We're a cookboy short. One of the lords found a rat in the soup. Hugh threw the boy downstairs. Broke his arm. Master John took him into the infirmary. He'll find it difficult to get work again.'

His expression was that of a watcher, detached and fateful; one who waits, unjudging, for destiny to be played out.

'He's a bad lad, that Finch,' said a voice from the hearth.

I turned and said: 'Good evening, Master Patch. I hope your eyes are improved.'

Nothing moved but the pale creased lips. 'You're a good lad, Piers, my son. You too, Master Nicholas, but there's bad in you.'

42

Silly old devil, I thought, saying: 'My sister could make you a lotion to put on your eyes, she's good with herbals. Shall I bring you some next time?' He seemed not to hear me.

Piers had his spectacles on, translating softly.

'. . . in the dark forest at dawning. The man climbs the hill, which is the true course of life, and the man is ascending it seeking the right way, alarmed for his soul. How old is your sister, Nicholas?'

'Seventeen.'

'The man meets with the leopard, its coat is dappled with the temptations of the flesh, the pleasures of the senses with their fair variety. And then the lion, which is pride, the disposition which is the root of the sins of violence. Is your sister beautiful, Nicholas?'

'More than that,' I said.

'And then he meets with the wolf, the type of avarice, that covetousness of earthly goods which turns the heart from the search for the goods of heaven.' He carefully smoothed down the page. 'I like your new suit,' he said, watching me with his old eyes.

'Whom does the man meet with next?' The boy knew far too much.

'With the divine Virgil, returned from ancient times, who construes the types of these three beasts which hinder the man's progress up the hill of virtue. They correspond with the triple Division of Sins; incontinence, violence, and fraud . . . Virgil's eleventh Canto, according to which the sinners of Hell are divided into three main classes.'

'You should be preaching at Paul's,' I said, and he smiled his little kind smile, shaking his head. He said: 'And you're all going to Bart's Fair?'

'Yes. You too, Piers, I hope.'

'Too noisy. And someone has to keep shop.'

From the hearth the old man said, loud and clear: 'They took my little maid away! They married her to that Welsh bastard. In the nunnery, she was so small, so cold. The tears I've shed for you, they've made me blind. My maiden, my nut-brown one, how you danced! And now you lie under the Welsh dung-pig and bleed in birth . . .'

43

'Who's he talking about?' I whispered. Piers got up and went to the hearth.

'Hush, Father,' he said. 'All's well. Don't cry.'

He wiped his father's cheeks and came back to sit with me.

'Don't let Finch lead you,' said the old man. 'Nicholas!' He was fumbling in his pouch, blindly he produced a pack of cards. 'Come here. Take a card.' Reluctantly I obeyed.

'What is it?' I told him. He dropped some cards. 'Ah!' he said. 'You're in love.'

And blindingly it came. David and Jonathan, incorruptible, yet who knew what their love was like? Love such as the Templars were burned for? Love like that of the Hanse Traders, who, in their river fortress of the Steelyard, have no need or knowledge of women? My mother's words came back: he knows not what or who he is . . .

St Swithin's chimed. People were hurrying through the City with their preparations for the Marching Watch. I had seen the women and girls returning from the forest, weighed down with green boughs, and the men carrying lanterns for the procession. Trestles scraped on the cobbles, set up for the communal feast.

I felt for my purse, newly plump, looked down at my new boots with the fashionable round toes, and tried my best to forget how I came to be wearing them.

'Where the devil is Hugh?' I said.

'At Mistress Seward's,' Piers answered passively.

So he was collecting. Mistress Seward's shop was the one place I wouldn't go into, not even for Hugh and certainly not for the Frays, for part of me remembered how she had given me food as I went my beggarly way. But there were other shops I didn't mind so much, although the first time had been the worst.

'Just ask for Frays' dues,' Hugh had said. 'The last time they threatened my life. You're so tall and strong—they'll pay up. A quarter's yours, if you do it.' He looked again at my patched clothes. I couldn't bear his look and I went in. They had a bull mastiff which they set on me; it tore my sleeve and I had to clout it with a pan which the wife had thrown. I was cursed to Hell and back but they paid up, and the same day Hugh took me to his own tailor. My suit was blue broadcloth and the shirt rose-coloured silk. I had to be careful not to display them at home. The next

44

time was easier and it bought a new dress for Josina. She didn't know about it yet. A little seamstress was working on the measurements I'd given her and it would be ready in time for the Fair. It was gold, purest wool with a silk petticoat and a little matching cap. The Frays were pleased with my work—that meant nothing. I never liked the twins. But Hugh was pleased also, and that was a different matter. All the same, I was glad I hadn't been asked to collect for a while.

'They tried it with me, you know,' Piers said softly. 'When my mother and her brothers all died of the sweat. The twins came after me and Hugh. He went to them. I was only ten, young enough to pick pockets for them, but I'd met Master John. He told me of God's design.'

'Mind his filthy temper!' said Patch. 'Bad lad. Ah, my Bessy! why did they send you to that cold place in the north?'

'It's all right, Father,' said Piers. 'He gets them mixed up,' he whispered. 'Henry Tudor's Queen, and an old love, who became a nun.'

'I saw a mad nun once,' I said. Strong and terrible, the memory. No new clothes, nor Dante Alighieri's mysteries, nor the calm presence of Piers could expunge it. I ached only for Finch.

At that moment he came in, kicking the door open, his arms full of flagons and pottles, and stood there laughing, in green, a feather in his cap. He looked like Robin Hood, a wicked, handsome Robin who didn't give a curse for the poor.

'Ho, Nichol-arse!' he said. 'Devil's elbow, what a crush out there! I could scarcely get through the people. Here, priest.' Piers got up and took the flagons. 'That should see us through the week . . . if we ever get any more trade. That bloody boy,' he said mildly, strolling over to the hearth. He lifted one of the poultices from Patch's eye. Milky pearl shone on the eyeball. Hugh let the dressing drop again.

'You're going blind, old dad,' he said kindly.

'I know,' said Patch. 'But Nicholas's sister is going to cure me. She's seventeen, and passing fair.' He hadn't apparently missed a word of my conversation with Piers. He was not, I thought, half as daft, or even as blind, as he made out. Then he said piteously: 'Poor little maid!' and began to weep again, and again was comforted by Piers.

'He's got the devils tonight,' said Hugh, rolling up his eyes in impatience. 'Let's go out. But first, I've something to show you.' We went through the kitchens. From inside a cupboard door the bare foot of a cookboy was protruding; it withdrew convulsively as we passed. There the boys snatched their sleep in rat-ridden straw.

I followed him up a ladder to a loft overlooking the alley at the back of Eastchepe. Another door led from the loft into the upper rooms where the customers disported themselves after supper. A rope was coiled by the window.

'The escape route,' explained Finch. 'Satan's rib! the times I've seen great lords go out of that window, bare as worms . . . we're not licensed for *that* sport. I always tell the mayor's deputies the girls are here to serve. So they are.' His laugh was echoed by an irritable clucking sound. With great tenderness he withdrew from a cage a little game-cock, and brought it to the window. He cradled the bird against his chest and with his free hand feinted at it. The beak struck like an adder, once, twice, almost piercing his glove, but his hand was even quicker in withdrawal.

'Quiet, my darling,' he said. 'You beauty.'

He shook off the glove and began to stroke the bird, whose taloned feet lay limply against his heart. Its legs were breeched with feathers the colour of hellfire. On a ledge lay its long spurs, honed like razors with tiny leather bands attached.

'Isn't he fine?' I nodded. The slender hand with its ruby ring went on stroking. The bird fluttered, then was still, for an instant a membrane flicked over its eyes. I watched the stroking hand, and his intent profile. I moved closer, breathing in dust and straw and an acrid scent almost of blood. He bent and touched his lips to the bird's fiery poll.

'Watch your eyes,' I said nervously.

'He won't harm me. Will you, my beautiful boy?'

My chest felt tight. He said: 'Stand out of the light, Nicholas,' and I stepped away as if stung. By the spurs sat a little bowl of barley and a flask.

'Mix it in,' he said. 'Only a few drops.' The scent of fermented mead rushed up my nose. The bird pecked the grains avidly from his palm.

'It's madness to give them too much,'' he said. 'Some fools

46

send them into the pit so drunk they can't stand, let alone fight. Just a little, there, my love . . .' his soft endearments went on.

It felt very heavy in the loft, as if thunder were about. The tightness in my chest rose to my throat. I asked:

'You're not pitting him tonight?'

'Ah no. I wouldn't waste him on the Marching Watch. They've no really good cocks. The real competition is at the Fair in August.' He smiled at me. 'You can lay your shirt on him then, Nicholas.'

He kissed the bird's head again, and replaced it gently in the cage; it bated and struck at the bars. Quiet, sweet boy. In the dimness I could see the perfect curve of his lips, the gleam of his eyes. I felt sick. I looked away, to the coiled rope down which the naked lords fled by night . . . there had been ropes piled like sleeping serpents, a rope about my waist to save me from the sea's hurling pull . . . the deck pitched beneath me in an unremembered time. I said desperately:

'What do you call him?'

'Nemo,' said Hugh. 'Because he's nobody. Like me.' His voice was bitter. He dusted damp barley off his hands. I had never probed the reasons why he sought my company so avidly. Now it was clear. Attainted and poor though I was, I was a knight's son, a gentleman. As for myself . . . I didn't know what it was I wanted from him. I only knew that I yearned for him with a passion so rooted in sorrow and madness that I was jealous of a little bird.

'Come on, Nicholay,' said Finch. 'I think I've caught old Patch's devils. And your face is as long as a corpse-cart.'

We went back down the ladder. Piers, clad in a butler's apron, was decanting the wine. From the cupboard I could hear a cook-boy snivelling.

'Don't get too drunk, priest,' Hugh said. Piers half-smiled at an ancient joke. 'Enjoy yourselves,' he said. His eyes touched mine briefly, then he looked down again at his flagons.

It was a fine evening. The sky was green-gold over the rooftops where the carved gables grew so close you could shake hands across the street. Lanterns had been lit for the Watch, every housedoor was dressed with branches and garlands of green birch, long fennel and St John's Wort, lilies in honour of the saint. The ways were thronged with people, in and out of the taverns. Gangs of prentices swarmed through Eastchepe and the nightwalkers had come from Southwark. We went towards Candlewick, and stood on the corner of Mart Lane. Tables set with ale and meats stood outside nearly all the houses. A few steps from where London Stone stood in its iron cage a bonfire had been lit, reflecting the glow from Ludgate Hill. There, the first of the fires had been kindled, and the twelve Livery Companies had started their procession.

Ranks of armed men, mustered and paid for by their Guilds, were coming down the hill. A thousand cressets, carried for a fee by poor men, set the sky alight and gleamed on the green boughs and the peoples' faces. The noise of trumpets grew from a gnat's whine to a surge of blazing sound which shook the street to the rhythm of drums and the fine whistle of fifes. The guild aldermen were in full armour and rode beautiful horses under painted banners. The Mercers' Guild flew the face of the Virgin on its gilt-tasselled standard. The Merchant Taylors bore the Lamb of God, etched in gold and white on a green ground. The file swept on, the Vintners, Ironmongers, Fishmongers, Haberdashers, Salters, Dyers, all making their own music, a proud disharmony. Among torch-bearers rode the Mayor, his sword-bearer preceding him, and following his party came the Watches of the sheriffs—the file plunged and flickered by between the flower-strewn tables and the cheering citizens. From west to east bon-fires blazed; all along the Standing Watch composed of armed aldermen lined the street. Notabilities rode by; they slipped past almost dreamlike in the flamelight and the shouting. King's men—Sir Reynold Bray, Sir Robert Clifford, Sir William and Lord Thomas Stanley, Sir Jasper Tudor, the King's uncle. Jewelled, they surged on in a stream of golden light. I smelt their riches and remembered them . . . from the old, the worst day . . .

Suffolk and Oxford's entourage passed, with a pack of great wolfhounds following the horses. Then the Church, finely robed: Cardinal Morton's pack. The banner of St John swept high and almost as wide as the street. Gold crosses, holy relics and the jewels of the religious threw back the cressets' light and the fires marching through the City. The end of the procession passed by the London Stone.

'We could go to the Eagle,' said Hugh, as the noise died. 'Did I tell you? Christ be praised, Agnes has gone back to Kent.'

My father came from Kent, I thought. I said: 'What about your son?' Had he ever seen him?

'Ah. Was he my son?' He gave me a terrible wink. 'It's a wise child, Nicholas.'

The last tabor throbbed through my skin; the dying fife iced my ears. 'He was though, wasn't he?' I said. He nodded, took my arm. 'Come on. I'm hungry.'

'Hugh, I'd like to go somewhere quiet.' He began to laugh.

'Of all nights,' he said. 'You want the moon. Still. Leave it to me.'

He turned sharply south down Fish Street, past St Swithin's, into Thames Street, to where Dowgate broke the wall of London. I could smell the river, fish-guts, garlic from a Venetian ship tied up at Galley Quay. The river gleamed darkly. Bonfires that had been lit on the further bank in Southwark doubled and bobbed with the lapping tide. Hugh ran down the steps, calling to a cruising boatman. Twopence to cross, the boatman cried, because it was a holiday.

'Thief,' Hugh muttered. 'One penny!' he yelled.

'Toss!' cried the boatman. The distant masts of the foreign ship were gilded by the watch-fires. Those other masts had been swinging against a dark sky and white sheets of water. Where? When? Hugh won the toss, and paid the penny.

'Get in the boat,' he said. 'Stop dreaming.' I nearly stepped straight into the Thames. The boatman took us over, laughing at Hugh's jokes.

We went to the Tabard. Only a few people were eating there. The booth where we sat was almost concealed at the end of a long low room; I wondered if it had ever been occupied by great Chaucer. This put me in mind of Piers and his learning. The leopard, its spots and dappling denoting the fair variety of the senses . . . a pretty redhaired girl in a clean kirtle served us; I was paying but she gave all her attention to Hugh. He seemed preoccupied, although he ate and drank with his usual gusto. My legs felt cold. Across the river, the whole evening was eerie, sad changing, as if time were running away, and I felt a panic fear. You're not eating, he said, and leaned back in the booth, folding his hands round his cup in the way I loved.

49

'Would you like to visit one of the stews?' he said suddenly. They're not for me. You can pick up the pox. The foreign sailors bring it, but . . .'

I thought: I love you so much I want you to share my pain.

I said: 'I saw a mad nun once.'

He refilled our cups and sat back. 'All nuns are mad, I should think. In need of a good swiving or two. I should think they are mad.'

I put my trembling hands under the bench.

'Tell me, then,' he said. 'Tell me about the mad nun. We've plenty of time.'

Bedesman had carried me to Leicester, I said, and he frowned, because he didn't know who Bedesman was and for another thing he could hardly hear, so I had to begin again, and he came to sit with me in the booth. I felt his warmth and could look at him. His face remained still during the telling, and sometimes I looked at his lips so that there should be a little beauty and comfort to support me, and this is how I told him, although not as plainly as I tell it now.

The week before Bosworth Field, my father had sent a letter by fast courier telling my mother on no account to leave Westminster until she saw him again, that the Tudor's invasion had begun, his forces coming up from Dale in Pembrokeshire, but that Richard had a great army and we should soon be reunited. It was a short letter and we read it after he was dead. Disobedient, we had all followed the King's army to Nottingham. Margetta knew our father would be angry, so we lay low at an inn until a page of ours who had enlisted as a baggage-boy, sent word that the royal army was moving off towards Leicester through the forest which was crawling with Henry's rebels, and that it might be better if we stayed where we were until all was over. But Margetta disguised us all as friars. We laughed as we donned our monkish robes. Josina was the smallest friar and Edmund not much bigger, but I passed for a holy man and my mother, astride a big black horse with her cowl over her face, even blessed the few folk we met on our ride. It was a hard fast journey for Bedesman; we had to keep an eye out for the rebel force and not lose King Richard's army at the same time. Josina started a fever and as

50

soon as we reached Leicester we put her to bed in the infirmary of St Mary. Then we waited at a lodging-house, to hear if battle were to be joined.

Behind us in a farm cart on the road were Mistress Brecher and her daughter-in-law, yeomen farmers' wives who had followed camp from Devon to Sherwood Forest; they had left their crops to rot, to ride behind their men, Master William Brecher and his son, Thomas, who was eighteen. These women shared our lodging at Leicester. I liked the young wife. I was fourteen, and she a year older. She was with child. We were all quite merry because the rumours of battle were all so faint and we knew we should soon be with the men again. It was good weather, if thundery. I was worried that I had damaged Bedesman's wind, riding so far and fast. I spent most of the time talking to him, and he bunted me with his velvet nose to show I was forgiven.

The little Brecher wife came into the stable with me that morning to admire him. I told her to be careful as he was a stallion, yet he acted like a gentleman and let her give him an apple. The apples were very good in Leicester that month, early ripe in the thundery heat, as everything came to ripeness and to death.

The lodging-house was not far from the White Boar where King Richard spent his last but one night—there are no White Boars today, King Henry had them all painted blue—with the busy market place outside. The little wife told me she was going to call her child Thomas for her husband, whose first campaign this was. She was telling me this, and caressing Bedesman, when I looked out over the stable door and saw a cloud of dust in the distance. People were shouting, running, in fear or curiosity, and that little blossomy cloud growing nearer, and the sun strangely, suddenly high, as if it wished this day over, placed away among the days that are lost and gone. The dust-cloud took shape and became mailed men, riders coming hard and shouting, a great confused force—it was like one of the hordes in the Bible, in the heavy dusty sun. They came over Bow Bridge packed together and I saw the Red Dragon banner of the Tudors. Even then it made no sense until I heard a boy's voice crying, wild with excited fear:

'It's over! All over!'

51

Mistress Brecher came out of the lodging, a comely woman in a smock, and the little wife, crying in fright, rushed to her. Margetta and Edmund came running towards me, white-faced. I cried out: 'What's happening?' and Margetta answered:

'They're saying Tudor's victorious . . . see his standard!' Then, gasping: 'Oh sweet lord Christ protect your father! Mark, oh Mark!'

I looked down the road and saw the prisoners coming, shackled together between an armed escort carrying the Dragon of Cadwallader, men crying, wounded. And then a little way behind, a mule bearing the naked body of King Richard. He'd been hacked and mutilated so that his arms hung down one side of the beast with blood dripping from the fingers, and his maimed legs and feet on the other. His head, with a great gash extending down his dead face, swung and lolled. Behind him came the little nun.

She was mad, and running, grief itself. She ran as fast as she could behind the body of the King, but they pricked the mule forward and went faster so she tripped and fell, and rose up, tears and blood and spittle mingling on her face as she tried to touch his dangling hands or his long gory hair. Richard, Richard. She cried his name a hundred times to my witness. Richard, my lord, my love, and fell again, and wildly laughing got up, and the people began to mock and throw dung at her. Then she tore at her habit and wimple until they hung in shreds about her thin naked shoulders and shaven head. She fell again, and a big lad came and carried her away. By this time they had thrown the King's body down in the market-place and people were crowding, taught by Henry to jeer and spit.

I saw that my father was one of the prisoners, so was Mistress Brecher's husband and the little wife's, a huge young man with gaps in his front teeth.

(I looked at Hugh. I said insanely: 'How do you keep your teeth so white?'

'I rub them with hazelwood and a cloth. Go on.')

We waited at the lodging-house. Margetta sent to the new King's envoys, begging for a pardon for my father. She offered all our estates (which were forfeit anyway). I think she even offered one man her body. She wrote to Sir James but he always swore the letter went astray. She asked in vain for a private audience with Tudor. It was a week later when they brought the prisoners out of Leicester Gaol. They had built a proper scaffold for traitors. A fire was lit in a nearby brazier. We stood in a line, the two Brecher women, Margetta and Edmund and I, one on her either side, and we saw them come out, in chains.

(Hugh poured me some wine. I knocked it over; my hand was jumping about like a rat. He moved his legs out of the way of the flood.)

My father had his arm round the young Brecher; though the boy was taller and bigger, he seemed only half-conscious. My father looked at us all with love and pain. He pursed his pale lips as if to chide us for having followed him. Without touching my mother I felt her trembling. Then a herald read out the charges. Margetta moved forward towards the scaffold; a pikeman stopped her. I saw my father kiss the Brecher boy farewell.

They put the rope round the elder Brecher's neck first. His wife had been as silent as we, but now she began to cry, tugging at Margetta's sleeve.

'Lady, what they going to do? He's done naught . . . he's no traitor! He fought for the King! Oh, Lord Jesus, save us!' Tugging at Margetta's sleeve as if she alone had the power to stop what they were doing now to William Brecher and his son, whose little wife had fallen in a fit, and to my father. They hanged them, at least, they half hanged them and then . . .

We were alone in the Tabard, save for the landlord with his tallysticks. The redhaired girl had gone. I looked at Finch.

'Hugh,' I said.

'Yes.' He cleared his throat. 'They took them down alive and then they stripped and gelded them. They cut open the belly and pulled the entrails out and threw them in the fire. Sometimes they take the heart too, but they're usually dead by then.'

I put my face down on the table, swimming with spilt drink. Finch tugged up my head by the hair.

'Now look at you,' he said. He cleaned my face with his napkin. The landlord stood by with the reckoning. I felt for my purse and shoved a lot of money across.

'Hugh,' I said, 'I should like to get exceedingly drunk.'

'So you shall,' he answered. 'But we must go now or we shan't get a boat.'

53

'I don't want to go home tonight,' I said.

He helped me up. My legs were icy. I stood like a stone.

'Hugh,' I said, 'I haven't told you the worst.'

'We'll miss the boat,' he said.

'When my father was dying—when they'd done all you said, I turned to my mother to take her in my arms. I thought she was going to fall down like the little Brecher wife. She pushed me away. She turned to Edmund. He was only ten years old. I heard her say, "Edmund, my son, my son." She pushed me away, Hugh.'

We were out in the street. There was a bear-baiting in one of the river meadows and crowds of people. We were soon across the river. I couldn't stop shivering. I didn't feel warm, then, in the Eagle, I felt hot. Robin Fray was particularly friendly, and sat with his arm round my neck. I didn't like it. He and his brother Simon told us the drink was on the house as it was Marching Watch night. Robin had a scar on his top lip; it gave him a bit of a sneer. I must have noticed it before but it seemed new and livid that night. Hugh told them I wanted to get drunk and all three of them did their best by me. By the end the room was heaving like the deck of that ship I rode on long ago. I nearly snared that memory for one moment, with the third flagon of Rhenish churning in my head. Then I recall Hugh and Piers carrying me upstairs at the cookshop. Hugh was swearing. 'He may be skinny but he's no lightweight.' 'Mind his head,' said Piers. 'It's his damn long shanks,' said Hugh, beginning to laugh. I felt Hugh hauling off my boots and Piers unlacing my shirt. And then blackness with the soft bed under my sore back (I'd fallen down several times after we left the Eagle), and a little red ray of sense bringing the dire knowledge that I'd not kissed Josina good-night. Struggling to get out of bed and go to her, and nearly falling on my head in the foreign darkness, and Hugh's arm hauling me back, his sleepy voice cursing me. 'Good-night, my sweetheart,' I said. He said: 'Good-night. Don't you dare be sick in my bed.'

And one last thought, that almost sobered me with its midnight logic: It should have been Piers to whom I told that story.

The bell sounded unfamiliar. It was not St Paul which usually woke me and was followed by St Anthony in Watling Street, but St Swithin's, harsher and closer. Every stroke was like an axe cleaving my head. I lay praying for the bell to stop. Very carefully I uncovered bursting eyeballs. Beside me Hugh Finch was deeply asleep on his back, his head resting against my shoulder. His face was as tranquil and smooth as Bedesman's hide, uncreased by trouble. His black lashes were fast on his cheeks. I wondered if he were dreaming. Edmund had terrible dreams, twisting and moaning. Sometimes, worried, I lit the candle, but he never told me his dreams and I had long since given up asking.

Sweet God! he was so beautiful in his deep sleep. My headache cooled; the bell ebbed into silence. I love you, Finch, I said without sound. My heart beat hard. Tears came to my eyes. Cartwheels started to rumble in the street, people cried: 'Fresh milk! Strawberries fair and ripe!' I lay still and looked at him, wanting and not wanting him to wake, for he was mine in that moment, his ruthless wit quietened, his gentian eyes locked in the caves of sleep. His face unblemished even by the sensual leopard, or the vainglorious lion, or the lean she-wolf of avarice . . . like a child he slept on, and in lonely sadness I loved him.

Very softly I laid my lips to his temple. Outside someone called: 'Lord's bread! hot bread!' At a pewterer's stall down the street, the man started hurling his wares about, enough to wake the dead. I took my lips away and lay trembling. Still he slept, as if enchanted. I heard Piers outside, talking with the breadman. A missel thrush sang a short crystalline anthem. My heart shook my body. I laid my hand on Finch's hard warm belly. Then I saw his eyelids move and knew he was awake.

Mind his filthy temper, the old man had said. I waited in sublime terror for him to leap up and knock me senseless with one of his lightning blows.

'They lay and slept like drunken swine,' said a doomed voice in the doorway. Piers had two mugs of ale and a loaf balanced across their rim.

'Don't be insolent, priest,' said Hugh, still with eyes closed.

'Lydgate,' said Piers amiably. ' "The Fall of Princes." '

Hugh sat up suddenly, I rolled away, burying my face in the bolster. I heard Piers put the bread and ale down on the night table.

55

'Is the old dad up?' Hugh asked.

'Gone to Westminster,' Piers replied. 'He says his eyes are good today. I've saddled his horse for him.'

'One of these days he'll fall off into Town Ditch,' said Finch. He leaned over me. 'Good morning, Nicholas,' he shouted. 'I think he's dead,' he said to Piers. 'Wake up, you sot.'

I feigned, stretching and blinking in an addled way.

'Fetch cold water, Piers,' said Hugh. 'Never again! It's like trying to sleep with a mad bull. Falling in and out of bed all night.'

I sat up. 'I'm awake.' I couldn't look at Hugh. I said, with my face on fire, 'Forgive . . .' and he said softly: 'Wait till he's gone.' Piers blundered downstairs, to the noise of the cookboys riddling out the ovens. Hugh was offering me a tankard of ale. His look was very direct and I dreaded it.

'Here,' he said.

'I don't want it.'

'So be it.' He propped his back against the bolster and drank off his ale, then mine, in a couple of long swallows. He tore off a piece of bread and chewed it thoughtfully.

'I'm sorry,' I said. He shook his head, went on staring ahead, chewing. If he doesn't speak I shall go mad, I thought.

'I want you to know . . .' I began. He suddenly hurled his bit of bread with great violence into the corner of the room. He swore a string of frightful oaths, some of them quite new to me. Then he lunged round and grabbed me by the hair. I thought: Now he's going to knock out the few good teeth I have left.

'It would have to be you,' he said. 'I'd have killed anyone else. What in Hell do you want? Do you know what you want? I'll tell you what you don't want. You don't want *me*!' in such a rage that it was somehow strangely calming.

I said: 'I love you more than any person in the world. Except one.'

He let go of my hair and sat back, folding his arms.

'That's different,' he said. 'I know, and I'm glad.'

'I shall always love you,' I said. 'Until the day of my death.'

'Or mine,' he said softly, and a shudder ran through me, for it was unlike him to talk of death.

'Oh, Hugh,' I said in great misery, 'tell me.'

56

'I'll tell you,' he said. He looked at me, his blue eyes undulled even after last night's drinking. 'Did you see the scar on Robin's mouth, when he had his face close to yours? Well, I did that. Years ago.'

I knew then why I had disliked the twins. My dislike exploded into loathing.

'They both had me,' he said. 'By force. Because I was so pretty.' He chuckled. 'Even while my bitch of a mother was alive. I doubt she'd have cared, she was too occupied persecuting the old dad. Robin used to hold me and Simon . . . I used to bite them. Then one day I acquired my little blade.'

He kept it honed fine enough to shave with. It had finches embossed on the haft.

'They never touched me again,' he said.

'How can you bear to be with them? Drink with them, work for them?'

He shrugged. 'It's in the past. I forget what's past. Sometimes I even forget what I did yesterday. It's the best way.'

I wish I could, I thought.

He smiled at me. 'And that,' he said distinctly, 'is why I love women so much. If I couldn't have a woman, from choice a new one every week, I'd end up like Witless Walter.'

He settled back and began to talk of women, quietly but with as much passion as Piers talked about the saints and philosophers, or as Edmund and my mother talked behind fast oak of their mysterious cause.

'First, I don't like harlots. They're unclean, also they're cold. I like a woman to warm to me in love. In modest women there's heat they never dream of. I hate women who chase me. That Agnes—who bore my whelp—she wanted to marry me. Different women; I like to bring them to the same condition, to leave them changed.'

He closed his eyes. 'I was fourteen, the day I slashed Robin's mouth, I went out and took a woman twice my age. A friend of my mother's. I've never been refused. I never shall be. With some, I play the innocent, I beg their pity. Some like to be ravished. It all ends the same.'

One of Piers's apothegms came to me, and in the Latin of St

Jerome, too. *Diaboli virtus in lumbis est*—The Devil's strength lies in the loins.

'The higher born the woman the more lust I feel. I'd like to lie with a lady, so clean, with little hands and feet. I'd take an abbess if she were pretty. I'd swive the Queen herself if I got the chance.'

'Better not let the old dad hear you,' I said faintly.

He laughed, but his voice trembled.

'The priest told me I'll burn in Hell. I'll pay my dues, then. I'll burn.'

I still loved him but things were changed. The watchfires were out. Through the window came the dead bonfires' acrid stench. He got out of bed.

'I'm glad you love me,' he said. 'But not the other. It's a crime against nature, Nicholas, and the law can burn you for it. I only want you to be happy.' His voice had never been so kind. He came back, dressed in shirt and hose, and sat on the bed.

'Are you going to lie there all day?' He twisted my nose painfully.

'You look thoughtful,' he said. 'You don't go with whores, do you? They can make you ill. Take care of your body. It's the only one God gave you.'

'I don't . . .' I began. He leaned and looked at me intently.

'Christ's nails.'

'That's it,' I said miserably. 'I never have.'

I waited for his laughter, but it was as if I'd told him I had some dreadful disease. 'Christ's beard,' he said. 'How old are you? Twenty?'

I had no skill, no wit. Now this.

He laughed, just a little, then. 'Oh, Nicholay! No wonder you. . . no wonder. What you've missed. But I'll cure you. By God, I'll do it today.' Lacing his doublet, thinking deeply, while I slid out of bed and dressed hurriedly. Outside someone was calling: 'Peascods fresh and young!'

'This evening,' he said, while I stood shivering in the sunshine. 'Meet me around sunset. When they start to ring for Compline.'

I swallowed. 'Here?'

'No, no! I never bring them here. Not with my priestly brother and those bloody boys . . . Paul's churchyard.'

'The preachers! The people . . .' And he answered impatiently:

'They'll all have gone to supper, or prayer. And don't drink a lot of ale. Or your rooster won't crow.'

He was preparing me, as he prepared his bird Nemo for the pit.

I went home, saying farewell to Piers on the way out. I thought his eyes were troubled. A blackbird was singing sweetly in our medlar tree, and Jankin and John were in the stables. The cob was lame again. Edmund was in the parlour, his face looking drawn. I was surprised to see him not at his work. He greeted me viciously.

'I suppose you've started whoring now,' he said.

I had to smile at this, enraging him. He pushed past me, nearly knocking me flat against the wall. I shut the door and held it fast before he could quit the room.

'Edmund, why can't we be friends again?'

The grey white-ringed eyes stripped me with scorn.

'We share nothing these days,' I said, 'and I seem constantly to offend you.'

'There are things you are not fit to share,' he said in his gruff voice. 'And I'd die rather than share your life. The gutter's your home.'

'How dare you,' I said.

'I dare,' he answered. 'I'm going to dare things above your dreams. If you have any dreams left.'

He struck my hand aside. Like Finch, he was swift and strong.

'Share your dreams with me then,' I said, and he laughed like a dog about to bite.

'Sweet Mother Mary! and have them blabbed all over East-chepe? Please God, I'll soon be gone.' There was uncertainty in his voice. I thought: Poor Edmund! what the devil are they planning for him, my mother and the mysterious Taylor? Then I remembered what Finch was planning for me, and grew sick with dread. Suddenly Josina entered, her thistledown hair loose. She was carrying some little pots of unguent and strips of clean linen. She had started plucking her eyebrows; it made her forehead very long and white.

'Show me,' she said to Edmund. Obediently he held out his hands. Across the palm and fingers the skin was seared from

59

drawing back the heavy bowstring. All his fingers were cut and calloused.

'Your gloves are too thin.' Josina frowned. 'Now it's beginning to fester.'

She applied balm and bound his wounds.

'What is it this time?' he asked.

'Dog-daisy.'

'*Bellis perennis.*'

'Margaret's herb.'

'*Fleur de Pâques*,' I said.

'You win, Nicholas,' she said. 'Keep it thus, Edmund.'

'Thank you, my lady.' Tenderly he kissed her cheek. He always addressed her with great formality. His stern guard dropped, his love showed. But she was mine, and he knew it. He bowed to her, glared at me, and left the room.

'Welcome home,' she said. 'I missed you.'

I embraced her. She smelt lemony-fresh, the perfume she distilled from the vervain plant.

'You have a headache.' She looked in my eyes. 'Did you see the Marching Watch? I heard them go by, and wished I was out there.'

'It was an unhappy evening.' She laid a strip of linen cool and wet on my brow as I sat down. My headache eased.

'Where's Mother?'

'In the solar, writing letters. There were some men here last night. They'd come a long way, the horses were very tired. They stayed for hours, locked in with Mother. I took them some ale. They drank the usual toast. Loyalty. Plantagenet for ever. The cause.'

My mother sails close to the wind, I thought.

'Who were they? Did you hear anything?'

'I heard Lord Lovell's name.'

'I thought he was dead,' I said slowly. Lovell was one of the few who had escaped after the battle. He had been King Richard's best friend and councillor. We had had no news of him for years.

'And when they were leaving I heard Mother say something I didn't understand. "The Boy will soon be ready, I believe." I knew she wasn't talking about Edmund. They answered: "Yes. Christ preserve him, and may we meet him soon."'

We looked at one another, frowning.

'Are you going out again?' she asked. 'Will you be late home?'

'Yes,' I said dully, 'and no.' I thought how drab and ill fitting her dress was, and wondered how the seamstress was getting on with my gift.

'I'll see you at dinner, my love.' I ascended, tapped at the solar door. My mother was surrounded by letters, some tied and sealed. She was wearing a tarnished green and gold dress. She had worn it at York, when the people were crazed with joy as Richard entered the city, singing his praises, coming to thank him for his beneficence to the city and people. Not even his brother King Edward had been owed so much. My mother's hands shook as she rolled a parchment. Last night's supper lay untouched. She had been up all night.

'Oh, Nicholas,' (still rolling and sealing), 'send Jankin to me. Is the cob's foot mended?'

Not a sign that she knew I had been from home all night. Not a flicker to acknowledge my tearing anxieties, my sick dreams.

'Nicholas.' She looked up suddenly. 'Do you go regularly to confession, do you hear Mass? Do you practise at the butts?'

She wasn't listening even when I answered no to all three. The grey eyes were far off. The green and gold dress shimmered in my sight. She had been carrying her son Richard when she wore that dress in York. She had had a hard time bearing the child.

Out of Hell came a vision of the little Brecher wife. She had miscarried after the execution, still lying on the cobbles among the tumult. I had heard her moaning and seen the bright blood patterning her skirt. Fresh horror struck me. Supposing this woman tonight gets with child through me and comes here demanding recompense. God help me.

'Nicholas,' said my mother, taking a fresh quill, 'we're lamentably short of soap, also feed for the horses. Attend to it.'

I bowed, pricked by her apathy. I thought: I'll do it. I'll go to Paul's churchyard tonight and have that woman. Devil damn the consequences.

They were ringing Compline when I entered the churchyard. A very fat preacher was up on the block, talking about Jeremiah. I wondered if Jeremiah's holy knees ever knocked together like mine did now. In this place, seven years ago, Bishop Shaw had preached his sermon 'Bastard slips shall take no root' when the princes, King Edward's sons, had been declared illegitimate, shortly before Richard's coronation. I remember thinking then: It must be hard to be a bastard, even a royal one. The sun was going down towards Westminster. The preacher ended his sermon with a blessing on the King and Queen and three-year-old Prince Arthur, the new Prince of Wales. Then he hitched his robe and waddled off. I sat down on the tomb of an ancient abbot and waited.

An owl hooted in the westerly trees. Very faintly in the cloister the monks began the service, the reader singing the responses for the versicle and then the choir's echo. It was days since I had heard Compline. *In manus tuas, Domine.* They sang like ghosts through the thick stone. I had climbed the hill of virtue to St Paul's. I looked now for the dappled leopard of the flesh. A beggar in the corner of the churchyard hopped away on crutches. I was alone. Sunset blazed on the tree-boles, and far above was a mackerel sky. The grass on the hill-top shimmered with gold. From the buttresses, like soldiers snatching rest during a siege, shadows lay down. And from out of them in the eastern corner came Finch, with a woman.

Freshly shaven, finely dressed, he was holding her hand and smiling slightly. She was chattering, pointing to the nest of some house-martins; it was shaped like a swarm of bees under a flying buttress of the church. They were both smiling, but his smile contained something unspeakable and a chill speared me as I rose and went to meet them.

When her russet hood fell back I recognized the redhaired girl from the Tabard. I wondered how he had persuaded her to come, for to my knowledge they had not met before last night and then, what with my long tale of woe, he had scarcely spoken other than to give her our order. He must have been over to Southwark today to get her. He held her hand lightly, but I knew long before she did, that he had her in chains. I had not realized how small or pretty she was. Her dress was immaculate, her red hair coiled up in pleats and braids. Her eyes were green, her complexion like fresh milk, she smiled politely. She was, perhaps a little older than I.

Finch nodded at me over her head, and I fell into step as they walked into the deepest alcove of the church wall. The monks' voices ebbed and flowed like sea-tides far away. We stepped into the alcove where we were screened from all eyes by buttresses and vaulting, our feet in long dry grass. The girl was chattering again. Finch brushed his hand down the wall to see that it was clean. His eyes looked into mine; they were very dark blue and pitiless. He put his back to the wall and swiftly drew the girl against him, holding her by the arms, her back against his chest. She fell silent.

'Now, sweetheart,' said Finch, 'this is my friend, Harry,' (with a wink at me). 'I want you to do him a little favour.'

I stood there paralysed, while she twisted her head round anxiously to look up at him. He raised one hand and loosened her carefully coiled hair. Her hood fell to the ground.

'No, my love,' he said. 'Not me. Not yet. Him.'

To this day I swear she had no notion what she had come to. She must have been so enchanted when the fine gentleman asked her over the river. She was a good woman. Finch frowned at me; his lips moved in silence.

'Kiss her, you fool.'

I stepped forward. Either she disliked the look of me intensely or my terror infected her, for without warning she began to scream. Finch's hand came over her face; over her eyes, as if he were hooding a falcon.

'Quiet, my sweet,' he said, and she was.

He glared at me. I came close and clumsily put my lips on hers. As I bent I felt Finch's breath against my ear.

'What's amiss?' he whispered.

The girl jerked her lips away. I thought: Apart from my sister, it's five years since I kissed a girl, and that was the little Brecher wife, that morning in the stable—I kissed her for fun while she was stroking Bedesman, and she put her arms round me and we laughed at her big belly keeping us apart . . .

Finch had his hand behind the girl's back, unlacing her gown. She writhed feebly, whispering: 'Lord Jesus! help me!' The dress fell, she was wearing a spotless white shift and long hose with garters. She tried to cover herself, bunching the shift together. He stripped her deftly; one moment she was clothed, the next, bare as a worm. I fixed my eyes above, on the house martins' nest.

63

'Look at her!' he said.

Her body was almost whiter than the shift. He held her firmly; I looked at her breasts and the little red beard below her belly. The monks were singing of the infinite mercy of God. My loins stirred faintly. Finch's face blurred. Let us go, I said silently. For God's love, let us go, Finch. Over her head his lips said: Go on. He had hooked his feet inside her spread ankles. Trembling, I exposed my hapless body and pressed against her. She struggled, he bent and kissed her neck, and she was still.

'Bend your knees,' he said. I knew he was dying to laugh. Whatever remnant of desire there was in me withered.

'Satan take you!' he said terribly. 'Just this once, then.'

He leaned more firmly against the wall, putting his arms round both me and the girl. He kissed my mouth, as if searching a wound. His lips were far softer than hers and the kiss almost drew out my soul. It was the last moment of my love for him and in it flared a terrible lust, flooding my loins so that I entered without difficulty, taking her as if I were taking him, in shame, in sickness, in sadness, till death do us part . . . the sea washed over me for an instant and I saw the swaying foam-battered masts and a bearded sailor's face and heard him say clearly: 'This poor little bastard!' I cried out sharply and came back, spent and ill, with the woman trembling and in tears, and Finch still clutching us, congratulating me with his wicked eyes. I looked in his eyes and I saw the Devil.

I reeled away, lacing my points all wrong, fastening my doublet. I leaned against the wall, then heard his voice, soft as cream, talking to the girl. Quiet, my love, all's well. Come now, to me.

"Watch, Harry!' I heard him say.

'My name is Nicholas,' I said to the wall. Nicholas, who threw gold to a poor man to spare his daughters from whoredom. Nicholas, who fired the sea and beat the Devil. The monks had finished their Office.

'Turn round, Nicholas,' said his voice.

Poor Witless Nick turned and saw Finch lay the girl on the ground. The lovely evening died; the sun limned the grasses with rose. It was very quiet, save for the owl and the sounds from the brittle grass—his soft voice and her constant moaning, like the

64

sounds made by the little Brecher wife miscarrying her child on the cobbles of Leicester. I wanted to look away; I could not even close my eyes, not even when he took her as a dog takes a bitch but with less tenderness. I knew that I stood on holy ground in company with the Devil, although she held him as if she were in the Pit and he her only salvation, her arms tight about his neck; in her frenzy she even tore out some of his hair. He was possessed, and the thing in him possessed her. He pulled her on top of him so that I should see her shame, and she convulsed like an otter dying on a spear. She had come to us a modest, happy little wench. Within half an hour he changed her into a whore.

When he had finished she stayed in the grass, and I knew that if all the monks had come from cloister, or the dead abbots had risen from their tombs, she would still have lain there, with her white body and her red hair streaming, shameless in her defilement.

He put himself quickly to rights, and wiped his pale face. Then he came and took my arm.

'I need ale,' he said.

I shook him off and went quickly to the far side of the churchyard and vomited in the grass. My face streamed with tears. Shivering, I heard him come up behind me.

'Are you ill?' He sounded worried. 'Do you want to go somewhere quiet? Not the Eagle . . .'

I rubbed the tears away before I turned to face him. I tried to speak; my tongue got stuck.

'What?' He leaned, puzzled. He looked tired, very young. Not the Devil now, but certainly his instrument.

'Goodbye, Finch,' I said.

I walked away down Ludgate Hill. I remember thinking I should have gone back and comforted the girl, found her clothes, asked her pardon, but I couldn't have touched her. I went quickly, afraid that Finch would follow me. I didn't know where I was going. Somehow I found myself on Cornhill. Witless Walter was in the cage. One of the mayor's deputies stood nearby and I gave him some money. He climbed the ladder and let Walter out of the cage. Walter came galloping after me like a foal, babbling. I shoved him away. I gave him some money too. But it was too late.

I found a tavern and ordered a drink, but couldn't swallow. I left, afraid that Finch might come in, and walked in fear through the City, but I did not see him. Finally I went home, in darkness. The cressets of the Watch flickered on the corner of Soper Lane; they moved away up into Poultry to look for felons and prentices out after curfew.

Edmund wasn't in our chamber, for which I thanked God. He had been to Bachelor's Acre and now I could hear him talking in my mother's solar. I went in stealth past Josina's door, unfit to kiss her.

I shall never speak to him again, I thought. I never want to see him again. I said it aloud. And we shall not be going to Bart's Fair. Josina will be disappointed, but it must be so.

I lay on the bed and wept. For the first time I was alarmed for my soul.

Piers, all goodness and wisdom, the Devil used him too. For the Old One is so subtle, he puts innocent words in the mouth which, when part of the whole pattern, are like a viper's bite—injuring one member, then spreading through the body until death. And the Devil is so beautiful; Lucifer was the brightest star.

I started hearing mass again and went to confession. Kneeling in the box at St Anthony's, I told the priest I had been drunken, had neglected my duty to God, had been guilty of avarice and fraud and robbing the poor; proud and envious, I had entertained unkind thoughts of my brother, and had lain with a woman not my wife. The priest gave me enough penances to last me a month, and I made a substantial donation to the church. I was too afraid to confess my feelings for Finch, and the brief black season of my love was over.

June melted into a hot penitent July, then August, month of death, sorrow and pestilence. Darkness fell on our house as in every August, with my mother constantly at prayer for my father's soul and those who died with him, and for Richard himself; she draped the raison of *Loyaulte me lie* with black as if it were Passiontide.

I also went to archery practice to please my mother, who never noticed. She was more preoccupied than ever; when not praying, she was writing letters. I shot at Moorfields under the eye of a dour sergeant who had been at Barnet and Tewkesbury, and I was his despair. I loosed the arrow either too soon or too late. Nine times out of ten I was wide of the mark. The sergeant cursed me: 'Oh damn you, Master Archer!' he'd cry, and that would make me want to laugh sadly, with my name so ill-fitting, and his biting comments that my father who had fought so valiantly when only seventeen would be ashamed of me. That I doubted: his kind ghost was with me during those hot aching days. I tried to be civil to Edmund, asking him how things went with him at work and in the cause, of which I still knew nothing. He ignored my overtures.

I thought often of Finch, with loathing. At times I caught myself muttering: I hate you, Finch. God curse you. And then it would come upon me, like a night-thief, how grievously I missed him. His jests, the way he looked sitting opposite me in a tavern, how clean he was, cleaner than I in some ways, with his constant tubs and his cakes of fine Bristol soap (as if he were trying always to wash something away), and the way he had looked while I told my story, quiet, his blue eyes shadowed. The discretion he had employed when we awoke together—not raging at me until Piers had left. One thing I never dwelt on was the way he had kissed me in Paul's churchyard. He had said he would cure me, and he had, too well. I never wanted to set eyes on him again.

By then there had been three notes from him. All said more or less the same: Where are you? Life's no fun without you. Come and see me. Always signed with the exquisite little bird. At one time I had dreaded meeting him face to face, round a corner or coming out of a tavern (I never went in taverns now), but I had only seen him twice and on both occasions he had not seen me. Once he was going through Soper Lane, probably off to collect Frays' dues, and another time, I glanced down the courtyard of the Eagle and saw him with the twins. He had a blonde woman on his lap and was pouring wine for them all. Sometimes I could make myself shiver with loathing. I was in this state the day I met Piers, coming out of the Whittington Library on Newgate.

I had Josina's dress under my arm in a parcel. The seamstress had had it proudly displayed on one of her young silkmaids, whose measurements were the same as my sister's. I was very drawn to the silkmaid. She smiled at me, and was tiny like Josina with the same medlar breasts, but black-haired, dark-eyed like a

Spanish woman. She flirted up and down wearing the dress and brushed against me out of the sight of her employer, looking at me with her large fruity eyes. I wanted her very badly. And I could have had her and loved her, I know that now, only I was too downcast to do anything about it.

It was not until I looked properly at the gown in the light that I realized it was wrong. Despite my vows to the priest, I nearly said Devil damn!

'I asked for gold cloth. This is white.'

The seamstress was agitated. She took a fold of the gown between her needle-pocked fingers as if hopeful of changing the colour by alchemy.

'White, sir, you said. Trimmed with gold.'

'No. Gold. White petticoat. And a gold cap.'

The seamstress pursed her mouth, her eyes anguished. The little silkmaid stopped preening.

'White, sir, you said.' Then the seamstress burst into tears, and the dark Spanish treasure looked about to join her, so I said desperately: 'Very well. White it shall be. But next time, please remember my orders.' They were so grateful they sat me down and brought me ale, and the silkmaid hovered, waiting in vain for me to make an assignation, and the business was thus concluded. Walking through Newgate I met Piers, he called my name. I hastened away, but he came panting up to me. He was from Hugh's house; I thought of Hugh, the bad things, his foul mouth, his dedicated lechery, his cruelty to the cookboys. Then I thought of his tender stroking of the little fighting-cock, and the way he'd thrust gold at me because he wished to see me well dressed, and his words: 'I'm glad you love me, I only want you to be happy.' And the whole pattern blurred and I was lost. The only weapon I could call on was my whispered hatred.

Piers called me again. Suddenly I thought: He isn't even of Finch's blood. No harm can grow from this good person. So I stopped and turned. His face glowed from the libraries of joy, his hands were covered with paint and ink.

'You go so fast!' Blinking, with warm weak eyes. 'I've thought of you often. Are you well?'

'Good day, Piers,' I said stiffly. 'I'm well enough,' and made to go on. He caught my sleeve. I hardly ever wore the ill-gotten suits these days and the sleeve he held was the one the dog had torn when I was collecting for Finch.

'Stay a moment,' he said. 'I liked talking with you when you came to see us.'

Across the meadow in Smithfield, St Bart's bell let out a tremendous boom. It seemed to shake the nearby cloister and library.

'What are you studying these days?'

'Oh, Nicholas'—his face became rapt—'something so wonderful—beyond this world. Meister Eckhart . . . the Eternal Birth. It puts everything so sharp and clear.'

'Good,' I said. 'Farewell, Piers; my respects to your father.'

'Very well,' he said, then unexpectedly: 'Remember that I pray for you. I am your true bedesman, Nicholas.'

I was so touched by this that I came back. He said: 'Would you like to see the library? We can talk there, if we don't make too much noise.'

The library was through the cloister and very peaceful. A great room with a hammerbeam roof and stained glass lights which shed jewelled squares and lozenges on the manuscripts and rolls. There were one or two of Caxton's printed books chained to lecterns. Monks sat together in the double-setters, following texts line by line with hands like veined old leaves. Piers and I sat down.

'Well,' I said. 'Are you going to show me Meister Eckhart?'

He shook his head. 'Not yet. We'd need time . . . it's too marvellous for haste. But . . . have you ever heard of the Hooks of God?"

Only as one of Finch's terrible oaths, I thought.

'God the Fisherman,' Piers whispered. 'Oh, Nicholas! the divine fisher's hook searching for our souls and bringing us to the net of His Love . . .' He smiled very sweetly. 'It would apply especially to you, for St Nicholas went out with the fishermen, as I told you. The love of God is like a fisher's hook. He who is caught by it is held by the strongest bond and yet the stress is pleasant. He who takes this sweet burden on himself comes nearer to the true aim than by any harsh ordinance devised by man. Moreover he can sweetly bear all that happens to him. All

69

that God inflicts he can take cheerfully . . . you are God's own, by this dear bond.'

He bent his head. 'It's too much for me,' he said.

He looked up, rubbing his sore eyes. 'I'm sad that you quarrelled with Hugh,' he said. 'He has few friends.'

That I can well believe, I thought. My hatred rose like bile. 'I don't think we need trouble about Hugh,' I said.

'He's wretchedly unhappy,' said Piers. 'He misses you. He's beating the boys worse than ever. One said the other day he'd rather be a leper in the lazar-house than work for us; he broke his time and ran away. Hugh . . . he's even shed a few tears.'

'Never!' I said loudly. One of the monks turned round and hushed me. I whispered: 'He couldn't weep if he tried.'

'Oh yes, he can,' Piers said softly. 'When I was very small . . . my uncles used to take him away and hurt him. Sometimes he cried half the night.'

Those were the words that did the damage. I felt my heart move sickly. I still felt I could murder the twins.

'The other day I mentioned you. He swore at me, but he wept. He loves you, Nicholas.'

'How are your father's eyes?' I said coldly.

'They're always worse in August. He was asking where the lotion was your sister was going to send him.' Then he said quickly: 'Why did you and Hugh quarrel? Was it over a woman?'

'You could say that.'

'What happened?'

'I can't tell you, Piers.'

He said: 'Whatever it was, he'll have forgotten about it by now. He only wants to see you.' He looked at my parcel. 'What have you there?'

'A gown for my sister.' (Bought with the tears and sweat of honest folk. Frays' dues. I'd like to give them their dues.)

'And you're unhappy too,' said Piers quietly.

I couldn't answer.

'Would you like to talk with Master John? Nicholas, he's so kind and wise. He doesn't judge.' He pointed at a little oak door under an ogee-shaped arch. 'I could take you to him now.'

'Thank you, Piers. No. I've nothing to tell. Anyway, I go to my own chaplain at St Anthony's.'

70

'This woman—why don't you go and see her, then? Sometimes a woman can mend matters between men.'

Sweet God! go to the Tabard? Is she still there? Perhaps she's dead, or gone mad, or bearing my bastard or Hugh's, perhaps she's still lying, bare as a worm . . .

Piers got up saying he must go back to the shop, for customers were expected. We parted outside the library, and I, turmoiled, went down Chepeside and home. I thought with sorrow of the redhaired girl. If things had been different, perhaps we could have been friends, even lovers. Suddenly, as never before, I longed for a wife, to love and be loved. I knew now what a woman looked like, could imagine the enchanting little silkmaid without her clothes. It made me sad. I felt despoiled. Finch, how I hate you.

I laid the parcel on Josina's bed, and loitered within earshot. Presently the silence was broken by her cry of joy. She rushed out and flung herself on me, showering me with thanks, and she never asked how I had earned the money.

'I shall be the most beautiful woman at Bart's Fair.' Then her brows came together, and her lips trembled. 'I'd forgotten,' she said quietly, 'that we are not going after all.'

For an instant I was tempted. No. We would be bound to meet Finch, and I never wanted to see him again as long as I drew breath.

'Never mind, my dove,' I said. 'It'll serve for your wedding day. Put it in your dower chest.'

'My wedding day!' she said gloomily. 'The gown won't fit me by then. I'll be forty years old, and long past children.'

She went quietly back to her chamber. There was still no dowry. I wished my mother would write to Sir James, but she was even less likely to have the stomach for such dealings now. I could almost smell the plot cooking, the plan concerning the mysterious Boy, and Edmund, and another half-forgotten name: Sir Edward Brampton. Only last week I'd heard her mention Brampton to Edmund, with that quiver in her voice, token of the cause. Brampton was a Portuguese Jew whom King Edward had converted to the faith. He had been one of King Richard's most trusted followers, but strangely, had not fought at Bosworth. His name gave weight to my mother's cause, and added to the enigma.

71

I was downcast. I wanted to punish myself further. That is the reason I took Piers's advice. I went down to Galley Quay and took a boat to Southwark, to the Tabard. I had to wait outside for five minutes for I thought I might be sick. Then I entered and sat down in the booth we had occupied the night of the Marching Watch. The servitors were busy. I kept my eyes down until someone came to stand by me in a white apron.

'Your pleasure, sir?' Red hair, green eyes, a pleasant smile. She had a tureen of boiling soup in her hands. I looked up and waited for her to pour it over my head.

I let the light fall fully on my face. She smiled at me, absolutely without recognition. I'm the man who raped you, I wanted to shout. Kill me. She was happy, she was tranquil, she was not with child that I could see. I'm the man who watched you in transports of shame and lust, I wanted to yell. I cleared my throat: this should make things certain.

'My name is Nicholas,' I said.

'Good morning, Master Nicholas,' said the girl. 'We have fine roast ribs of beef, or a good pike taken from the river an hour ago. What would you like?'

She turned round to two little serving-boys hurrying past—she tapped one lightly on the head with a spoon, admonishing him for spilling soup. Then her face came back, still cordial, if a little impatient.

'We're quite busy, sir,' she said. 'Will you order?'

I got up and blundered past her, out of the inn. Gaping, I watched her through the window. She was laughing and shaking her head. She went to serve some men at another booth. Did I imagine that she flaunted her hips a little more than previously? For my life, I couldn't tell. I only knew that she was unharmed, and more certainly that the memory of Finch, if memory there was, had wiped me completely from her mind.

Back home, I found Josina in her knot garden. I hate you, Finch, I thought. But it is only Christian to succour the sick.

'Sister,' I said, 'could you make some eye lotion for an old man going blind?'

'Easily.' She moved to where the little stream flowed into the pond and the Yellow Flag grew with its dagger leaves. She uprooted one whole plant and brought it to me.

'Fleur de lys,' she said. 'The flower of France.'

'Dragon flower.'

'Jacob's Sword.'

'*Flambe d'eau.*'

'You win,' she said. 'I'll distil it now.' She moved towards the house. 'Is the old man coming here?'

'No,' I said. 'I will deliver it.'

Even before I opened the cookshop door I knew he was inside. There was something about his presence so vital it could burst invisibly through thick oak. I carried Josina's little flask of distilled flowers as if it were a thunderflash. I kicked the door open with unnecessary violence; it crashed back and Finch, who was standing alone by the hearth, looked round, startled.

I had imagined we might circle one another like strange suspicious dogs for a while, and a diffident conversation ending in an awkward truce. Nothing like that happened. He came to me and I went to him and we were in one another's arms. Laughing, laughing, and he hit me so hard on the back I began to cough and choke, and he hit me again, nearly knocking me down. Then he pulled my hair, and punched my jaw, and cried: 'Oh, Nicholay! you skinny devil!' and rushed to the kitchen to get a flagon of wine, and if there weren't tears in his eyes there certainly were in mine. I knew then that he needed me as much as I needed him; he needed me to share and bear his sins, and perhaps to eat his sins when he was dead.

He was pale and had lost weight. But his eyes were still the most beautiful, next to Josina's, and his laugh the loudest, and his language the foulest, and when he got the wine I heard him smack a cookboy's head just for sport, and we sat down and talked for an hour, then he took me to see Nemo.

Previously, I had been afraid of Nemo. But when he took the fiery little bird out of his cage and put him in my arms so that I could hold him while he trimmed his talons, my fear fled. He told me to stroke him, and the bird quietened magically, while Hugh tenderly sharpened the wicked talons with his little knife. 'I'll have to fine the claws again before Bart's,' he said, 'and hackle him properly. He's in good trim, isn't he?' Then he started to

73

laugh again and his eyes glowed at me in the dim loftlight. And he said without preamble: 'How's the lovemaking?'

'Hugh, there's a little silkmaid, a real beauty . . .' and I described her, and he said mischievously:

'Mind I don't get there before you—where did you say she worked?' and I gave him a blow in the chest and said: 'Devil damn! as if I'd tell you!'

When we finished laughing, he said seriously: 'Nicholas. How would you like to handle Nemo at Bart's for me? I'll have to be round and about while we're there—there's a lot of side bets I want to place. Look—he's taken to you—you can pit him for me if you like.'

His precious bird. I said: 'I'll be delighted, Hugh.'

We went tumbling down the loft-ladder again, and had some more wine. I could hear Piers in the side parlour, talking to customers. Hugh picked up the flask of lotion. He sniffed it and pulled a face.

'What the devil's this?'

'My sister made it. For the old dad's eyes.'

He replaced the cork. He said: 'Oh yes. I remember.'

It was the week before the Fair.

I even remember the weather that day, when Josina and Edmund and I went out together. It was the kind that had hung over us at Leicester during the battle-week. There was thunder about. The day was so sultry that the birds stopped singing in the trees along the road we took through Newgate to the great ward of Farringdon; the ward that stretches south-west down to the Temple and the Strand and river, and north and north-west to Smithfield and the Priory of St Bartholomew in whose precincts the Fair was always held.

Josina rode the cob. During the past weeks it had seen more of the road than its stable, with my mother constantly sending Jankin off with her secret letters. Jankin was ordered to accompany us to the Fair. He came on foot; a big amiable man armed with a stout staff, which annoyed me, for I fancied myself well able to protect us all. Edmund and I rode two other thin nags from our stable.

In her quiet way my sister was of course beside herself. She never asked why I had changed my mind at the last moment. Perhaps she feared I might change it again. It was five years since she had left the house for any sort of celebration. The only outings she had had were three visits to my father's tomb, and once with my mother to Winchester where Sir James was lodged, for my mother wanted him to see what a beauty Josina had become and how the years were slipping away with her youth, yet there was still no dowry.

I said a beauty, but when I saw her dressed in the gown I was lost for words. She was like a small perfect lily-flower. Her hair was hidden under the little gold cap, her neck a flower-stem. I thought: it was worth it. All the shame and crime, for if those shopkeepers could see her, they would not grudge their stolen earnings. I think I was more Witless Nick that day than ever before or since.

I took her little hands, the nails cut straight across like a child's, and said: 'Iseult. You are Iseult.'

'Ah, Tristan!' So long since we had played. Iseult at the court of King Mark, in sadness, despite the jewels and purple cloth of Hungary and Thessaly . . . with Tristan ever near, until the coming of the wicked dwarf and Tristan betrayed, and Iseult doomed, thrown to the lepers . . . She lifted her pale flower-face for me to kiss her.

'I'm unworthy,' I said.

'Madness!' She put her arms round my neck and soundly kissed me. I thought: Until I've searched the world and found her equal, I shall never marry. The parlour door opened.

'Careful! Here comes King Mark.'

Edmund appeared. He looked quite spruce. He was carrying his tall yew bow and a quiver full of arrows fletched with parchment. He saw Josina, swallowed several times and said gruffly: 'Sweet Mother Mary!' Then he knelt at her feet, kissed her hands, shaking his head and muttering. I was pleased to see him shocked and ravished by something I had wrought, though it was Josina who was beauty, not the dress.

He was in good spirits, for him. All week he had been on the Acre, practising for the contest. The fletcher had given him leave from work. Edmund seemed to be able to do as he pleased with the fletcher, who was also in mourning this week. I had an inkling

75

that he was also an active part of the plan. I said kindly to Edmund: 'I wish you all good fortune today. Those other boys don't stand a chance.'

He looked at me suspiciously. Then his face cleared.

"Thank you, Nicholas. You look very grand. I hope you win some money.'

I was wearing my best suit, black broadcloth, the doublet slashed to show my white silk shirt. I wanted to look well to escort Josina. I also wished I could win a little money; my purse was not at its healthiest, since I had stopped collecting Frays' dues. But I had enough for today.

'Is Dame Philip coming with us?' Edmund asked.

'She is not!' I winked at Josina. Fairs are for the young, Dame Philip had said, and she was, like my mother, dressed in black this week. As soon as we had gone out, they would be off to St Anthony's for a vigil likely to last all day and possibly half the night. Dame Philip could sleep in church as well as anywhere.

Together we went along and tapped at the solar door. My mother had taken my father's sword out of a chest, and was standing, hands folded on its hilt, her head bent. She had been weeping. I felt so sorry for her, and the bright day clouded a trifle. Her black hood fell half over her face, and she looked like the friar again, riding to Leicester.

'We're away now, madam,' I said. She looked at me vaguely, then at Josina, muttering: 'Black and white. A raven and a swan,' and for a moment I was alarmed that constant mourning and sleepless nights and plans had attacked her wits. Then she beckoned to Edmund; he went forward and knelt. He placed his hand over hers, on the hilt of the sword. It was a private moment. Josina and I might not have been there. She said: 'God's blessing go with you, my dear son.' She kissed his brow. Distinctly I heard her whisper. 'Prove yourself today. Soon, now. Be patient a little longer.'

Jankin had brought the sidesaddle for the cob. I lifted Josina up and draped her lily-whiteness in a cloak. Edmund and I mounted. Jankin grinned at me.

'Don't you gallop away, sir. I'm not too fast on my legs.'

We went steadily towards Newgate. The sun had climbed half way up the spire of St Anthony's. The yellow sky seemed to press down on us; the birds were quiet. I thought about Nemo. Finch had been feeding him with great science for the pit; he'd been up in the loft nearly all day every day. I'd seen him giving Nemo raw offals, tiny pieces of beefsteak, every hour on the hour. Little bowls of fresh blood and occasionally the mead-soaked barley. Nemo was set to kill, and I only hoped I could handle him right.

We came into the ward of Farringdon and saw ahead the civic procession going to open the Fair. The town crier went first, ringing his bell, and then, in a whirl of dust and a lilting medley of hoofs and belled bridles, the Mayor in scarlet with his sword-bearer and officers. Following them came the banner of St Bartholomew the Great, tasselled and jewelled and held so high that it brushed against the heavy green branches overhead. As the gap between us and the procession narrowed, the trumpets began to sound, a silver, flaunting bray, and the drummers struck their tabors, fierce as firecrackers, the rat-a-tat piercing the heavy air. This is how it must be to ride to battle, I thought, and bowed for an instant to my father's memory.

Swarms of barefoot children were following the procession, and barking dogs by the dozen. Josina's cob was still going well, she sat lightly, her body turned gracefully in the sidesaddle. Her head was up, her face pink. 'Take the cloak off,' I said suddenly. 'Let them all see you,' and she shrugged out of it and threw it to Jankin. I glanced behind. Edmund had his bow slung over his back, his quiver at his belt. Scores of people were on the road behind us, riding, walking, driving carts. There were several lords among the throng, the spears and banners of their escort caught the sunlight. Alewives and artisans came striding along. On the horizon behind loomed the standard of the Butchers' Guild, for this was their day, Bartholomew their patron saint.

Also on the road were being driven two or three bulls—a small white one, a larger red-and-white and a black bull. Fiercely horned, they snorted and drove with their heads at the dust. Behind them on a cart in a big cage sat the mastiffs and terriers that would be used for the bull-baiting. And further back, roaming uneasily in another cage were a couple of shabby old bears.

A juggler ran past, throwing up three golden apples, followed by a man with a soot-blackened face, leading two chained apes. A young man spurred his horse past. He wore a gold collar over a fur-trimmed mantle of blue sarcenet. I knew him: he was the lordling who had bought Bedesman, and I wanted to weep, for he was not riding Bedesman today.

'Nicholas, be happy,' said Josina, faint over the bawling trumpets and drums and the shouting crowd that had nearly caught up with us. I managed to smile at her. My kind lily, my Iseult, my beloved white lady. We had nearly reached the entrance to the precincts of St Bart's. Ancient tombs lay ahead. The Mayor was already through in splendour. A mountebank came tossing somersaults, flipping back and forth like a blown leaf. Josina urged the cob forward so she could ride near me. 'Be happy, Nicholas!' I caught up her left hand from the bridle and kissed it. At that instant I saw Finch. His eyes were on us. He was in his forest green attire. Beside him, shaking with fear of him, was one of the cookboys with Nemo in his cage. I raised my hand, and mouthed to Finch: 'I'll see you later.' His face seemed deathly pale. He's worried about Nemo's contest, I thought. He nodded, looked away.

Edmund said: 'Who was that?'

'A friend.'

Edmund shifted his bow more comfortably. The scar on the back of his hand was vivid today. It stood out like a brand. Witless Walter came riding by into the precinct, borne on the back of someone's dray, and full of babbling joy. I had had to avoid Walter since the night I had given him money, or he would have allowed me no peace. It wasn't money he wanted; he only wanted what he thought was conversation. Beggars hobbled in front of our horses. They were what the Mayor deplored as 'sturdy cripples', and quite shameless. I saw one man strap up a perfectly sound leg and swing away on crutches, while a blind man capably counted coins he'd gained on the road. I wondered if Patch were coming, but Piers had told me that the old man disliked fairs; they reminded him of one May Day when he'd met his lost love. I still couldn't fathom whether he spoke of the Queen or the girl who became a nun.

The precinct was about a mile square. To the east were the post and rail enclosures for the bull- and bear-baiting, and the cockpit. Ahead, dwarfed by distance, were the archery butts with the loges

78

for the judges set up nearby. Edmund's eyes went to them. To me they were vague shapes, but Edmund's magic eyes picked out the stuffed and gaudy popinjays on their posts, the forty-foot targets, and the standing butts. A little to the west behind the archery range, the dense forest began and woodland encroached on the field on three sides.

'How many heats are there?' I asked him.

'Three, I think, but you hear so many different tales. I know the last is the running, when they drive out the deer.'

'What time does your contest start?'

'Soon, I trust. But the prizes aren't awarded until near sundown.'

'And you'll be there to receive them all,' I said. He almost smiled at me. Perhaps after today we should be friends again.

We left the horses under some trees. People thronged the meadow. Stalls had been set up; chapmen, cheapjacks, sweet-sellers, ale and wine booths, drapers and jewellers showing their wares, butchers carving meat. Friars and monks went ambling about. Prentices linked arms and ran through the crowd. The young lord with the gold collar tethered his horse near ours, leaving a boy to guard it. I looked carefully at the horse. No, it was not my honey-coated Bedesman; I knew he was dead. The town crier rang his bell. He stood near the entrance of the precinct, holding a decorated staff crowned with a great gilt glove.

'What's that?' asked Josina over the yammering bell.

'It's to show that strangers and merchants may enter the City as long as they respect its Charter. He's going to open the Fair.'

The bell stopped. The crier bawled: 'Hear ye! The glove is up!' and folk rushed towards the stalls. Drink began to flow. Clear spaces appeared in the meadow, instantly filled by jugglers throwing up burning brands, women balancing themselves on swords driven into the ground, men with performing monkeys. A troupe of wrestlers, stripped to the waist, prepared for the first bout of a day-long contest.

The bulls were led in and tethered ready for baiting and the two ancient bears were unloaded, still caged, from the cart. Dogs fought, children screamed.

Edmund said nervously: 'Nicholas, I think I'd better go and see my sergeant from the Acre. He's over there.' He pointed to the archery range. I could see only a cloudy knot of figures. 'I must ask his advice.'

'Then join us for dinner. There.' They were laying long tables in the middle of the meadow. In between them an ox was roasting, its horns carefully arranged to lie over the edge of the firepit. The horns must remain undamaged; part of the day's mystery. This was an old place. Long ago, other festivals were held here, when the sacrifice had been more than dead oxen.

A great cry went up from the entrance to the precinct.

'Rahere is coming!'

The old Rahere had been dead for three hundred years. This was a man dressed as the King's Fool who became Abbot of St Bartholomew's. He capered in, a tall man in motley, jeering at the people, and there was something real and menacing about his mockery, his face was cruel as he struck out with his little gilded doll. Behind him came a pretty lad dressed as Maid Marian, then a whole train of weird mummers, men inside animal skins, stilt-walkers and the Hobby, whose appearance made Josina gasp and terrified some nearby children. The Hobby could have been one man or two, dancing under an immense gown which hung to the ground and was starred with cabalistic symbols. From the Hobby's chest protruded the neck and head of a meek little horse, but the Hobby's face was a grotesque, lolling mask with evil eyes and snapping jaws. It had a flowing mane and tail, and its black hands waved through holes in its mantle. It came prancing through the people. Women screamed and scattered; men guffawed, knowing themselves safe from the Hobby's power. The Hobby came straight to Josina and caught her round the waist, pulling her beneath its gown. She vanished completely. Jankin raised his staff and looked at me. I shook my head.

'It's only sport.' Josina reappeared from under the Hobby's gown. She was laughing, if a bit pale.

'If he's spoiled my gown, I'll . . .' But it was still pristine white.

'Praise God, the blacking doesn't come off his hands. What did he say to you under there?'

She was blushing. 'He said. "Now you'll have many children!" and I said: "I'd rather be wed first, sir!" and he laughed.'

'That was quick. But stay by me, poppet. Tell me what you'd like.'

Jankin cleared his throat. I thought: The poor soul sees as little life as Josina, living at our house. I said: 'You can leave my lady with me, Jankin. Go and have a drink.' I'd seen him looking gloomily at the ale-stall. I put money in his fist. Off he went.

Rahere was up on a block in the centre, haranguing the people. He had an abbot's mitre on his head. We strolled over, but it was difficult to catch his mocking sermon over the din. The noises of a troupe of bagpipers warred with a band playing fife and shawm, and the drums went banging on. The sun began to rise suddenly and surprisingly high, as if it were anxious to have this day over and done. Rahere ranted on, the cruel-faced Fool on his block, with his little gilded doll. The ox-horns hung on the edge of the burning pit. The bulls waiting to be baited bellowed and tore the ground with their weaponed heads. It was a day of horns.

Wherever she went, eyes followed her, some unseen by me. I swear she could, dowry or no, have snared any of the young Lancastrian lords who flocked the fairground. Even the pretty women looked at her with hatred. Sublimely innocent, un-conscious of admiration or envy, she went with me like a queen. When we passed some prentices, one of them groaned loudly and pretended to fall on his dagger. Her lips twitched; she understood that much.

'How foolish they are.'

'I'd say they were uncommonly wise.' I put my arm about her. In the same moment I saw my silkmaid and she saw me. Her black Spanish eyes filled with tears, and she dived through the crush, looking very pretty in blue with a yellow hood. I thought of chasing her, to explain who Josina was, but it was too late. The day was growing very hot. Men sweated over the pit where the ox was nearly cooked. They had chopped off its head behind the horns, which lay cooling on the ground. We took a little walk to see our horses were safe; the lordling's horse-boy had gone to sleep on the edge of the wood. Avenues of sunlight filtered into the leafy wood, like cloisters leading to the naves of dark cathedrals, where great oaks grew massed together for miles. The scent of bruised grass mingled with burning wood-ash, the warm smell of horses, Josina's vervain perfume, the cloying tang from the sweet-stalls. We saw Jankin sitting on a bench with a full mug

81

in his hand, grinning contentedly as he talked with a group of yeomen.

At sight of me he got to his feet.

'Sit down, Jankin. Join us for dinner if you like.' He sat, looking relieved.

I bought Josina a trumpery little necklet at the trinket stall. It took her fancy though I didn't care for it; the jewels were glass. But she could have what she liked. Oh yes, this day of horns and fire was hers, as well as belonging to St Bart and the Butchers' Guild and Rahere, who stalked through the crowd like an avenging angel, followed by his unholy, masked company. The wrestlers were in full bout near the baiting area and the cockpit, an oval patch fenced about with wattle. I couldn't see Finch. We watched the Cornish wrestling for a while. The prentices were shouting and yelling. Bets were being placed and increased so fast it was hard to keep a tally. 'Four marks on Trevennick!' someone bawled. 'Double!' cried a known voice. I looked past the sweating grapplers in the ring and saw the Fray twins, their heavy faces flushed, their little eyes avid.

'Let's go and see Edmund.' By means of shoving I opened a way to the archery butts. The markers were clearly etched against the leafy trees and little paths leading into the forest. Edmund was listening to his sergeant. The contest had been put back for an hour, and I felt sorry for Edmund. The sergeant talked on.

'Remember, you lad. Never draw with the strength of the arm, always the strength of the body. Keep your right at rest on the nerve. Press your whole weight into the horns of the bow.'

Edmund nodded. I saw his fist clenched tight by his side. The sergeant went to instruct others, and Edmund came to us.

'It's this damnable waiting.' He looked so like my father! That anxious face in the last days at Westminster when the King was ill and his reputation ruined and all our fortunes blowing in the wind.

Josina said: 'Shall I stay with you? You can tell them I'm your wife!' and laughed.

'I wish you were,' he said.

'Be careful,' I told her. The archers were practising, their flying arrows thudding heavily into the straw butts. 'Stand back. I must leave you. I have to see about a cockfight.'

'I'll stay with Edmund,' she said, 'until dinner'.

There was still no sign of Finch. But I saw my silkmaid again, and she had acquired an admirer, a tall young man who looked as if he couldn't believe his good fortune. He had his arm about her and it looked as if they were going towards the wood. At the wrestling ring, the Cornishmen were groaning and panting. No holds or hitches allowed below the belt, and no kicking. Trevennick had just kicked his opponent in the backside.

'Striking with the side of the foot only!' roared the marshal, and the Cornishmen swore at him in their strange tongue. The watchers roared; someone doubled his bet on the fouled wrestler, Polcarne. The Frays raised their hands to me in greeting. I nodded coldly. Polcarne suddenly rushed in and threw his opponent who landed with two hips and a shoulder squarely on the ground. The marshal bounded into the ring and knelt to judge the fall.

'I went in for this last year,' said Finch's voice. He stood suddenly close to me. 'Not Cornish—Cumberland. Greek wrestling.'

'Where have you been?' I asked. 'I didn't see you anywhere.'

'But I saw you,' he said. 'Riding in. And again, five minutes ago. Going up to the butts.'

'Are you well, Hugh?' I said. He had the most peculiar air. His eyes were feverish. He looked ill, unsmiling.

Trevennick made another foul; he caught Polcarne in a groin-hitch and threw him. The crowd went wild with rage. Robin Fray was wagering against his brother on Polcarne, laying twelve marks. The twins looked across at us. Finch raised his hand, shouted 'Double!' to Simon. The marshal ran into the ring again and gave Trevennick a final warning.

'Yes. Greek wrestling,' said Hugh. 'I won. By a foul too. He tried to bite my nose off. Guess where I bit him. I won.'

'You would.' He smiled at last, put his arm through mine, his forest green against my black.

'Where's Nemo?'

He looked round. 'I left him with that bloody boy.' The cookboy, aged about eight, was a new one, with a pretty face. He stood a little distance behind. Under a tree was Nemo's cage. The bird was in it. Quiet.

83

'You swine,' said Finch to the boy. 'I told you to put him somewhere cool.' He smacked the boy's face. The boy darted behind me, his desperate hands clutching my belt. Finch turned back to watch the wrestlers.

'Don't hit him, Hugh,' I said. 'Look, Nemo is in the shade.'

'Don't what?' he said. His eyes were quite blank, very dark blue. Sweet Christ, I thought. He's forgotten already. I know he forgets, but this is strange, he must be ill. Polcarne heaved his opponent in the air and brought him down with an earth-shaking crash. He pressed Trevennick down, two shoulders and one hip, and held him there. The marshal dived in and pronounced a true fall. The crowd cheered and cursed. Polcarne strutted.

'There,' I said. 'You've won.'

'I always do.' He gave a little shudder.

I knelt down to look at Nemo. He was magnificent. Finch had hackled him to perfection. All his flowing tail-feathers had been sheared, his wings were exquisitely trimmed to a fine rounded line. His eyes were a warning. His beak and claws were as sharp as Finch's little knife and his plumage the colour of Hell.

'You still want me to handle him,' I said in awe.

'Yes, Nicholas. You're my cockmaster for today. Don't give him any more meat. Just the barley. And this, the strongest of all. Only a few drops.' He took a tiny flask from his pouch. The odour almost blinded me.

'Sweet God,' I said. '*Aqua vitæ.*'

'Yes. It'll make him mad. No other bird could beat him.'

'I think I need a drink as well,' I said. I picked up the cage. We went to an ale booth. I slid a coin into the little cookboy's hand. Finch saw me; he saw everything.

'You're soft, Nicholas,' he said.

'I'm not. I feel sorry for the poor devil.'

Finch laughed, scowling. 'Pretty, isn't he?' he said viciously. So all his talk of forgetting and forgiving the Frays was mere panache. In that moment I almost understood him. He called for wine. I put Nemo's cage under the bench. There were things I wanted to ask Finch about the cockfight. If he were white with nervousness over it, so was I, and there was poor Edmund, shaking for his honour up at the butts. It was a strange day, not as I'd imagined it.

'How much shall I lay on him? Do you want me to place any bets?'

'No, I told you. I'll place my own side bets. I must be round and about. There are some wonderful cocks. Some lords have brought twenty apiece. As for your stake—it's your money. But I want Nemo to fight Bellerophon. He's the real cream today. If you have to wait for an hour, he must be pitted against Bellerophon.'

'Oh God, Hugh,' I said. 'Do you trust me?'

His eyes were violet blue, their whites bright as silver. His black hair was trimmed and curled, his pale face tight. He said the strangest thing:

'I trust you, Nicholas. I trust you never to trust me.'

I shook my head and poured him some wine, ministering to him as he usually cossetted me; he took the cup and gazed into its red heart, not tasting it. I thought: He's like a stranger. Not a joke, hardly an oath. But he looks as wonderful as ever, more handsome perhaps through his abstractedness and the way his eyes change all the time. I wish I looked like him. I wish I could have had the silkmaid. The sun was climbing.

'Dinner,' I said, getting up. 'Come on, Hugh.' I gave Nemo's cage to the little boy; he fell in obediently behind. Finch rose from the bench like a sleepwalker. I linked his arm and we went to where I could see Josina and Edmund sitting at the long table. Jankin was there, further down, with a full tankard. Near the table, Finch jibbed like a horse at a graveyard.

'No,' he muttered. 'I can't stay.'

Now I was furious. I gave him a sharp dig in the ribs. 'Go on, Finch, damn you. Sit down with us, and be civil.'

He made to go round the bottom of the table and sit near Jankin. I manœuvred him to the other side and forced him on to the bench beside Edmund. I sat opposite with Josina and made the introductions. Edmund, his hands clenched with thoughts of the contest, muttered a greeting. Finch muttered something back. They stared at one another for an instant, the gentian eyes and the white-ringed other-worldly eyes meeting. Josina inclined her long neck and smiled. Finch got up to bow to her and sat down again. The cooks and servers came with trenchers of bread and plates piled with roast ox. Jugs of wine and ale appeared, and savoury coffins of pastry filled with leeks, like the ones we had once eaten in the Greyhound. And now the two people I loved best were with me, at the same table.

Edmund said: 'I can't eat, Nicholas. I'm sorry.'

'Leave it. You'll shoot better on an empty belly.'

I poured us some wine. Neither he nor Finch touched it. Josina drank, and ate her dinner with enjoyment. Then, leaning her head against my shoulder, she said softly:

'Pourquoi est-ce-que ton ami est si triste?'

She often spoke to me the beautiful courtly French we had used at Westminster. She turned her laughing eyes on Finch. He looked at her, then down at his untouched food, then away. Devil damn me if I know, I thought.

'We're the only ones eating,' I said to her. I felt quite the lord of the manor, did Witless Nick, with his little company of guests. I leaned down the table and called: 'Drink up, Jankin!' and he thanked me, raising his tankard. A trumpet sounded. Edmund turned even paler than Finch.

'The signal,' he said faintly. 'The contest begins.'

'And I must go,' said Finch. 'I'll see you later, Nicholas.' He rose, bowed to us all and walked away as if devils were after him. He passed Rahere, who came sneering through the people with his demonic entourage. He had discarded the abott's mitre and, pagan and terrifying, was wearing the ox-horns on his head.

'So sad, your friend,' said Josina. 'So quiet and sad.'

'He's not himself,' I said, watching his forest green merge with the crowd. There was much I had wanted to ask him about Nemo. The cookboy stood by, waiting for orders. I told him to take the bird to the cockpit. I gave him another coin.

Josina and I went up to the butts where the first heat was beginning. We stood well back, watching Edmund. About forty young archers waited their turn in a line at the Flemish butts. The Mayor and aldermen sat up in the loges, the nearby forest cast a cool shadow. Some children were chasing in and out of the trees and the Master of Archery sent his footmen to shoo them away. The young men stood on the 30-foot marker. The butts were quartered in blue and red squares. Edmund was calm. The trumpet sounded, the Archery Master called a command and the first bowman stepped forward.

They were all very good indeed. Edmund's turn came ninth; he

86

rested his bow on the ground for a moment. His lips moved, he crossed himself with the scarred hand. Then he raised his bow, thrust his whole body sidelong into its horns, his heel dug firm, his head steady, his fingers delicate veterans of the bowstring. The muscle in his shoulder waxed to the size of an orange. I never saw the arrow fly, but heard it strike the right quarter of the butt, then saw it shaking there, deep and true. There was silence as he reloaded. He drew again; the breath hissed from his lungs a second before the arrow hit the centre of the top left quarter. There was a little murmur from the Mayor's loge. He took a fresh arrow, working fast, drew and loosed, and the wand fled, impaling itself dead centre in the lower right quarter. He drew again, his small slender body forcing itself into the thrust, and the last arrow homed into the last quarter.

The Archery Master's men ran forward to judge his work. It was a faultless pattern of impaled wands. They took out measuring rods, and turned to smile at Edmund. He lowered his bow slowly. The Mayor leaned down from his loge and said something to one of his officers. Then he clapped his hands and the patter of applause began, like sudden heavy rain. Edmund stepped away and came to us.

'That's only the beginning,' he said.

'Matchless, Edmund,' I said. 'You'll win.'

'For the love of God! Nicholas, if you're going to talk that way, you'd best go.'

The archer following him had botched his performance. His arrow hung from the marker like a dead man's hand. He laughed and cursed. Jankin had come to stand behind us, ale-mug still in his fist like an extension of his body.

'By Christ!' he muttered. 'Our boy's a marvel.'

'Hold your tongue, Jankin,' said Edmund dementedly. 'Your pardon, Jankin. Sweet Mother Mary!'

'Would you like us to leave you?' I said. The last archer was drawing; his pattern was good so far, but as I watched his arrow pierced the right quarter too low. The marshals measured it and shook their heads. He turned away, grinning. He was richly dressed; to him it was a pastime. The straw butts were dismantled. Propped against the loge were the posts with the stuffed popinjays. They seemed an impossible distance from where the line was finally drawn. The sun was tipping towards the west.

'I'll have to go in a few minutes. I'll return as soon as I can.' Edmund shook his head, not listening.

In the loge, the Mayor's servants were bringing refreshment. The trumpets sounded. A herald jumped up on a bale.

'My lord Mayor will retire for half an hour. All archers competing be ready for the second trial after that time.'

'Dear God.' Edmund looked at me imploringly. He gripped my hand. 'I think I shall spew. I'm so ashamed.' He looked queasily towards the wood. 'Shall I come with you?' I asked. He shook his head and went towards the trees. Jankin had gone back to his cronies at the ale-stall. He's drinking deep, I thought, but he gets so little pleasure. Edmund returned, wiping his face. Josina leaned against me. She said: 'Oh, if only I could sit down!'

I looked at the grass. People, children and loving couples were sprawled. I looked at her white dress. Then I spied a bench near a sweet-stall where some old women were taking the sun, hoods and wimples nodding as they murdered someone's reputation. Not far from the bench was Jankin's broad back.

'Do you want to sit down, Edmund?' Sweat was on his lip, his eyes were flared, blind-looking. He worried me, so did the thought of Nemo. It was time I went to the cockpit.

'Come on then, sweetheart.' I sat Josina down on the end of the bench. The crones made room for her without drawing breath from their gossip. She gasped with relief, and kicked off her little shoes.

The sun tipped further towards the west. The sky was a heavy blue, patched with lemon thunderclouds. I didn't like leaving her, but Edmund was near, wandering about, having a terse word with the other archers, and Jankin was close at hand.

'I will come back soon,' I told her.

She smiled up at me. Her little round lily-face. It haunts me now.

'There will be a main of cocks, in five minutes!' The man went through the fairground, ringing his bell. 'Cocks on sod, in five minutes!' I pushed my way through. At the bull-baiting the people were so thick I couldn't move for moments. The white bull was being baited. It was brave. Two terriers already lay on the ground, one dead, the other writhing in its entrails. A small grey mastiff had the bull by the dewlaps, jaws clenched there as if for eternity. The white bull bellowed and pawed and swung its head about. The mastiff leeched on, four feet off the ground, lunging like a blown banner as the bull groaned in fury. I knew the dog; the people had set it on me when I went collecting Fray's dues. Folk were shouting: 'Six marks on the mastiff!' 'Double! Twelve marks, he's a game one.' The bull caught one of the dogs on its horns as it leaped, tossing it out of the ring, and impaled a second, sent into the ring too fast, like a worm on a fish-hook. Suddenly, unbeckoned, Piers's words came into my mind. 'Have you ever heard of the Hooks of God? God, the Divine Fisherman . . .'

'That's a good dog!' said Finch, close to me. Again I hadn't seen him coming. He called to the bull-baiting marshal: 'I lay two marks on the mastiff!' The marshal nodded. Finch looked at me, still ash-pale.

'Where in hell have you been?' he demanded. 'The main is beginning.'

'Hugh,' I said. 'are you ill?'

'Never better.' He laughed. The mastiff's jaws were clenching tighter, the bull's maddened bellow sounded over the spectators' howls. The bull was beginning to bleed, red stained its white breast. It went down on one knee. Someone sent in another dog, it glanced off the horns and screamed like a woman. Then it ran out of the ring. The bull was kneeling properly now, trying to scrub the mastiff off with its head. Hugh turned to a man nearby and said: 'Hold my stake in this, Miles.' He took my elbow and steered me to the cockpit.

'Don't worry about Nemo, Hugh, he's a marvellous bird,' I said, feeling sorry for him.

'He must fight Bellerophon. Even if you have to wait there all day, see that he fights Bellerophon.'

The cookboy was under a tree with Nemo's cage, and the Fray twins, who greeted me affably. Finch went to where the pit master sat on a trestle overlooking the fight area. I saw him talking, gesturing with his long hands, his eyes dark in his pale face. The pit master bent and spoke to a henchman, who went off into the crowd, to return, nodding. Finch came back, drawing me aside from the Frays.

'It's arranged. Bellerophon it is,' he said softly. 'I'm off to place my side bets now. Don't leave Nemo, will you? I don't trust that wretched boy.'

He looked me straight in the face, and to my amazement there were tears in his eyes. 'Forgive me, Nicholas,' he said, then turned and went away. I thought: If this is cockfighting, it certainly unhinges a man.

The Frays came to stand close, and with Hugh gone, I was almost glad of their support. Men were bringing the first pair of birds out of their cages. A black cock and a red, equally matched, spurred and game. The crowd thickened behind me. I could not have left the pit area if I'd wished now. The cocks' owners stood at the fence, gentling their birds. I felt for the little flask of *aqua vitæ* and for my purse, which had survived the day's pickpockets so far. I wasn't going to bet yet. Only on Nemo.

I said uncertainly to Simon Fray: 'When the time comes, do I . . . throw Nemo into the ring?' I made a vague tossing gesture. The twins roared with laughter.

'By the devil's nose,' said Robin. 'You'll do no such thing. You'll get him disqualified.'

The pit master was declaring the rules.

'Every man to show and put the cock into the pit with a fair hackle, not too near shorn or cut or any other fraud, under pain of forfeit. Every cock matched shall fight as he is first shown in the pit without shearing or cutting any feathers afterwards to disadvantage without the consent of both parties that made the match, on pain of forfeit. When two cocks are set to fight and one of them runs away before they have struck three mouthing blows, it shall be judged no battle to the betters . . . when a battle is set and both cocks refuse to fight ten times, according to the law, then a fresh cock to be hovelled and set to each cock, and if one fights and the other refuses, then the fighting cock to win the battle . . . between every setting-to they shall stay until twenty is counted before they set-to again . . . on pain of forfeit.'

'Watch,' said Simon. The owners of the first cocks were lowering their birds into the ring. 'You set them so, bill to bill.'

'Like lovers,' said Robin heavily. He leaned his forearm against mine. 'Before the real struggle begins.'

The next hour turned like a wheel of speed and flying feathers and shouted oaths and cheering, the little black and red birds, pair after pair jetting through the dust of the pit so fast the eye was defied, themselves becoming a feathered wheel, an embrace of beak and talon and spur, a hopping leaping plumed collision of fast and drunken death. All had been primed on mead or spirits. Their hackled feathers lifted them only a desperate few inches above the pit floor, soon flecked with blood and dusty feathers. Wagers battered the air—four marks, twelve marks, and a penny apiece over. There were fouls and frauds, disqualifications, rages. About half an hour through, a small red cock struck its beak right through its adversary's gizzard, jumping on top of the felled bird with a crow of triumph. I watched thirty pairs fight; it would soon be Nemo's turn. I took a moment to wonder how Edmund was faring. Very faintly I had heard the trumpet, but how long ago I had no idea. I'd lost sense of time. I thought I saw Finch's forest green in the crowd, saw him smack his palm on that of another man, settling the wager. The cookboy was standing behind me, jumping in the air to get a view of the pit. I turned and told him to go to the butts and find out what passed with my brother, and he wormed on hands and knees through the crowd.

I took Nemo out of his cage and fixed his spurs. He was restless now and I gentled him, stroking his hackle as Finch had taught me. Robin held the bowl of barley and Simon uncorked the flask of *aqua vitae*. The cookboy came crawling back and stood up.

'Your brother won the second heat,' he declared. 'Then the Mayor asked him into his loge for some wine. He's still in there.'

I gave the boy another coin. No time to rejoice for Edmund yet. The pit master was shouting: my heart jumped in my chest.

'His lordship's Bellerophon. Set against Master Finch's Nemo.'

I poured the *aqua vitae* into the barley. Nemo pecked it avidly. In seconds his little terrible eye filled with raging blood, and a rank smell arose from him. Terror and delight shot through me. And in my ear, so clearly that I turned round to acknowledge him, came Finch's voice. *Just a little, there my love. Ah, you're so fine, so fair* . . . Just his voice, in my head. The man in green turned and pushed through the people. Not Finch after all, but an older, shorter man.

'Hugh should be here to see this,' said Robin Fray.

91

'He's too nervous,' I said. 'Who owns Bellerophon?'

'I do,' said a voice. I looked. Sweet Christ! it was the lordling who had bought Bedesman. The same, arrogant, insouciant, pampered. He looked at Nemo disdainfully.

'Is this the bird?' he asked. 'It has no quality.'

The pit master heard him and shouted: 'Stop cavilling, my lord. The fight is fixed. Set to.'

'Will you wager?' said the lordling to me.

'Yes. Ten marks.' Higher than I meant to go.

The lordling said: 'Double.' I smacked his palm. I would like to have smacked his face. 'It's a lawful bet!' called the pit master.

Robin was wagering against Simon, five marks, and a penny apiece over. The pit master was holding Hugh's stake, they said. The sun was westering. Soon they would be running the deer for Edmund's last trial. Sweet Mother Mary be with him. He always prayed for help to her.

The lordling went to the pit-side and lowered his bird. Set them bill to bill, said Simon in my ear. I put Nemo in the pit. The two birds stood still.

'Dear Christ,' said Robin. 'He's going to mantle. He's going to crow.' Both actions would disqualify him. But Nemo stood still and silent, his hackles never moved. Then he launched himself on Bellerophon. They both struck the three mouthing blows. Then Bellerophon ran away. I heard the lordling swear. I thought of Bedesman. I went mad.

'Double your wager?' I called to him. He had his bird back in his hands, counting to twenty. I clutched Nemo to my chest. I could feel his heart beating like mine. The lordling nodded.

'Forty marks,' I said. 'And a penny apiece over.'

'Lawful bet!' called the pit master.

I set Nemo again. He went for Bellerophon, three mouthing blows, strike, strike, strike, with his sharp beak and talons and upraised spurs, his hackles the colour of Hell. Bellerophon returned the blows gamely. For an instant they were a plumed ball, dust and blood flew up. Bellerophon backed into the corner. Nemo made a little growling noise. I went mad again.

'Double your stake?' I said to the lord. His friends, wearing satin and gold collars, were looking at me, whispering.

'Can you afford it?' said the lordling, and his friends smiled at his wit.

'I change my mind,' I said to the pit master. 'One hundred marks on Nemo.'

'Double,' said the lordling.

'And again,' I said. 'And a penny apiece over.' Nemo was growling in my arms. One of his spurs had nicked a hole in my doublet. I was mad, gaming mad. The Frays were looking at me almost in horror. I couldn't afford a tenth of the stake. I would have to sell the horses before we went home. I would have to sell my clothes and Edmund's, and Josina's dress. We would all be going home bare as worms. I set Nemo at Bellerophon. They flew at each other, six inches above the ground, plenty of pluck and bottom in them both, said Robin Fray. The lordling put his knuckles between his teeth. Nemo struck the three blows and had them returned. His spur rowelled Bellerophon's breast. The two birds rolled over in the blood-flecked dust. Nemo struck at his opponent's eye; red jetted, Bellerophon wavered for an instant and Nemo had him down, raking his breast with claw and spur, pecking his poll to shreds. He stood on Bellerophon as he died, fanfaring his triumph. The spectators erupted. It was the best battle of the day.

The lordling picked his dead bird out of the pit. I leaned and took up Nemo. There was blood on his hackle but it was not his blood. His heart was like a tabor. He pecked me savagely and I quietened him. Before I put him in the cage I kissed his head, like Finch did. The lordling came over to me.

'God's bowels,' was all he could say.

'Pay up,' I said.

'God's eyes,' said the lordling, looking at Nemo. 'That's a prince among cocks. I'll buy him. I'd like to breed from him. Name your figure, Master Finch.'

'I'm not Finch.' My voice shook. 'I'm Sir Mark d'Archier's son. He died for King Richard. The bird is not for sale.'

The lord raised his brows and put a purse into my shaking hand. It was a leather purse with buck's heads embossed on it, the Stanley arms. Traitor's arms. There were over two hundred pounds sterling there. Years since I had seen so much money.

Never had I held so much. My knees turned to wax and I clutched Robin's arm.

A little celebration, the Frays said. They armed me out through the crush. I hated them but I was glad they were there. As we passed the lordling I said: 'Bedesman,' and he raised his brows again. He had lost a lot of money to a madman. I wanted to weep. I looked down with love at Nemo, I thought of Finch with love. It was almost as if Finch had bought Bedesman back for me, a sweet vengeance. I squinted up at the sun, dipping behind the treetops. At the nearest ale-stall, we talked about Nemo. Finch had bred him. He should be here. Again I thought I saw him in the crowd. Again the green-suited man turned and it was not Finch. You'd better get your pockets sewn up, said the twins. I answered: 'I wish I could find my silkmaid, she'd do it for me.' In the distance a trumpet sounded; the sun winked like a gold angel behind the tips of the forest and slid down. I bought the Frays another drink. They bought me one. I bought the cookboy a drink and gave him some more money. I felt I should never rise from that bench again. I could hear cheering from the archery range, where most of the people were now gathered, although many had started for home; carts and horses were streaming away. Rahere walked by still wearing his horns. He looked sombre, enthralled by his own power. I sent the cookboy off to see what was happening. He came back at speed.

'Your brother has won.' His little pleased face. To him, Witless Nick was God. 'He's Champion Archer.'

I handed him Nemo's cage and told him to say farewell to Finch. I arrived in time to see Edmund coming down from the Mayor's loge, carrying a gold wand and a purse of money. He looked drained and happy. I embraced him, and he allowed it. 'Oh, Nicholas.' He rested his head against my chest and wiped his eyes, then, himself again, said gruffly: 'Where's my sister?'

'With you, of course.' A little chill began to expunge the glories of both cockfight and championship. 'She must be with Jankin.' But Jankin was still on his bench, fast asleep, the front of his jerkin sticky with spilled ale. His staff lay idle, beside an upturned tankard.

'Look for her,' I said to Edmund. I started off, ready to comb the fairground, but he held me back. 'Wait,' he said. Jumping on

94

a bale of straw. 'I'll use my eyes.' His white-ringed eyes dilated in the evening light. He scanned the whole precinct, faces, horses, the two maimed and one dead bull being taken away through the tomb-lined exit. The eyes came to rest where the horses were tethered, and he smiled, for the first time in five years.

'I see her,' he said. 'Standing by the cob. Her feet hurt her. She has one shoe off.'

We went over and roused Jankin. He was as drunk as I had been the night of the Marching Watch. We hauled his arms round our shoulders, Edmund cursed him. Edmund had his bow and gold wand to carry, also his purse of money. In the end I slung Jankin over my shoulders, his weight half-killed me. Josina stood still by the cob. Her face was to the east, her head haloed by the setting sun. 'I won,' Edmund said, 'and I won,' I said. 'We're rich!' Jankin stirred and nearly fell head first off the horse over which I had cast him. Edmund and I both swore.

Josina said very quietly: 'Will someone please help me up? I'd like to go home now, please.'

I left Edmund steadying Jankin and lifted her on to the cob. Her waist felt hot and silky in the white dress. She was holding one shoe in her hand and I put it on for her as she sat in the sidesaddle. Her toes were grassy; a blade or two was stuck between them. I kissed her foot. She drew it up as if burned.

We reached home just before nightfall. I had never felt so tired. It hadn't helped having to walk by the horse bearing Jankin. He'd woken up on the way and said, his face swaying upside down by the horse's belly: 'Was a very good day, sir. Nice young fellow. Gave me plenty to drink,' and went to sleep again.

Dame Philip and my mother were still at St Anthony's where John had escorted them. Edmund and I had to bed down the horses, while Josina went into the house. We put Jankin to dream off his ale in the stable. I asked Edmund if he'd enjoyed the day.

'It was a strange day,' he said. 'Yes.' It had been very strange, with everything not quite in true . . . yet very profitable.

'Would you go again?' I asked him.

'I might. But next year I'll not be here.'

In the lanternlit stable, his white eyes flared with secrets.

'Edmund,' I said, 'please tell me why you're going away.'

'I can't'.

'Don't you trust me'?

'Yes. I think I do.' I was so pleased. Friends again.

'Can't you give me the essence?'

'Do you swear on our father's soul to tell no one?'

'I swear.'

'We're going to bring back Plantagenet.' I looked quickly at Jankin's supine snoring form. 'It's all right,' Edmund said. 'Jankin takes the letters to Taylor's agent.' He whispered: 'We're going to bring down Henry Tudor. That is why I have to be one of the élite archers. To defend Plantagenet when he comes.'

'And who is Plantagenet?'

'I cannot say. Never a word, Nicholas. Least of all to Mother. She would be furious that I told.'

'Thank you for trusting me,' I said humbly. I went with him into the house, so tired I could scarcely stand. 'Are you coming to bed?'

'No. I'll wait up for Mother, to tell her I won, and give her the purse.'

'For the cause?' I asked softly, and he nodded. I said: 'I'm so proud of you, Edmund,' and left him, in the good moment of our friendship.

Josina had taken a chill at the Fair; she stayed in bed next morning while Dame Philip ministered to her, between naps. We were all cordial together, my mother and Edmund and I, she so pleased over his success and Edmund and I reliving it with our little secret, and his eyes no longer hostile, but accepting all my shortcomings and knowing he had my prayers. It had rained heavily overnight but the sun was shining when I went out to buy provisions and of course to call on Finch and ask after Nemo.

Piers was in the parlour, polishing some silver. The old man was still at Westminster, for the King had gone to Dover to see about his French war. That meant that Patch could have the Queen to himself, to talk quietly of the old days under cover of a frail jest—of her beloved father and uncle and the lost happy times. Piers told me this is what they did; he said it was a mercy King Henry reckoned Patch such a dotard as to be harmless.

I went into the clean parlour that hid the filthy kitchens. Piers was breathing on the silver and attacking it with hidecloth. From the kitchen I could hear squeaking like mice, breathy rustles of damped-down excitement and hilarity from the cookboys, a rare sound. Piers's face was grey with weariness. I told him about the Fair.

'I'm glad you had a good time,' he said. He covered his eyes and sighed. Another ripple of mirth came from the kitchen. 'Hugh's upstairs,' he told me.

'They sound very lively,' I said. 'And you look worn out.'

'I've had no sleep.' He jerked his thumb towards the rafters. 'I don't think Hugh's been to bed. Every time I closed my eyes, I heard him walking up and down, going out, banging the front door, coming in again. I don't know how he expects me to work,' he said without rancour. 'Go up and see him.'

The cookboys hushed as I passed through, but when he saw who it was, the pretty little boy I had treated at the Fair ran to me, smiling. I sent him back to scrubbing the table with a sharp word and went up. Finch's door was locked. I hammered on it.

'Who's there?' he called.

'Nicholas.' There was a long silence.

'Are you all right?'

'Of course I am. Let me in, Hugh.'

After a moment he admitted me. He wasn't so pale as yesterday, but he was equally as strange. His bedroom was in chaos. Every suit of clothes he owned was flung down on the bed. Boots lay all over the place, and a pack half filled with his gear was on the floor. I moved some shirts off the bed and sat down. He was walking quickly about, hurling things into the pack. His eyes were everywhere, out of the window, up at the ceiling, once or twice he muttered to himself.

'It was a good day, wasn't it?' I said.

'Excellent.' He glanced at me quickly. His black hair was tousled, his eyes looked dull and smudged. 'How are things at home?'

'Very good. Edmund is in top fettle, my sister has a cold, but nothing serious, and even my mother seems to love me today.'

He went on packing. I asked the obvious question.

'Are you going somewhere?'

'Yes, I thought I might.' He looked out of the window, frowning. 'You handled Nemo well, Nicholas. Thank you.'

97

'It was wonderful. I won a lot of money on him. How is he?'

'A bit tired. Unmarked.'

'Where are you going, Hugh?'

'Ireland.'

I gaped at him. 'Ireland? Who do you know in Ireland?' I felt suddenly low-spirited. It was only just over a week since we had made up the quarrel. 'I'll miss you.'

He threw a pair of soft leather boots into the pack, crushing them down. 'No you won't,' he said. 'And I don't know anyone in Ireland, but I can always get to know them. Anyway,' he said, 'I may be in a little trouble here.'

'Trouble with the law?' I knew he'd fallen foul last year and had in fact spent a week in Fleet Prison, which he'd hated for its dirt and squalor. The Frays had bribed the magistrates and bought him out. He muttered something in reply and went on packing. He seemed to be taking a lot of money with him. I wondered if he were running off with Frays' dues. I hoped he was.

'How long will you be gone?'

He shrugged. 'Weeks, months, years.' He knotted a thin rope round the pack, tugging at the ends with his strong white teeth. 'I've hired a horse to go to Bristol. I can get a ship from there.'

I got up and looked out of the window. Sure enough, there stood a saddled horse. I thought: I really shall miss him. Why can't he keep out of trouble? I thought of him on board ship; I knew what it was like, the racing waves, the crack and flutter of sail, the mariners shouting through spray.

'You are a miserable devil, Finch,' I said, 'leaving me like this.'

'Don't be so witless!' he cried in sudden rage. 'Just think. You might never have met me but for that night when I fell down outside the Eagle.'

True, I thought. And there was the strange little voice in my head saying *let him lie*.

'I thought we were friends.'

We are, damn you!' he shouted. He hurled spare boots and clothes into a chest and slammed the lid.

'Are you taking Nemo?' I asked.

'No, Piers can see to him. Or that snivelling little swine downstairs. The pretty one. The twins'll be after him, just you watch.' There was such hurt in his voice. Again I thought: Oh

98

no, you don't forget, in spite of your boasts, so you must prove and prove yourself a man, until you die . . . At least, those are my thoughts, remembered now. They faded, to be gathered up long afterwards, replaced by: At least he's coming back. He wouldn't leave his precious bird for ever.

'While you're away,' I said, 'I'll come and visit Nemo.'

'Yes. Piers would like that.'

'I wish you could have seen Nemo kill Bellerophon,' I said. He was at the window, staring at the saddled horse.

'Did you win much?' he asked.

''A little fortune. I feel I owe you something, Hugh.'

He turned round, his face was white again. 'Don't be a fool.' Once more there were tears in his eyes. I wish I could comfort him, I thought. Then he said: 'Do you remember the first time we went to the Greyhound?'

'I was thinking of it yesterday, at the Fair.'

'I gave you some money.'

'Yes. You wouldn't loan me any. But you gave me two angels.'

'Will you give me them back?'

I stared at him. Then I got out my purse and handed him the coins. He put them away.

'That's it. I don't want you in my debt, Nicholas.'

I shook my head, lost. I said, as he picked up his pack: 'You'll feel better when you're in Ireland. It will be good for you to get away from this place for a while.'

He put the pack down and grabbed me savagely in his arms. He gave me a couple of his painful blows on the back. 'Goodbye. I'm off.'

He slung the pack over his shoulder, felt for the knife at his belt, jammed his velvet cap on his head, and stormed out of the door and down the stairs. I heard him cursing the boys in farewell as he went through the kitchen. Already I felt the lack of him. The air took a little time to settle from his turbulent presence, and the room whispered to itself. The horse's hoofs clipped the cobbles, diminishing down the street. My bewilderment began. Piers couldn't help me; when I saw him on the way out, he spread his hands, then went on polishing his silver, smiling his kind, fateful little smile.

★

October came in sharply, with a chill of mist to make one wish for wool. I learned, when calling at the seamstress's shop to ask about her, that my silkmaid had left to be married, somewhat hastily, to the tall young man at the Fair. A wealthy merchant's son, said the seamstress, fluttering her pepperpot fingers; she'll have a beautiful house, but who will do my fine work now? And so another door closed. Not a happy month, October; I missed Hugh and I was bored. Yet it was the last month of my peace.

I went to confession at St Anthony's. With little to confess, I made up a few sins so as not to waste the priest's time. I still had my winnings from the cockfight intact, and knew how I would like to use them but was afraid to broach the subject to my mother, who was now so fraught with fresh perilous excitement over the cause that it was almost impossible to talk to her. At Mass, her white face was aflame with dedication in the candlelight, while I knelt praying solemnly with Edmund and Dame Philip who only woke up for the Elevation of the Host. Josina kept her brow bent on her little white hands, and was silent.

October 2 was the birthday of King Richard. We mourned him and my mother expressed the wish to drink the health of his soul, and sent me for wine to the ordinary with the cob and a cart. I went to the side entrance of the Eagle, with no intention of entering. Secretly I had never been fond of the place. But I glanced down the courtyard and into the lit room at men arm-wrestling, dogs squabbling, wenches flaunting with orders and being mauled by the customers. Greasy rushes, spilled ale, a den of bitter homeliness; a halfway house between boredom and sin. The Fray twins were in there, their big faces hot and laughing, and they had captured the pretty cookboy. He sat between them, looking from one to the other like a pert, bewildered little bird. They were making him drunk. I'd no wish to get into a brawl, and yet, seeing Simon Fray roughly hug the little boy, I found myself inside the Eagle, standing by their bench.

They looked up with guarded welcome. I nodded to them, then took the boy by his collar, yanking him to his feet, out of Simon's grip. The boy started choking from the pressure on his throat.

'Knave,' I said. 'Master Piers is looking for you. How dare you leave your duties?'

100

I didn't look at the Frays. I gave the boy a clip round the head to add pith to my part. I marched him out of the inn. Quite easy, I thought, trembling outside. Sweet God! I put the boy in the cart, lecturing him all the way to the cookshop, and pushing him into Piers's custody with a final exposition of men's brutishness. By now the boy was howling in fright.

Half way through October came the night when Edmund and I talked in whispers until after midnight in the dark. He had fallen asleep early and dreamed, rolling and groaning so dreadfully that I woke him and he was grateful. I asked him and at last he told me.

'Leicester,' he said. 'That's what I dream about. Accursed Leicester. Oh, Nicholas, I did love my father so.'

'So did I,' I said softly.

'He was so good. So stern. When he told me I was going away to Barnard Castle, I felt lonely and afraid. But I'd only to look at him and remember how brave he was, and it all vanished. I saw how pleased he was with me.'

'You were about eight.'

'Was I?'

'Yes.' I tried hard to remember where he could have been, that day I was shut out, at Westminster.

'Edmund,' I said in the darkness, 'do you think our mother really loves me?'

'I'd think so,' he said, after a moment. 'She always professed she would,' and the silence grew very chill. I felt confused and afraid. It was such a strange answer. It was too late to pursue the matter; Edmund was saying:

'It will all be put right. We will be avenged on Tudor for Bosworth Field and for Leicester. And for the slanders against King Richard. Do you remember him, Nicholas?'

'Not very well.'

'I do, as clearly as I remember my father. I went in his apartments once. The King showed me his Book of Hours. His own prayer. The page was all stained where someone had wept over it. Tudor owns that book now. I wish I could remember the prayer. I can only see one line: "Thou, who didst save Susannah from false accusation . . ." that's where the tearstains were. And then it ended something like this: "By the blessings which Thou hast brought me, since Thou hast made me of nought and hast

101

redeemed me, bringing me from everlasting Hell to eternal life, I beseech Thee, sweetest Lord Jesu, that Thou wilt deliver me from evil . . . and after this transient life wilt lead me to Thee, O God of Life and Truth.'''

He sighed deeply. I asked: 'Have you any idea when you leave here?'

'With fortune, next month. It all depends on what we have from Taylor over the next few weeks. Before All Souls Day.'

'Is Taylor still at Rouen?'

'As far as we know. But his agent left last month for Scotland. We shall know more soon. You've told no one, have you, Nicholas?'

'I swore. I keep faith.'

We were quiet for a while. I said: 'Edmund. You remember that money I won at the cockfight.'

'Yes. On your friend's bird. I didn't like your friend.'

'Would you like some of it, for the cause?'

He said: 'I'll ask Mother—it would have to be anonymous. She still thinks you don't know.'

'Perhaps we'll forget it, then.' Again, I was left out. I swallowed the hurt.

'I was thinking of another use for it, anyway,' I said. He didn't answer. I felt wakeful. My mind roved back over our conversation. He was just like my father, so outraged over the rumour that Richard had had his nephews done to death. I could scarcely remember Richard's face. I certainly couldn't remember the princes. I'd seen them at a distance no more than half a dozen times.

'Edmund,' I said, 'what did Prince Edward and Prince Richard of York look like? When you were with them at Barnard Castle?'

There was no reply. He had fallen asleep. Neither of us knew how much would one day depend on his answer.

So the end of October approached, with misty days dragging like a wheel in mud. All Saints and All Souls—the Day of the Dead. And Josina in our mother's bower, a few days before that sombre festival. Old Dame Philip nodded in a corner of the room. She slept because there was little else to do. She had food and a bed and she had brought my mother into this world, so her place was sure. Her duties were few; Josina could mend and sew quicker, distil herbs better and attend my mother, when she wished it, with greater skill.

My mother sat before an ancient silver mirror while Josina plied the comb. I stood and looked at our reflection. There were pieces of us missing where the silver had worn. My mother was wearing a scarlet dress of worn velvet with trumpet sleeves. Late afternoon sun fell on her pearly neck and face. She stared at her own eyes in the silver; the sea storm was there, contained, but ready to lash the grey into black. She stared without seeing, mind fixed on some heady star. Josina ran the comb down, smoothing its passage through the long black hair pied with streaks of white. I looked at our faces; my mother's mouth was full and pale, Josina's smaller, the same shape but an unfurled bud. My own lips were much longer, thinner. Josina had split her dress a little under the arm and her tender skin showed as she raised her hands to the parting in my mother's hair.

It was weeks since she had kissed me like she used to do. I had put her coolness down to my new friendship with Edmund, fancying her jealous. For years I had cosseted her with love-names, whispering and laughing in private, honey language. Now Edmund and I sought one another out whenever we could, talking about his prowess in archery, and, as much as he dared, about the cause. Sir Edward Brampton was indeed part of it, although at present in Portugal. Who Plantagenet was I had yet to learn. It was as if Edmund and I were anxious to make up for the years of dislike, and perhaps Josina had lost a little from this.

In the mirror, she kept her eyes down. It was a long time since I had seen her eyes properly. But she was never unkind; she was incapable of so being. She was quiet, as always. She kept herself occupied, nurturing and distilling the yield of her knot garden, spinning, weaving and dyeing her meagre crop of flax, brewing medicines and ale in her little stillroom crammed with flasks in various stages of fermentation. In her leisure time, previously always spent with me, she would go alone to the foot of the garden by the little stream and sit by the willow tree, with her black cat on her lap. I knew better than to intrude. In September I had come up behind her, kissing the soft crown of her hair, and she had risen quickly, saying:

103

'Please, Nicholas. Do not touch me.'

I had left her, too bewildered to be hurt, although the hurt came later and was accepted as all things are, but I felt strangely guilty, wondering how I had offended her. It was concerning her that I had entered my mother's sanctum.

'Madam,' I said, louder than intended; Dame Philip jolted awake. My mother's eyes met mine.

'It's bad luck,' she remarked, 'to speak through a mirror.'

'I now have a little money,' I said. 'I would like to make a contribution.' She looked startled, fearful for her secrets.

'To Josina's dowry,' I said. My sister's combing hands stilled.

'Was this money lawfully gained?' asked my mother. I was dumb. Josina started combing again. She spoke up softly.

'He won it at a cockfight at the Fair.'

She caught the comb on a tangle, my mother winced. Josina smoothed the piece of hair in apology, her white eyelids still down.

'Gaming,' said my mother. What scorn.

'Ay.'

'How much?' she said, staring at her own eyes in the mirror. I told her, twining my fingers behind my back.

'Josina may have it all.'

My mother gave a bitter laugh, that seemed to contain all our lost glories and great estate.

'Such riches!' I felt my temper rise. 'Is that the price you place on my daughter? Look at her! She's beyond rubies!'

Through welling tears of rage I thought: Yes, she's peerless. My sister, loved above all other. Do they think I wish her married and gone from me? I went quickly away, and in the garden wandered among the agrimony, the bugleflower, the spreading sour pennyroyal, the Knight's Pondweed, the Madonna lily. All wilting, dying, reminders of how not so long ago she and I used happily to cling and tease one another. A dark trout or two rose murkily in the little pond and gaped at me. Witless Nick, their wondering mouths said.

I heard her light step behind me. The mist-wreathed sun was low. The nights were coming down early, as if anxious to take their toll of the golden summer just gone. With joy and relief I felt

104

her fingers curl round mine, and looked down at her. The gilded hair now in one rich plait, the white lids down. I wanted to see her again in the white dress, walking like a queen.

'I am sorry I offended you and Mother,' I said.

'Nicholas.' Her honey voice, as of old. 'It was so kind. Thank you.'

'I know it was not enough. I'd give you heaven and earth. You could have my life.'

I took her unresisting into my arms and held her close. Sadness enfolded us, an unknown sadness that had to do with the misty sunset and the dead summer and the winter of our years. I no longer wished she were my wife. I felt as if I were her father.

'Josina . . . about your dowry. Do you think Sir James . . .'

She left my arms and was leaning against the willow almost before I realized it.

'I shall never marry.' Her face was turned away. 'I know it now.'

She knelt and began to gather some herb, tugging at the roots savagely, her hands covered with earth. Then she said: 'Nicholas, if you have any money to spare . . .'

'Anything. All of it, my dove.'

'You could buy me a lute.'

'Surely you had a lute.'

I watched her, her little rounded body, her thick fairy-gold plait, her small hands soiled like a grave-digger's.

'I left it behind, the last time we went to Leicester. I'd like a new one, Nicholas.'

I went straight away up Ludgate Hill past Paul's towards the Middle and Inner Temple where lawyers were going about the last business of the day. Near Fleet I found a little music shop about which Piers had told me. John Bore stocked everything. Once, Owen Tudor, grandfather of the King, had his Welsh harps strung there. I bought the lute; good sycamore with lilies carved into its belly and gilded strings. It was costly and I was glad. The sun was spreading blood and gold along the horizon when I returned; the gillies under the garden wall were lost in shadow. Josina set the lute in tune, and sang the saddest song I have ever heard in my life.

105

'Now care is come unto my heart,
The nights they fall, the days they pass,
All joys and I are rent apart,
My only cry: alas, alas.

Now grief is come unto my soul,
My only cry: alas, alas.
I'll sing to pay this endless toll,
The nights they fall, the days they pass.'

Pain and hopelessness were in its note, like the song of a bird who has flown too far and returned to find her eggs cold in the nest.

My memory cringes as I approach the Day of the Dead. Old wounds are touched to rawness. I see myself, useless of habit, living from day to day with an empty mind, while November sent in a whirling thrust of fog to flush us into nightmare. Somewhere the Devil was laughing, as he must have laughed watching me pick Finch out of the gutter what seemed so long ago. He must have been sick with laughter, watching us all with his pitiless brimstone eyes.

Edmund had had his long-awaited call. He told me about it in bed when the house was quiet, just after the Matins bell had sounded from St Anthony's. He lit the candle and propped himself on his elbow. His eyes were bright, serene. A courier had come, as anonymously and unobtrusively as all the others, staying only long enough to drink a toast with my mother and snatch some food before departing again on his laboured horse.

'Taylor sent a message from Rouen,' Edmund whispered. 'I leave on All Souls Day.'

His contained exultation infected me but I was worried. He was so young, the mission was surely dangerous. I hoped he wouldn't be too much alone in it.

'How many others are there?'

'Twenty. We are to be called the White Rose Archers. Our work will be to protect Plantagenet.'

'Can you tell me now who he is?'

He bent close, his breath sour with excitement.

106

'Richard, Duke of York, of course. The younger of the princes. He may have been declared bastard but he has far better claim to England than Tudor. It should have been Prince Edward, but something befell him on the sea crossing.' He gripped my shoulder. 'Never a word. Or I'll return and cut out your tongue from wherever I am.' He smiled as he said it. The trust was still between us.

'I never knew they were taken abroad.' I thought of ship-lanterns swinging in a gale, a rope round my waist to save me from the sea. Where? When?

'Brampton took them before the battle, so they should be safe from Tudor. It was one of King Richard's last orders. Tudor was so afraid of them; he knew his claim was false. He rules by tyranny, the unholy usurper. But we'll bring him down. We'll do to him what they did to Richard and our father. The times are changing, Nicholas. The light is coming.'

He looked like a good, unspoiled young priest. His eyes flamed white and his ardour made me shiver.

'Do you know where you're going?'

'They'll come for me. I may be for France, for she supports us in this, also Brittany. Or even Portugal. Our allies are everywhere. I'll go where they wish.'

'Edmund. Please take some of my money, for the cause.'

'No. You may need it, Nicholas. At least until we are restored and back at Westminster, at the court of Richard the Fourth. When we've hung Tudor's bowels on the highest tree.'

I gripped his hand; the arrow-head scar glowed white. 'May God be with you,' I said. 'I hated us being enemies.'

'We were never that,' he answered. 'I didn't like your ways. I still don't like your friend. I hated to see you drunk, or going whoring.'

'I never went whoring,' I said.

'One day I shall be married,' he said. 'And get children to carry on our name. After my work is done.'

'And so shall I,' I said. As I spoke a coldness assailed me; the candle wavered as if from the chill of my thought. The future passed over me, a barren warning; pigs rooted on my grave.

'What is it you want most? Our restoration, or vengeance?'

'Both', he said. 'All is equal.'

107

I looked closely at him. He had the black hair of my mother, and was pale, like Josina these days. He had my mother's tight full mouth and my father's eyes. We were not in the least alike. I loved him for looking like my father. I wished we hadn't wasted time, quarrelling.

'Put out the light,' I said. 'You must rest. God keep you, Edmund, this night and always.'

'Amen.' He snuffed the candle. 'You also, Nicholas.'

'I have the most unhappy feeling, Edmund,' I said. But he was already asleep and soon so was I.

I went to see Nemo and Piers, who looked less weary in Finch's absence. I heard the weird unbelievable sound of the cookboys singing. Even the kitchens looked better, with less filth about and the ovens hot and bright. Nemo was baiting. He refused the meat I offered him. His plumage looked dull and the membrane flicked across his eye. He brightened a little when I stroked his hackle, but he was certainly not the game killer I had seen at the Fair.

'He misses his master.' Piers kicked some wood shavings across the loft. 'They complement each other, he and Hugh.' Yes, I thought: both swift and ruthless, bright-coloured. In the parlour Patch was back from Westminster. He was dressed not in jester's outfit, but in ordinary clothes. He stretched his skinny veined legs in their pale hose in the hearth. He was shuffling cards very dexterously, and his first words gave me a shock.

'So, Master Nicholas,' he said, 'I hear there's another rebellion a-making.'

I looked wildly at Piers but he was sitting at the table and unrolling some manuscripts. I wondered in panic whether I had at some time betrayed Edmund. I was sure I hadn't, even when drunk, but the old man's look, filmily acute, wrapped me in chaos.

'Is there?' I managed to say. 'Such things hold no interest for me, Master Patch.'

'Very wise,' he said. 'Stick to drinking, Nicholas.'

'Would you like wine, Nicholas?' said Piers. 'I'm forgetting my manners.' I shook my head.

'One would think,' said Patch, 'that folk would have learned their lesson, after the Lambert Simnel affair. I saw Simnel yesterday. He makes a good pot-washer, for a prince.'

He looked hard at me. The pearly film on his eyes seemed less. I remarked on it.

'Yes, your sister's lotion did me great good.' He laughed softly. 'I see all I need to see, Master Nicholas. Who's the figurehead this time? Young Warwick again? No, he's in the Tower, mad as a loon, and the people have seen him face to face. So it will be one of the Lords Bastard. That's who I'd choose, were I leading a rebellion. Wouldn't you, young master?'

I said nothing. Nervously I watched him rise and lean against the mantel. His back was quite straight, he pointed a dancer's toe in the hearth. I remembered that he had been a good dancer once.

'I met your father,' he said. 'First, at Middleham. Those were the good days. The moors, the sun, the hawking. Richard and his lovely Duchess. I gave Anne to him, you know. I found her hidden away because of her riches, in a place like this, her hands worn from rough work. Richard was always grateful to me. He loved her, and not for her riches. He was good to everyone. Too good.'

'You met my father then.'

'Yes. Before you were born. He came with his keen eyes to Middleham, bringing news of the call to arms in France. The Treaty of Picquigny. A fine disgrace, when King Edward sold us out to Louis of France . . . there were riots, the army was so discontented!' He was shuffling cards with his quick veined hands. He said softly: 'Have you naught to tell me, Nicholas? No news with which I could cheer my Queen?'

I said steadily: 'I know nothing. There is nothing,' then something moved in me; a wish to comfort him and half a wish to reveal my partisanship. 'The other night I was talking with . . . someone . . . about King Richard. His Book of Hours. There were tearstains on the prayer, just where the line occurs: "Thou, who didst save Susannah from false accusation . . ."'

The old man turned his head swiftly away, leaning it against the mantel. I heard him whisper: 'Oh, Jesu. Jesu.'

He said: 'I shouldn't weep. It's bad for my eyes.' He kept his head turned. 'It's when I remember . . . Dickon, his kindness, his justice. They gave him no kindness, no justice. And even in

109

death, no mercy.' He shivered, then turned, spreading out the fan of cards. He said: 'Take a card, Nicholas.'

It was the Angry Moon.

'Oh, that's bad,' said Patch. 'Do you believe in the Devil? Of course you do. I saw the Devil, more than once. When I was young, he never left me alone. A merry little fellow. I had to work hard to rid myself of him, but he went away in the end.'

He sat down and closed his eyes. Behind me I could hear Piers reading aloud, muttering apothegms, a maddening habit of his.

'*Angelicus juvenis senibus satanizat in annis*—An angelic boyhood becomes a satanic old age. Erasmus. From a proverb invented by Satan.'

'*Furore iraque mentem præcipitant*—Fury and anger carry the mind away. Virgil, *Aeneid*, Book Two.

'I must be off,' I said.

'*Maximum remedium est iræ mora.* Seneca: *De Ira.* The greatest remedy for anger is delay.'

'I'm not angry,' I said. He smiled, fiddling with the rivet on his slipping spectacles. On the bench he had his treasure spread out, carefully copied. Meister Eckhart. 'Don't tell me,' he said. 'Once more you haven't time to learn. Oh, Nicholas.'

'I will one day.' I looked between his inky hands and saw the word 'penitence'. Then: 'Fasting, watching, praying, kneeling, being disciplined, the body is too strong for the spirit. Food, drink and comforts are all against the spirit. The spirit's race and kin are all in heaven. To assist the spirit in its distress, to weaken the flesh for its struggle against the spirit, penances are put on like a bridle . . . but if you wish to make the flesh a thousand times more subject, put on it the bridle of love.'

'Look!' Piers said softly, pointing. 'Love is like a fisherman's hook. When one has found this way, he looks for no other. To hang on this hook is to be so utterly captured that feet and hands and mouth and eyes, the heart and all a man is and has, becomes God's own. Love is strong as death and harder than hell. Love cannot endure anything anywhere that is not God. Whoever is caught in this net, love does it, and love alone.'

'The part about penitence seems very hard.' I thought of the days to come when we should be restored, with all our lands, good clothes and comforts.

110

'It's not hard at all,' said Piers. I realized not for the first time how thin he was, how fatigued his face, as if he never slept. 'It is the sweetest bond. "Wait only for this hook and you will be caught up into blessing, and the more you're caught, the more you will be set free."'

'I think I'd like some wine after all,' I said. 'And a cup would do you no harm.'

He went and fetched a flagon. I heard the cookboys greet him joyfully. I looked idly at his pile of papers. Half hidden under the writings of Dante was a creased roll, a few lines in the most execrable handwriting in the world.

'You didn't tell me you'd heard from Hugh,' I said.

'I quite forgot.' He gave Patch a cup of wine and poured some for me. 'It's rather a strange letter. There's something in it about you.' He picked it up and strained his eyes over it. '. . . Hmmm, see Jessop about candles for Christmas, oh, that's nothing . . . then something about Nemo. I can hardly read it myself. Ah, here it is. Ask Nicholas . . . if all is well at home. If I hear nothing, expect me soon.'

He smoothed the letter and looked at me. 'What do you make of it? Is all well at home?'

'All's much the same,' I said. 'Where did he write from?'

'A tavern in Bristol. A carter brought it. Dated last week.'

'So he's in England. Do you think he ever went to Ireland?' I said.

'Yes, he did,' said Piers. 'He writes about Cork in the letter. He had a good time there, apparently.'

I rose to leave. The old man had gone to sleep. At the door, Piers took my hand.

'I still pray for you, Nicholas.'

'Yes, Piers, do that,' and I grinned at him. 'Pray for me, and for all sinners.'

No doubt that wanton remark raised another guffaw from the Devil. It was time for him to alight upon us.

By All Saints, Josina had added a new verse to her song.

> 'Now doubt is come unto my heart,
> Where once was bliss, where once was joy,
> I think not on the courtly art,

111

Such musing does my soul annoy.
My only song: alas, alas,
The nights they fall, the days they pass.'

The morning was the best part of that day. Thin sunlight streamed through mist. Josina was in the garden, sitting. Singing. Edmund and I could hear her from our chamber where I was helping him make ready for the morrow. He had a small chest for his sea crossing, shaped to take our father's sword under layers of clothing. I had bought him a thick Welsh wool cloak from the best draper in Candlewick Street. It was plenty long enough and reached almost to his ankles. Josina had made him a woollen hood and his hands were finally healed, the palms and fingers tougher than his leather gloves. He had his passwords, money, knife and bow. All he lacked now were his final orders and his White Rose livery, which would be issued when and wherever he disembarked abroad. He had said farewell to the fletcher with tears. Yorkist and Plantagenet to the heart, the fletcher looked on Edmund as nothing less noble than a crusader.

We worked quietly together, while that little dolorous song came threading through the mist. She sang it a dozen times and its minor key began to eat at our wits. Edmund went to the window and looked out at her. 'I think she's sad because I'm leaving,' he said. I lidded and locked the sea-chest. I was sad too.

'She's coming in,' said Edmund.

She moved slowly up the garden, her lute drooping in her hand. She brushed her fingers across her eyes as if to clear them of mist. She passed under the gable and into the house, going into her little stillroom.

In my pocket a guilty secret crackled, one which it would not do to let Edmund see; I was anxious for nothing to disrupt our harmony at this late stage. But I knew I had to go out, ever since the boy brought the note, early, to my hands. As I passed the stillroom door I heard Josina clattering jars and pots about, noisily, for her. Impulse made me enter. Something that smelled noxious was boiling on the fire, and she was decanting a greyish liquid from one phial to another. My entry startled her and she dropped one of the phials.

'Now I'll have to make some more,' she said as if to herself.

'What is it?' I picked up the other phial and made to taste it. She snatched it from me. It smelled like decaying corpses. She turned her back on me, her hands trembling.

'I'm glad the lute gives you pleasure,' I said. 'But I wish you'd let it play merrier tunes.' She went on pouring, stirring, silent. The smell grew overpowering, and I was glad to be from the room and in the air, walking towards Eastchepe, where sun battled with the mist. The note in my pocket said simply: I AM BAK. And the little bird beneath it could have flown straight off the paper.

I walked slap into him on the corner of Soper Lane, just as the sun emerged triumphant. I'd forgotten how he looked, and his beauty came once more as a shock. He was tanned from the sea-voyage, which made his eyes more violet-blue than ever. Butter wouldn't have melted under the delicate line of his lips. His hair fell in blue-black rings on to the shoulders of a new sapphire velvet suit. We embraced on the corner of the Lane, people bumped and cursed us. 'You miserable swine, Finch,' I said. 'You skinny devil, Nicholay,' he said, and tugged my hair until I yelped. He held me so agonizingly tight for a moment I pitied his women. But then, they probably liked it.

'Drink,' he said, taking my arm.

'The Boar's Head,' I demanded. I wanted to steer clear of the Eagle after the business with the cookboy. We sat down among the lords. Servitors rushed to attend us. We ordered Burgundy. My blood sang with joy. I wanted to shout. Devil damn you, Finch, for leaving me alone so long. Damn you for coming back to plague and infect me. I wanted to do something desperate. I would like to have gone out with him, found two pretty women and taken them somewhere quiet. I even suggested this, as he knocked back his first cup of wine, grinning across the table.

'I'm done with women,' he said, and wiped his mouth. 'Did you ever get your silkmaid?'

'The bitch got married,' I said, and could have bitten out my tongue at my ugly word. 'Did I hear you right just now?'

'Ask me next week,' he laughed. 'You're lucky to see me in one piece. Satan's teeth! those Irish women. Like fiends. I could show you my back . . .' For a moment I thought he was going to shed his clothes there and then. 'I was clawed half to death.'

'Begin at the beginning.'

113

'The ship was awful. I was sick all the time. I thought I should die. But I liked Cork. I even got work there.'

I couldn't believe my ears. 'You worked?'

'Well, you could call it that. I met this cloth merchant in an inn. He paid young men to wear suits made up of his cloth—show it off to the townspeople. All I had to do was dress up and walk up and down. It was great sport. Especially when the ladies came and felt the texture of the merchandise. You should have come with me. He'd have given you employment too. We need never have come back.'

'You never asked me,' I said. 'I wish you had.'

'Well, I came back,' he said and looked into his cup, then straight at me over its rim. 'I came back to see you, you know. I must be mad.'

'Tell me some more.' Suddenly I found swallowing difficult. From him that was an open declaration of love and need.

'I got paid commission on the suits I sold. It was costly, beautiful cloth. All the Irish lords wanted it. Strange people. They wear beards. They'll pick a fight with you for looking the wrong way. One of them took me up, though, invited me to his house. Over six feet tall, that chieftain. His wife was the most glorious creature—long black hair down to her bum. Dear God.'

'Were you the only person showing off the clothes?'

'There was another, but he ran off with the suit on his back. I did hear something, though, that might interest you. Knowing your family's politics. There's to be some kind of a rising against King Henry. The man I took over from—not the thief, but another—he left because they came for him and took him to France. He'd come from Portugal in the first place. MacMorrough's servant told me this. They said this young man—how much is truth I couldn't say—was the spit of young Richard of York.' He shrugged. 'It's nothing to me, but I know how your mother feels. It might put her in a good humour.'

'Do you know who it was that took the young man away?'

He thought for a moment, hands clasped round his cup.

'Taylor,' he said. 'John Taylor, of Rouen. And there was a Breton, called Meno.'

I was very tempted to say yes, this is all correct, and that *was* Richard of York. I mastered the temptation.

114

'I never saw him, of course. I fancied the Irish were a bit chary of it all. They'd had their bellyful with Simnel—remember how they crowned him and made themselves a laughing-stock in front of Henry? Devil damn!' he said suddenly. 'Politics bore me. Drink up. How are things at home?'

'Unaltered,' I said, still thinking: I must tell Edmund all this. Hugh smiled radiantly and called for another flagon.

'My sister's a bit melancholy, though,' I said. He said quickly: 'I want to tell you about . . . about MacMorrough's wife. It's very droll.' He dived into his wine-cup as if it were the last in the world. 'Tell me about the Irish women,' I said. 'How are they different from English?'

'They're like savages. They seem to have a lot of power over their men—not docile like our women. The north-west of Ireland was long ago ruled by a terrible Queen, of the same name as MacMorrough's wife. Maeve. She used to cut bits off her menfolk if they didn't obey and I can believe it.' I was beginning to chuckle. 'I was in Leinster, so I can't imagine what Connaught's like. All the high-born ladies used to come up to me in the street and stroke the cloth. No shame. MacMorrough's wife was beautiful. But she had these awful talons. She quite frightened me.' He winked.

'Never,' I said.

'No. Nicholas, she used to scream and wail like a banshee in bed. I'm sure they heard her in Munster. I had to hit her to keep her quiet. She hit me back, too. You'd never get an English-woman doing that. Well, I was with Maeve one night . . .' He stopped, his eyes glazed over, 'Christ! she was lovely . . . and she was shrieking and tearing the skin off my back, and her husband came home. He was supposed to be in Dublin for the week. What with the noise she was making we didn't hear him until he was outside the door. I had to jump out of the window . . .'

'Bare as a worm,' I said.

'Yes. And then he came after me with a bloody great thing, like a spiked mace without the spikes, and made of wood . . .'

'A shillelagh,' I said.

'That's it. Maeve threw my gear out to me, and I put it on and never stopped running until I got to Wexford. I thought it was time to come home. To the good influence of my Nicholay.'

115

'Finch,' I said, 'I never knew you were a coward. Lecher, yes. Villain, yes. Coward, no.'

'Oh, but I am,' he said, looking at me with innocent eyes. 'Didn't you know?'

'Tell it all over again,' I said, and he did, with embellishments. Then he sat back laughing, enjoying my laughter.

It was the last jest we were ever to share.

The mist came down early. By the time we had supper, an elaborate meal as it was Edmund's last night at home, it lay in veils over the house and garden, a low river-mist, thinning as it rose. The watery moon fought through it. Our table was bright with lamps and candles. My mother sat at the head, facing Edmund, Dame Philip and Josina opposite me. My mother and Edmund were pale; this made Josina's lack of colour unnoticeable. She was wearing the white dress and kept her eyes downcast, while my mother talked incessantly. Edmund and I got on with our meal and Josina pushed her knife about her plate and crumbled bread. Jankin and John waited on us as usual. The meal dragged. My mother kept lifting food to her lips and putting it down again, talking of the old days and covertly of the time to come. We drank wine, thinner and less heady than that I had had earlier that day. It was wine left over from King Richard's birthday.

I thought: This is ridiculous, as my mother spoke about the cause in riddles that a child could fathom. So I stood, and lifted my goblet.

'Madam,' I said, 'I propose a toast. The health of my brother Edmund. Success to the cause, and all prosperity to Plantagenet. May the brave men who surround him find their rightful place. Safety attend them. God be with them.'

She lifted stormy eyes. Shocked approval crept through the storm. She rose slowly, as did Edmund and Dame Philip. Josina sat on, crumbling her bread.

'It is a good toast, Nicholas,' said my mother. 'Let us drink it to the dregs.'

Josina got up; it seemed she could not stand very straight. Then Edmund's voice made me look down the table.

116

'Nicholas is loyal, madam,' he said. 'He's with us in all we do. And he has kept faith.'

'Have you?' she asked. I bowed.

'I have said nothing, although more than once I have been provoked.'

'Nicholas,' she said. 'Edmund. Daughter. Dame. We salute Plantagenet. Death to Tudor. Loyalty for ever.'

In solemn silence we drank. Josina gave a little choking cough and I looked at her with sympathy. She was sitting down again, eyes veiled. Then I thought: I must tell them about Cork. I gave them the essence, and watched their glances of triumph and for the first time, shared. I could tell them the name of the Breton— Meno—probably because it was an anagram of Finch's bird. I also told them the Irish seemed unimpressed, after their previous disillusion over Lambert Simnel. 'This is most useful,' said my mother. Yes, I thought, and had you trusted me earlier I might have gleaned more for you, from Patch and who knows how many other secret sources. The candles gleamed on their rapt, taut faces. Dame Philip guzzled wine and nodded, soothed by the rare kindly atmosphere. Josina sank down in her chair, turning her head sharply towards Dame Philip. I thought: The hag does little to cosset her these days. When we are restored at Westminster I will find her the cleverest, most able maid in London.

The candles licked my mother's scarlet dress to a sheen. She looked supple and young. Every detail of that evening stays. I wore my black broadcloth, and Edmund, murrey, and Josina looked like the ghost of a lily. I was cracking a nut between my hands when Edmund said:

'This means then that I shall be going to France or Portugal. The cause has reached so far.' He looked at me. 'Nicholas, your source is reliable, I trust?'

'Completely. It came from someone quite uncommitted, and was told to me in passing, on his return from Ireland.'

'Let us hear his name,' said my mother.

I felt my face redden. 'I'm sorry, Edmund. It's someone you don't care for. But he is reliable.'

'Oh,' he said with disgust. 'Him. I hate him. I only saw him once, but I hate him. Don't ask me why.'

'Who is this?' asked my mother.

'Nicholas's friend,' Edmund said. 'We met him at the Fair.'

Josina knocked her wine over. The cup was almost full and made a large stain on the cloth. Then she got up and left the room so fast Jankin had only just enough time to open the door for her. I glared at Dame Philip, who was scattering salt on the wine-stain. Attend her, I mouthed. I could hear Josina walking about with a heavy step above our heads. My mother had ignored the interruption and was wanting to hear again what was being said in Cork, when the prince had left, how he looked. I could tell her no more, I said, and thought I should go up to my sister. Impatiently my mother gave me leave. As I left the room she was devoutly gazing down the table at Edmund, and Dame Philip was nodding off.

Josina was not in her chamber. Jankin had lighted candles on the landing, and I took them up. The flames trailed and smoked. I heard Josina's cat crying as if it were being hurt. I swept the light along the landing. The sound came from my room. The cat was not there, but Josina was, lit by misty moonlight, and it was she who was making that tortured sound. She was taking two or three little steps at a time, turning, gasping, tearing at the girdle of her dress, with one hand down her back to unfasten the laces. I set down the candles, crying: 'What's the matter?'

She flung herself round, clawing at my arms. 'Take it off,' she whispered. 'I must get the dress off. I can't stand the pain any longer.' She bent, clutching her belly. I tore at her dress, and it fell; she stood there groaning in her white shift, clasping herself, sweat shining on her face. She threw back her head and cried: 'God help me! Sweet Mary! Help me!'

In all my days I had never been so terrified. She was in agony; it lashed at me, full of the unknown. I tried to hold her; she writhed in my arms. Her body felt different, full, and there was a dreadful smell on her breath.

'Oh God!' I cried. 'What is it?'

Crazed, she reeled from me, slid crouching down the wall, her hair streaming over her naked shoulders and face. 'I'll get Dame Philip,' I said, and she screamed: 'Nicholas! Don't leave me!' I knelt with her and she collapsed against me. Again I asked her: 'What's the matter?' She quietened for a moment and I held her while she panted with pain. Then she raised her tortured face.

118

'I thought . . . at first I thought it was the Hobby.'

She has gone mad, I thought. I'd heard of women succumbing to melancholy. I should have seen a warning in that dreadful little song.

'That monster . . . at the Fair . . . said I'd have children . . .'

'Oh, my poor Josina,' I said.

She clawed at herself again and groaned. The smell grew stronger on her breath. Then she started babbling. 'I was sure it was the Hobby . . . over the weeks I thought . . . it couldn't have been just the Hobby . . .' Her shuddering became mine, a grave-chill composed of fears too big for me to encompass.

'Tell me about the Hobby.'

'He touched my face, under his gown. I thought of that when I knew I was with child.'

Far away I heard myself saying: 'No, my love. You don't get with child from that.'

Another spasm took her, she gasped and cried in my arms. I still didn't believe her. Melancholy, I told myself; she's been cooped too long in this house. Then she gave a terrible shriek and writhed away, clawing up the wall so she could stand. I saw a long red stain beginning on the front of her shift, red drops splashing on the floor. Some fell on my shoes. Before me again was the little Brecher wife, the big belly and the blood. Behind me the door opened; someone stood in the dark passage. The red patch was spreading on the front of her shift, dripping off the hem.

'The herb pennyroyal,' she whispered. I caught her and carried her moaning to the bed. 'When I was sure . . . I took the double measure . . . and another, then another.' She began to weep. 'A child. No husband. No dowry. The shame.'

I laid her down. My teeth were chattering. Even if she were bleeding to death, I had to ask her. I wanted to hear her say she had been ravished by a stranger. God help me, I wanted her to tell me that.

'What happened at the Fair?'

Out it came. Yes, she knew in her heart that the innocent Hobby with his devil's face could not be blamed. She told me quickly and lucidly, bleeding all over my bed.

It was so hot on that bench with the old women. He had come, so quiet and sad (*sometimes, I play the innocent, I beg their pity*), while I was so long away at the cockpit and Edmund in the mayor's loge and Jankin asleep (*nice young fellow, gave me plenty to drink*)—then just a little walk, through the trees over the sweet bruised grass, in the cool forest out of the crowds. Squirrels, she said, there were squirrels, like dainty dancing courtiers, and fallen trees. He had picked her up and carried her—'just like you do, Nicholas'—he had been worried all the time about her gown so white. When he first saw her, riding in, he had thought he had died and was in heaven. She had never seen such eyes. Then he took her hands and . . .

'He asked me if I would please kiss him, for no one had kissed him since his mother had died.'

'Oh, dear sweet Jesus,' I said, and began to weep.

'And then—' I looked at the red and white shift, like the Brecher wife, the mad nun's face, the bodies of my father and the King, the worst things in the world. And all my doing. No, Josina. Have pity on us. But she made me her confessor. I managed not to hear some of it by thinking how I would kill him. I had decided to kill him some minutes ago.

I said: 'Tell me this. Did he hurt you?'

If he had hurt her, I would make him beg for death, and go beyond that. Otherwise I had decided to kill him quickly, and rid the world.

'No. He was gentle, like you. He said it might hurt a little, but no more than cutting one's finger . . . it was true. He said it was love.'

'That's not love,' I said, weeping.

'And then—' she gasped in pain as she said the worst thing of all— 'I wanted it never to end.'

I bowed my head. For a moment I hated her. My Iseult, thrown to the lepers. But who had set her among them?

Edmund, in the dark doorway said quietly: 'Finch. Bloody, bastard Finch.'

I said: 'Stay with her. I'll fetch Mother and Dame Philip.'

Josina was screaming for me not to leave her. I couldn't have left her, I loved her as I never loved her before. All my hatred ran away and burned within, feeding a rage so strong it was almost love, compounded of the knowledge that I had thrown her in the Devil's path, and that his instrument had seized her as a prize. So blonde, so beautiful. Crawling from the gutter to lay the hands of lust on her, just as I had once laid hands on him. The guilt was mine. To destroy it I had to destroy him or myself.

Dame Philip and my mother were in the room with candles. Dame Philip, alert at last, her old function restored, went to work. My mother sat down at the bedhead and took Josina's head on her breast. Her eyes probed mine. For a terrible moment I read her, saw her remembering—how I was always kissing, touching Josina. However low of me her opinion, she could not think that.

'No, madam,' I said. 'But all the same, the guilt is mine.'

'Get out,' she said. 'And you, Edmund. This is no place for men.'

I detached my hand from Josina's just as she quietened and Dame Philip, with expert pressures, expelled from my sister the bloody little swab that had been Finch's child. Dame Philip said: 'That's good. That's it. My dove, my dove. Christ aid us all. The shame.'

Edmund stood at the top of the stairs, his head bent on his hands on the newel-post in the dark. I went by him without a word, out into the thinning mist, round to the stables. No Bedesman there, to assuage my grief. No grief, only fury. I took my knife and sharpened it on the whetstone. I honed it so fine and went on honing it long after it could have cut a blade of grass in two. I was groaning in a rapture of fury. Then as I watched the blade spark in the stable lantern, another knife landed on the stone beside it and kept time with my strokes.

'Go away, Edmund. This is my affair.'

He went on sharpening, hissing through his teeth. Wearing the cloak I had bought him, he seemed taller and bigger in the mist and gloom. One of Piers's proverbs skipped unbidden through my mind. *Noli pugnare duobus*. 'It is not chivalry,' I said, 'to make him fight against two adversaries.'

'Chivalry,' said Edmund, 'is dead.' The pupils of his eyes had shrunk to the size of a bird's. We were both trembling as if we stood in snow.

'My sister,' he said. 'Sweet Mother Mary!'

'She's my sister too. She's mine.'

'She's more mine than she is yours,' said Edmund. 'Oh, that

121

whore's son. Come, Nicholas. Let's send his filthy soul to the flames.'

I went after him into the street. I thought: Please God, let the old man be gone to Westminster, and let Piers be out. Edmund will spare none in that house. I walked with him that well-known way that I had travelled in joy and love and madness, through the streets mist-cold and full of writhing ghost-shapes, not thinking or speaking, my mind a blade pointed towards the enemy. And not a soul about, not even the Watch, the dark ways lit only by the moonshine—the angry moon.

From across the street I looked at the door of the cookshop and should not have been amazed to see it burst into flames from the rage of my thought. It opened and Piers came out, removing his spectacles to rub his eyes. Edward lunged forward and I caught his arm.

'Wait.' Piers went off round the corner. We moved forward. The door was open. I pushed Edmund violently away from it. For the last time, I whispered, 'This is my quarrel!'

I entered, thrusting him aside. The greatest remedy for anger is delay, said a voice in my head. *Furore iraque* . . . Quiet! There he is, standing by the hearth.

He was in shirt and hose, leaning down with a spill to light a candle. Fireglow limned him round, the slender back, the long hand with the ruby ring, bringing the light carefully up to the candle. He didn't turn. He said: 'That was quick, Piers. Did you forget the money?' He lit the candle, then another, and the familiar room loomed into bright life. Edmund gave a little groan of rage, and Finch turned his head and saw us, our stance, our faces. He threw the spill gently into the fire. Then he hooked his thumb and finger into his belt, just above his knife-hilt.

'I see him,' said Edmund, a little bloody lilt in his voice. 'I'll take him.'

Then he swore at Finch, a stream of obscene insults that even Finch could not have bettered. I wondered vaguely where he had learned them and thought: The Acre. Archery is enough to teach anyone to swear. That's how cold my mind was, now. Finch stood looking at me. Edmund's loathing voice quivered into silence.

122

'So she told you, Nicholas,' said Hugh Finch. 'I somehow thought it would be today.'

I said: 'I've come to kill you, Finch. But first I want to hear your confession.'

He was no coward after all. He stood there and simply asked us to end him.

'Yes. I had your little sister, Nicholas. I took her in the forest at Bart's Fair. She's very lovely. I had to have her. She loved it. Virgins often do.'

Because he was so sure it would be me, he still did not go for his knife. I had mine ready in my hand and knew I had to get him first. But then Edmund threw off his cloak, threw it over my knife-hand, and sprang across the room with a yell like a wild beast. He had his knife upraised, and in that sick moment I thought: Sweet God! keep your guard up, Edmund . . . I saw the firelight gleam on Finch's drawn blade, and Edmund ran on to it. The blade vanished upward under his ribs: his rush carried him forward on to it and on to Finch's outstretched palm pushing him back. As he fell backwards the knife came out of his body, gleaming darkly and he went down, rolling under the table. And I remember thinking: He should have brought his bow, used his keen sight . . . as I walked slowly across to come up close to Finch, so there should be no mistake and I could look into his face as I took his life or he took mine.

He held the blade away from his side, and some of Edmund's blood rolled off the tip. There was blood on my shoes from what Finch had done to my sister. I looked into his face as I brought my knife up slowly. He looked very young. Very tired and, unbelievably, very sad. I tossed the knife up in my hand and guarded my body with my other arm.

Finch said: 'I warned you never to trust me. Now just look what you've done.'

His face wavered. I could see his lips move, but caught only a few words.

'I belong to you, you know,' he said. 'I always have done. You can do what you will with me, now.'

I raised my blade, letting it shine in his eyes. He watched it in a kind of fascination, intrigued by death. His knife hand never moved. He smiled slightly.

123

'You won't kill me, Nicholas,' he said. 'You love me.'

'Not any more,' I said. His knife came up then, but so slowly it was easy to knock it away. I struck at his face, at one of his beautiful eyes, the left one that once I, enthralled, had kissed. My blade went deep into the soft cavity and into his brain. I felt the tip jar against bone, my palm flat against the end of the knife-hilt. He died instantly, I knew as, in an absurd attempt to save him from harm, I caught him close as he fell, going down with him to the floor. I knew he was dead and that this was our one and only true embrace. Then I withdrew the knife from his eye. Blood rushed into the socket, half his face became instantly covered in blood, and more ran from his nostrils and mouth in thin dark threads.

'Oh, Finch,' I said softly, 'Oh, Hugh.'

He lay quiet, almost in the hearth. I had never seen anyone so dead. It was as if he had lived with such vitality that even his death had to be more climacteric than anyone else's. His long hands were relaxed, He had died unhouselled, and he had talked to me about the flames of Hell. I began to shiver. Behind me I heard Edmund moan, and I crawled over to him. My hands were covered with Finch's blood and I tasted it on my lips. I took Edmund close in my arms. His doublet was sodden red and by now I was bloody from head to foot; my sister's blood on my shoes, Edmund's and Hugh's blood on my hands and face and clothing. And I was myself completely unmarked. Just look what you've done, he'd said.

The white light was fading from Edmund's eyes. They stared over my head. I stroked his hair and kissed him. He whispered: 'It's so dark . . .'

Silence. Then he said, quite merrily: 'Father!' and was silent again. In the deep quiet I heard a terrified little whisper and a bolt drawn close. The cookboys in the kitchen must have heard everything and were protecting themselves from murder. I looked down at Edmund. His eyes were ordinary in death, and I closed them, then dragged him gently from under the table. I brought his cloak and laid it over him. I sat down on the floor and waited. Piers came in, carrying a flagon of wine.

Anyone else would have cried out or sworn in the face of such a scene. I stood up and moved away from the two dead bodies so that he should have a full view in the candle and firelight and the

124

lantern he brought in from the street. He saw all, and drew a little sharp breath. He put the flagon down and came to me.

'Are you hurt, Nicholas?' he said softly. He looked me up and down, at all the blood. Try as I might, no words came. He pulled out the bench for me as if it was an ordinary day. His calm was weird. He lit more candles; it was like daylight in there by now. He went to the hearth and bent to Hugh. 'He's dead,' he said. Then he drew the cloak back gently from Edmund's face. 'And so is he. This is your brother?' he asked. Three times I tried to answer, and finally succeeded.

'My brother. It should be me lying there.'

'That's not for you to say,' Piers said gently. 'Hugh killed him?'

'And I killed Hugh. Your brother, Piers.'

'My half brother. Poor Hugh. He was so wretched. You did him a service.' He knelt by Edmund, crossing himself. 'But this is different. This is a tragedy I had not foreseen.'

'How much did you foresee?' The room was swirling, the candles dancing in figures of eight.

'Most of it, though not these deaths. From the moment you said you had a beautiful sister. Now. We must protect you.'

'Protect me?' I tried in vain to stand. 'Piers. I wish you'd kill me.'

He came and placed his hand on my shoulder, a very heavy young hand. 'Be still, Nicholas,' he said sternly. 'Do as I say. Bolt the door behind me. Answer only when you hear my voice.'

'You're going to fetch the Night Watch'.

'No. I'm going to fetch Master John from the Greyfriars. He'll know what to do. I shall try not to be long.'

At the door he turned and said firmly: 'It was a street brawl. They were killed by persons unknown.'

I bolted the door behind him, then went to where Edmund lay, his keen eyes closed for ever. I touched the scar on his hand and thought: When my mother learns of this, I too shall die tonight. And the thought was miraculously calming. Hell is remote, for this is Hell on earth.

Then I knelt by Finch. His face was smooth, where the maimed side was turned away, and younger than Edmund's. The fire was dying; it had grown very chill. I bent and kissed his cold lips. I

125

thought I heard his laughter. I envied his stillness, and was alarmed for his soul. His soul, hidden by his beauty like the foul kitchens behind the spotless parlour; his callous cruelties, his secret shames and his honesty—yes, honesty, for he had shown and told me that with him no woman was safe. Whichever way, the fault was mine. He had loved and needed me. I had rewarded him thus, and sent my knightly brother with him.

I sat there with the candles burning down and heard St Swithin's strike, but I could not count the hours. I sat with two dead men and my own conscience, and if I could have willed myself to die I would have done it. Finch's voice was all round me and once I thought he moved, but even the dried blood on his face was chill. I thought of the Irish woman, Maeve. If she knew, she would probably mourn the lover who had pleased her so. I thought of Finch's son by the girl Agnes, the poor little bastard he had never seen. And lastly I thought of Josina, for she too had loved him for a moment, and he, or I, had brought her to ruin.

After a long time I heard scratching at the door. I opened, and Piers entered with Master John. I had heard so much of the scholar and teacher I had imagined an æsthete, tall and grim. But Master John was a round, merry-faced little man, although his face was far from merry now. He was as calm as Piers as he surveyed the dolorous sights in the room. He bent over Edmund and then Hugh, seeing if they were beyond life. Then he came back to us. I had to sit down again and Piers kept his heavy hand on my shoulder.

'Is this Nicholas, Piers?' asked Master John, and Piers nodded.

'Did they die in their sins, Nicholas?' he asked me. I whispered: 'Yes, Father, they died in their sins, and I live in mine.'

'Is it too late?' Piers asked him.

'Yes, my son. Their spirits have departed. There can be no absolution and no public requiem. But we can pray for them. Leave me with them, please. He took out his breviary, open at the Office for the Dead. Piers and I went to the kitchen door. He tapped softly and called: 'Boys. Open please. All's well,' and presently the bolt was drawn and a terrified cookboy admitted us. The boys were clinging together in their cupboard. Piers and I sat at the table. He put his hand on my shoulder again and kept it

126

there. I closed my eyes and let the strength of his mighty will surround me.

After a long time Master John let us return. He had laid the bodies side by side. 'Now I will make the arrangements for Hugh,' he said. And I knew with great sadness that none would ever come seeking vengeance for Hugh Finch's murder.

'And your brother?' said Master John to me.

'I must take him home to his mother.'

'I'll get the horse and cart,' Piers said. 'And I'll come with you, Nicholas.'

'No,' I answered. 'This is something I must do alone.'

The fog smoked and rushed about me as I drove with Edmund's body towards Watling Street. The cart-lantern swung gently and fog swirled about it, a ghost's breath. Here and there the moth-grey cloud opened as a breeze arose. I could still feel Piers's hand on my shoulder. He and Master John had taken Hugh to the Greyfriars for burial. There I shall stay till morning, Piers had said. To pray for you, Nicholas. As I approached Watling Street I heard St Anthony's toll Matins. It was All Souls, the Day of the Dead.

Piers had told me something else, thinking to comfort me and bringing greater pain. Just before we parted, he told me that Hugh had made his will; he had had it drawn up in July, when I hated him so. It was a strange thing for him to have done, but he had left everything to me—his money, his clothes and jewellery—and Nemo. As I left, Piers had taken the ruby ring from Hugh's finger and silently given it to me. I did not expect ever to see Piers again, but when I said this he merely smiled and said: 'Remember. Love is strong as death and harder than hell. Love cannot endure anywhere that is not God. And I am still your true bedesman.' He was praying now; I felt his prayer all round me, fighting back the fog and mist.

I took the horse and cart round to our stables and put it with ours. Then I took Edmund's body, still wrapped in his cloak, and carried it into the house. There were lights upstairs, and one in the parlour, but no voices. The parlour was empty. I laid Edmund on the table and arranged the cloak about his body. I put a candle at his head and another at his feet for his Wake-Night. I took the

127

ruby ring out of my pocket and slid it on my right hand. Then I went upstairs to Josina's room, for a last sight of her.

Piers had washed the blood off my face and hands and the blood on my clothes had dried indistinguishably into the black. I would not have liked to frighten Josina, after all her misery. I could hear Dame Philip now, talking gravely in my mother's solar. A little light was burning on the side table by Josina's bed. She turned her head on the pillow towards me. Her face was no longer small and round; it was pointed, quite gaunt. I looked hard at her, to punish myself more. I gave her my hand to hold, she looked down at it and recognized the ruby ring. Tears filled her eyes and she turned her head away sharply. 'I love you,' I whispered. 'So much. But it's too late to weep now. Sleep, my darling.'

In my room I unlocked Edmund's sea-chest and withdrew our father's sword. I went down again and sat in the hall. After a short time I heard my mother coming downstairs, her candle preceded her with flickers and shadows and trailed gleams over her red dress and her loose hair. I stood up so her light should fall on me.

'Where's Edmund?'

I pushed open the parlour door for her and followed her in. I laid my father's sword down on a chest. Edmund's face looked smooth and fine in the candlelight; disembodied above the dark cloak. It was the first thing she saw. My mind was cold. First, she will scream. That will distress Josina. But she did not. Her back became very straight, and she stood looking at Edmund's dead face for a long time. When she turned, her face was almost that of a demon, her eyelids fluttered, I could see only the whites of her eyes. A spur of froth appeared at one corner of her mouth. She took two steps towards me and spoke very low.

'Your doing?'

I whispered: 'Yes.'

'You? You killed my son?'

'No. But it is still my doing.'

She clenched her fist and struck me in the face, so hard that I fell to the floor. Blood sprang from my nose, my blood at last, I welcomed its taste. I got up slowly and she struck me again, cutting my cheek open with her ring. And again and again. I felt each blow a few seconds after it landed. This was not what I

128

craved. I wanted death. Then she started to rave at me, in an animal's growl.

'You whoreson bastard. Murderer! Traitor! Cain! You vile, loathsome harlot's son!'

Somehow I felt apart from the scene, up, watching from the far corner of the room, near the ceiling. I felt puzzled. She, who was of such noble blood, calling me a harlot's son. She insulted herself. From up in the corner my spirit watched the tall, tow-headed young man with the bleeding face frown, and heard him speak.

'No, Mother!' and then I was suddenly back in my shoes, feeling her spittle jetting in my eyes. 'I am still your son.'

Then she did scream; it had been bottled up for twenty years.

'You are *not* my son! You bastard! Beggar! You're no son of mine, you murderer! Look at you!' and she smacked my face with the stinging flat of her hand. 'How could you be my son, you false viper! God curse the day your father ever bade me take you in!' And then she whirled away to throw her arms across Edmund, cradling his dead face, weeping as I never wish to hear anyone weep again this side of the grave. Oh, Edmund, she cried. My beloved Edmund. Ah, my sweet son! And she began calling him by my father's name: Mark, oh, Mark.

She mourned so dolorously that I had to move forward and touch her. Had she been my worst enemy I could not have borne the sounds she made. It was the collapse of all her hopes—it was the sound of widows of the world, bereaved mothers, men disembowelled, the howl of werewolves, all punctuated by sobs as rhythmic and inexorable as a grave-digger's spade. She will die from it, and it is I who am supposed to die. 'Mother,' I said, because her words had meant nothing beside my present grief. 'Mother.'

Soon, her lamenting lessened. She turned to me, a hag, a witch, with her piebald hair streaming and a drift of it in her fingers where she had torn it out.

'I am not your mother,' she said. 'You are the fruit of one night's folly on your father's part, when he was exiled abroad with Richard of Gloucester. Your mother was a whore.'

Even the candles grew agitated, their flames shivering at the news.

'He asked me to bring you up as my own and I agreed not to

tell you. I have never broken that promise, though it went hard with me. That harlot! we were betrothed . . . he was unfaithful . . . ah, Mark, my love . . .' and her eyes rolled up again. I feared she would fall in a fit as she cursed me again, and cursed my mother, the whore.

'Edmund knew,' I whispered.

'Yes, and only Edmund. Were you not such a wicked fool you would have guessed yourself. Have you never dreamed you were beneath my family?'

'And I was born abroad . . .' I said. My tears fell and fell. I wiped them impatiently away. I was remembering Leicester, when she had rejected me. Now I knew why.

'You came by ship to England when you were two years old. There was a storm . . . the ship nearly foundered. Would to God you had been drowned. Would to God you had never been born. I curse you with my last breath.' In a panting, whispered scream. 'I curse you, bastard Joachin. You were baptized Joachin—your father renamed you Nicholas. Your evil ways have ruined my daughter and killed my beloved son. You have destroyed my family. May you never find peace on earth or in heaven.' Then she put her hand to her head and sank against the table.

I took up my father's sword and gave it into her lax hand. I knelt close and ripped my shirt open to the waist. Her knuckles paled on the sword-hilt as she raised the weapon to my heart. I closed my eyes and waited. Then I heard the sword clatter to the floor.

'I cannot,' she whispered. 'You are of Mark's blood. I can harm nothing that is his.'

'Madam,' I said. 'Margetta.' I opened my eyes. 'I beg you, kill me or forgive me.'

'I cannot kill you. And I shall never forgive you as long as I breathe.' She went back to Edmund, crooning, weeping, stroking his head.

After a time I said: 'I do not ask forgiveness, then. I only ask to be allowed to atone.'

'How can you atone?' Her voice was tired and sad. Her rage had burnt into ashes.

'I will do anything. I will go to Hell and back to atone. Margetta. Give me a penance.' Piers was still praying for me; his prayer was inside my head, coming all the way from the Greyfriars . . . 'to assist the spirit in its distress, penances are put on it like a bridle . . . put on the flesh the bridle of love . . .'

'It is long since anyone called me Margetta,' she whispered. 'As you did just then.'

'My lady,' I said. 'Give me a penance. Let me atone.'

She looked steadily at me with her ravaged face. The storm in her eyes was stilled, the cause was slipping from her grasp. Yet a little flicker of intensity came back as she looked at me.

'They will be coming for Edmund today,' she said softly. 'To fight for the cause. To protect Plantagenet. I promised them my son. He is dead.'

I rose at last, swaying on my feet.

'But I live,' I said. 'I will go in his place. His loyalty shall be mine, Margetta. I pledge life and death. Let me go.'

She said: 'You will never see Josina again. When she is recovered she shall become a nun. She has no chance of marriage now. In cloister, she will be safe from the world and its deceits. That shall be your penance.'

'It's not enough,' I said. 'Let me go. To defend Plantagenet.'

And perhaps, through God's mercy, to die, I thought. She was taking Edmund's cloak from him, carefully lifting his light body to withdraw it. She brought the cloak to me and placed it about my shoulders; it was exactly the right length. Then, looking in my eyes with pleading and hatred, she told me what I was to do. I was to follow, to glory or to the grave, the rightful King of England, Richard Plantagenet.

Part 2

1492-1495

Ferrum tuetur principem. Melius fides.—The sword
protects the prince. Better still, loyalty.

Seneca: *Octavia*

To stand on the battlements of Amboise was like being on the summit of the world. The breeze-cooled sunlight lay on my bare head and on the White Rose emblem on my tunic breast. Up here all was whiteness—the château's bastions and walls sweeping down to terraces and turrets of opalescent stone. Far below were the courtiers' exquisite small buildings, and beyond the lawns and rose-gardens the Loire ran broad and green. A barge was passing and the King of France's moored pleasure-boat rocked on the swell. The tree-covered Île d'Or sat calmly mid-river. On the banks, willow and alder shed their leaves; the tiny figures of gardeners chased them with brooms. Tinier still were strolling peacocks, their beauty dimmed by distance.

The château stood across the main road to Spain, and the bridge below was heavily guarded. To the west, the distant tower of St Gratien at Tours rose from a shroud of trees full of birds making ready to depart. Autumn was almost upon us, and looking across at the dark and endless royal forest, my instinct felt the unseen fall of summer.

Silent I stood, with two other silent men on the battlements of a foreign castle, framed by beauty in the dying year. Not on guard, barely armed, in a madness of apathy. For nothing can ever be presaged. As I left England I had thought: I shall do this and that, I shall perhaps be redeemed a little. I had never expected happiness, yet I had visualized a regime of tense occupation, enough to outlaw the past. The hope that I might be honourably killed was a bad jest. None of us had yet been called upon to defend Plantagenet, although he was indeed here at Amboise, a guest of Charles VIII of France. I and my companions had spent the past two years with scarcely the sight of a drawn sword, save for a little skirmish in Ireland which came to nothing. Watching, from Irish duns and manors, and now from French battlements, because at this hour there was nothing else to do.

Maurice Fitzdesmond leaned and spat, his lob landing neatly on the head of a stone griffin. He would spit for a wager. I had met him in Kildare, when I first left what was no longer my home. Short, tough and bearded, he was related to the great Fitzgerald,

Earl of Desmond, whose allegiance to York and Plantagenet was legendary. The old Queen, Elizabeth Woodville, an entrenched Lancastrian despite her marriage to King Edward, had, twenty years ago, had three members of Desmond's family butchered. When in June, Maurice had heard of Elizabeth's death in Bermondsey Sanctuary, he had been drunk for a day and a night of savage celebration. It was easy to get drunk at Amboise.

I liked Maurice. I did not know if he liked me. Certainly he had no reason to like me today. Last night I had dreamed again, and had woken everyone in our chamber. Wim Schenk, who had joined us from Flanders six months ago, stood next to me. He also had had his sleep murdered by me; in the beginning, they had had to endure the sound of my dreams weekly. Now it was more like every two months. Sometimes, waking, I allowed myself to think of Edmund. I had come to the conclusion that Edmund out of sheer frustrated zeal would have challenged or killed someone by now. And now . . . never. I looked down at my own clenched hand. The ruby ring stared back, sombre as spilled blood.

'Shall we go below?' said Wim. 'The sun is dying.'

We passed the chapel of St. Hubert, went under the decorated ogee-shaped arch and down the spiral, through galleries and halls to emerge near the armoury. Amboise was heavily fortified and maintained. The smiths were banging away, steel hissed on stone. Gardeners glared at us as we walked on the cherished lawn; we were foreigners, Englishmen, born with tails, the entourage of some mysterious prince. Eating like locusts at the château's store.

'The King,' said Maurice. There came a bull's bellow of laughter. The gardeners scattered, gathering up rakes and brooms. Through a rose arbour came a lady, running like a hound, skirts up, hair flying. King Charles, arms spread, lurched into view. The lady glanced round, stumbled and, losing ground, shrieked.

'Holy Virgin,' Maurice said, peering. 'Is it the same one?'

Wim was laughing himself purple. 'La Duchesse Madeleine,' he managed to say. 'He'll catch her this time.' At that moment the King hurled himself at the lady's knees, bringing her down for an instant on the grass. She gave him a great shove and leaped up. King Charles continued his pursuit, hands and feet pointing in all directions. His oversized skull jerked on his thin neck like a

136

palsied old man's. It was hard to believe he was only twenty-three. His face was dominated by a drooping nose between small wild eyes, his mouth hung open. He twitched and stammered. One might have taken him for an imbecile, and been fatally wrong.

'Now he has her,' said Maurice.

The pretty Duchess's flight was balked by a shrub. Charles lifted her off her feet. Again she writhed free and ran towards the river. He tripped her at the top of the slope and they rolled together; she laughed and screamed, then began biting and kissing his enormous ears. Their rolling was halted in time by the roots of a willow.

'He has six toes on each foot,' whispered Wim. 'His valet told me.'

We were accustomed to these sights—almost daily we saw him in pursuit of some courtesan who always managed not to run too fast.

We had been in France for over half a year. Before that it had been Ireland (the last place Edmund or I would have expected). Back to Cork where it all began, gathering followers, with Plantagenet hidden and cherished in a house owned by Kildare, the Deputy Lieutenant of Ireland, and then to Kerry, and a few months in Munster. I had not been seasick on the crossing. I had ridden that deck grimly as if borne on a deathship to Hell. The spray had whipped me, scalding my face with ice. At night I stood gripping the salt sheets, watching the stars sway over the topmast, thinking to see the faces of the dead written there in light.

I had been accepted as a spoke in the great wheel that was to roll us all to victory. I wore the livery—the Rose of York stitched to the skyblue broadcloth. Plantagenet for ever. This was our watchword, shared by some Irishmen in Cork, and in the great draughty castle of Kildare. The Earl was a handsome man, fiercely independent, but for all that he spoke fearlessly of the cause, he was wary of Henry Tudor and swore never to set foot in England, although Tudor professed a wish to welcome him. The Earl, precarious in his office, smelled treachery. The wild country, fraught with feuding chieftains and divided loyalties, clung desperately to the tatters of liberty, and Kildare never disguised his rebel's heart.

A little court formed round Plantagenet. There was John

Atwater, Mayor of Cork, and his son Thomas. Thomas Astwood, one-time steward of Marton Abbey, was appointed the prince's esquire. John Taylor was with us for a short while before departing again to Rouen. The little Breton merchant, Pierre-Jean Meno, who had introduced Plantagenet to the Irish, went with him. There were others: quiet, hasty men who rode fast, hiding their dangerous livery beneath night-cloaks: John Heron, a bankrupt London mercer; Nicholas Ashley, a gloomy, thin-faced scrivener, much overworked (letters still flowed between the partisans), and Edward Skelton. Maurice, Wim and myself were part of the team of White Rose Archers.

Sir Edward Brampton was with us briefly. He was playing a perilous double game; Tudor had sent him a general pardon for his Yorkist loyalties while Brampton was in Portugal, and this had been accepted. For a time Brampton returned to Westminster, then departed again abroad. There was no sign of Lord Lovell. No one asked many questions during those early days in the echoing halls of Kildare.

And with the passing months came the knowledge that the whole of Ireland was not prepared to rise in support of our cause. Five years ago they had thrown their hearts into the rebellion initiated by Abbot Sante. Believing Lambert Simnel to be George of Clarence's son, the Earl of Warwick, they had crowned him Edward the Sixth in Christ Church, Dublin, parading him in a crown borrowed from a statue of the Virgin. While Henry Tudor released, for a few hours, the real Warwick from the Tower so that people could gape at the witless lad, the Irish welcomed 2,000 Austrian mercenaries provided by Margaret of Burgundy, Warwick's aunt. The army was led by Lovell and Lincoln, who had been named heir by King Richard, and who was probably involved for his own gains. The ensuing battle at Stoke, from which Lovell fled and at which Lincoln and four thousand others were killed, began the Irish disillusionment. Lambert's unmasking as an impostor completed it; it would be a long time before Ireland, as a whole, trusted the dream of York restored.

Looking back, I wondered whether Henry Tudor knew then of our plans. How many whisperings had there been like those in the Watling Street house? how many paid ears to the door—how many false servants? Did he know then that the true Plantagenet,

138

no organ-maker's son like Simnel, was ready? That we had among us the living testament to Sir Edward Brampton's loyalty to King Richard? Whether at this juncture Henry knew or not, he was much preoccupied with his long-planned invasion of France. I had heard the Earl of Kildare and Brampton talking about it, eighteen months earlier.

'Brittany,' said Sir Edward. 'That's what irks his Majesty.'

The Earl let out a few Irish curses, presumably directed at Henry.

'For sure, she's a prize, with all those good harbours directly to windward of England. What news of the lady?'

He had been speaking of the Duchess Anne of Brittany, the most desirable heiress in Europe. Marriage to her would bring with it the last great feudal fief independent of the French crown.

'She still favours Maximilian of Austria,' Brampton had answered. 'Indeed, with his estates, he'd warrant her immunity from any French invasion.' (The Austrian duke owned large territories in Flanders through his earlier marriage to Mary of Burgundy.) 'Tudor would rather see her wed to Austria than France.'

'A pity,' said Kildare, 'that your great monarch can't marry her himself.'

'Too late, even if he could. She's already gone through a proxy marriage. Wolfgang von Polheim went to Rennes as Maximilian's chamberlain. Thrust his bare leg up to the knee in the Duchess's bed. That's how it's done in Austria. The French laughed themselves sick.'

I looked to where Charles of France was helping his light o' love to her feet. He began to lead her up the slope where a small deputation was coming to meet him. I thought: The French had soon stopped laughing, so had Maximilian, who at the time of the proxy marriage was trying to quell a rebellion among his Hungarian subjects. Charles, ugly, charming, powerful Charles, had swiftly reminded all parties of the Treaty of Vergers, which prohibited the heiress of Brittany from marrying without the consent of the French king. Little Anne had been besieged at Rennes and she was now Charles's wife. I glanced up at the ivory turrets that housed the royal ladies. She was there now— entertaining Plantagenet.

139

The deputation came on, headed by the Sieur de Concressault. Tall and cadaverous, he had been appointed head of our prince's personal French retinue. In springtime he had ridden into the forest to escort us to Amboise. We had been fatigued from the long ride across Normandy and Maine, yet we knew that at last we had a perch to roost on, a powerful sovereign glad to be our ally. Within a green cavern our parties had met; John Taylor and Brampton had ridden forward and offered the letters of introduction to Charles's court, negotiations for which had been the work of one Stephen Frion. Frion had lately held the office of secretary in French affairs to King Henry. (He too was at Amboise, loath, for the moment, to return to England.)

De Concressault had dismounted to greet our prince. In the spring breeze pennons flickered and the standard of Plantagenet sprang to life. Worked in gold thread on a blue ground, it depicted two little boys, one escaping from a tomb and the other from the jaws of a wolf. The wolf wore a Red Rose behind its ear; its face was a lupine version of King Henry's, its significance unmistakable.

The bodyguard which de Concressault summoned to Plantagenet's service numbered one hundred men, armed *cap-à-pie*. They took us fast through the forest. Within the château, Plantagenet went forward to the dais and the French king rose to embrace him. Throughout the speeches of welcome in which Plantagenet was acknowledged for his royal blood, all one hundred of the French armed men had remained, and throughout the banquet which followed, and the installation in our sumptuous apartments. Not until three months ago had it become apparent that half their number had been withdrawn. The force had dwindled to twenty-five, and now there were only six. Now, watching de Concressault's grim face as he had urgent speech with the King, a creeping doubt stirred in me. Charles was still kind, hospitable; this paradoxically gave vigour to the doubt, as if these were final kindnesses. We were fed and wined (venison and boar from the forest of Blois, and the vintage of the Loire slopes; musicians, revels, the pattern of life at Amboise seemed unchanged). Until this moment.

I thought of the wolf with the boy fleeing its jaws; of the hatred that had attainted all King Richard's followers; of Henry Tudor's grudge over Brittany. I guessed the reason for de Concressault's granite looks, and for once I was right. He handed to the King a sheaf of despatches that could not wait for the council chamber. Charles unrolled the first document with twitching hands. The royal head gave a palsied jerk. Under the pretence of brushing dead leaves from his clothing, the pretty Duchess was trying to read over Charles's shoulder. He shrugged her away, his face darkening, and let out a bellowing soldier's oath.

'By St Denis! A pox and a murrain on Henry of England!'

We sidled round the edge of the lawn so we could hear.

'*Mon roi*,' said de Concressault, rising from his knee. 'It was only to be expected.'

The French king's face worked like a crying baby's. Then he tittered, tossed the parchment in the air and kicked it away.

'I riled him over Brittany,' he said merrily 'It must burn him like thorns. And now—does he think to thwart me? Use up my forces? My forces gathered for my Italian campaign? To counteract his puny invasion?'

De Concressault picked up the parchment.

'Not so puny, *grand seigneur*. Two days ago, 26,000 men landed at Calais and laid siege to Boulogne.'

'I'll not waste my army,' said King Charles. 'I'll buy him. Come.'

He turned and walked rapidly towards the château. My doubt fledged itself in fear. I went quickly to find Sir Edward Brampton, or John Taylor or Atwater, anyone older and wiser who could tell me the worst of this news and Charles's reception of it.

I knew from months at Amboise that the French king's paramount desire was his planned conquest of Italy—a campaign which would take him again into the military life he loved and see him supreme over the realm of Naples, which he considered his by dynastic right. All over his demesne Italian modes were aped with great covetousness. Ladies sang Neapolitan songs, wore clothes and shoes of Italian design, read Florentine romances. While the king mustered his armies in pursuit of the dream which would bring Italy more tangibly into his House.

In Brampton's chamber my fears were reinforced. He was terse and busy, signing shoals of urgent letters and flinging them to relays of messengers, but he had time to give me audience.

141

'Sir, no one makes war in winter.' I had learned that much. 'I thought we were safe.'

He glared up at me through smoking seals and tapers.

'Safe? Have you forgotten the last attack on France, when English fought French at Calais over the betrothal of Queen Anne to Maximilian? The annexation of Brittany? Have you forgotten Spain's interest in such matters?' He was usually kind, but he was very worried. 'Have you forgotten the Treaty of Medina del Campo?'

That had meant little to me, three years ago, when I had heard the announcement in Paul's churchyard. It was a treaty drawn up between Henry Tudor and Ferdinand and Isabella of Spain which required the two realms to engage in mutual alliance in the event of war against France. The terms had included the prospective betrothal of Henry's son Arthur with the Infanta Catalina of Spain.

'Spain would be happy to ally herself with England in conquest of the French northern territories. She would take up arms if only to see Charles prevented from becoming ruler of Italy. As for the Papal States, his Holiness Alexander Borgia sits in the middle, full of alarm . . .'

'Charles said, just now,' I whispered, "I'll not fight Tudor. I will buy him." '

'Money there'll be,' said Brampton grimly. His face was tired; there was grey in his hair. 'But a certain person will be part of the price.'

'Plantagenet.' The wolf's jaws gaped in my mind. Red rose, struggling boy. Sir Edward got up. I bowed for his exit.

'Look to him,' he said. 'He is your master, and precious.'

In the hall, people were congregating for supper. Loire salmon, Florentine music, Burgundy brew. And safety. For how much longer?

I knew, as surely as winter approached, that King Charles, mindful only of safeguarding his Italian adventure from Spanish forces, would care as little for my master's future as men did for the fate of the Wandering Jew. And with that one I often felt an affinity, for he was also outcast and, some said, a murderer.

I stood before the high altar in St Paul's. It looked as tall as a

142

mountain. Despite many candles, the church was very dark. As always, Master John was the officiating priest. He bustled about at the altar. And as always, I could not move from where I stood, but a glance round showed the nave to be full. Everyone was there, including the redhaired girl from the Tabard. Her green eyes glittered. 'Oh, fairest day!' she said. 'I love a wedding!' Beside her was Mistress Seward, weeping, with a tray of pies. The lordling was there, and he had tethered Bedesman to a pillar. Piers was somewhere too; his soft frantic prayer was mixed with Nemo's petulant growling and the beat of his wings against the cage. Master John was consecrating the Host. Faint singing came from the clerestory.

Finch stood at my left hand, smiling faintly. Staring ahead, he said: 'You keep the rings, Nicholas. Give them to me,' and I clutched them, one ruby, one plain, and shook my head, trying in vain to move my feet. A black friar, cowled, joined Master John at the altar. Terror scorched me. Behind, the great door of Paul's opened with a groan.

'The bride comes,' said Master John.

She came to us, gleaming white, her downy hair free. She smiled, and began to sing her song, then whispered: 'I must finish the anthem, before the blood comes . . . and gasped, looking down to where the rich stain patched white with red, like my father's body, and I knew that he too was somewhere in church, imprisoned by shadows.

'Give me the rings, Nicholas,' said Finch, and Master John thundered: 'Obey!' and Nemo hissed and growled and the redhaired girl giggled. Then Finch turned to me as he always did, his face calm and fair save for the blood-filled eye where my knife protruded. He kissed me and said: 'Forgive me, Nicholas. Nothing matters now. I belong to you for ever . . .' Master John began to dance with rage, holding the chalice high, and the black friar threw off the cowl revealing Margetta with the foam of fury on her lips. Feet came drumming down the nave; my brother with upraised sword, and I cried: 'No, Edmund!' and Master John and Margetta railed at me in concert: 'Damn you, villain!' and the priest threw the chalice of wine over me. Cold as snow, it soaked me to the marrow.

I opened my eyes. Maurice hurled the empty water pitcher

across the room where it crashed against a pile of harness, stacked ready for the time we might join battle. 'Rot you,' he said with clenched teeth. 'You should be exorcized,' and there was a groan of assent from the half-dozen other men sitting up in bed.

'It's the howling,' said someone. 'Like a wild dog. Heathen madman.'

'What's the hour?' I whispered.

'Between midnight and dawn,' said Wim Schenk wearily, lying down again.

I stared up at the dark ceiling with its Italianate bosses. I lay fast in the dream's newborn horror. Maurice leaned over, still cursing me.

'Tonight was the worst ever. Men's souls could shrivel from those sounds. Who, in the Virgin's name, is Margetta? I was dreaming of Beatrice. Not often do I get the luck.'

Someone blew out the light. Drenched in icy blackness, I realized today was All Souls, the Day of the Dead. Small wonder I had dreamed. Maurice was grumbling about me to young Tom Atwater.

'They say that reciting the Gospel of St John works well,' said Atwater. 'Or beating with a whip made from porpoise skin. My cousin was taken with shouting-sickness. They gave him bishopwort, lupin and fennel, boiled in ale and the nine masses said over it.'

Then he said: 'He died. But some said it should have been given as a bath, not for drinking.'

Maurice muttered: 'If he were to go on pilgrimage . . .'

Atwater said: 'But there are few enough to support the prince as it is.'

'But what use is *he*?' There was the rasp of flint; the candle bloomed again. 'There's no place for fools and dreamers here. With Henry of England three full weeks in France, backed by a willing army . . . they'll follow him, he built them a great brewery at Portsmouth before they sailed, with promises of more if they returned in glory. Bloody Tudor,' he added. 'I had news of Kildare. The Earl's in danger of losing his lieutenancy. Tudor hasn't forgotten he's loyal to our cause. While here we lie, waiting to see who calls the tune, French Charles, or Tudor.'

144

'Will the French treat with Tudor?' I heard Atwater say. 'Does the Italian campaign mean so much?'

'Bishop Fox and Baron Daubeney are still at Étaples. The talks between them and Charles's emissaries have been going on for days. God alone knows the outcome.'

'By St Brigid,' said Atwater. 'Could we only send an assassin to Étaples. To creep into Tudor's tent!'

'Send our dreamer.' I felt Maurice glowering at me. 'I doubt he would know which end to hold the knife.'

The water-soaked coverlet was stiffening over me with a rime of ice. Atwater said: 'You're hard on him, Maurice.'

'These are hard times. He is elfshotten.'

Atwater said very softly: 'We must cleave together. Especially now.' He lay down, sighing. The icy fog of morning filtered through the wall slits. The candle fizzed and brightened. I was elfshotten. The flying venom of old magic . . . no wonder Maurice spits so often and so far, the only way to combat the sailing evil in the air . . .

I heard him leave the chamber, then I must have dozed, for a drop of wax on my hand from the candle brought me upright. He carried a dry cloth and a silver vessel. He began to scrub at my bare chest.

'No sense in taking a chill,' he said gruffly, almost skinning me with his efforts. He tried to wring the water from my hair.

'It could have been worse,' I said.

'Yes. It could have been the *pot de chambre*.' He peered at me closely. 'You can't help having demons. What are they like? Why do they come? I dream only of Beatrice.'

He set the cup down and began writing in the liquid with the tip of his dagger, jabbering an incantation.

'What is it?' I looked in the cup.

'Wormwood in wine, et cetera. From the Lorica of Gildas. I must begin again, you've broken the chant. This is the worm chant, a thousand years old, against the nine onfliers . . .' Gabble, gabble. 'Have pity, so that neither the mortality of this year nor the vanity of the world may bring this man down with it.

'These nine darts against nine venoms,
Now these nine herbs avail against nine spirits of evil,
Through blessed Matthew, Mark, Luke and John, Amen.'

145

He gave a final stir, then spat in the mixture. 'Drink.' The potion went down like gall and gave me a hot feeling in my nose. Maurice nodded, satisfied. 'The charm works well with horses,' he remarked inconsequentially. 'Are you cured?'

'Much,' I said, sitting rigid. 'What were you saying to Tom about Fox and Daubeney at Étaples?'

'Och. Bishop Fox is a clever prating prelate, and Giles Daubeney an eel of a man. They, if any of Tudor's men, can persuade Charles to negotiate. Mark me, Charles would rather pay money than risk men in a hazardous winter engagement.'

The sweet bell of St. Hubert's chapel began to toll Prime. I began hurriedly to dress. The wine in Maurice's potion bred a shifting cheerfulness. Maurice lingered, still anxious to make amends.

'Shall we play tennis today? King Charles said we could use the court whenever we liked.' We went amiably to the chapel, Maurice recalling to me a famous hurling match in Kerry, when four players and thirteen spectators had been killed.

I had only played royal tennis a few times. The court was Charles's pride, its floor of smooth Caen stone dyed, like the walls, with soot and bullock's blood to a glowing grey. High windows ran along each wall, and the play line denoting the upper limit of strike was worked in gold leaf. Pentices sloped upwards from the inner to the outer battery wall, inlaid with mosaics. On both hazard and service sides the court was marked in crimson paint with the fourteen chase lines. Because of my height, I had the advantage of being able to strike clean over the high side of the net at either end; Maurice played best midcourt where the net was lowest. Word had spread that the foreigners were playing, and, as we spun for service, that vital advantage called *l'âme du jeu*, a handful of spectators were taking their seats. They watched from galleries behind the opening of the *dedans* on the service side, and from alcoves above the first, second and winning galleries and the low doorway dividing them. Suspended from the winning gallery was a silver bell, placed to register a lucky strike. Coins chinked; wagers were laid. The marker climbed to his box beside the first gallery. Maurice said:

146

'What shall we play for? The usual, *denier d'or* per point? Four points a game, four games a set?'

'Yes. Fifteen a point, sixty per game. *Double d'or.*'

In the galleries the few courtiers rose to bow for Queen Anne. It was an unexpected honour that she should come to watch our lowly game. She was surrounded by ladies, and Maurice blushed to the roots of his beard. Beatrice, his dream-companion, was in attendance. In her rose velvet gown she outshone the Queen. Anne of Brittany looked older than sixteen. Illness and long, fasting hours of piety had sapped her beauty. Her gown was trimmed with the Breton ermine, the skirt cut to disguise a malformed left leg. From above she beckoned us to rise from our knees.

'Gentlemen, we shall enjoy the sport,' said the little Queen. 'Although we do not approve of these heavy wagers.'

There was no answer to this, and, as she limped to her seat, bags of money were still being passed to the stakeholders. Maurice won the toss, and took his position for service. Fog was drifting through the enclosure. I stood in the hazard. Behind was the grille, set in close by the projecting tambour, off which a deflected ball could shoot into the winning gallery on my right. I had to guard the tambour and the grille, another winning opening. Maurice served along the side pentice. I had forgotten he was left-handed, and the ball flew off the side wall, spinning back along the pentice opposite. I failed to return it. Maurice grinned, his head turned to seek Beatrice. She had a lace handkerchief draped over the side of the gallery like a favour; it moved in encouragement. I gripped my battoir and crouched to receive the next blistering service, catching it on a volley and striking it almost into the *dedans* opening. His next service hit the tambour and spun off into the winning area behind me. The following service was also unreturnable.

Again he glanced at Beatrice, sitting between the Queen and the pretty Duchess in the gallery. I was one game down and 60 sous poorer. I had to try to make a good chase, using a full backswing, keeping the battoir held just above wrist level. I cut the stroke off hard and short, aiming for the chase line marked from the second gallery, and Maurice whacked the ball back so hard into the winning area that the seasoned leather split and flock spilled out like someone's guts. He shouted: '*L'esteuf!*' and a boy released a new ball into the channel beneath the marker's box.

'Double your stake?' he called, and for a moment I was back at fatal Bart's Fair. I shook my head, coiling low for another shattering service. The ball loped past my head and struck the grille with a boom. *Trente-l'œuf.* I lumbered up into the second hazard chase. The fog-slick floor shone like a dull river. I struck the ball high and obliquely. It hit the side of the *dedans* pentice and fell, unreturnable, between wall and floor; sheer luck, but the point was mine. 'Dead nick!' called the marker, in English. A long rally followed, won by me; I decided on discretion. I shouted: '*Bisque!*' and the game was mine. Maurice nodded in approval. The *bisque* is a desperate, double-edged measure, but it sometimes wins. We changed ends. Immediately my play improved. I drove the heavy ball straight at the grille, then at the tambour where it flew into the winning gallery. I won game and set. There was a spatter of applause. More money changed hands. The fog glided in through the galleries like a thief.

Seeing Maurice moving about on the hazard side, cutting the ball heavily, paler now, how important it was for him to win, came to me forcibly. He must shine for Beatrice, small though the game was. I did not want him to win, for he, unlike myself, had no need to seek victory or self-redemption. He was clean and whole, with no more worries than the outcome of an old sport once played by bored monks in cloister. I put all my bitterness and power behind the stroke. The ball landed with a trickle almost at the back wall. 'Better than half a yard,' called the marker. It was a good chase.

I then served two faults and a few minutes later found myself back in the hazard full of disproportionate anger. My shirt was clammy with fog and sweat. I parried Maurice's service and we beat the ball back and forth, using the whole court, plodding stickily over slimy ground from the pass line on my side to the nineteenth chase on his. The game seemed eternal, like one of the long battles which we should by now have fought and won. I lowered my battoir and beckoned. Maurice came to meet me at the net.

'I suggest cramped odds,' I said.

148

'Touch-no-walls?'

'Bar the winning openings.'

'Good. I relish difficulty.'

The marker listened and nodded, and Maurice struck his twisting left-handed service. The ball slunk past my ear and disappeared into the winning gallery where it struck the bell and hung in the netting. At the next service, my wild volley skimmed my opponent's head. The ball made straight for the *dedans* opening. Maurice turned to lob it in flight. His foot slipped. He reeled crazily, clawed at the side wall and in a flurry of arms and legs tumbled out through the low doorway. His head struck the lintel with a crack, and he disappeared. People began laughing. When I reached him, he was white; an egg-sized lump was sprouting above his eye, he had fallen on his left arm, which was limp and twisted. He rolled his eyes upwards and swore at the door.

'Someone will kill himself on that one day,' he said.

'Maurice, I'm sorry.'

'Not your fault. But there'll be no more tennis for a while.' He was sweating in pain.

'I'll get a doctor.' Already a man in a mantle powdered with the Breton ermine was kneeling beside us. He took hold of the arm and Maurice gave a yell.

'Don't bleed me!' he cried. 'For Christ's love. It's an Egyptian Day.'

'Teach me not,' said the doctor testily. 'The fourth day of the moon. Be still.'

At that moment he was rudely pushed aside by a whirl of rosy skirts. Beatrice flung herself down and took Maurice's bruised head to her breast. Through pain, his eyes found mine with a look that said *it was worth it*. Envy and sadness such as I had not felt for months made me feel faint. Yes, it was worth it. Even if he never used that arm again for tennis, or fighting, he loved and was loved, and all that was never to be my portion.

I visited him after supper. He was in bed with a poultice on his brow. The Queen's physician had bound up his arm with elmbark and white of egg. Pained but jubilant, he had Beatrice's handkerchief tucked under the bolster.

'The fool still wanted to bleed me,' he grumbled happily. 'It's death on the *Dies mali*, with the moon waxing and the tide

149

flowing. Like eating goose in Ireland.' He yawned; they had given him mandragora. Guilt filled me as I looked at him; again, my especial demons had used me for hurting.

Leaving him, I met Stephen Frion and Thomas Astwood, Plantagenet's chief esquire. They both had the same worn, uneasy look, like Sir Edward Brampton. 'Playing tennis, at a time like this!' the look said.

'Make ready.' A page was climbing the stair behind us with a salver of bread and wine. 'Had you forgotten? Master Fitz-desmond was to take the tour of duty from tonight with our lord prince. You must serve him instead.'

Sweet God, I said softly to myself. In the past two years I had never yet watched by Plantagenet of a night. There had been more than enough willing for that work. But I knew enough for the prospect to fill me with dismay.

'Be lively,' said Stephen Frion. 'He hates to be kept waiting.'

It was night, November, full of ghouls and gloom.

I knew what to do. Like my father, I had been Gentleman Usher of the Bedchamber, but unlike him I had never served kings, or aspiring kings. I had however slept guard by Sir Edward Brampton during the past months and that had not been an onerous duty, save that Sir Edward snored like a thundercloud. Plantagenet's apartment was far more sumptuous than Brampton's; part of the new building initiated by King Charles, it had every appurtenance of grace. When I entered with the page, everything was in disorder. Much of the prince's wardrobe was scattered over the floor and his bed, with its cloth of gold hangings and brocade coverlet. An empty wine jug was on its side, and there was a jumble of armour—pauldrons, a hauberk, and a battle-helm, as grim as if there were a severed head inside, sat in the middle of the carpet.

I took the bread and wine from the boy, and thrust the empty flagon into his arms. In the hearth, the fire had burned down. I said, 'Hurry, build a blaze,' and he hurled on wood and puffed with bellows. I stowed fine wool and velvet garments into chests, straightened the coverlet and cleared away the battle-harness.

A picture of St Sebastian, quilled with arrows, hung over the bed. On the night table was a Book of Hours loaned by Queen

150

Anne, in red leather tasselled with gold. It lay open at St Appollonia being put to the torture, a picture which always gave me toothache instead of curing it.

I lit candles, while the page pulled out my trestle from under the bed. Oh, sweet God, I thought suddenly. Supposing I dream again tonight and disturb him . . . I set the Night Livery beside the Book of Hours. I made more light, and the wall hangings gleamed like running fires. Plantagenet's heritage: the White Rose, the Falcon of York, the boy fleeing the tomb, the wolf balked of its prey. The leopards of England, gold on blue, flicked their tails under a little draught.

'That's it, well done,' I said to the boy, who I suspected was laughing at the antics of this tall silly Englishman. Voices were outside the door, as Stephen Frion and Thomas Astwood escorted the prince to bed.

He had been taking wine with King Charles, but it had not enlivened him. His face looked cold and wan; his voice as he bade Frion and Astwood good-night was almost a whisper.

'God keep you, gentlemen, through this night,' and then: 'My father, God assoil him, used always to bless his courtiers before retiring.'

They bowed and left him. The page followed, shutting the door with a bang. A twinge shot through one of my back teeth, and the prince hunched his shoulders at the noise. I rose from my knee and he turned to face me, giving the hint of a nod of greeting.

I had not been so close to him in months. Now, uncrowded by his French bodyguard, I saw him clearly. I can resurrect his true image like the crystal colours of the Book of Hours.

He was about a hand taller than I, as tall as his father King Edward had been but more slender, elegant. He was fair, with the gilt hair peculiar to the Plantagenets. Only Richard had been dark; all the others, George of Clarence, Margaret, now Duchess of Burgundy, were golden folk. His mother, Elizabeth Woodville, was famed for her fairness. He carried himself well; I could imagine him parading in the streets of Cork. His ringed hands were those of a graceful gentleman.

The shape of his face tallied with what little I could remember of King Edward's. The mouth was full and curled. The large pale blue eyes glittered, but to the left eye there had perhaps been

151

some old injury. The lid drooped protectively, giving a knowing, secretive look. I did not want to look at it; some old pain might lurk there, and the thought disturbed me.

He frowned, pulling off his velvet cap. 'Permit me, your Grace,' and I went behind to help him off with his long mantle, azure velvet trimmed with fox.

'I am known as Prince Richard in this chamber,' he said coldly. He glared at me with his good eye. He was wearing a short jacket of figured satin, the stuff forbidden by Edward the Fourth to all below the rank of knight. It was slashed deeply to the waist, showing a tight stomacher in cloth of gold. His sleeves were buttoned to a wide velvet cuff. He had long buskins of tawny Spanish leather, a gold collar lay over his chest. I had seldom seen such beautiful clothes. Yet as I helped him out of them I thought him very thin, and his flesh beneath the fine cloth was cool and rigid. I knew he was about three years younger than I, but he looked older. He held his chin high and lines like scars framed his mouth. He stood warming himself before the fire. Kneeling, I tried to air his bedgown as the book of courtesy decreed. The logs had burnt up fiercely and a spark jumped, driven by a demon. I slapped at the little black hole that appeared. The sooner he's safe abed the better, I thought nervously, whipping the gown over his head. He emerged tousled as a child, one blue eye steady, the other veiled, mysterious.

'Do I know your name?' he said severely. 'Maybe I know your father.'

'He died,' I said. 'A traitor's death. Because he fought for King Richard. A lot of us died a little that day.' My voice wavered like the flames, growing thin in the chimney.

'Ah!' said the prince, turning his other side to the fire. 'My royal uncle. An ambitious man. He was bound by desire to rule. Yet' (judicially) 'in all other actions he was fair. He loved the honour of the realm, the comfort of the people. But he courted death. And death crushed him.' He laughed, a strange laugh. Distaste ran through me.

Leaving the fire, he walked to the bed and the Book of Hours. 'Saint Appollonia!' he looked down at the picture and laughed again. 'My brother prayed to her a lot. His jaw festered and he died. She must have been sleeping.' He picked up the book and

152

wandered back to me. 'Read the history to me again. That is, if you can read.'

In that moment I hated him and his swaggering hauteur, thinking: I had a brother too, you must have known him. He was with you at Barnard Castle, and though young he was champion archer. Oh yes, Prince Richard, you with your cherished life and royal-fed veins, my brother, burning with poverty and zeal, was born to be your slave, and I ended him. I glanced up at him as he stood clasping the closed book, and thought: You are not the kind one talks to, man to prince. There were some princes who welcomed confidence and friendship from lesser men. My father had said that these little touches enhanced kingliness. Not you! with your sea-cold eye and your winter laugh. All I want is to have this night over without dreams, yours or mine, so let us to bed, Prince Richard.

He had spotted the tiny hole in his bedgown and cried: 'You've burnt it, you knave! God's Blessed Lady! from what midden did they recruit you to our service?'

I bit my tongue. He strode away, mounted to his couch and I drew the covers over him. Even with his grand stature the bed dwarfed him. His golden hair was the only focus of light among the shadows. He closed his eyes, and in the candlelight his shut face looked vulnerable, but only for a moment.

'I'm thirsty,' he demanded. I came and poured wine into a silver goblet, held it out, and violently he struck it from my hand. Drink splashed all over me and puddled darkly on the Turkish carpet.

'Do you know nothing?' said his icy voice. As I bent to pick up the cup I wondered: why is he behaving like this? (I'll not let him get me down.) A tiny light shone in my mind. He acts so because it is what he has been taught. How a king behaves. But he's wrong! I remembered my father's tales of King Edward's jocund follies and easy wit; the confidences and shared agonies of King Richard during that sick night of whispers when my father nursed him . . . Charles of France too, who only last month had on impulse shown me his aviary with the jewel-bright birds from the East, teaching me how to mimic their calls. Steadily I poured more wine.

'Taste it!' he said. 'Would you witness my death?'

'Surely, great prince,' I said, not caring much if I spoke out of turn, 'the King of France is your friend and his butlers beyond reproach. Even the page . . .'

'You're a fool as well as a knave,' he snapped. 'Of course the King is my friend. But there are agents—all over the château. Taste it.'

It was good, sweet and full. I waited for death throes. Then I said: 'Tudor agents? Here?'

'Throughout the world,' he said grimly, and drank at last. 'I'll sleep,' he declared. I went round the chamber snuffing candles and poking my sword behind the arras. The firefly eyes of the wolf and the leopards glowed, coming out like stars from the banners; the gold fleurs-de-lys swam in the darkened blue of the ceiling. I stretched on my pallet, and heard the prince's breathing, too regular for sleep. Soon he was bolt upright again, calling for his jewel-coffer in which to put away his rings. I took charge of sapphires, pearls, enamel roses; he looked at me as if I were likely to abscond with the lot. Then we lay down again.

I had by now decided to stay wakeful for fear of dreaming. Anyway I was here to watch over him and was determined that he should find no further fault. I let my eyes roam the ceiling. Between the fluting and the carved bosses, there were twenty-four lilies from east to west. Stone oak leaves branched up the corner buttresses, and a fresco of little Breton ermines held a frozen gallop along the edge of the ceiling. Over the hood of the fireplace was a yawning hippopotamus wearing a crown of grapes. Little night sounds filtered in; the distant chink of the masons' tools as they worked on a new wing for the château; the faint squeal of hoist and pulley as a block was lifted into place. Charles was so impatient that he paid the men double to labour night long by torchlight; they heated the stones to make them workable in winter. St Hubert's chapel bell sounded the hour. A peacock cried, followed by a lion's roar from the menagerie.

'I'm cold,' said the prince. I got up and fed the fire, stirring up a great blaze. The room brightened so I could see his face. There was a gleam of sweat on his pale brow. Sweet God! don't let him be ill. He'd likely demand a cup of my blood as medicine. I lay down quietly, my thoughts ran steadily on. I thought of our coming to Amboise, escorted by de Concressault. We had entered

154

through a vaulted corridor opening on to an enclosed terrace, hung with scores of tapestries. Above was a sky-blue awning painted with sun, moon and stars. Then, the Tour des Minimes, riding up and up its extraordinary broad spiral ramp, until we had a view of the forest. Our horses had gone well during the ascent, but had hated coming down.

And there, I decided, lay the horizon of my memory. Nothing beyond that, no Watling Street, guilt or sadness, even in these night hours. The times I had put myself to school thus! and always in vain. Deep in his bed, the prince gave a little groan. Was he, too, struggling to chase comfortable thoughts through the valley of night? His face was turned into the shadows, his breathing almost silent. There was a little leering devil crouched in stone up in one corner of the ceiling. As I watched, he hopped to the middle of the row of racing ermines and then back again. I put my fingers in the corners of my eyes and stared widely. He was crouching again. The fire spluttered, somewhere a dog howled. Chip, chip, went the distant masons, like someone building a scaffold. The fire shifted, darkening the room. Unease surrounded me, anxiety not only from myself but from the man in the bed. And I thought, suddenly: Was this how my father once lay, tense and doubting, beside King Richard?

Again I saw my father's face after that grim white night with the sick king. His grave words to us all: 'Never listen to rumour. It is the devil's iron' . . . And another quotation, the king's echoing of someone in the lost past: '*Omnia fui et nihil expedit*—I have been all things and it availed nothing.'

'I am Richard Plantagenet, rightful king of England.'

Freezing sweat bathed me. The voice was so sepulchral that I imagined the devil on the ceiling had found a tongue, or the ghost in my head—a spirit, using the stones of this fretful chamber as a sounding-board for life and speech . . .

'I am the king.' The voice came from the bed. My relief was so great I could have wept. He was fast asleep, yet his voice was distinct. So he had night demons too! He said something else, in a tongue like that of Wim Schenk, the Fleming. Then Latin—and my flesh crawled. It came from the Order of Burial.

'*Libera me, Domine, de morte aeterna in die illa tremenda* . . . when Thou shalt come to judge the world by fire!'

155

Then, banging his head on the bolster: 'I am Richard of England.'

Such a weary, tormented voice, that I said softly:

'Yes. You are Richard, King of England. Save your Grace.'

He rolled, choked and sighed, and passed into deeper sleep. Despite my resolution I must have slept too, for what seemed the next minute I was staring into blackness, the fire dead, a chill on the room. There was an expression that Patch used to describe this time of night; the hour between dog and wolf. And perhaps for the first time since we had been in France, I felt fear.

We were outlaws, objects of Henry Tudor's retribution. Now I was certain he had known of the cause since the beginning. King Charles had said, laughing: 'I'll not fight him, I'll buy him.' When Charles laughed it usually meant he was deadly serious. What was it Henry Tudor wanted, as much, perhaps, as Brittany? Why, his rival, the upstart prince whom everyone had thought dead. The Yorkist bastard, to whom he would doubtless give a harsher sentence than that of kitchen slave . . . it would be death for us all. I was icy with fear, trembling with shame, and the dog and the wolf had me clipped close between night-black jaws.

Here was a desperate irony. For had I not prayed to be killed and thus purged of my crimes? My father would often quote a maxim of Tacitus: It is sin to leave the field alive after the leader is fallen. He would have been proud to die in the field. Instead . . . Leicester filled me again with its horror. I had witnessed the birth of fear on my father's face; I had seen his courage change to an emotion so strong, so inhuman, that even he, with all his purity, could not outmatch it. I tried to salve my own shame with the remembrance. My eyes closed against all thought.

I felt the cobbles under my feet and heard the tumult of the crowd and the little Brecher woman shrieking above it. Her husband's entrails were a mottled skein to his knees. His head lolled in the halter, but he was still alive and sentient. As the executioner moved on to my father, I thought clearly: This is the worst, I shall not wake—it will kill my soul. Margetta turned and flung her arms round Edmund. The butcher on the scaffold craned to listen to the sounds I was making. His black hair fell in curls, and one eye was a blood-filled hole. He raised his knife, and blew me a kiss.

156

Hands gripped me, firm, arousing. Candlelight bloomed. The chamber was shocked and still from the echoes of my howling.

'All's well,' said Plantagenet, swallowing a little tremor in his voice. 'Sit up. I'll get more light.'

Dazed, I watched as in his night-robe he fed candles. His hands shook. The vaulted ceiling bloomed; the fleurs-de-lys seemed to have shortened their trefoils. The ermines looked aghast and cringing, and I could have sworn the little devil had his hands over his ears.

'They've gone now,' said the prince, a little wildly. He came and sat down on the trestle. He poured wine, his hands still shook. 'Drink. The ghouls have gone. Salute their passing.'

'My lord.'

'Go on, it will revive you. Drink!'—with no trace of his former abrasiveness. I obeyed and he watched, chafing his nervous hands together.

'They will never leave me,' I heard myself say. 'Even in death, perhaps they'll plague me.'

'You did frighten me,' he said. Then, curiously: 'You were cursing someone. Cursing, yelling.'

'I was dreaming of my father.'

'Cursing him? Didn't you love your father?'

I bent my head. Tears splashed into the wine. Disbelievingly I felt his hand, very gentle, on my head.

'Weep,' I heard him say. 'It releases the evil humours from the brain. I used to weep a lot once.' The hand stayed, consoling, restraining, as one might gentle an unschooled horse.

'Oh, my liege lord,' I said.

'Sweet Jesus! how you frightened me,' he repeated. 'Tell me about your father.'

I whispered to him a little and felt the hand on my head fill with thoughts.

'Ah yes,' he said at last. 'Well, soon you can avenge him.'

'When?' I whispered, 'Prince Richard, when will this waiting end?'

He withdrew his hand and sat hunched on the edge of the trestle.

'I pray God, in a little while,' he said.

I set the wine-cup down and said falteringly: 'My prince, I

157

believe that we may soon leave Amboise.' And told him what we had conjectured from overhearing King Charles and what Sir Edward Brampton had said. 'I believe the price for peace with Tudor may be you, my lord,' I finished. For some reason I had imagined he might dismiss this as fancy, but his face grew old and stark, and his good eye blinked rapidly.

'No,' he said. 'I cannot believe it. All saw how we were welcomed here. Fox and Daubeney will not be able to coerce the ambassadors. This is wild talk from frightened men who listen to the songs of Tudor agents. Charles would not deliver me into the jaws of the wolf.'

'The other day I heard,' I murmured, 'talk of the Deputy Lieutenant of Ireland being stripped of his office—with Tudor being so angry . . .'

'So!' he said crisply. 'What has that to do with us? Laws which alarm the peat-bog barons have no teeth here in the courts of Europe! France knows the worth of a true Plantagenet, rightful heir to England. Charles and I are kinsmen!'

In a silence the watchman called Prime, although outside it was black as hell, and the fog still clung like a slander.

'Are you restored?' he asked. 'Finish the wine. I must go to the morning Office.'

I felt full of gratitude. I also felt the need to share with him another hurtful memory.

'Prince Richard,' I said, as he rose. 'You would remember my brother. He was with you at Barnard Castle. A wonderful archer. A dark boy, very agile and devout . . .'

He set the candlestick down with a bang. The light jumped crazily.

'Sweet Jesu!' he said furiously. 'There was a pox of little knaves. Every Tom sent his son to toady favour with the blood royal. How should I remember one especial wretch?'

So it was over, too good to last. I was sad, for it had cost me dear to mention poor Edmund. The prince snapped elegant fingers, bidding me attend him. First, the privy—parting the curtains with my sword against assassins. It had silver appointments and a new-fangled shaft invented by Charles; this angled sharply on its course to the moat (thus avoiding, during siege, a stray arrow in the fundament). Then the ablutions and a new

158

suit—cloth of gold with trailing sleeves over a doublet of murrey. A sapphire rose for his thumb and a gold ring for his ear (in the Italian fashion). During the robing, I said humbly: 'I thank your Grace for his patience,' but he did not deign to reply.

But I shall not forget, I thought. Not that brief tenderness. The curse of a long memory can sometimes turn to blessing.

I walked behind him to the chapel built astride the ramparts. Torches had been lit against the pitchy dawn. New flames blazed in the two fireplaces where folk were warming themselves. Over the door was carved an image of St Hubert, confronting in the forest the stag with Christ crucified between its horns. Opposite him, Christopher bore Our Saviour over the stream.

Throughout the Office, people talked more than usual, there was a distinct, high-key hum to the conversation. King Charles entered late, accompanied by the English and French ambassadors who had been at Étaples. Freshly dressed and shaven, they had been at Amboise for some hours. De Concressault came last, stalking like a black-garbed heron. A chill galloped over my body.

The prince stayed praying for some time. As people left the chapel the murmuring became a loud excitement. Escorting Plantagenet out, we were brought face to face with a small deputation: Stephen Frion, Thomas Astwood, de Concressault. One or two partisans of ours, looking aghast; Stephen Frion seemed to have swelled in importance and like all the Frenchmen with him, looked far from unhappy. Astwood looked merely resigned. But de Concressault was gloating. Addressing my master, he said:

'*Grand seigneur*, I have some delicate news for you. King Charles begs me to inform you that the negotiations at Étaples have been concluded. A Treaty drawn up between England and our sovereign lord will be disclosed to you. If your Grace would follow . . .'

Stephen Frion fell into step beside me. He had always been courteous, as the prime negotiator of our *entrée* to the French court. Now the malice in his eyes showed what that courtesy had cost him. He said, hissing with satisfaction:

'Cursed English! your days at Amboise are done! Moving on, my friend, moving on!'

It transpired that King Charles had bought Henry, after much

159

wrangling. We learned the price very shortly: 745,000 gold crowns, and no further sanctuary offered to the rebel Richard, pretender to Henry's throne.

Winter whirled and beat about us. It was snowing so hard that the horses' hoofprints filled up almost as soon as they were made. It brought the strange feeling that we were ghosts, riding invisibly in a white ghost-land. Yet almost every man in our thirty-strong company was merry. Behind me I heard Wim saying the weather would improve the further north we went.

'They don't have hard winters in Flanders,' he sang. He was obviously pleased to be going home. 'The sea tames the weather. The fens fill up and float it all away.'

This sounded fanciful. I pulled my muffler closer about my face, where a devil in my back tooth employed his little prong. Above, the flaccid banners of York and the rebel standard wept snow, and the wind flicked whiteness into our faces. Wearing half-armour and the prince's livery, I rode in the forefront. I had a good horse, but she was as soaked as I. We had travelled nearly a hundred miles in seven days, and only now had the weather shown its teeth.

Behind me and the standard-bearer rode the prince, flanked by John and Thomas Atwater. Plantagenet was wrapped to the stirrups in a cloak. What could be seen of his face was pink and hearty. His eye drooped as usual but this day it could have been in a friendly wink. One of his valets, an odious youth named Philip Proud, was exercising his lovely tenor voice in a song of the Burgundian, Gilles Mureau.

> 'Grâce attentant ou la mort pour tous mes
> 'J'ay trop esté d'esperance abusé
> 'Labour en vain ou j'ay mon temps usé.'

A song of death, yet he made it sound like a wedding ballad. That, and the snow-hushed hoofs, the creaking rasp of mail and the steamy coughing of the horses were the only sounds. We rode as fast as possible, direct through Blois, keeping within shelter of the forests while avoiding Orléans and Chartres. We had crossed the rising Seine by a rough bridge near Elbeuf. Nearby to the east

160

lay Gisors. We had been lost three times, and hoped we were now heading for Amiens.

There was danger on this ride, and although the snow hid our tracks it slowed our progress. We had slept nights at monasteries, where gold gave us an *entrée* (new Yorkist partisans, riding with us now, had arrived with fresh funds before our departure from Amboise), but the scowling monks and stone-faced abbots fed and sheltered us with scant charity.

'Speak French, even among yourselves,' John Taylor had warned. 'And it would do no harm to furl those banners.'

But the prince would not hear of it. He was Richard, rightful king of England, so the limp banners preceded us into unfriendly cloisters.

'We are no longer France's honoured guests,' said Taylor. 'They know us for the trouble we are.'

'News gallops,' I said. The agents were still at work, Tudor's, and others. On occasion we had been followed by a riding party moving quietly to one side of a bare forest. Doubtless King Charles had sent this to ensure we went on our way from his kingdom.

'Also,' remarked Taylor, 'the French have not forgiven Harry's wars. It's barely a lifetime since these lands rang with English steel.'

I dismissed this. Agincourt was a hoofprint filled by the snows of time.

I wished that I had Maurice to talk to. His arm had not healed well and he had gone back to Ireland, to do what he could for the Earl of Kildare, who had been finally stripped of his lieutenancy. When Maurice heard that Kildare intended to go to London and beg Tudor's pardon, his shame was great. He was so preoccupied that his touching farewell to Beatrice was cut short. 'I'll write,' he pledged, 'if I can find a loyal messenger.' He vowed to raise money for the prince, and embraced me, showing no grudge for the physical hurt I had inflicted.

'Be wary,' he said. 'Trust none. Tell the prince I said so.'

'He knows. I still taste his wine.'

Lately I had slept guard over Plantagenet on several calm nights. There had been no more dreams, or intimacies. We had been exiled from France, but he was full of new hope. Few of us realized, during the month's grace allowed us by Charles, that my master had been sending many letters north of Amboise, mostly written by his own hand.

We had been packing up, the royal wardrobe, relics, books, gold and jewels, and at any moment I expected to see Tudor's armed escort, come to hale us back to England. However, a messenger arrived as I stood guard over valuables outside the prince's chamber. A sandy, flat-faced man with an accent that dipped and rose like the oars of a boat; the accent of Flanders. He told me he was the servant of Seigneur Roderick de Lalaing of Tournai, and gave me a letter for Richard of York. 'He's expecting it.' He cocked his brow. 'You will be coming? You will be welcome, Englishman.' And from his slanting, sand-rimmed eyes up and down the tapestries he somehow, mysteriously, intimated how much he and his countrymen detested the French. When Plantagenet read the sealed roll, the last tensions smoothed from his face.

We crowded into the council chamber for the leave-taking. All of us, including the new contingent of partisans from England, and most of the French court with Queen Anne, her ladies, priests and scribes. It was as if an invisible line had been drawn on the floor between us. Stephen Frion was firmly on the other side, reasserting his Tudor loyalties. He was not alone; quite a few of our original followers had turned tail and returned to England. Near to Frion was a man I remembered seeing in London, on the Night of the Marching Watch, that sad, mad night, when the lords rode through town . . .

Sir Robert Clifford. He had been one of the English ambassadors at Étaples with Daubeney and Fox. He looked unchanged; cool eyes and a neat beard out of which an old sword-scar ran like a small dry river. I knew he was one of King Henry's chief advisers and a close friend of the Stanleys. Yet as Charles repeated the terms of the Treaty to the assembly there was none of the satisfaction on Clifford's face that I might have expected.

Charles was full of emotion. He crossed the invisible line to embrace Plantagenet with all the passion in his misshapen frame. The prince had to bend to meet him. Had our future not been so anxious I should have laughed at the sight.

'My dear cousin!' he cried. 'My heart dies, but what can I do?

The Treaty stipulates that neither King Henry nor I harbour one another's rebels. By St Denis! a sad day.'

'The Treaty is fair,' said the prince evenly. 'I am happy there will not now be war in France. I believe, *mon roi*, that it has cost you dear.'

While Charles protested gallantly that the keenest blow was losing Plantagenet's company, I thought how the terms of the Treaty would bring Tudor a steady income of 50,000 francs a year. He loved money. But what the gentlemen who had come to France in hope of plunder would feel was a different matter. As for Parliament, which had paid him to go to war . . . he would not be popular after this.

'I wish you all supremacy in your Italian campaign,' said Prince Richard. Then, calmly, 'When I am restored to the throne of England . . .'

Someone beyond the invisible line laughed and then fell into coughing.

He never faltered. I watched him with some admiration. He said, standing tall and graceful, his hand on his sword-hilt:

'. . . I will deem it honour to visit you again, so I may admire the treasure you bring from your new conquest.'

Charles wagged his ugly head. His eyes were sympathetic.

'My cousin,' he said seriously, 'where will you go? What of your destiny?'

There was no mistaking his emotions this time. His histrionics were over. It was evident that although the Treaty with Henry had been signed to their mutual advantage, he was loath to surrender the person of Plantagenet along with the vast bribe. Perhaps there was loyalty in him for his erstwhile guest. Perhaps he resented the thought of Henry having all his own way. He had returned to the dais and sat there, chewing sadly on his thumb.

The prince stepped forward. From inside the bell of his sleeve he produced the letter from Sir Roderick de Lalaing of Flanders.

'My destiny is secure,' he said quietly. 'Read, Majesty.'

A kind of knowing mirth followed the path of Charles's eyes as they flicked down the roll. He showed no surprise, he looked rather as if he had won a certain wager.

'My heart is glad,' said Charles.

Plantagenet, one foot on the dais, spoke loud and clear for all to hear.

'As you see, *mon roi*, I am invited to seek sanctuary at the court of Flanders by my beloved aunt, the Duchess Margaret of York, widow of Duke Charles the Bold of Burgundy. This great lady is the sister of my late father King Edward of England. She has been cognizant of my fate throughout our enterprise. Her prayers and blessings have always been with me. Now that she hears of my present plight, she is ready to embrace my cause for the restoration of my rightful inheritance.'

I glanced at Sir Robert Clifford, expecting to see him girding himself for the gallop back to England with this news for Henry Tudor and Sir William Stanley and Cardinal Morton and all who desired Plantagenet's downfall. But he, too, looked unsurprised.

'God speed,' King Charles said, his narrow eyes shining with mirth or tears (one could never tell which with him). 'I will have masses said for your safety.'

Now we ploughed on through the whiteness to Flanders, another foreign land. The snow choked my eyes. Suddenly Margetta's words, unbidden, came back.

'You came by ship to England when you were two years old. Would to God you had been drowned . . . had never been born. I curse you with my last breath.'

And last, most dreadful: 'May you never find peace, on earth or in heaven.'

I glanced round at Plantagenet. He was squinting with his good eye against the lines of falling snow. There was not a soul about to ask for Amiens. Even the shadowy escort seemed to have vanished.

Let me atone, I had said to her. Let me serve him. And what had I done so far? I had never yet fleshed my sword in his defence. The little skirmish in Ireland at the beginning had been shameful, our small force being defeated by the armies of two of Henry's commanders, James Ormond and Thomas Garth. We had had to flee for our lives. I had done nothing for him in France, save give him a bad night. How would I do in Flanders? Our party was flagging. The animals loaded with valuables and gear were tired. We seemed lost and solitary, and there was a decided lowering of our spirits.

About a league further on the blizzard ceased. We came to a group of cottages built beside a flooded stream. They seemed deserted though smoke from their fires hung low over the thatches. In the doorway of the last dwelling a man in a fleece jerkin stood watching us ride by. I reined in and called: 'Amiens?' jerking my head towards the invisible road.

The man took in our colours, our English manner, then unlaced himself and yellowed the snow with a copious stream. Steam rose, an insult. Then he went inside, banging the door.

'Soon be in Flanders,' piped Wim, his voice woeful now.

On we rode through sparse, glittering forest. There had been a small avalanche and snow was deeply drifted. And we saw, protruding from a solid cloud of snow, a dead man's hand, blue and crooked like a giant bird's claw. Unhappy traveller, I thought. Travelling where? Looking back, I saw that the prince was shivering violently, despite his cloak.

Swiftly I stripped my mantle; he accepted it with a nod. I brushed a few stray snowflakes from the White Rose on my tunic and rode back to the head of the cavalcade. Soon I was shivering too. But if his destiny was, as he said, assured, so was mine—to serve him. I did not like him, yet I remembered his compassion in the night. I did not understand him fully—yet neither, I felt, did any of us. He was a cipher of greatness, the frail, displaced anchor of our wanderings. My mare put down her wet head and strode on into the mouth of a little rocky pass between two white hills. The day was shortening.

'It must be past noon,' said John Taylor. The company reined in, the horses blowing out clouds of vapour in the blanched air. Soon we would need a place to rest.

'There be caves up there,' said young Atwater, scanning the hillside. A starved blackbird flew shrilly from a thorn tree. The feeling that we were being watched returned strongly.

'The prince! In a cave!' John Taylor was shocked.

'At least it's dry.' I pricked my mount and led the way into the gully. Suddenly, to my left, the hillside started moving. Wedges of snow, stones, dirt, sprayed down across my path. The air became vibrant with shouts and hoofbeats. The next instant a party of horsemen came charging down the hill. A crossbow quarrel hummed its heavy song past my ear, ploughed through my hat and carried on, taking hat and a tuft of my yellow hair and pinning them neatly to the bole of an oak.

I was too surprised even to reach for my sword, and sat there, trying to hold my frightened mount, while a fierce pack surrounded me. Vaguely I knew that the rest of our company was cursing and drawing weapons—I heard the steely slither. Then I heard John Taylor crying wildly: 'Put up! they're too many!' and howls of argument in the confusion.

There were twice our number in the ambush party and they held off my companions with spears and axes. The rest ringed me round. I sat on my plunging mare, my hair in my eyes, feeling exceedingly silly. A trickle of warm blood ran from my scalp. It began to snow again.

I looked into the face of the leader. I had never seen him or his fellows before. Blood ran into my left eye and made it twitch. I sat up straight, still unafraid, but curious. The man was stout, redfaced and scarred by past journeys and affrays, and armed to the gills. His page carried the royal banner of Tudor. We stared at one another. Behind me I heard shouts and blows on steel. The ruddy man took his gaze from me and shouted above the sounds.

'Don't kill them! Disarm them and let them loose.'

More steely scuffling, and the fretful neigh of the horses. They were taking the horses; a loose one ran past, harness flaying the air and disappeared round a bend of the hillside. The pack-mules followed, lumbering under our goods. The man said to me, formally:

'Sir, I arrest you, in the name of his Majesty King Henry. You will be escorted to Calais, whence you will take ship to England to be put to the question.'

As he spoke he looked at me eagerly, my tabard so rosily white, my blondness, my height. He said (though I had not uttered):

'Sir, don't dissemble. Are you not the rebel and traitor calling himself Richard Plantagenet?'

Snow filled my mouth as it opened wide. The devil in my hind tooth gave a vicious jab. I said calmly:

'Sir, I am.'

The inn which they commandeered was called *L'Auberge au Chien Rouge*. It lay outside the walls of St Omer, south-east of Calais, and I was taken there, wrists chained, at a fast pace despite

166

the weather. Snow lit its gables, and flowers of frost starred the red coat of the hound on the inn-sign creaking under the blizzard. The men settled themselves in the main room among the pigs and fowls brought in from the weather, and watched the windows. I was taken aloft to the best chamber, with a good bed, and a heavy oak door which was made fast upon me.

I spent most of my time lying down, trying to fathom my own actions. Why? I had not even hesitated. It had seemed natural. Yet it would have been even more natural to swing round and point, like Judas. That's your man. I, my lord, am but his humble henchman. But now I was the prince, a barb in Henry Tudor's pride, soon to be put to the question. Only the weather kept us from Calais and home. It was snowing worse than ever; the inn and its environs were full of cursing men and restive horses. There were footsteps up and down, grumbling, and the roaring of the ruddy man. All the while my tooth ached fiendishly.

To be put to the question. I wondered, and did not wonder, what that might mean. Kings do not care to be shown as foolish, any more than lesser men such as my captor. What would the great Henry say when I was before the throne? Oh, he could be merciful, witness Lambert Simnel. I would be for the Tower, that unspeakable fortress of pomp and pain. A louse jumped on the bolster and I smashed it. So would Tudor doubtless smash me, the counterfeit prince. Bad enough dealing with a real Plantagenet. I should be afraid. I found myself instead beginning to chuckle, I rolled about and laughed aloud. Wild thoughts, laced with pain arose. Had Edmund been in my place he could never have done this; his looks were wrong. But I am not the prince and can prove it. Maybe Tudor will release me, reprimanded, into London. I'll go down and regale Finch with such a night of laughter . . .

The sign of the red dog whined and swung in the bitter wind. Were the demons now to plague me waking as in sleep? Did Master John ever breathe a requiem over that lonely grave at the Greyfriars? Did the Devil keep, for his instrument, an especial hot corner of Hell? I sprang up. I was the prince, with no past, and would be treated as such. Seizing a ewer, I crashed it against the door, bellowing, and heard an answering cry. After a moment, the bolts shot back. Two of the armed men stood there.

'I'm famished!' I cried untruthfully. 'Bring me the best! And wine! Much wine! Is this how you treat a king's son? Send a boy to attend me!' All this in top voice, though it sent lightnings through my tooth. Recalling Plantagenet's petulance, I hurled the ewer through the doorway. Both men ducked and the vessel went clanging down the stairs, finding an eventual target, which howled.

After minutes in which I strode and cursed and kicked the furniture, a boy, pop-eyed with alarm, entered with a tray. I had been given a roasted fowl, clary, and some custard tarts. Eating, my mad merry humour subsided, for I began to think of the others. Through the window I saw snow steadily falling, and packed along the sill. John Taylor, the Atwaters, Wim, and above all, my master—denuded of horses, baggage and money (there were always itinerant robbers); freezing, starved, even the cock-sure song of Philip Proud stilled. I thought of the dead traveller's stiff blue hand pointing to Paradise and pushed my food away. It would be just my way if all other lives were forfeit and I were spared, like the useless flotsam from a sea-wreck.

The boy, about twelve, sat crosslegged regarding me. His mouth hung open, he sniffled. Twin snail-trails from his nose festooned his upper lip. Playing my part, I should have asked him to taste the wine, and was glad I had forgotten.

'Sweet God! You're disgusting!' I said. He blinked. A long tongue curled up to lick his leaking nostrils.

'Stop that!' I cried. The boy grinned. Suddenly I remembered how Piers would cosset in secret the most noisome of the cook-boys, comforting their bruised bodies, slipping them bits of food so that they loved him like dogs . . .

'You're hungry?' I shoved the half-eaten fowl across and he was up and on it in one bound. He licked the plate clean, adding grease to his encrusted face. I glimpsed my own face in the up-raised metal. I looked desperate. Blood from my torn scalp had dried all round one eye, my hair stood on end and my jaw was swollen from the evil tooth. I used the fingerbowl to wash in, then ordered the boy to remove my boots, caked with frozen snow. He obliged, catapulting across the room when the tight boot yielded.

'Who is the red-faced knight?' I asked him.

'Sir Geoffrey,' he answered through his clogged nose.

'Sir Geoffrey who? Address me as your Grace!'

168

'Don't know. Grace!' He sat down again, hugging my boots.
'What's your name?' I asked, without much hope.
'Walter,' he grinned.

It would be. Witless Walter. They filled the world. He depressed me inordinately and I bade him go. Outside the gable gleamed with the weird night light of snow. Faintly, I heard hoofs outside and the chink of a bridle, then hammering on the inn door. There was a soft waiting stillness, token that the snow had stopped. I rested my aching cheek against my hand, tried to suck away the taste of blood and pus, and thought again of my friends. I was safe, if only for the moment, and they were lost. So I began kneeling to pray for them all, especially for the prince, that he should not be wasted in the whiteness and by God's grace, find somehow a safe passage to his aunt in Flanders. We had been so near the border . . . could they by chance have toiled through drifts to journey's end? No. Like all the lives which, in their misfortune, touched my own, they were finished and done.

Feet clumped upstairs, halting outside the door. The agitated voice of my captor said clearly:

'No! My orders were to leave him! The King . . .'

'Pox take you,' said another voice. 'Stand away. His Majesty will only thank me for sparing him trouble.'

I stood up. The bolt slammed back. My hand went to my empty scabbard, for I was sure they were coming to kill me. They burst in, the red-faced Sir Geoffrey expostulating with a shorter, dark knight.

'So,' said the stranger, staring at me.

Choleric, Sir Geoffrey cried: 'Leave him! I have orders! It must be a public confession! It must be proclaimed in London, before witnesses!'

'You squawk like a farrowing sow,' said the other. 'You'll have your reward, never fear. The King does not renege on promises.'

'God's life! I took him! Three hundred crowns is mine for that, to say nothing of spreading the word in Flanders.'

'Quiet,' said the dark one. He sat down on the chest, wrapping his fur mantle about him, and stared at me again.

'So. Royal whelp.'

I bowed slightly, and said, with frost: 'Will you name yourself, sir?'

169

'My name is of no matter. I am, as are we all, a servant of King Henry. What ails your face?'

'Toothache.' Memory rushed on me. 'My brother, the prince Edward, suffered likewise. A family malady.'

A kind of brooding glow fired his black eyes. He said abruptly:

'Tell me, what did your mother call you, master? Was it Pieter? Pieterkin? Or has your false Flemish tongue forgotten?'

'Leave him!' growled the red-faced man. 'It must be public, with scribes and witnesses . . .'

The other held up his hand. 'Come, let me help you,' he said to me softly. 'It will be easier for you later on. What did your mother call you? Does she still live? Who schooled you first? When did you assume royalty?'

I did not attempt to follow his drift. I held fast to my masquerade.

'My mother the Queen died last June, as you well know. She always called me Dickon.'

My interrogator rose slowly, hunching his collar like a dragon's ruff. Before he could speak again a new set of feet came pounding upstairs and raised voices cut the silence.

'Not Clifford! Never! When did you learn this?' The voice bounced up and down the stair, almost a shriek of surprised dismay. Then a string of luminous oaths. Both men turned to listen. They looked at one another. The dark man said, though the heart seemed to have gone out of him:

'I shall send for the priest. To him you can make full confession and pray for the mercy of God and the King.'

'I need no false priest,' I said. 'And I have no confession to make. I will see the King's majesty and he will see me. In London.' The prince's skin fit me close and tight.

Someone was banging on the door, and the inn, from cellar to attic, seemed to echo with the name: Clifford, Clifford.

'Tomorrow,' said the dark man to me warningly.

'Tomorrow,' said red face in fury, 'we will be for Calais. Come snow or tempest.'

They left, and for hours the voices continued, drumming up and down. I lay and nursed my raging face. Pain was exhausting me and I drank a lot of wine to ease it. Just before stupor engulfed me I wondered vaguely who false Flemish Pieterkin had been.

170

Then I prayed once more for the welfare of my prince.

The sound of water woke me. I saw in the murky dawn the red dog now shining with wet and a steady pouring from the gable. From below came the clash of helms and hauberks being donned and voices husky with short sleep. A horse whickered irritably as it was led into the dank morning. I leaned through the window and spat out foul blood-tasting matter. Below, a pikeman stood with a lantern. Rain floated against its ray like a myriad frail insects. The man did not seem very alert. For a wild moment I wondered whether it would be possible to drop down, steal one of the horses standing in line in the yard, and flee. Directionless, unarmed, through strange terrain? The idea died. Too late, as well—several armed men had joined the solitary guard. They were mounting up. Then I heard Sir Geoffrey roaring and saw his harnessed shape blunder out into the yard. The first riders were urging their mounts out towards the open country. Sir Geoffrey grabbed one horse by its bridle and the beast reared up and away, its hoofs churning the slush. To my amazement, he drew his sword and slashed at the rider, who raised his shield. The blade bounced off it, ringing. Sir Geoffrey was bawling as more men, leading horses, and hopping to mount, burst through the rain.

'Dogs! Come back! Paltry, soapy sons of cowards! I'll see you hanged. Stand, I say!'

He grasped a rider's stirrup and was dragged a few yards. 'Traitor! Cur!' The horseman, kicking his legs out wildly, cursed him back. Again I heard Clifford's name. The first few riders had already vanished into the rain, leaving a trail of churned mud. I felt almost sorry for red-face as he staggered back. 'I'll burn your hearts!' he moaned. 'I'll eat your livers! Oh, damn you, and damn Clifford!'

I turned and picked up my half-armour which bore a patina of damp and was ready to rust. Slowly I buckled it on and was wrapped by chill. The devil in my tooth heated up his irons for another day's work. Shivering, I wondered if my mantle had helped to shield Plantagenet from a cold death in the snow. Then the dark man, looking hungry and disquieted, entered. He brought with him a priest, and came straight up to my ear.

'Where were you born?' he murmured.

171

'In London,' I said, and my heart jolted, for I had almost told the truth. 'I'll answer no more questions.'

'Confess then,' he breathed. 'Confess to Sir Priest here how you were led astray and fell into treason against the King's Majesty.'

I sat down, mute. He drew his poignard and held it to my face. 'I'll slit your skin,' he murmured. 'For every drop of blood I'll have a word of truth.' He touched the point to my right eye. 'I'll send you stumbling and mewing in the dark like a day-old cat.' The tip of the blade touched my eyeball. Its grey length filled the world. I sat still, rocked by a racing heartbeat.

Next moment Sir Geoffrey was in the room. The knife vanished. Sweat trickled down my sides. He was babbling about the deserters.

'We must be away. Two days to Calais, and the road may be flooded.'

They bundled me downstairs and out into the yard, scattering landlord, animals, and the half-wit boy. They put chains on my wrists as I sat shuddering on my horse. The idiot boy waved at me, remembering the chicken. We moved off down the drenched road; I counted our escort, now but a quarter of its former strength. We rode across meadows patched black and white by the thaw and entered an oak wood where bare branches yielded their snow in rushing falls. I took a great glob of snow squarely on the head and it slid slowly down my neck, while I raised my manacled hands vainly. The men-at-arms who rode alongside me hooted with laughter. Spray shot up from the horse's hoofs as the thaw left lakes in the amber mud. Water ran down inside my collar and lay trapped between shirt and armour. My legs were drenched, my boots looked about to fall apart. The road, eroded by frost and snow, was pocked by gullies into which the horses stumbled. All the while my tooth roared and raged. We left the wood and met a cataract which leaped down a bank of hills to our right. The horse beneath me shivered; its coat steamed like a kettle and so did I.

Sir Geoffrey, who was riding ahead as fast as possible, must, somewhere beneath that choler, have had charity. He glanced back at me with bulging eyes and roared to a servant, who rode back to me with a bundle.

'He says you're to wear this,' he panted. 'Says you'll take a chill

172

before we get there.' It seemed I must be delivered whole and sound to Henry.

He removed my manacles and I unrolled the bundle. It was a cloak, the most beautiful I had ever seen.

'Woven in Flanders, knave!' Scowling, my dark tormentor edged his mount near mine. 'Perhaps that will mend your memory, traitor dog.'

I had long ceased trying to understand him, and scarcely heard him, for I was examining the cloak. It was of the finest, lightest English wool, yet so stoutly made it was almost rainproof. The weft was the coppery colour of fishing-boat sails at sunset. The double warp threads were a lively, spicy purple like the whortleberries that had given their juice for it, and a crackling yellow, the colour of young tips of heather. Across the width ran an intricate broken line of monk's-belt patterning, up and down, in, out, side by side and back again, spelling out those singing colours which should by rights have quarrelled but did not, and, bordering the sleeves and collar in new delight, a row of honey-suckle shapes—square flowers of perfect geometry yet fresh and free as a child's song.

I looked at it and into it, and suddenly it was as though every little bead and knot, every bright, rain-silvered colour, every patch of detailed threadwork repeated crosswise and in a glowing octagon seen again and again, the small scenes each so complete in themselves yet part of the whole language of the cloak, from its silver buckle to its flaunting fringe (drawn out at the last by a blithe unwearied hand proud of its work)—it was as if all this was spread out to form a map worked for my life and peace—almost my peace eternal. The feel of the garment was like a comforting hand in darkness, its colours were magic, and as I swung it about my drowning form I felt it warm me like love.

Even as my manacles were replaced, I felt there were no miseries, past or future. It was as if this soft mosaic of love (I felt it pouring from every stronghold of its warp and weft) had become myself, and I the cloak. From neck to boots I was bathed in a mystery of utter safety.

'Thank you, my lord,' I called, but Sir Geoffrey was gazing ahead at a sheet of flood water laid across our path, and a low rumbling denoted fresh curses about to be birthed. The hills, now to our left, poured with a torrent. Ahead a valley lay drowned, topped with patches of melting snow. Stray branches sailed by like boats. Red-face mourned, calling on the denizens of heaven and hell. He sent one of his depleted company to ride to an eminence and survey the western prospect. He returned, drenched, skating his horse down the bank to report that the flood stretched to the horizon.

'We should have made for Boulogne and gone by sea round the coast,' said the dark man. He looked at me with loathing, as if I had witched up the flood.

'Too late.' The red-faced knight waved us eastward, over a causeway through marshland. So that was the road to Calais, I thought, which he was hoping to strike again higher up. We must be fairly near the Flemish border. The road rose, more woodland came in view. The mud was so thick that our pace slowed considerably. The ground was churned, as if another company had passed this way. Hillocks dotted with thorn trees, black-mawed caves and boulders, rose to the right of the wood as we entered its dripping tunnel. I jogged along between two of the armed men. A dozen sensations pierced my fatigue; the warmth of the cloak, the agony of my tooth, the turgid beating of my heart. I closed my eyes and rested against the saddle-horn. The next instant hell erupted all around, as fifty men plunged from ambush, yelling, bearing arms and banners, coming straight at us with flailing axes and broadswords and a forest of tilted lances. Like a blow between the eyes, I recognized the standard of Sir Robert Clifford.

Jubilant in his disaffection from the majesty of Tudor, he led fifty men into our ill-formed ranks. I saw him kill Sir Geoffrey outright with a two-handed chop of his sword between neck and shoulder, while his bodyguard laid about them, smashing their way through our party. Both my guards were slain, one clubbed in the head with a spiked mace, the other stabbed between the rivets of his hauberk. The dark man blundered to my side on his shrilling, terrified horse, and seized my mount's bridle. Leading me at a gallop, he started back down the greasy road. We were brought up short by half a dozen mailed men bearing longbows. Behind, at the mouth of the wood, the unequal battle briefly raged with the cries and crashes of armoured men as they hit the sodden ground. Three others of my one-time guard fled into the wood, pursued by Clifford's soldiers through the bare branches; after a moment came their dying screams. Then there was quiet, broken by the dripping thaw and the wheezing of the horses.

Still holding my bridle, my captor turned our horses. I saw a mass of dead and wounded men. One, dragging a half-severed foot, was worming into the bushes; apart from that there was no movement. Sir Robert Clifford dismounted and took off his helm. He had shaved off his beard and the old battle-scar was a white tributary from his mouth. Two esquires hovered near him.

'Search their gear,' he told them, and they ran to tear down the saddle-bags, hurling their contents on the ground. From Sir Geoffrey's pack an esquire drew out a sheaf of parchments wrapped in leather. These Clifford unfurled and studied. His lips compressed, the scar puckered into a knot. While he was reading, I felt the dark man's hand in my hair, and the coldness of his knife against my throat. I also heard the unmistakable glide and click of the half-dozen men behind us notching their arrows.

Clifford let the parchments drop to the ground.

'Burn them,' he said.

I felt the dark man's breath, foul with rage, blow past my nostrils. 'Clifford,' he said thunderously, 'those letters are the property of our sovereign lord King Henry. You are culpable of high treason.'

'My lord, you're the traitor,' said Clifford mildly. 'By these documents you were set to discredit our true sovereign, Richard, soon by God's grace to be King Richard the Fourth of England.' He turned to address his followers, while the esquire got a damp blue fire burning and laid the papers on the flames. I heard the strained breathing of the archers at my back, holding their strings taut.

'Hear ye,' Clifford said. 'Those were the testaments of foreign agents paid to lie on the matter of our prince's origin. Letters culled from the sewers of Europe and bound for Westminster. Filth to be spread to slander Plantagenet. God be praised I was able to intercept them. Lies though they are, they are grist to a mill of liars.'

I felt the knife biting into my throat. Beside me the dark man trembled with rage.

'You may have destroyed the affidavits,' he rasped, 'but I hold

175

the cause of your bloody actions in my hand.' He yanked my head back. 'Here is your false, feigned Plantagenet! Let us pass to Calais. Let me deliver him to his Majesty. Or by Christ's crown, I'll kill him now, and rob you traitors of your figurehead!'

Clifford began to laugh. With my head wrenched back I couldn't see him, but heard him laugh until he choked and spat on the ground.

'No,' Clifford said, when he could utter. 'Prince Richard is leagues away, waiting to be welcomed at the court of his aunt. What you have there is, I think, his servant. No one of note.'

My hair was released, I was face to face with my captor. It was like looking into Hell-mouth. Clifford was still chuckling. I thought, yes, laugh, my lord, while he kills me anyway through sheer spleen, and I was right, for he raised the dagger high, his eyes screwed up in blind murder. Then I saw Clifford's little nod to the men behind us and felt the thud of sixty pounds of hard-held arrow homing into my captor's back. The point pierced his mail hauberk and emerged, tipped with garnet drops, at his heart. He was grasping my neck as he fell and brought me down, rolling almost to Clifford's feet. The esquires helped me up.

'Well!' said Sir Robert, looking at me.

'Thank you, my lord.' Mud had fouled the beautiful cloak and I rubbed at it.

'You were lucky,' Clifford said. 'Had we not chased these knaves to secure the treason they carried—by the Virgin! Tell me, what had you planned to say to Henry Tudor?'

My rescue had been pure chance. Lucky indeed!

'It was a cunning thing you did.' He studied me. 'Are you a professional decoy? You look like the prince in certain lights. Release his hands,' and a man-at-arms came from the ranks to unshackle me. Now I recognized some of the deserters from the *Chien Rouge*. But this man—I stared at his tabard. Three bucks' heads—the Stanley device. Sir Robert still watched me.

'These are men from the Calais garrison,' he said. 'Honourable and loyal. They would rather follow the true king than the usurper Tudor.'

It was too much to contemplate, that Stanley should be part of this double game . . . Stanley, who had fought for Tudor, had with his own hands crowned him on Bosworth Field. True, it was whispered that Stanley bore a grudge, saying that Henry had not rewarded him sufficiently, but Stanley, deserting his royal master? The man moved back into the ranks. Clifford turned his horse. 'Ride,' he told the esquires. 'Tell the prince we come, with his servant.' He looked at the strewn mangled bodies. 'Strip these carrion.'

The birds of battle were already perching overhead, bearing down twigs with their black, avid weight. Somewhere a wolf howled. The trees dripped; the thaw would soon wash away the blood.

Night, and another inn, just inside the Flemish border. A roaring fire and a place to strip and dry the cloak, Wim slapping my back, the Atwaters, Astwood, Roderick de Lalaing's flat-faced emissary, all gripping my forearm in greeting. Even Philip Proud tuned his voice to my praise. They wanted to hear everything, tongues overrunning, wanting to tell. Praise God that Clifford, who had embraced his new allegiance as soon as the Treaty of Étaples was signed, had come upon them all in the snow on his way to Flanders. Praise God that he had found me! Only then, I asked: how was the prince?

'He has retired,' Wim said, toasting me in mulled ale. 'I waited on him tonight . . . very impatient. He wants to see you.'

I went up and tapped on his chamber door. He was alone, in a white robe starred with gold lilies. The fire was half up the chimney and shooting sparks. Tapers and torches threw a whirl of celebration over the walls. The glitter danced on him like a fountain, the hooded eye kept its secrets. I knelt. He smiled at me, telling me to rise.

'That was a very brave thing you did,' he said. 'A thing of honour.'

'It was but a whim on my part, Prince Richard,' I said.

'A whim?' He raised his brows sharply. 'I cannot believe you. With no thought for yourself, you saved me.'

'No, highness. Foolishness. Nothing. If it served you, I'm glad.'

He looked me over, shaking his head. 'Did they harm you?'

'Threats. No more. One of them would have blinded me, I think, to get some fantastical confession.'

His hand flew halfway to his left eye, then dropped. He fears pain, I thought suddenly. Most do, but he more than most.

'How can I reward you?' he said. 'You are a man of honour and courage. I shall not forget. But tell me—why did you do it?'

I did it for you, I thought, surprised. Perhaps the cause, which had had Margetta and Edmund in thrall, had caught my own soul at last. But that addle-witted act, conceived by the prick of the moment, was for you and you alone. I said nothing.

He said: 'Money,' and put a heavy purse in my hand. 'There'll be more, when I come into my inheritance. Riches for all my loyal ones. And further. You shall be my secret envoy, entrusted with matters close to me. From this day, Nicholas.'

It was the first time he had named me. The firelight blazed about his tall straight figure, gleaming on his hair and white robe. To my chagrin I felt tears springing. I had had a vision of him dead in the snow. I was almost enraged with him for having worried me. Only now did the emotions unfelt during my escapade threaten to swamp me.

'Your Grace does me honour,' I said. 'You have been kind to me. Not only now, but in a time you may have forgotten.' And I put the purse back firmly in his hand.

'All men have bad dreams,' he said acutely. He cut the air with his hand. 'This is a good country, where we shall be safe as my father the king was before me. Yet there will be dangers none the less.'

'I will gladly share them.'

'Ah, Nicholas! Your father would have been proud.' He looked hard at me. 'Don't weep. Rejoice. There must be something I can do . . . Tell me, what do you need?'

Tears, and agonized laughter, choked me.

'Yes, Highness. There is something. Have we a barber-surgeon here? Or failing that, a blacksmith? To draw this God-rotten, birth-cursed, howling hell-imp of a tooth of mine?'

Later, with a blissful, black hole in my gum where the devil had been routed, two things came to my mind. During our talk I had failed to describe to him the strange questioning I had suffered, the hints, doubtless reiterated in the burned letters, of some false Fleming called Pieterkin. But then, he had not asked. Possibly he

178

had had no need. He had his own agents and spies. He now had the most powerful adherents; Clifford, and, incredible notion, the Tudor's own kinsman, Sir William Stanley. He would be *au fait* with rumour. It was of no moment—he was safe. Warmth wrapped me at the knowledge. Warmth, like that of the loving cloak.

The other thing I discovered for the first time that night was that if I spread the cloak over me on the bed, no demons could enter. I blessed the mystic joy it brought me. I was not to know that one day the feel of it would bring more sorrow than a shroud.

Margaret of York, Duchess of Burgundy, had been a beauty. Even now, past her fiftieth year, she was fairer than many of her young attendants. Her clothes were the most gorgeous I had seen since the old days at Westminster. Her mantle was cloth of gold over silver tissue faced with snowy speckled ermine. Across her breast lay sapphires and pigeon's-blood rubies and a pendant of margeurites in white enamel and diamonds blazing in the thousand torches that lit every colonnade of the Prinsenhof. She walked with majesty, mint gold hair flowing free beneath her coronet like a maiden's. She was lithe and taut as if she had borne no children.

This was the greatest lady of Flanders, sister of Edward the Fourth. Before our prince's birth she had left England to marry Charles of Charolais. He had been dead for fifteen years—killed in a battle against the alpine spearmen of Switzerland. This was Margaret Plantagenet who had supported and schemed for the restoration of her nephew and the downthrow of Tudor, even from the beginning—before Ireland, when I had first heard of him.

Banners, like strange flowering trees, grew on the walls of the Prinsenhof. Many of the devices belonged to English lords, and behind the dais, the Lion of Flanders rippled with wasp waist and flaming tongue. Beside it hung the device which Edward the Fourth had given to his son with the Dukedom of York—the silver falcon within a fetterlock, its hinge open to show that Edward had forced the door of kingship in conquest of Lancaster.

This was the first public reception Margaret had given since we entered Bruges, with Flemings lining the ways, brandishing white

179

rose pennons and cheering. I would never forget that ride, not only because the prince entered like a Cæsar, but because of a private, inexplicable joy, similar to that felt when first I donned the cloak. It was still with me as, in the prince's train, I began to approach the dais of the Duchess Margaret.

The faces and insignia passed like a dream of homage: Thomas Astwood, the Atwaters, Pierre-Jean Meno, John Taylor, Simon Mountford (an old partisan of King Richard), Sir Robert Clifford, Sir William Barley, Sir William Daubeney, brother to the lord who had been at the Treaty of Étaples; Sir Thomas Thwates, Sir Thomas Cressener. There were Irishmen, daring Henry's wrath: Butlers, Geraldines, Fitzgeralds. Envoys from Sir Edward Brampton, now at some secret work on our behalf in England. And couriers from Sir William Stanley, bringing funds and gifts.

There was a crowd of Austrians and Flemings, keepers of the growing arsenal of weapons to be used in the prince's service. And present were those who were heart-sick of the pincer grip Henry and his Chancellor Morton were laying on England. There were Yorkists weary of hiding from the King's revenge within Sanctuary. And men who were taxed to the point of bankruptcy and hoped for better days. Men who remembered King Edward and longed to see his son enthroned. Men who had fought for Henry and found him ingrate. There were even those who, when he was exiled from France, had deserted the prince, but now that his star was rising, had returned. Hundreds filled the hall; the torches breathed out heat. A stench of pitch mingled with sweat, spices, and the sappy green smell of trodden rushes from the fens.

Close against me I felt a fierce nudging. An urgent whisper blew to my ear.

'How fine he looks! God speed our beloved king!'

Dark eyes in a small sallow face were fixed on Plantagenet. Our newest member of the company was Antoine de la Force, small, fiery, zealous. Had all our adherents shared his frenzy, we should already have been swimming the North Sea to scale all Henry's towers without discipline or plan. Since the departure of Philip Proud, who had packed his lute and simply disappeared as soon as we arrived in Bruges, Antoine had been appointed valet to the prince. He had been found lying across the threshhold of the prince's apartment, as if inviting him to wipe his feet.

180

'My father loved King Richard,' he said, dropping great tears. 'When he was lord of the North, he served him, and his only sorrow was not to die with him. Now he's old and sick. I offer you my life, great Duke.'

He was taken in and proved himself adept as a valet, so swift and quiet he seemed scarcely there at all. He was given to passionate whispering, and reminded me strongly of Edmund. His loyalty was so patent that even the prince asked no further questions.

On the dais, Margaret sat with her attendant lords: Henri, Bishop of Cambrai, jowled like a sea-monster; Sir Roderick de Lalaing, wearing the Order of the Golden Fleece, and most prominent, the Archduke Maximilian of Austria, the same who had been cheated by French Charles of marriage with the heiress of Brittany. He had been widower for ten years since Mary of Burgundy had fallen from her horse. He was magnificent in cloth of gold and silver, like his stepmother, the Duchess. On his long red-gold hair was a velvet cap rimmed with diamonds. His face was made frightful by a monstrous nose, bowed and broken from an accident in the chamois-hunt. At his side stood his son, Duke Philip, and his golden-haired daughter, Margaret.

As Plantagenet approached, Maximilian bowed, saying deeply: 'Welcome, most noble prince.' The Bishop of Cambrai held up a trinity of blessing fingers. But the Duchess Margaret came quickly forward, her jewels and her eyes giving off radiance. She left the dais and drew up Plantagenet from his knee. She embraced him tightly, then, still holding him to her, she faced the assembly. Their faces were much alike; she could have been his mother.

'My lords and friends. Join me in welcome. For this my beloved nephew has come to our shores at last.'

Her large eyes were dark with tears, but she smiled, showing sharp little teeth. Her voice surged down the hall, sometimes in direct address to all, at others as if for the prince alone.

'Your coming here ravishes my soul. This is your haven. Others have cast you out. For gold!'

She spoke with contempt of Charles of France.

'Not for the riches of heaven would I betray this flower of Plantagenet. This is the last hope of my noble House!' She kissed

181

him on the mouth, then festooned him with a heavy gold collar.

'England will smile again under this great prince.'

He answered her. Excitement had enhanced him. He looked sovereign of the hour.

'Beloved Madame, most gracious aunt. My lady, you were ever the favourite sister of the king my father. This was always his chosen harbour, his refuge . . .'

She interrupted, her body an unstable, iridescent skein of silver and gold.

'Yes! More than twenty years ago your father came, exiled by usurping Lancaster! Flanders opened her arms, as I do. Flanders gave succour, as she will now. Present the guard,' and a line of thirty halberdiers in murrey and blue formed on either side of the prince.

'Each of these lays his life beneath your feet,' said the Duchess. Maximilian smiled approvingly from the shadow of his terrible nose.

'As I do,' whispered Antoine de la Force.

And I, I thought. There was the infection of glory in the hall, desperate and defiant, emanating from around the dais. All about were lit faces, tiny murmured storms of assent.

'. . . until we drive King Henry forever from England,' he was saying. Henry's name unleashed harpies in the Duchess. A diamond mist of spittle left her lips.

'Tudor! That ravening baseborn wolf! that *huckster*!'

'Madame,' said the prince quickly, 'it's true he oppresses the English people, causing great misery. It is my desire . . .'

'Tudor!' cried Margaret. 'He's like a greedy usurer against the lion-hearted Plantagenets! You are England's saviour . . .' she seized his hand. 'I charge you to remember how your father left this court an exile and returned a king. How with his force he entered Ravenspur and marched on London to scourge the might of Lancaster!'

Quiet and clear, he said: 'Though I was not then born, Madame, I will do likewise. Return, and claim my right.'

'Tear him from his throne!' she said. 'That shaky throne got by treachery and murder—for murderer he is, of your uncle on the battlefield, and of your mother, the widowed Elizabeth, immured till death . . .'

182

'With your aid, I will avenge them,' he said. His face was troubled; he looked suddenly very weary.

'The bells will ring for you in London.'

'And in York.'

'And Scarborough,' she said. 'Fairest of towns. My memory's joy.'

'When I am crowned,' he said, 'Scarborough shall be your town. I will hand you the keys myself, as I hope for heaven.'

'I thank God,' said Margaret, 'that I am spared to see these days beginning. Once,' and the pride went from her voice, 'I did all I could to uphold a poor counterfeit wretch whose claim to kingship was null. Simnel was a blunted sword with which I sought to lame Tudor. I was wrong and I was misled. But before God I swear I never knew the true Plantagenet was living!'

The prince began to speak formally to the assembly.

'I will keep faith with all. I am full of gratitude for the loyalty I see before me. I know you have lost goods and lands for daring this allegiance, and for setting your faces against the king, that your names have been cried traitor in St Paul's and that you are on the roll of the king's enemies. I know the risks you bear.' He drew his sword and kissed the hilt gracefully. 'I swear by this token of knighthood that I will not fail you. I promise further to pardon freely any of my subjects who have transgressed against me in loyalty to Tudor. I will reward all who uphold me. I know, good, gracious people, the hazards you would dare, and I embrace them with you as a loving kinsman.'

Antoine whispered: 'There's talk that Tudor may banish the Flemings from England for this. And there's rumour of an embargo on the wool trade . . . Tudor's so angry . . .'

'And, noble Irishmen'—his eyes found Geraldines, Butlers, Fitzgeralds in the hall—'I am your debtor, for the pains and harassment you have sustained under the English king. I pledge you, by the secrets of my blood and birthright, that I shall make you a glorious and free nation; when I am king.'

He stepped back, head high, one eye glowing, the other veiled and sad. The Duchess cried: 'Homage! to the White Rose of York!'

The throng pressed forward in a barely restrained rush. I rose hurriedly to save being trodden under, my sleeve was caught fast in eager fingers. An oval face looked up at me, the skin smooth as buttermilk. 'Meneer' the lady whispered.

She spoke to me in English with the singsong accents of the Flemings, accents I would one day long to hear above all other. By her apparel she was a high-born lady, but her demeanour was wanton.

'I have watched you for days, meneer. Up to now I do not dare. Now I dare.'

I was filled with dismay. Her eyes were amorous and I wanted no part of her, beautiful though she was. I feared the unease she bred within the shuttered cage that was myself. I moved away.

'*Madame, je m'excuse*,' I said, and suddenly saw flint in the swooning gaze, and cursed myself for speaking French. The Flemings, we had discovered, had a long memory. Old French atrocities like the Battle of the Golden Spurs ran in their minds like fresh blood.

'But wait,' she said as I turned from her, 'you must help me. You sleep near the Duke of York, for whom I . . . I am sick with love.'

I looked quickly at the chequered tiles under my feet, praying she had not read my mistaken conceits.

'Does the prince like music?' she asked. 'I sing well—Binchois, Hans van Ghizeghem, Dufay . . . Bring me to him tonight, I pray. He is mightier than Maximilian,' and as if she had spoken it, I knew she had been the Archduke's mistress and that high favour as much as love came into her passion.

'He likes music,' I said, and she came close again.

'My mother knew his father the King.' She lowered her eyes.

Like mother, like daughter. When my own father was Gentleman Usher to Edward, one of his duties was to secrete his night companions, and many a broken night had my father.

I told her where to meet me after the evening Office. I imagined the prince would be pleased, although I knew little of his amorous life. As a young child he had been married to the four-year-old Lady Anne Mowbray, but she had died.

During supper I held the napkins for him, while he was feasted by Margaret and the great Maximilian who showed him deference in all things, and he seemed in a mood to be pleased, as if he had already come home in glory.

184

'The lady asked me if your Grace were married or trothplight,' I said lightly, when we had him prepared for bed. 'She has a case of love.'

Antoine glowered as he stowed damask shirts away. He had protested at the lady being given *entrée*, fearing she might be a poisoner.

'I trust you told her I was a bachelor,' said Plantagenet merrily.

'She is waiting,' I said gently. He had forgotten his marriage to Anne Mowbray and no wonder, with all those years gone down-river. He said: 'Antoine. Bid her to me in an hour. I want to speak with you, Nicholas.'

He had been writing a letter in his own hand. It lay on the night table, the fine mesh of italic script black in the candles. He sealed the letter with his ring, imprinting precisely the shape of the falcon in the fetterlock. Everything he did now was steady, his hands were firm, his eyes less tired. Confidence sat on him like new armour. He then took from a coffer a purse of considerable weight, for when I stowed it inside my doublet it dragged at the cloth. A couple of gold coins he put loose in my hand. I was suddenly reminded of my old avarice, and that Finch's fortune, whatever it was, lay unclaimed in the London notary's office. I should have brought it as a contribution to the cause. I read the superscription above the seal.

For Vrouw Jehan W. of Tournai. By the hand of
Nathaniel Osbeck, at lodging in Bruges.

The purse hung like a heavy heart beneath my own. The prince was wealthy now—perhaps at his wealthiest. The Duchess Margaret had already given him 800,000 crowns. This purse was so fat it would pay for the muster of many troops. Yet I guessed it was an intimate gift.

'This repays a debt,' he was saying, as if to himself. 'They were so kind to me, long ago. Guard it well. Nathaniel Osbeck will take it and the letter to Tournai. You should find him down by the quayside. He is related to my friends. It's years since I saw them, when Brampton brought me to them in my flight. Osbeck is comptroller of Tournai and associated with the Dean of boatmen over the Schelt. He will pass on this *goud*.' He laughed. 'I find I am thinking in Flemish again.'

185

'It's very like English, Prince Richard,' I said, putting the letter in my pocket. You only had to ask *'Waar is de Lange Straat,'* and instant directions to the Long Street followed. Ask in French, and you were ignored.

'This is a secret matter, Nicholas,' he said. 'You can take Antoine. No one else.' He turned his back but I heard him say softly, 'I would not have them think I had forgotten. None shall ever find me ungrateful.'

I went out and put letter and money in a safe place until the morning. Passing through the antechamber, I saw the lady going in, armed with a ribboned lute. I met one other person: Thomas Astwood, esquire, one of our long-time adherents. I straightened my doublet and the purse bulged like a canker. His eyes went to it, and somehow I knew he had been listening at the door.

When first I knew Bruges, she had passed the flowering of her greatness as the Zwyn, silting up, had begun to block the commercial waterways and the land took its toll from the sea. She had been a city not without mischief in the old days of the Karls, the sea-going freeholders who had never been bound by serfdom. Fierce feuds against the nobility had raged and been resolved as Karls intermarried with great families until Charles the Good had been murdered in the Church of St Donatian. The Dean, an Erembald Karl, had slandered him, calling him a scullion's son.

Even now there were days of unrest, risings against Archduke Maximilian, extravagant, always in debt. His father, the Holy Roman Emperor Ferdinand of Austria, was mortally ill and Maximilian was desperate for money to secure his own election as Emperor when Ferdinand died. Antoine, who seemed cognizant of the ramifications of court policy told me:

'The Flemings only tolerate Maximilian's taxes in respect to his widow. Mary was a saint.'

It was a cold bright day with the wind raising tiny quirks on the waters of the canals and the sun gold on their greenness.

'I've heard him called the *premier chevalier* in Christendom,' I said. I was wearing the cloak, the sun swooned among its colours and the wind found no entry. Beneath it the purse of gold clung to my body. A sheathed poignard sat above it and I had the letter tucked in my belt, while Antoine, earnest on the prince's mission, bristled with arms.

From the Prinsenhof as we walked was not far to the Markt, the great trading place dominated by the Cloth Hall and the Cranenburg fortress. In Bruges, there were the same dark little courts and alleys as in London, but seeming somehow more honest; an unexpected grove of trees, a flash of water, cleaner, freer, prouder. The Cloth Hall with its square belfry (the simple flutings of its ogives giving the brickwork a marble sheen) seemed that day to speak of freedom of the soul; in the *beffroi* the vast bell hung waiting to summon the Brugeois to arms against any that threatened their heartland, and up there, behind iron gates, lay the Citizens' Charter, won from their overlords long ago in blood.

Away from the square the town was a labyrinth of leafy cobbled streets where waterways ran like green blood through a vibrant heart. Outside the ramparts giant black windmills spun circles about a circle, for Bruges was built in an almost perfect round. We walked by the waters, where barges and other craft moved through a drift of swans and cygnets parting to paddle languidly away. We crossed one of the many bridges in wind and sunshine. The moving gold rippled on the wall of a house which stood as if it had been born in water. From the lost mystery of its foundations to its high stepped gables it stood firm among lapping amber, lit by dancing water-light. A woman threw back shutters and emptied a pail into the canal. For a moment the wind and water stilled, and it seemed that the foundations of the house went down for a thousand fathoms. Deep were timbered gables, window-boxes, flowers in secret bud, mullions glinting, and the woman's twin, shaking out her pail, down there in the inverted green and gold.

Over the bridge came nuns from the Duchess's Béguinage. A new breeze threatened the huge white coifs that blinkered them. They shrieked, clutched their headgear and bustled by. Antoine remarked on their prettiness, or what could be seen of it.

'I've yet to see an ugly woman here,' I said.

We came to the Bourgplaats, crammed with people, shaking from the iron wheels of the traders' carts. There was of course poverty—beggars and cripples, especially towards the Waterhalle, a long dock and warehouse on the west side of the Markt. There

187

the sluggish Zwyn brought the barges from the port of Damme; there the carracks of the world unloaded wealth and the smell of far places. The pungency of cardamom, coriander, fenugreek and pepper from the Ind, the cool perfume of silks and jasmine and ambergris, rich reapings of the Orient. Steel blades from Damascus, carpets from China. But the prime prosperity of Flanders lay in the tightly bound sarplers of English wool. Fleece on fleece, bringing work to the looms of ten thousand pretty women.

Along the wide water between Bruges and Sluys, the locks imprisoned the tide and upriver came these riches. We walked to the Scapenhuis, the aldermen's lodging south-west of the Bourgplaats. Like a stone jewel nearby stood an ancient chapel. I asked a passer-by its name.

'Der Heilig Bloedbaziliek,' he said. 'Built to house the vial of the Holy Blood. Thierry of Alsace brought it back from the Holy Land three centuries ago. Citizens have fought and murdered over it . . . one time it was thought lost for ever. It's on show at the May Festival. You're English? Be welcome.'

He also told us that the neighbouring fortress was once the palace of Baldwin of the Iron Arm, and that a miracle was commemorated in the chapel of Our Lady of Succour. A woman due to be hanged for murder was saved by the intercession of a dove, holding written proof of her innocence in its beak . . .

'But you should see inside the church of Our Lady,' he said. 'Onze Lieve Vrouwenkerk' I repeated it till I got it right. The Flemish came so easy. I felt light, untroubled. For the first time in recent memory I felt like entering a tavern.

'The prince's money,' said Antoine unhappily.

I laughed, and patted the bulge. 'It's safe.' We went down a quiet street lined with tall elms coming into leaf, each green frond doubled by water like the rosy bricks of the merchants' houses. Someone was playing a soft gittern behind shutters. We reached a fish market where the catch lay in silver heaps, and I asked directions to the Dyver, turned a corner and there it was, the estuary busy with boats, carts on the street flanked by tall flat houses with small inquisitive windows. From the largest of these houses suddenly erupted, with a wide roar of laughter, two watermen in smocks and clogs. They bowled along the quayside, laughing and hitting one another. The house door opened on to a long low room full of roistering bargees and townsfolk and the smell of woodsmoke and spiced sausages. Antoine followed me inside. I had to stoop to enter the tavern, and while the landlord came forward in welcome, I had my hand upon the doorframe. It was honeycombed with carvings, margeurites, touched with gilt paint; they climbed among leaves on the black oaken door. The hard flowers greeted me, their wood acknowledged my touch. Marguerite—*bellis perennis*—Margaret's Herb—Margetta. The equation slipped into my mind, words whispered from another's heart, and I knew with certainty that I had been here before.

The bustling little host took pains to make us happy, asking had we noted the beauties of his city, or the Gruuthus near Our Lady's Church where King Edward had once found refuge so that the two nations were for ever allies, and would we drink ale because the imported wines were costly, and not all that good?

It was noisy and crowded, with folk jostling for space on the benches. There were Italians, Spaniards, Greeks, and two yellow men with long silky plaits who played silently with amber counters. Antoine was jumping about for fear of pickpockets.

'There is a private chamber upstairs,' offered the landlord. 'Another English meneer is there, alone.'

We followed him up. I knew these stairs, knew that there was a dip and knot in the one before the top, that round the corner the white wall had a painted design of swallows, that the door on which the landlord would knock had a great crack down the oak. That there were two steps down into the room and a lion flanked by swans carved on the fireplace. There were thoughts here too, familiar; not mine, but like another's memories. In the dark passage there were fierce feelings—drunkenness, laughter and lust, blowing like a hot, ancient wind. My head sang with the unknown. Then my father, a strong ghost, came unbidden into my mind and I knew he had been in this place and what I felt was memory generated in his blood and mine. It was true, and somehow terrible.

I stepped into the room. Philip Proud, my master's one-time valet, sat with feet on the table and a flagon of wine. Although we had never been friends, he rose effusively to greet me. He was rigged like an earl in cloth of Rennes and Cordovan velvet. Every finger sported a ring. He was flushed, bright of eye.

'*Mon cher* Nicholas!' He waved his cup. 'Jehan, another flagon. Make it two.' He beckoned Antoine and me to sit at the table.

'Ale will do very well,' I said, frowning.

The landlord shrugged and quit the room. I pulled out the bench and sat. Antoine remained uneasily standing. Philip Proud gleamed up, eyes darting like birds.

'Well!' he said. 'I can't say that I expected you, of all people. Not after those heroics of yours in the snow. But you're welcome, Nicholas. Have you word for me from Astwood? This is a tricky game, by God.'

I stared at him.

'I see you still wear that motley garment.' He flicked a corner of the cloak with his cup, revealing the purse for a moment. 'Have you brought me some money? This business gets costly. Tell your friend to sit. He makes me nervous.'

The landlord returned. 'I've brought both wine and ale.' I went on staring across the table at Philip Proud. No one answered and the landlord went crossly away. Antoine standing close behind me began to tremble. I looked deeply at Philip Proud. His gleeful flush faded; conspiracy hung about him like a tarnished chain.

'Jesu, mercy,' he said softly. He scrabbled to retrieve the moment, slopping out wine into three cups while the flush returned, so that his face looked suddenly raw. 'Here, drink,' he said with a high laugh. 'Tell me your news. Does the Duke prosper? How is Margaret's court? I hear it's full of willing women . . .'

I stared on. His prattle died.

'What is this costly business?' I said. Behind me Antoine was grinding little curses like pebbles between his teeth, while Philip, full of brass, declared that drinking was costly, so were fine clothes, and Plantagenet had never paid him enough, but now he had a new master.

'What new master?' I leaned across the table, smelling fear mixed with wine. 'What costly business? What has Astwood to do with it? What new master?'

'Merchant . . . spice merchant . . .' Proud's eyes bulged at me.

190

'Traitor. Tudor spy.' I felt Antoine pressing against me, quivering like a limer certain of the quarry. I put my hand on his wrist. His sword was half out of the scabbard.

'Tell me, Philip,' I said.

'I've told you!' He was shrill. A vein on his brow beat hard. 'Clothes, whores. Fine lodging . . . you can have sport in this town, join me, I'll show . . .'

I was gripping Antoine's wrist tight. 'Let me kill the traitor,' he was moaning. I could scarcely hold him. I said quite gently:

'But Philip, I need no other master. Richard, rightful king of England, is my good lordship. I trusted he were yours too,' and watched him, waiting. There came a change. He stopped flinching and babbling and his face went white again. He stood up, and smashed his goblet down on the table.

'Fools! Accursed fools, both of you!' he whispered. 'Listen to me. You call me traitor? It's your precious master who's the traitor—your popinjay prince who struts and prates of his royal blood . . . Sweet Jesus!' He lunged forward. 'Do you know, you witless crew, who it is you left your homes and your safety for? and put your family's lives at risk? Have you seen the colour of this card you're all gambling with? Prince? That's no royalty up there cozening Margaret of Burgundy in the Prinsenhof, though, sweet living Christ, she'd like to think he is! That's the son of a poor Flemish waterman from Tournai, and his name's little Pieter Warbeck! Perkin—Warbeck! Prince Perkin!'

I still gripped Antoine's wrist, but I couldn't hold him much longer. I said:

'You should be hanged for treason, Proud. I would do it myself, and I will when I bring you back to face my lord.'

We were all on our feet by now, and there was a little part of my mind, quite detached, which said: What if he speaks truth? What of the letter for Tournai, written in secret? And those other letters destroyed by Clifford in the snow-forest? Then another part of my mind rode in, like a message on a shining sword. He lies. Be still.

'You'll not take me back,' said Philip Proud. 'I pity you and all the others, to be duped by this barge-boy. I'll be in London when Henry sends you to the gallows and I'll say—I warned them. I'll be there when they stick Perkin Warbeck's ugly face on a spike on the Bridge—and who'll be the traitor then?'

'Proud,' I said, 'I have power to arrest you in the Duke of York's name, and this I do.'

He said, with a bitter laugh: 'You crazed wretch! The Duke of York is dead and mouldering these past nine years, and his brother. The world knows it. Cardinal Morton told the world—how Dickon Crouchback had those boys snuffed out one dark night in the Tower!'

Antoine's blade came up in an arc; on its way to Philip's face it scored a gouge in the table-top. With his other hand he jerked the table and it crashed on its side. Pots and flagons hurtled all ways, spraying the walls with wine. Philip Proud was on guard like a Milanese assassin, a dagger in each hand. His back was to the window. He dodged the wild sword-slash and stood at bay. I had my own knife out, but I wanted him alive. Antoine edged along the table. I moved to cut Proud off.

'I'll have your tongue,' said Antoine. 'Slice it out . . . make you eat it.' Gasping: 'Base liar. May King Richard strike you down from Heaven.'

'From Hell, rather,' said Philip Proud rudely, and laughed in fright as Antoine sprang over the table, launching a two-handed cut which would have beheaded Proud had he not dipped and weaved, bringing up sharply one of his wicked little knives. The blade ripped through Antoine's sleeve, opening his forearm to the bone, and he dropped his weapon. I went at Proud with my dagger. He took two nimble steps backwards and said quickly, holding up his blades: 'Don't blame me when they hang you,' then turned quickly and thrust his elbow at the window which flew open. He leaped on the sill, balanced there and then jumped, barely clearing the building, for he left his cloak hanging on a gable. After a moment the splash came as he entered the canal. Antoine, dripping blood, and I looked out in time to see Proud hauling himself over the side of a boat rowed by two men. With strong strokes they bore him away, and the craft disappeared under a bridge.

'Let me bind you,' I said, feeling stunned.

'It's stopped.' Antoine had his kerchief tied tightly round the vein. 'Sweet Christ. I never even marked him. Those foul lies. That most noble king, God rest him.'

'Morton's lies,' I said, schooled by my father. 'Rumours bred close to the throne. How else could Henry keep his crown, married to the princes' sister?'

Little Philip Proud, I thought, with his songs of death. How many more were there like him, living lordly? For a moment even I had believed him. The spring day seeemed to darken a little.

'I'll go back,' said Antoine. 'Nicholas, we must tell the prince of this, and warn him about Astwood. Astwood of all people! Sweet Christ.'

I righted the table. Blood and wine were pooled on the floor.

'I must pay the reckoning,' I said. 'They will think little of English manners. And then find Osbeck's lodging.'

I told Antoine to go back to the palace through the Markt and along the Geldmuntstraat past the Mint. I directed him intuitively, as if the streets of Bruges ran like veins in my heart. It was not until I was out of the inn and a fair way along the quayside that I realized I had lost the prince's letter.

I returned to the upper room where a group of Spaniards were now drinking and searched in vain. The letter must have been brushed from my belt by someone in the crowd. Surely there could be nothing in it that could harm the prince, I told myself. Deeply downcast, I was more concerned with the image of my own folly. I served him gladly, but there were times when it seemed I did not serve him very well.

There was a troupe of musicians standing beneath a linden, singing about the death of a maiden by drowning in the canal, and one of them broke off to point me to the Groene Rey and Stonecutters' Quay, where lay the weavers' shop over which Nathaniel Osbeck lodged. The weavers' was a very long building with lancet windows behind which were white-capped women, visible at work from the quay in line with the law of Flanders. A small alley ran beside the house, and, through a side door, a porter took me up some stairs, through a maze of passages punctuated with iron-bound doors, and eventually to a room where Nathaniel Osbeck was dressing to go out.

He had a broad sea-burned face and was in a hurry. I had only just caught him in time; he was returning to Tournai that day.

I delivered the purse of gold, and began to stammer who had sent it, and for whom.

'There was a letter.' I felt sweat in the roots of my hair.

'From the Duke of York?' He raised his brows. 'My kinswoman will wish to know what he said. Can you remember?'

'He sent his heartfelt thanks. He said it was a debt of honour, and he would not wish the lady to think him ungrateful.'

'Ah!' He seemed satisfied, and scrawled me a receipt. 'Don't lose *this*, meneer,' he said kindly, and winked at the English dolt. 'My humble duty to his Grace. Our prayers are always with him.'

All this was said in hurried, heavily accented English while he fastened his jerkin with swift thick fingers, pulled on sea-boots, and strapped a money-belt about his waist. He then took an enormous sword from a chest and girded it on.

'Would that I could stay and entertain you,' he said, swinging into a salt-stained cloak. 'But I must leave this cursed place. By the Holy Blood, I shall be glad to see Tournai again.'

'But Bruges is the fairest town,' I said.

'It was,' he said. 'God prosper you, meneer.' He was through the door, pointing. 'That way, and down the stairs. Christ save you and your royal master. Farewell.' Thumping his boots along the passage, he was gone. We had spoken together for barely five minutes and most of that had been blessings. I felt oddly cheated, and curious. But the gold was safe. Leaving the room I faced a row of doors, all blankly waiting for me to choose. I opened one at random, and found myself staring at a roomful of gaping little girls.

Their ages were from about eight to eleven. Each sat before a spinning-wheel crowned by a distaff laden with greyish fleece. In their midst, elevated by a square pulpit, sat their grand mistress, an iron-faced hag holding a long cane. Many pairs of round eyes watched me but the work never stopped. The wheels spun, under the play of the small hands the weft came shimmering out on to the spindle. Each spindle, which was attached to the floor and had an eye through which the weft could pass, grew infinitesimally fatter as I watched. Like little frenzied spiders the girls spun and fed the twisting spindle with an eternal skein, coaxing the weft

194

over their fingers while the muted creak and chirr-r sounded like some vague mourning of lost playtimes.

One of them smiled at me over her floating hands. As if in judgement, the weft snapped. The wheel slowed, the spindle whirled to an angry halt. In the pulpit the overseer rose. Her long cane struck unerringly on the crown of the child's head. She resumed her seat, not a word spoken. The others spun faster. The girl repaired the thread deftly, tears running down her silent face. I closed the door, upset by the little tragedy, and turned to face an elderly man, blue dust on his clothing, blue beneath his fingernails. So thin that he looked like a walking suit of clothes. He seemed embarrassed and tried to brush the blue off himself, while asking if I were lost, in English.

'You come to buy? I go only to the Wulhuis—the Wool Exchange—on Fridays. But the samples are below. Come, I will show you over the house. How much is wanted? Best cloth from here to Antwerp. I am master here. Hannes van Grynghem, at your orders.'

'God give you good adventure,' I said. 'I am not here to buy.'

'I show you anyway,' he said gloomily. 'It was once a fine business. You should have seen it thirty years ago. You are too young.' He spread his hands, obviously resigned, like Osbeck, to some unknown recession. I followed him, and he made continual apologies for his appearance. He had been in the fulling mill and other workshops and had not yet changed his clothes. Life was busy, life was hard, and if meneer only knew, there were scant earthly rewards.

'You saw the spinsters. That woman—she is a demon. At times she tries to rule even me. The little ones work well. There are outworkers, of course, to spin and card the wool, but *ach*! ten in one family from the baby to the grandmother, all working on one warp, irregular spinning—some soft, some hard—makes a weak thread, always breaking. And weak thread makes uneven cloth.' He continued to brush at his jerkin.

'And some of them are dishonest.' He led me down twisted stairs. 'They weight the spun wool before it comes to be woven. The staplers are no better. Many a sarpler of wool I've had off the quay full of lambs' tails, stones, ironware. What can a man do? The world is wicked.'

195

An unpleasant smell was abroad. Dust, rancid grease, fierce dyes, soot, sweat, madder, alum and warm metal. The air seemed solid with mysteries. The stench increased as we went out into a tiny covered yard and through a low door. The weaver pulled his collar over his nose. 'This is the combing room,' he said indistinctly.

Charcoal smoke filled the room, almost obscuring the forms of men and boys. They swam about their duties, coughing horribly. Their overseer appeared briefly out of a hellish cloud, sweat tracking lividly on his grimed face, and spoke to the weaver before plunging back into the murk.

'They gain high wages,' said Hannes van Grynghem. 'Carding and combing is done there. The worsted is made from the long combed wool, the cloth from short carded wool.' He picked up a fold of my cloak. 'This is worsted. Beautiful.'

Through another door, youths were tending looms and handling mountainous fleeces. Journeymen, he said. 'Not to enter, or they will start complaining. There the wool is sized and beamed on to the loom. I have three prentices, all the guild allows.'

He walked faster, throwing open more doors, feeding me knowledge. The types of cloth sounded like a song: bays, says, mockado, tapestry, stament, carsays. The coarsest to the finest. The cloth was scoured in the canal and dried in lofts, beaten free of dust, picked of debris, carded or combed, spun, sized and loomed, woven, scoured and fulled, teased, sheared and dyed. He showed me the shed where prentices scraped the woven cloth with teazles and cropped close the nap, and the fulled cloth was stretched on tenterhooks and pressed between plates and sealed for the Markt. He showed me cloth dyed in the wool after washing but before weaving. He clawed at the woad under his nails and finished the tour in a rush.

'I should have brought you first to where it all begins. The sorting of long from short fleeces. As God will sort our crimes in Heaven. The perfect principle of the wool trade. Just as fullers' earth is to the weaver God's most precious treasure, so is a perfect piece of cloth most pleasing to God.'

We were in the last passage and I could hear the sounds of the street. He said with regret: 'I never showed you the dyeing room, where the colours are made. Next time. You will be welcome.'

'I don't expect to buy,' I said. He stopped at the last door. 'No matter. Look, you pass through here . . .' At that moment a young woman slid soundlessly past and into the room, whence came low voices and a yelp of mirth. '. . . and out into the street. In there are my very best weavers. My nieces, all of them.' And he turned his eyes as if for help to heaven. The door flew open, the girl reappeared. A very pretty girl, in a white cap.

'Uncle Hannes!' she cried. 'Katje is coughing again. Beer, Uncle Hannes, for the love of St Basil. We must have beer, dear Uncle.'

She started to stroke her uncle's blue arm; he looked pleased and cross.

'Back to work!' he said. 'This is an Englishman, of rank. What will he think of you?'

Elegant, loose-boned as a stoat, the girl made a deep curtsey. 'God greet you,' she whispered. 'Beer, Uncle. Friede is coughing too.'

Defeat dropped on the weaver. 'Very well. You are bad girls. Show meneer the way out.'

She took my arm and turned me like a horse. 'I am Marijka,' she murmured, and from her great brown eyes gave me a blistering look, which convinced me all the amorous tales about Flemish women were true. With fright and joy, I let her lead me into the room. It was small and lit from the street. Piles of spun wool were stacked in corners, some dyed in different colours, some plain. There were two broad and two narrow looms. A pair of girls sat at each of the broad looms, working steadily, throwing the shuttle across the warp deftly and beating together the weft threads. There is no music in the world like those taboring shuttles—to me. The narrow loom which Marijka had left stood idle, as did one nearest the window. The water-light from the canal shone in and rocked gently on the walls, coloured by iridescent reflections from the piled dyed wool. The girls were singing softly in a patois and coughing as the wool fibres tickled their lungs. Beside each loom sat a small boy, winding the yarn as it was worked by the women. When I entered with Marijka all work ceased.

'We can have beer,' she cried, and gave coins to one of the boys

197

who darted out into the street. 'Look!' she cried, all mischief. 'I've brought you an Englishman! Look at his hair.'

They began politely to speak my language—not that it mattered—I seemed to understand them anyway.

'Saffron colour!' cried one of the broad-loom weavers, a little round blue-eyed wench.

The swarthy girl who shared her loom, peeped up at me with naughty, slanting eyes.

'Like gold,' she murmured. 'Dyed with onion skins.'

They all cast themselves about laughing at this. Then they began to rise from their looms and look me over.

'And so tall! I am Katje,' said the little one.

'He's the tallest in the world,' said the dark one. 'My name is Adeliza.'

'And I'm Rosa,' said a blonde, stroking my sleeve with delicate fingers.

A pale one who looked the youngest coughed bitterly and said: 'Friede, meneer. God give you your heart's wishes.' It was a formal courtesy, but somehow it moved me deeply.

'And God be in this place,' I said when I had chance.

'Isn't he handsome!' declared the first girl, turning me about in a proprietorial way. I felt as if I were blushing from crown to toes. The boy returned with beer, and Adeliza hurled some wool off a bench and thrust a full mug in my hand. 'Sit, meneer. Tell us your name.' They all began to talk excitedly. I wondered what Uncle Hannes would say as they abandoned work and crowded round me, pulling up their stools.

'My name is Nicholas.' Even that had had to come in for praise and comment; patron of sailors and children. They were rather like children themselves.

'Are you staying at the English house?' Rosa asked. 'Do you come from the Bourse—the paved street, where all the foreign merchants live?'

'Have you heard this song?' Katje interrupted, and was howled down. Rosa asked: 'Have you been to the top of the tower? You can see Oudenberg, the fortress of Blankenburg, Ghent, Nieuport, Damme and Sluys, on a fine day. The devil burnt the tower down once. There's a great black beam where he set fire to it with his breath.'

198

'I'll take you up the tower,' Adeliza said slyly.

'We could take him on Sunday,' said Marijka. 'We don't work on Sunday.'

'No one works on Sunday,' Rosa told me. 'The spinsters don't even work on Saturday. My cousin was a spinster and worked on Saturday. She was dead next day, and went to Hell.'

'How do you know?' I said, alarmed.

'Oh, she came back,' said Rosa, winking at the others. 'She showed her burned hand, and sang: "See what in Hell I won, Because on Saturday I spun"!'

She burst out laughing and was taken with a cough which she doused with beer.

'Don't tease my Englishman,' said Marijka. Abruptly she rose and came to sit on my knee. She was very light and warm, and wound her arms round my neck. I took a draught of beer. I was dreaming, a good dream for once.

'Are you staying long in Bruges?' she asked softly. We could take you to the Waterhuis . . .'

'Don't go, meneer,' said little Friede. 'They will walk you on the collapsing bridge. Then they will lead you past spurting walls, so you are soaked through again.'

'I must not stay,' I said. 'You will be in trouble with your uncle.'

'Oh no,' they said. 'This is a good place. He's kind to us.'

'He's a good master,' said Marijka. 'Krista had a bad master'—she jerked her head towards the unoccupied loom by the window—'before she came here. He made her work all hours.'

'Who is Krista?' Idly I asked the most fateful words of my life.

'Uncle Hannes is related to her cousin,' said Marijka, shifting her delicious weight. 'So she is one of the family. But he had to do battle with the Guild to get her here. She was very ill.'

'Is she old?' I pictured a frail elderly dame.

'She's eighteen, the same as I,' said Katje. 'She's gone to Ten Wijngaarde this morning. The nuns wash the wool for us, and Krista collects it.'

'This is her work,' said Marijka suddenly. She took a fold of my cloak in her fingers. 'I remember when she wove it, to her own design. She did it in her own time.'

199

'Without Uncle's knowledge,' said sly Adeliza.

'You will never see another pattern like it,' said Rosa. 'I recognized it at once.'

'She stole the wool,' said Adeliza. Instantly Marijka leaped from my lap and ran at her, hand raised. The others restrained her quickly, with soothing cries.

'She did not,' Marijka said angrily, sitting down on me again. 'That was all broken weft, which she mended and dyed. She wove in the knots to cover the damage. One more word, Adeliza, and I'll tear your loom apart.'

'We love Krista,' Rosa said.

'She is so kind,' said Friede. 'And so beautiful.'

'So are you all,' I told them. 'What is Ten Wijngaarde?'

'It's the Béguinage,' Marijka said. 'The Prinselijk Begijnhof—the royal nunnery. Near the Minnewater—that's where they wash the wool. Very quiet, where noble ladies go for retirement. Many tall elms shade it.'

'I must visit there, when I get time away from the Prinsenhof,' I said. Then Marijka got up quietly and sat away from me. There was a dreadful silence.

'You never told us you were in the service of . . . Maximilian,' someone said. The name dragged out, like a corpse from a river. I looked at the girls one by one. The light had gone out of their merry eyes.

'You have a grudge against the Archduke?' My voice dropped heavily into the quiet.

'We would rather not say.' Marijka turned to arrange the warp in order on the loom. 'We must go on with our work now, meneer.'

'Ladies,' I said, desperately wanting back the warmth and fun. How I had upset them I had no notion. 'I'm not in Maximilian's service.' And I told them briefly of my reason for being here, and the name of my master. Marijka had her shuttle raised and the boy was waiting to wind, but slowly she put the shuttle down, and to my relief, smiled.

'But do you know nothing of our history? Then you are only lately come here. Haven't you sensed how sad and restive the people are?'

'Bruges is beautiful,' I said.

'No more—thanks to that *verdamnt* Maxi.'

'He's a fiend from Hell, Maxi,' said Adeliza.

'He'll be Holy Roman Emperor when his father dies,' I said.

'Yes!' Marijka rose from her loom. 'And that ambition has nearly ended Bruges! He's crushed her heart. Holy Bruges, once called the Staple of Europe! Maxi's greed for money and power and high estate, Maxi's tyranny, has turned Bruges into a shorn starving beast!'

'He's in league with the Devil, men say,' said Friede.

Gradually the story of his crimes emerged. Bruges, her resources already weakened by the silting up of the estuary, was under great persecution. Two years earlier the Archduke's excesses had brought about an uprising, when Maximilian, taxing the people almost out of existence, had brought in Austrian troops to enforce his demands.

'There were soldiers everywhere,' said Rosa. 'One day the garrison forces from Damme and Oudenburg arrived and . . . *Heilig Jesus*! it was a foreign invasion. They killed the merchants, wrecked the markets . . .'

'The women suffered most,' said Friede sadly. 'My mother was raped. She hid me in the cellar, I was lucky. But my sister was raped to death by twenty Austrian soldiers.' She began to cry, softly.

'Nearly all the merchants' wives were ravished,' said Katje. 'Then they cut the dresses off them and drove them from the town. They cut off all supplies. We starved.'

'We ate our dogs,' said Rosa. 'In the end you had to pay high prices for a rat.'

'They tasted best boiled, with garlic and spices,' and Marijka began to laugh, and the little ripple of laughter spread to Friede, who dried her eyes, while the sun returned to the chamber's lapping, water-coloured walls.

'Maximilian appointed the Count of Nassau his lieutenant. The town had to give him a formal apology.'

'In the church, the sacred body of St Donatian wept blood.'

'People still starve. There is a terrible governor now, Jean de Tinteville.'

'An apostate monk,' said Adeliza. 'Cruel, debauched, a tyrant.'

'The rebellion was started by an Englishman,' Marijka looked

201

at me, but fondly again. 'His name was Edward Nicholas. He led a mob into the Council house and killed the burgomaster. Then they imprisoned Maxi in the Cranenburg but only for a little while. Afterwards Edward Nicholas was hanged in the Markt.'

'Roland le Fèvre was appointed treasurer to rob the people,' said Rosa. 'Bruges lost nearly all her relics, silver, gold, all went to fill Maxi's coffers.'

'And trade is dying,' said Friede. 'There are only half the number of merchants from abroad.'

'And I thought it all so beautiful,' I said with sadness.

'Things are not often what they seem.'

'Surely, Margaret of Burgundy . . .' I said.

'For all her glory, she is powerless in civic matters, and she contents herself in striving over her own affairs,' Marijka said.

'Of which my master, my lord Duke, is one,' I reminded them. Adeliza said anxiously: 'You'll not tell? We shouldn't have talked like this. God have mercy, we could be burned. Many women were burned two years ago, outside the town. The smoke drifted across the river for days.'

'I will never tell,' I said. 'I'll die first. Let me pay for the beer.'

Marijka got up and put her arms about me, she kissed me on the mouth. 'We trust you,' she said. 'Forgive our fear.'

Her head blotted out the window. She stood hugging me as I sat. I could only sense that the door on to the street had opened by the smell of the sunlit canal and the cool draught. There was no hint that here came the pain and splendour of my destiny.

They all left me and ran to her, crying her name, Krista, Krista, as if she had been away for years not a morning. They embraced her like one who had been deemed dead, taking from her arms the heavy sack of washed and dried wool she bore. Outside a boy was leading away a horse and cart. For some minutes I could not see her face, as she stood against the open door, haloed by the water-gleam, but I saw she wore no cap and had fine, fairy-spun hair as lint-blonde as a babe's. She was very small, and too slender. I rose slowly from the bench.

I spoke aloud, low, unheard beneath the chatter. Crazed words which broke from me wantonly. 'Josina,' I said, 'my dove, my darling, Josina.' And then Krista came further into the room and I saw that she did not really resemble my loved, lost sister, for her features were stronger. Yet it was enough; it was as if a blade bore into my heart, bringing an agonizing felicity that was almost too much to endure.

Perhaps I was conditioned to fall in love by the praises which had heralded her—how good, how fair, how beloved. Perhaps the amorous tenor of Marijka's ways, the welcome given to me, the sunlit ambience of the day—perhaps all this predisposed me to fall in love at instant sight. I remember trying to reason thus, in the moments before being presented to Krista, then recognizing, like some holy truth, the reality. That I had loved her long before this meeting. That the magic cloak had been made by her for my wearing, as the unknown, unknowing harbinger of our love.

The sun shone endlessly in those first days of love. There was a double image of speedwell sky where the canals were clear. Snowy swans floated like replicas of the small soft clouds above, and all my evil dreams had spent their venom and departed for ever. Yet strangely, I neither expected nor hoped to see Krista again. That I loved her was enough. For weeks I had feasted on remembrance of our only meeting, every nuance, look and word; oddly passive, this is the way it was. I knew that by her existence she had sanctified my own, and was now the guardian of my spirit. I told myself that was enough; there can even be beauty in self-deception.

It was the day before the Festival of the Holy Blood. Antoine and I were strolling in the Prinsenhof gardens, following the progress of the court, and near enough to Prince Richard to serve his whim. The Archduke Maximilian walked with his arm amiably linked through the Duke's. To have an alliance with the Holy Roman Empire strengthened my master's cause immeasurably, and I imagined that soon we should be returning to England as invaders 'to stretch Tudor's neck on Tyburn tree', as Antoine was always musing. But so far no one seemed in haste to move, and for my part, time itself was a slow dance of love.

The Archduke had been out hawking in the fens. As he turned his great-nosed head to address the Duke, he looked like one of his own birds of prey, sated and gorgeous. Maximilian was one of the rare beings of Bruges in whom I could find no beauty. My view of him was tempered by the bitterness of the weavers, and little

Friede's tears. He had two of the hated ministers with him, dressed to outdo one another. Roland le Fèvre was sallow and bowed, Jean de Tinteville (the apostate monk) obese and lewd of eye. Maximilian took scant notice of them but continued talking with the Duke, while they kept close as if for protection. *Au fond*, they were frightened men; the people of Bruges had put one of their kind to death in the Markt five years earlier: the tyrant Pierre Lanchals. There were black swans (his device) on the canal at the corner of the Groene Rey—placed there by Maxi as a grim *in memoriam*. Lanchals had a fine tomb in St Donatian, and fifty citizens had been racked to death for the crime.

The Prinsenhof's great gate was surmounted by a tabernacle whitened by sunshine, with a statue of the Virgin, and images of Duke Philip the Good and St Andrew. The open court was lined with carved galleries and bath-houses. Mid-courtyard were two fountains decorated with saints and beasts. Into their basins leaped pure water brought directly from the Waterhuis. Daily a man on horseback worked the big wheel, keeping supplies flowing to the town conduits, the palace, and the celebrated Watergarden with its trick bridges and spouting images. The town filled and ran with crystal water. Love filled and ran in me, grateful, marvelling, expecting nothing.

I thought of Krista as we progressed towards the palace, past bays and parapets and a central tower with four slender turrets and a gallery from which one could see the town. We moved through stone arbours and galleries coiled about with statuary, past the chapel whose campanile tolled like a crisp coin falling. We came to the first of the two great gardens, where, as at Amboise, master gardeners had worked for perfection. Dozens of square lawns within walls, exotic trees and shrubs, pavilions, their willow trellises draped with vines, small fountains and little streams set among grassy walks. Over many years the Dukes of Burgundy had planted flowers from the blossomlands of Lille. Rows of eglantine and old sweet gillies, bushes of rosemary and lavender, red and white roses, an avenue of cherry trees, and violets like a blue and white sea. They bowed and sprang beneath our feet, and I thought of Krista.

I could hear Antoine muttering, rubbing his half-healed forearm. The gist of it was he still didn't trust Astwood. His fierce eyes were fixed on the rear view of Astwood's meagre frame, which moved on regardless. When Antoine returned bleeding from the encounter with Philip Proud, there had been a violent scene. He had assaulted Astwood outside the prince's chamber, accusing him of treason. Astwood had protested total ignorance, and guards had been called. It had taken a long time to soothe Astwood's feelings, and even now he bore a grudge.

'Why should Proud have mentioned him by name? You heard him, Nicholas.'

'The prince trusts Astwood.' I picked a young rose for my coat.

'Then the prince has changed, by God.'

It was true. He was easier. He no longer smelled Tudor agents under every bed, although he did send out a hunt for Philip Proud, which failed, it later being ascertained that Proud had fled to England on a returning woolship. I myself had had an awkward interview.

'You delivered my gold safely?' he asked me and I nodded, giving him the good wishes of Nathaniel Osbeck. Now was the time to tell him I had lost the letter. It was as if a drawbridge had gone up in my mouth. It was not so much fear as shame at my doltishness. Then he asked:

'What were the lies that Philip Proud had for your ears?'

It is no light thing to smear a royal duke's lineage, even in hearsay. I stammered and evaded, and he said: 'Don't dissemble, Nicholas. I'll not punish you for recounting another's treason.' So I told him.

'Vrouw Werbeque', he said thoughtfully. 'It was to her that my letter was sent. And Proud hinted that she was my mother?'

'Yes, your Grace.' Embarrassment burned me. What made things even more awkward was that this conversation took place in the bath. I was standing half-naked in the water, pouring scented herbals over him while he sat on a large sponge. It was the biggest bath in Europe, and when Philip the Good had imported it from Valenciennes they had had to break down the palace wall to bring it through.

'Clever of Tudor,' he murmured, his face foamy, his bright hair plastered down. 'To use my dear friends thus. The impertinent huckster. My noble aunt chooses apt words. Huckster.'

When I was drying him, he said: 'But I have no qualms over

205

Astwood. He has been with us from the beginning. I have questioned him and am satisfied as to his loyalty.'

Then he dismissed me, telling me to send in the lady. This was a new mistress. He lived like a paladin, yet as if in abeyance, like all of us. After the pledges and oaths at Margaret's welcoming banquet he had become calm, although he practised feats of arms daily, with the Archduke or his son, Philip.

These three were now seated talking in an arbour. Young Philip was as comely as a maid. I reckoned his looks came from his mother, and not for the first time, I wondered what my own mother had been like. Somehow I was sure she had been beautiful. Antoine was still talking, about his fears, and his carping impatience to be armed and away.

'We have a force, money, the Duchess's blessing. The Archduke has promised more Austrian troops. Why do we wait?'

'The force isn't large enough against that which Tudor could raise. Neither is the money enough. Maximilian isn't yet Holy Roman Emperor. When his father dies, he'll have suzerainty over all the Low Countries, eastern Burgundy, Savoy, northern Italy. All the electors, margraves, dukes, counts in the Empire will send men to his standard then. Just look how loving he is to Richard. That's why we wait.'

'How wise you are, Nicholas,' said Antoine.

I looked at him sharply. 'Would to God I were.'

'And so steady. I'd heard some tales—how you would scream out o'nights—that you were . . .' He blinked and faded.

'Possessed? Perhaps. No more.'

No more. Only sweet sleep and in the day a waking dream of her, feeling her in the knots and woollen jewels of the cloak. And the remembered clear light of her eye like flawless glass, sea-coloured like sun through a wave, darkening at times to the violet of a deep ocean. Sweet God! and her little hand that I held for a moment and kissed, the smooth back of it as white as her brow, the hidden scars and roughnesses of the palm, each one a landmark of her life among the weft and warp and looms, and the line of blue dye under her delicate nails . . . Krista. I had already found that saying it formed my lips into a smile, even when I didn't feel like smiling. It was a name shaped like the Saviour's.

Had she worn a ring? That, for my life, was one thing I

206

couldn't remember. Not that it was of consequence. I had no expectations. I was for the first time in my life going to be clever. I was not going to tempt destiny with any hopes of fulfilment. That was why I hadn't been back to the weaver's shop. Prince Richard had kept me busy. There was talk of Margaret moving her court for the summer. She never stayed long in Bruges, preferring Tournai or Antwerp. I might need to be ready to leave at once. There was no time to go out pleasure-bent in the town. All this I told myself, knowing that only part of it was true.

I was afraid to go back and see her. I would rather cling to my small indestructible private happiness. Better to love her from afar than confront her, court her, attempt the possession of any part of her soul or person. Better by far for her to remember me as the English gentleman whom her cousins teased and called handsome, than to know the true Nicholas Archer. The bastard, Joachin. Accursed, unworthy.

The Festival of the Holy Blood began before sunrise, the drums first, sweeping down the narrow streets like a heartbeat. As the first clean sunlight lit the canals, musicians joined in—fife and viol wailing high and sweet through town, and people began to stream out of their houses or fling wide shutters so that those disinclined to join the mob could watch from above, packed like fish in a basket.

At every vantage point folk, brightly best-dressed, gathered. In the Markt they climbed the belfry under the great spire and the statue of St Michael trampling a dragon, surged round the Waterhalle which straddled the dark waters of the Rey, and crowded on to the barges moored there. They climbed the stocks and pillory and the well surmounted by seven gilt statues. The Great Crane, with its treadmill and hoist, was motionless this day, a wine-cask still dangling from its arm. As the morning brightened, the Guild banners were seen. First came the aristocracy of trade: the cloth and linen merchants and mercers. Then the weavers' guild, shearers and fullers and dyers. The leather and metal workers, the needle-makers, the chandlers, the rosary-makers and the boatmen, and the powerful factors' guild. From the cloister behind St Donatian came the artists and illuminators, with banners like jewels.

207

The royal party from the Prinsenhof went ahead of the main procession, their route curving south-east along Steenstraat to the Boeverie Gate and the Hospice of St Julien where they were to dine. Maximilian, his family and ministers, had an armed guard riding with them. The Duchess Margaret travelled in a gold carriage with my master. The householders had been up all night, garlanding their dwellings with green leaves and flowers. Embroidered woollen banners so fine that they looked like silk were draped from the arch of the Paradise Porch of Our Lady and the hospital of St John opposite. The Guild House of the Archers of St Sebastian streamed with standards, likewise the Stadhuis next to the Chapel of the Holy Blood, from which dignitaries were emerging: the *hooftmannen*, town officials with the keys at their girdles, the burgomaster and *échevins*, and the sworn brotherhood of *vinders* and *sorgers*, mounting up with crossbowmen as escort; a standard-bearer carrying the Lion of Flanders, and the banner with three gold lions' heads borne by the *schild-drager*. Each officer bore a white wand and wore purple or crimson or saffron robes worked in the costliest wool.

Aldermen came from the Scapenhuis opposite St Donatian where coloured statues of the Counts of Flanders had been wreathed with blossoms. Standards blew above the turreted chessboard roof and even the clock had a garland. A mass of clergy followed and incense mingled with the smell of the canal and the flower-filled breeze. At the chapel of St Basil, the Blood, in its jewelled shrine, had been exhibited since before dawn. The last of the torches which had burned through the small hours was extinguished and the sun touched the shrine. Everyone was kneeling before it; the murmured music of paternosters hung on the air. Bishops, monks and priests formed a guard round the reliquary. The foremost prelate blessed the crowd, and declared:

'The blood is the veritable blood which flowed from the body of Christ, and which was sponged from His wounds by St Joseph of Arimathea, whence it was conserved in a goblet. All honour and praise this day and to God be glory, amen.'

The square, tasselled banners were raised to shine and sway as the measured procession started off towards the Markt. An anthem soared, censers flashed like leaping fishes. A mist of incense enveloped the street. The singing rose to meet the sound of pipes and drums. Little girls in white caps and tabards embroidered with the cross went singing the *Veni, Creator Spiritus*. After them came Adam and Eve dressed in skins, bearing a banner with the words: 'His blood shall redeem us,' then Cain and Abel, and after an interval, Abraham leading a ram and carrying faggots, with his son roped and walking behind. Then came Joseph with his bloodstained cloak, more priests, angels, devils and saints.

Mary and Joseph passed in a wagon with a painted cow and a bawling infant Christ. The Three Kings followed, and the child Jesus arguing with the doctors. After a long while, a little donkey bearing the bearded figure came into sight, with palm leaves and cries of glory. Then the furious mob, the ultimate sacrifice, with St Joseph and Nicodemus bearing the bowl in which the holy blood had been collected. Next, the guildsmen. I saw Uncle Hannes, walking beneath a gorgeous banner, and wondered if Krista had had a hand in its weaving.

Last came a company of mounted knights wearing the colours of Count Thierry of Alsace, bearing the blood back to Bruges from the Holy Land. Carried as escort to the Blood itself, came the relics from all the churches in the town. So, borne by two bishops, the glittering shrine moved on, wreathed in sacred smoke, garlanded with song. A canopy of scarlet silk was raised above it, and a guard of archers walked behind. Then came the town jester, a phalanx of giants and dwarfs, the nuns from the Béguinage, and a King Herod, hurrying, late for his part, with two of the Apostles.

I followed them through the Markt, jostled, close to the wall, and soon came to the Steen prison where, from a grating at ankle-level, felons languished and cried for alms. Along Zuidzandstraat, winding past the Capucin monastery of St Godelieve and a Godshuis, where folk lived and died on charity. Past the Waterhuis with its joke fountains and to the Boeverie Gate. The line of banners moved up on to the ramparts and turned south. The standards tautened, the black windmills rolled, and into view came a group of buildings surrounded by tall elms, a green lake and a graceful little bridge.

'That's the Begijnhof,' said the man walking next to me, 'and the Minnewater.'

209

So that was where the nuns washed the wool for Krista. My heart lurched and lifted. The Minnewater opened to form part of a harbour from the elms to the sea. We jostled on past the twin-towered Lock House, to the gate of St Catherine and another Godshuis, the Hertsberghe. North again up Ste Katelijnestraat and Mariastraat, past the precincts of Our Lady where the crowd was thickest, and back through town, circling the Street of the Holy Ghost and St Donatian. Again to St Julien, where the nobles were feasting. The procession, held up many times, had taken about three hours, and the sun was high.

With blessings from the bishops, and a final anthem, the Blood was returned to the chapel for another year. The crowd began to fragment. One of the Three Kings was wiping the blacking from his face, and Moses removed his false beard. The sacred part of the day was done; the alehouses prepared for trade. The jester cavorted, knocking off people's hats. Youths linked arms and swarmed down the street. Quickly the space before the chapel emptied, and I stood alone. Then someone called me. Marijka came running, cap askew, from the direction of the Markt. She greeted me with a kiss.

'We saw you,' she cried. 'We were waiting at Onze Lieve Vrouw. We tried to get to you but the people were too many.'

She gabbled on: wasn't the procession fine, Uncle Hannes looked well, did I see the fight in Mariastraat, six people in the canal, and how was I?

'We thought you would have come back to see us.'

'Too many duties.' I glanced to where other female figures came hastening, in hope, in dread, my mouth dry, my skin cold. I saw Friede, Rosa, Katje, and, hopping to retrieve a shoe, Adeliza. Not the other. My dreadful hope turned to disappointment.

'Krista has gone back to the workshop,' said Katje, smiling at me. 'She was tired, and wanted to sit down.'

Marijka clucked in annoyance. 'We lost her. Outside Our Lady, I said, look, there's Meneer Nicholas, and she was off, running like a dog. We must go back. Come with us. Uncle Hannes has gone to the Guild banquet. There's ale. We'll have sport.'

'My lord may need me,' I lied. Now I felt an unknown, craven dread. If I should see her, what then? Was memory false? Had I merely created a thing to love, building a tower out of smoke? We

210

had spoken only half a dozen words: 'God greet you, I am Krista van Sluys' (unlike the others she had given her full name). And her eyes falling to my cloak with a flicker of something more than pleasure—a tiny secret nod of affirmation like a witch whose spell has worked, saying: 'The garment looks well. It was difficult. I mixed the dyes myself,' and coming closer, delicately tracing with one finger a thread of russet. Then the calm upward look from her crystal eyes and the cool scent of her breath, sweet as flowers. The flavour of her nearness had been like walking in the green garth of a cloister at dawning.

I let Marijka lead me. A cockfight was taking place by the quay, with a close ring of watermen laying wagers. Sick with memory, I hurried Marijka past. 'He wants his ale!' she cried, and laughed me in through the door of the weavers' shop. There was Krista, sitting at the narrow loom with a pall of sunlight covering her as if the sun had time for no one else.

'Working on a holiday!' screamed Marijka. 'The Guild could fine you for this.'

Krista said, without looking up, 'It's the altar cloth for the Begijnhof. It should have been finished yesterday. Dame Friedelinde will be disappointed.'

'Look! I've brought my Englishman.' Marijka leaned her head against my shoulder. I moved from her, looking at Krista. No, I had neither dreamed nor imagined the rapture; it was redoubled in a timeless force. She turned her face from the sun to look right into my eyes through the wool-dust cloud that floated like glittering insects about the loom. I wanted to say: I don't belong to Marijka. I belong only to you. Then I realized there was no need. The mind behind those serene eyes knew mine, and her heart, my heart. It was as much a miracle as the Holy Blood.

The others came clattering in and Marijka hunted for flagons. After a time Krista resumed her work. I moved near her loom, entering the pool of sunlight as if I walked through water. Her posture grieved me, I saw her breast constricted by the work, her shoulders bowed, and she coughed from the whirling fibres. I wanted to lift her, straighten that cramped pose. I wanted so badly to kiss her small soft mouth that I grew unsteady with wanting. I watched her fingers, passing the warp deftly through the two sets of healds, lifting, with the small finger of her left hand, several

211

threads and passing the shuttle under, then with a swift jerk throwing the shuttle across the warp, driving home the weft threads with the batten. The unvarying clack as the shuttle hit the sides of the loom was like a beat for wild music.

She said: 'Would you be kind enough to wind the yarn for me? The boy ran away when the jugglers went past the window.'

I sat down on the little stool beside her.

'Just wind off the quill,' she said. 'My thanks.'

I wound, and the thread between us grew tight and full until I felt I should burst from the shimmering thread of love from me to her and back again. The clack of the shuttle beat out the rhythm of an old dance and I felt body as well as soul yearn for her without shame. I dreamed of her small working hands on my skin. Her eyelashes moved like reeds on lucent water. The sun lit tiny golden down on her pale cheek. Her neck was long and round. One blonde braid lay over her tender breast.

Marijka banged down a cup of ale on the floor beside me. She spoke; I could not answer. The precious minutes passed and the threadwork grew until I felt my heart near bursting and fancied that Krista and I sat sealed off together in a sunny world, for the others' voices as they grew merry with beer and jests came faintly. Soon they gave up trying to draw me into their gaiety and began to sing a rondel, and very pretty it must have been, but I did not hear it. At one point Krista's thread broke and I helped her mend it, for now I could do anything, all my clumsiness and follies in the past. As I leaned close and we knotted and smoothed the thread, my cheek almost touched hers. The very air between us caressed me.

'Will it show?' I asked, and her lips curved.

'*Ah, neen.*' She brushed the tapestry delicately. 'It will be beautiful, all the errors hidden.'

Yes, I thought. Fair cloth, new life, all the sins knotted off behind.

'Next time,' I dimly heard Adeliza say, 'we will take him to the fulling mill and toss him in the cloth until he's black. As a penance for neglecting us.'

Krista stopped weaving. She stretched her back and coughed. Her pale face was stained with rose. Painfully I said (for the cough hurt me, too):

212

'Work no more today. Please rest.'

It was very hot in the crowded room, filled with sunlight and beer-fumes and the drifting fibres.

'There's scant air in here,' I said, and turned to look into Marijka's furious face.

'*Het is echt hondweer*,' she said. 'Dog's weather!' Much as she loved Krista, I was her Englishman. The coughing was over, but Krista was very pale again. Terror made me bold. With a trembling hand I covered the hand that held the shuttle.

'Rest,' I said, '*als u blieft*.' Oh, my love, rest.

I guided her hand away from the shuttle. For a second she resisted. Then she smiled, our hands moved downward and I held on. Nothing short of Judgement would make me loose that hand.

'You're right,' she said. 'I'm foolish. I shall not finish it today.'

She looked at me fully, she bathed me in her look. I was sure she could hear my heart beating over a new bawdy song from the girls.

'I must go and tell Dame Friedelinde. I hope she will forgive me.'

She rose, making swift tidying movements to the loom, and brushed wool from her green gown.

'I will walk with you, if I may,' I said.

I waited for Marijka to scream: 'We'll all come!' but she didn't, thanks be to God.

'The streets will now be full of rogues,' I said.

And Krista, with a little smile and that look of still water, said: '*Ya, dank*. You are kind, Meneer Nicholas.'

Then we were outside, the girls' laughter fading and the bright day like a blow in our faces, and the small rough-smooth hand still in mine as I guided her along the quayside and into the mazes of town. I led her close to the house walls, placing my body between her and the street, which was thronged with cupshot folk. In places the cobbles were running with ale, and worse. We threaded through alleys and courts, past deep shining waters towards the Boeverie Gate. From the precincts of the Waterhuis youths came running, soaked, yelling with laughter and shaking themselves like dogs.

'They never weary of it—the water game,' she said, and I thought how weary she herself sounded, and looked down at the

213

shimmering flaxen plait against the soft neck, and felt my heart squeezed in a torture of tenderness. She spoke no more until we approached the little bridge with its three arches reflected in the Minnewater and saw the twin towers of the Lock House and then the Begijnhof with its stone feet in water and the elms, standing still to admire themselves.

'I shall not be long.' I watched her walk to the low door beyond the bridge. She had a very straight, flowing walk. A porteress let her in and she vanished from my sight. Standing on the bridge I gripped the parapet with both hands. Below was my own tow head and wavering white face. A pair of swans sailed under the bridge and wiped me out with a fan of green water.

In a kind of dream I stood there. It may have been ten minutes or an hour, a bubble of time that shone because she was near, and seemed to grow within me, swelling with joy and fear—always inexplicable fear, like the wasp in the apple, the serpent disguised as a fish. As she returned across the bridge, her almost noiseless step was a kind of alchemy, her face frail and lucent as a flower, and if her gait was fluid as the swans', her eyes seemed distant and noble as the swans' eyes, and she was no longer the weary lovesome weaver-girl but a goddess. I longed to cry: Protect me!

I said: 'I've been lonesome without you,' and it sounded like foolishness, but, sweet God! she gave me her hand again.

'Was Dame Friedelinde upset?'

'Ah, neen, she was most kind. She told me to go away and enjoy myself. She would have been out herself but she is very old. They are good ladies in the Begijnhof.'

I rubbed the little roundness of her thumb, gently.

'Are they all nuns there?'

'Some. But maidens can live there without vows, under the protection of the Church and the Duchess Margaret. Many went in at the height of the troubles, and they are afraid to come out.' She shuddered, and smiled. I found I was holding her hand far too tightly. My body was rigid.

'How well you speak my language,' I said.

This pleased her. 'My mother taught me. She has known many English people.'

'Do you live with her?' By now I was almost sure she was unmarried, but it was well to ask. She pointed east over the bridge.

214

'My home is not far. Yes, we live together, she and I. In great harmony.'

Again she looked up into my eyes, so true and bright it made me feel blind, as if I were the swan-speckled water and she the sun. Then, looking at my cloak, she said: 'I am glad it was you who bought it. Is it conceit for me to say it looks so well?'

'No conceit. It is the loveliest garment in Christendom. I did not buy it, however. It came to me in a time of great danger.'

'Ah.' She began once more to trace, line by line, the pattern. 'Tell me how the colours were made,' I whispered.

And she did, her finger moving softly, marking the map of my life, moving over my soul, erasing a sin here, emphasizing a brief happiness there, shivering my heart and body with the pressure of that one finger on the brightness of that which she had made for me.

'There for the red, I used sorrel roots, and for the golden-red, cutch rinse after the dyeing, and for the grey, the yellow iris. The dandelion made the magenta, and here was ladies' bedstraw. I took elder bark mordanted with copperas to make this thread of black. For the yellow-brown I went to the sea for the grey lichen that grows on the harbour wall. Elderberries gave the violet, and the green came from the wild mignonette.'

And for a heart-wrenching moment I was back in the Watling Street garden playing the herb game with my Josina. My love saw my face and her little, absorbed smile was wiped away.

'Ah, Nicholas,' she said simply, as if she knew. She turned to rest her other hand on the bridge and I saw suddenly how frail it was against the stonework. With passionate despair I thought of how those stones would remain after that hand was dust. Anger joined my sadness, for how dare that mindless stone outlast the beloved flesh . . . and neither of us spoke for ages. In truth, our unspoken words made me shake inside, they were so loaded with awe. An unsworn, unsigned compact, but as surely as the water swallowed the image of the houses and the elms trembled at their own beauty, it was there. Then I spoke at last.

'Lady. Krista. Krista . . . you are . . .'

Beautiful? Good? *Known?* Yes, known as mine, from some hidden place long ago. My fate, signed and sealed, delivered into that sadly mortal little hand resting on the bridge.

215

'We are strangers,' I said, swallowing my tumult. 'But I would rather we were not strangers. My family is a good one . . . I speak with honour. I would . . . have your favour . . . your esteem.' All this came out in churlish bursts, a kind of limp and sorry pleading. She let me continue, her gaze steadfast as a candle in the eye of a storm.

'Lady,' I said, the words emerging flat and naked. 'I swear you have my heart. From the first moment.'

By now I was gazing at the ground.

'By the holy passion of Christ, you have my most true and honourable love.'

And I looked up and saw tears.

'Forgive me,' she said, trembling. I felt the blood drain from my face. She was going to refuse me. She was betrothed to someone else.

Then she said, rushingly: 'Forgive me for running from you today outside Our Lady's church. Excuse me, *als u blieft* . . . for I was afraid.'

I said: 'Afraid? Of me?' I had both her hands now, guarding them from mortality. A swan clapped its great wings, water sucked against the supports of the bridge. Krista smiled with stunning tenderness.

'*Ah, neen*, never. One day I'll tell you. Perhaps. I longed to see you.'

I drew a breath which seemed to come from the soles of my feet. I felt the bridge rock beneath me, looked wildly about, saw the brickwork of the houses glow like gems, the floating weed in the canal like a merman's hair. The sky covered us, a pale blue bowl, and in it was a cloud shaped like a fish. I smelled flowers, the heaviness of the canal, sensed the distant secret ripeness of the vineyards. Everything clear and sharp and crying out to be remembered. And I thought: My life starts here.

At the Prinsenhof, I found folk in a fair humour. The prince and Maximilian had dined well. The Duchess was in her bower with her ladies. There was the faint tinsel sound of gittern and cithera and the beat of a tabor. The musician Josquin des Prés, whose patron Margaret was, had invented a dance in her honour. Now the bright notes of '*La Margarita*' swirled to touch my uplifted heart.

216

In the gardens I met Antoine, coming from the chapel where the campanile bell was tolling. This had been for him no holiday; he had dogged our master's steps, watchful for murderers.

'You pleasured yourself, then? Everyone has been drinking deep.'

I wanted to say yes, but not by drinking. I have been in Paradise. I felt he would not approve, thinking my mind had wandered from the cause. I wanted to tell him I was to be married, for, come death or damnation, I was determined to marry Krista. I had the notion that it would be some time before this came to pass. No matter; I could wait. I felt a lion, able to dare any hazard. The first gate was open; I had met her mother.

I had squired Krista home through the streets from which most folk had departed, walking as slowly as possible, with her hand in mine and her head leaning on my shoulder. Just before we reached her dwelling, I had made my hands a cup for her face and kissed her gently, and it was like taking a sacrament of flowers.

The path to her house was itself a tiny bridge over dark water. The door was arched and low, the knocker a lion's head. The door opened at our approach, as if we were expected. I learned later that Krista had described me to her mother with some ardour, giving me virtues I didn't possess and was never likely to.

The mother was tall. She could look me level in the eye. And her eyes were grey, clear glassy grey, with a black centre that swelled and bloomed by dim light or heady thoughts. A very bold eye had that lady. When young, she had been ravishing, now her breast and hips were heavy, languorous. There was still something seductive in her large grace as she leaned with her forearm against the lintel. She wore a tall starched cap. Her mouth was red and full, and her long fine face showed the print of hard times.

'*Wilkommen*,' she said, like a low bell. 'I am Anneke van Sluys.'

We went in. A tiled stove in the middle of the room, breathing out heat. A great bed heaped with quilts in the wall alcove. Two spinning-wheels—one still vibrating from Anneke's fingers. A black cat sitting on the table among the dishes, and a little brachet bitch curled by the stove. Webs of tapestry hanging everywhere. The floor dizzy diagonals of black and white, broken by woven carpets in peacock colours. How I loved that room.

217

I kissed the long hand of Anneke van Sluys, and for an instant felt weak, as if that hand were that of an enchantress. The vital forces of her life leaped to greet me; I felt her strength. In that moment I loved her; from her womb had sprung Krista. And she knew, for, laughing, she took my shoulders and said: 'We do thus in Flanders,' kissing my lips soundly. Then she looked deeply with her bold amorous grey look, as if we were long familiar. Together we sat on the settle, Krista set to arranging pots on the stove, every now and then her eyes sending a tender message to me.

'So you are in the service of the fugitive prince,' Anneke said. 'How long will you be in our country?'

'Always, I hope, Vrouw,' I said. There seemed no merit in dissembling. 'Always within sight of your fair daughter.'

'Ah!' she laughed. 'To love, and be young. God's greatest benison.'

'I do love her.' I felt myself tremble, heard Krista drop a couple of knives and knew that she too trembled. 'With the blood of my living heart. I love her, Vrouw van Sluys, and may I be damned eternally . . .'

'Hush!' she said. 'Such oaths! There is no need. I know all about love. Love and curses do not mix. Be still, Meneer Nicholas. It is good for Krista to have a lover. We have suffered these past years.' The grey eyes darkened. With her long foot she stroked the brachet bitch.

'I am widowed. My husband took part in the insurrection against the Austrians, when they killed Lanchals. They took Krista's father and others, and hanged them outside the Cranenburg.'

'So was my father hanged,' I said. 'Hanged for the crime of loyalty and the sin of courage. He was thirty-three.'

We were all silent. The bitch yawned, the cat jumped softly from the table. Spilled water hissed on the stove. I put out my hand. Anneke took it in both of hers, and I stopped trembling.

'Will you take supper?' she said. 'It's plain fare—not like the Prinsenhof.'

I refused, sadly. I had been away all day.

'But our house is yours,' she said. 'Our door will never be closed to you.' As I left the room I looked back and saw her, sitting thoughtful. Krista came with me to the door, and I kissed her again, hands, cheeks, lips, and she closed her eyes under my homage. Going home I was so intoxicated I nearly walked straight into the canal.

'There is a letter come for you.' Antoine's voice dragged me back. 'The comptroller has it in his office.'

'A letter?' I stared at him. 'Who brought it?'

'A courier came. One of Sir Robert Clifford's agents from London. He brought it with the other letters. The news is hot. Tudor now openly calls our prince an impostor: "the feigned lad, born in Tournai". He accuses him of conspiring with the Duchess and promising certain alien captains duchies, baronies and counties within England, so hoping to mount an invasion of the country. And the sooner the better, say I.'

I said nothing.

'Also,' continued Antoine (who must somehow have had a good look at this secret missive), 'Tudor declares that the impostor's antics don't cause him a moment's alarm.'

He burst into sardonic laughter, like a mad dog barking.

'What else?'

'The Earl of Kildare'—Antoine frowned savagely—'seems to have lost both mettle and loyalty. He's pleading now for Tudor's favour. He declares he can't understand why the King is so angry with him. It's all a plot by his enemies, he says, to involve him in treason, and he blames the Earl of Desmond.'

'If I prepare the prince's bath,' I said, 'will you fetch my letter?'

I collected the vials of rosewater essence and Antoine returned soon. The letter he handed me looked as if it had been through the fulling mill, so dirty and travelled was it, but the seal was sound. It was the common seal of the Greyfriars in Newgate, but the letter was from Piers.

The sight of the immaculate cursive script jolted me. I sat holding the letter, smoothing its split edges and the tattered ribbons of the seal. It came from bad old times. Then I had a vision of Piers's good little face and broke the seal. The letter was six months out of date.

'Right trusty and well beloved friend,' he began. Then he informed me that my kinsman, Sir James, had taken the news of our latest misfortune very heavily. (How in the world Piers found all this out I never did know.) In his displeasure, Sir James had sold the lease of the house on Watling Street. 'Your lady mother' (said Piers) 'had to take herself to the Minories, which nunly life suited her quite well.'

His next sentence drove me to my feet.

> There your lady mother, whom God assoil, died this week. Her end was peace. The funeral was of some magnificence and paid for by your kinsman. (Contrition on Sir James's part? I wondered.) She asked for burial in the church of your late parish and twelve poor men carried the coffin for alms. She left alms to the prisons of Newgate and Fleet, and the sum of fifty shillings bequeathed to each of her two menservants. She bequeathed two gold torches and some silver plate to the churches of St Paul and St Anthony and £6 to her confessor. To you she leaves the sum of £200 *for your father's sake* (underlined).

Somehow the will must have been made public, or Master John was in close communication with the blabbing nuns of the Minories. And for all her cheeseparing, Margetta must have had more money than we knew.

> She asked that you pray for her soul.

Briefly the black letters swam and blurred. Did this mean that her curse was lifted from me? I read on.

> You need have no dread that a certain matter be disclosed. We had plague in London. Among those who died were the brothers Fray. There was none to mourn the victims of a street brawl.

The room seemed to have chilled. I went to kick a log in the fireplace, thinking: Finch, you grow green in the tomb, and your murderer's ill-gotten money lies at the notary for collection. With that, and Margetta's amazing bequest, and my wages from the prince, there will be enough to make a home for Krista.

> Right good friend, I hardly know where to send this bill, which you might burn after reading. But Master Fletcher (the partisan to whom poor Edmund had been apprenticed) ad-

vised me as best he could, and is giving it to the bearer, who is for France. I pray that you keep in health and safety in Christ, and in the knowledge that I am for ever your true friend from the heart.

Piers of Eastchepe

Post Scriptum. Master John gives you his blessing. You have taken your road and I mine. I pray that you will come to the joy and peace that I find, beyond this world.

It sounded almost as if he were dead, but I knew it was his way of saying he was still given to God. Well, I was given to Krista, and it seemed almost the same thing. This soiled roll had been to Amboise, and then God knew where in Clifford's courier's satchel, and it brought Piers to me as if he were standing opposite, wise and quirky and sad.

The door opened suddenly and Richard of York entered, his pages skipping to catch the train of his long mantle, Thomas Astwood following with the Night Livery on a tray. Antoine and I divested him. He was rosy from the good holiday, bright-eyed. He stumbled a little as he walked towards the fire and I caught his elbow swiftly. He smiled brilliantly into my face. 'My trusty Nicholas!' he said. We realized he was cupshot. This made him loquacious and all the time we worked he was talking to us, as friendly and familiar as any of his Plantagenet forebears. Antoine hissed like a farrier. He hated the prince to be free-tongued, thinking him prey to traitors. The Duke stood nude before the fire. Still tall and graceful, he had grown a little paunch since being at Margaret's court. His good eye roved and rested on Piers's epistle.

'A letter?' he said pleasantly.

'Mine, sire.' Guilt seized me, but he didn't ask to read it.

'A whole pack of the things came today.' His mood hardened. 'God's blessed Lady! what wonderful things letters are!' He spat into the fire and sat down, spreading his hands to the warmth.

'Your Grace has cut his great toe,' said Antoine, kneeling.

'Dancing,' said the prince. 'My noble aunt wears the legs off all at court.'

'I'll get the marigold balm.' Antoine rose and went to the medicine coffer. The Duke's spread hands were trembling

221

violently. I knew his thoughts. *Feigned boy*. Feigned attitudes too—he and Tudor both. Tudor is greatly alarmed and angry. Even now in his cold Westminster (it was said he was too mean to light many fires) he rages grimly and plots counter-measures. Here, Plantagenet dances and drinks deep to show himself immune from the sneers and threats and the rumours of his base birth which come thundering across Europe from the dirtiest tavern to the highest throne. It is all a masquerade.

'Have you had news from home?' he asked me.

'My mother is dead, Sire.'

I draped his samite robe about him and he gripped my hand as it touched his shoulder, a brief clutch, full of instant compassion, doubly warming because it was so unexpected. There was a pile of coin on the coffer and he gestured to it.

'Have Masses said for her'. To Antoine, who was down, anointing his feet: 'This man risked life for me. Wearing my name, he faced my enemies. I asked him then if there was any boon'—he tilted his head to look at me from the lazy eye—'but you wanted nothing.'

As he rose I wondered if it were too late, for there was indeed a favour. I should need his permission to marry. Very few of the entourage had their wives with them and these were mainly the knights . . . ushers and stewards enjoyed little conjugal life. I knew without asking that here was one of the obstacles, dimly foreseen . . . the answer would be: Wait. Wait until our cause is brought to fulfilment, until Tudor is beaten and my right is gained. So I looked at the secret eye, and said nothing.

'You will all be rewarded,' he said, as he did nearly every month. 'Loyalty breeds wealth. I will carve my kingdom into a million parts to honour my friends. Even the humblest.'

'To serve your Grace is reward,' Antoine muttered.

I was thinking: As long as he gives me leave to visit Krista. As long as my tours of duty don't war with my heart. I was already planning—in two weeks I could contrive a day—in three, a day and a half. Summer in Bruges. To see her, hear her, hold her, unfold my heart. But what was my lord prince saying now?

'It will be good to move on for a while. It will give Tudor pause to wonder what we are about. Antoine, tomorrow you will start preparing for our journey—make inventory of my gear. Nicholas,

I charge you with the gewgaws. We leave in about ten days' time.'

'Where, Sire?' asked Antoine.

'Vienna. The Holy Roman Emperor's condition worsens daily. The Archduke Maximilian is anxious to be beside him. We must pray for an end to the Emperor's trial. There is no cure, yet he may linger for months.'

So saying, he sailed unsteadily out of the chamber towards his bath. It was a full minute before I could follow. Shaken to the roots, I understood for the first time why soldiers desert, and, grieving, knew also that this was not my way.

Written at Antwerp, at the House of the Merchant Adventurers, June, the ninth year of King Henry's reign.

I laid down my pen, looking at the page of love I had written. Outside, a storm stirred; dun-coloured clouds, heavy as my heart, gathered. So long, so many months without her. My mind could still hold her face, but I could no longer remember her voice, and this made me afraid. Strangely, the voice of Anneke, the mother, still rang mellowly in my consciousness. I listened for the sound of the chapman's bell down the street. He moved often between Antwerp and Bruges, and took my letters for a fee. All I could hear, however, was the growling of the Flemish mob, who gathered almost daily outside our lodging, near a statue of the giant, Druon.

Antoine said, at the window: 'They're very angry today,' and someone cried distinctly: 'Go home! *Verdamnt* English!'

They were justifiably enraged for they were being punished. Through the people, Margaret of Burgundy was being penalized by Tudor for her harbouring of the prince. Henry had struck at Flanders in the most harmful way by placing an embargo on all wool and cloth trade between the two countries. He had struck at the clothiers, the merchants, the guildsmen, the workers. They had welcomed us once; now their belts were tight, they longed to see our backs.

'Go home, English prince!' they howled. 'Your fault, that our children starve!'

Tudor, at his council in the Charterhouse, Richmond, had promised a lifting of the embargo once 'the feigned boy' was

223

handed into his custody. But here we were, waiting on the prince and his plans, wearing our White Roses, oiling our unused weapons. The Merchant Adventurers' House was large and gloomy and noisily placed in the centre of a street and I disliked it, fill it though I might with dreams.

'My soul craves your sight,' I had written. 'Each moment spent away from you is a link in a leaden chain about my heart . . .'

I was no poet, but I knew she would understand. I thought over the past few months. Our time in Vienna like a burgeoning wave breaking finally on the shore of the Emperor Ferdinand's winter death. His funeral, attended by the nobility of the Empire—a thousand black horses, golden tributes and sumptuous requiems, pomp more fitted for the entombment of a saint than a mortal man. Then Maximilian's enthronement as his successor—with my royal master closely in attendance. The proclamations and speeches—at one of which Plantagenet declared formally that should he die without issue, Maximilian should be his heir to the glories of England.

And then a grand whirling tour, showing off Plantagenet to the Holy Roman Empire. So many places, faces, banquets, vigils, so many suits of clothes and armour draped and burnished. So many horses held and peregrines flown. The world became a cockpit, full of spinning blazing supremacies. The glittering eyes of a hundred diadems, a thousand yawns on as many late nights. Too much wine, too much food; Rhenish, Burgundy, *vin grec*, ypocras and muscat, sturgeon and suckling-pig and sugar-woven subtleties. Too many days and nights. Too many horseshoes ridden down, and another year growing older, as we did.

And so long parted. Now that I had seen my devotion doubled in her face, like the elms in the still water, I was no more content to languish in my own loving thoughts. I had seen her twice more before leaving Bruges. We had walked beside the Minnewater, the *Lac d'Amour*. On St Anthony's Eve a maiden would see her future husband reflected there over her shoulder. 'Now you see him,' I said, and stood behind her, breathing her fragrance. I had laid my hand over her heart to feel its strong wild beat and knew that she burned for me, as I for her. During the months apart that burning had grown into a hard bright hurting stone within me. I longed for her with my body's worship.

224

The mob outside was chanting: 'Go back!' like a flock of angry geese. A flung pebble glanced off the window-pane.

'I must look to the prince,' said Antoine.

'He's with his councillors. Come away from there. They'll soon weary of shouting.'

The last time I saw her I had taken supper at the house—a pork stew with ginger, made by Anneke's enchantress hands. She, afterwards, smiling like a kindly witch, had taken herself off to visit a neighbour. Krista had sat on the settle, I at her feet, my head in her lap, with the brachet bitch snoring and the cat washing and the stove murmuring tales of home and safety, while Krista moved her fingers through my hair in endless tenderness. I asked her then why she had run from me the day of the Holy Blood.

'I was afraid.'

'But of what?' I looked and saw her sad and puzzled.

'Truly, I do not know,' she said. 'I longed to have you for my own heart's joy and comfort and yet I felt . . . it would be wrong.'

'How could it be wrong?' Then, suddenly bitter, full of old sins and secrets, I said: 'You knew I was not worthy. Christ in heaven knows that I love you, Krista, but I am not a good man.'

You had sprung from your seat, Krista, and rushing to hunt for—of all things—a mirror, had brought it back to me.

'Unworthy!' she said, in horror.

Yes, I answered, and it was a good, sad relief to tell her my past life had been like a loathsome disease. But she turned me to the small angel-rimmed glass and made me look. I hadn't studied my own face for a long time. I looked old. There were lines on my brow and beside my mouth. My cheeks were thin, cadaverous even—how could the weaver-girls have called me handsome? There was even a whitening of my tow-coloured hair, above the widow's peak on my forehead.

'See the good face, of a good man, loved by me,' she whispered, then kissed me ardently so that the room grew dim to my sight. I stood and held her as if to draw her right into my heart, and then we heard Anneke singing a loud merry song outside the door.

I had Krista's last letter to hand now. As well as words of love, she put in snips of news.

Today Uncle Hannes had a fierce quarrel with the factor. He

225

still holds the goods and takes the credit for longer than is lawful. As for the clothing business, I fear my uncle will soon be poor. He has had to lay off many of his workers and goes in dread of the Guild.

All this—because of Tudor's cursed embargo.

Last week Marijka went to the bath-house and got into trouble. She said it was an adventure—some young men stole her gown.

I thanked God that Krista never went to the bath-house, where the young and lively Brugeois indulged in ripe sports.

Several of our kinsmen have returned home from England. They were sent out of Norwich by order of the King's stewards. No Flemish persons are now allowed on English soil.

I took up my pen again and wrote a postscript about this.

Dearest of all, it grieves but does not surprise me. The English herald who came to visit the Duchess Margaret bore the King's threat. While our lord prince is harboured here, none of your countrymen can remain there. Could I undo the hurt I would.

I remembered the English herald well: Dr William Warham, a small bespectacled lawyer with a loud voice. We had been at Tournai briefly following the grand tour. Margaret, with the Duke of York enthroned beside her, had sat in her chamber in public assembly. Sir Edward Poynings, one of Tudor's diplomats, had been in charge of proclamations, but Warham made formal delivery. The lawful mouthpiece of majesty, he did not fear to look directly at Plantagenet, declaring that the young man was, in King Henry's view, of base birth and a false usurper of the name of Richard Duke of York, who long before had been murdered in the Tower.

Margaret's pallor began to be replaced by angry red. Had she not been such a strong woman, I would have feared for her; as it was, I feared somewhat for Dr Warham, who moved to other topics, some of them mightily obscure. Even Elizabeth Woodville came in for Tudor censure, having earned the King's displeasure by trusting her daughters, ten years earlier, to the care of the alleged murderer, Richard. The lawyer turned finally to Maximilian, begging him and his council not to suffer such impostors as this Pierrequin Werbeque, now masquerading as York. Had not King Henry sided with Maximilian earlier during the débâcle over Anne of Brittany? He concluded by offering Maximilian Tudor's support over any future conquest of France.

The proclamation was to be spread in Tournai, Bruges, Antwerp and Ghent. With the news of the proposed trade embargo, there was the first sign of movement among the assembly; the air grew subtly anxious. Then Margaret, pale and red by turns with anger, answered the ambassador with some force.

'I am not offended by your speech or presence,' she said icily, 'although some would say you have transcended the bounds—you are speaking for a fee, and I will reply.

'I intend to be the protectrix of this distressed prince, this true Plantagenet, to whom I give absolute credence. Of that you can assure your king. For the boy king Richard was conveyed away from England at the time of your master's usurpation of the throne, and now stands before you.

'Concerning the dispossessing of his mother, Elizabeth, this is nothing for your King to boast of. She was a fair and tender widow woman who was used unjustly. I will revenge her quarrel.' Her voice hardened. 'I am no further moved by your unseasonable oratory than I am afraid of Tudor's menaces. Let him do what he will. By your insinuation with my trusty friends to desist from their allegiance to my nephew and his lawful claim, you count us as perfidious as yourselves. It is known that the friends of Henry Tudor have been seen gladly to leave him in the midst of his enemies!

'Concerning your allegation against the Holy Roman Emperor of ingratitude, why, the petty revenges upon France by Henry Tudor are not to be compared to the Emperor's grand design: any conquest of France by England,' she said maliciously, 'will be lost as soon as it is gained. It has been so since the days of Henry the Fifth. You can only keep Calais, and that for shame of losing it.'

Dr Warham was a good diplomat. He stood there, insults bouncing off him.

227

'I offer a challenge to Henry,' said the Duchess, her little teeth bright with venom. 'Go back and tell your politic prince that whereas words are but womens' weapons, we determine to arm ourselves. And this prince, by God's assistance and my power, shall bid him defiance in his own kingdom with spear and shield, and make an equal combat the decider of both their titles.'

She rose. Her skirts rippled with the ecstasy of her temper. The ranks parted as she came down from the dais, her arm on that of Plantagenet. She confronted the ambassadors as in a close joust, and her face was old with rage.

'There is nothing your infinitely insolent sovereign can do to me and mine,' she said. 'Here I am absolute. Take your master's barbs back to him and have him use them to pick his foul Welsh teeth.'

My thoughts at the time had been: Tudor must fear our prince, to offer these extreme measures. Some months earlier he had declared that the impostor's May-games caused him not a moment's grief; that England was happy and peaceful, that even the Irish were quiet . . .

'*Are* the Irish quiet?' I asked Antoine now, as he stood watching the Flemings from the window.

'Kildare, I heard, went to England to beg Tudor's pardon. Several Irish gentlemen were with him. Henry feasted them and brought Lambert Simnel from the scullery to serve their wine. Mocking them—reminding them they'd once crowned him in Dublin. Tudor said: "You'll be crowning apes next."'

'How did they take that?'

'Oh, I believe they shuffled their feet a bit and then Kildare said something about the wine being good, so he'd drink it. Damned traitor.'

'Christ aid him.' I could not share Antoine's spleen. I looked again at Krista's little letter. 'Now I must seal this bill, best beloved, for the Werc Clocke is sounding,' she'd written, and my mind heard the sweet bell and saw her sitting to her loom, weaving her jewel-colours with no one there to kiss her.

'Tudor has appointed his new get—little Henry—Lord Lieutenant of Ireland,' said Antoine gloomily. 'The brat's only three. Holy Mother, what now?'

The noise outside was swelling, like a drunken hive. A knot of

Flemings had seized our White Rose standard and were trying to tear it to shreds. Three of the prince's guard were tugging on the other end, like pups at play. I drew my sword, praying I wouldn't have to use it on the people I liked so much, and Antoine and I ran downstairs. Blows were being struck—I pushed a little man, whose contorted face was familiar, away from the standard; he cannoned off the wall and came at me with his fist, clouting me heavily on the nose. Licking blood, I stared at him. It was Wim Schenk, our one-time partisan.

'Wim!' I cried, 'Why?'

'My country comes first.' He swung at me again. 'I'm sorry, Nicholas. Take your Prince Perkin home and give us back our livelihood!' He hit me, blacking my eye, and I pushed him backwards into the arms of his friends, still screaming round the torn standard like gulls over flotsam.

There was a sudden clatter and a horseman came thrusting through the press. He spurred up to the door, scattering people, and fell from his mount. Filthy with travel, he was loaded with despatches.

'Prince Richard,' he gasped, as I bundled him in through the door. 'I must see him.'

I knew the man—he had ridden on messages from Nick Ashley and John Heron between London and Amboise on occasions. 'Dire news,' he grunted. 'Take me to the prince.'

'He's with his council,' I said. 'What is it, for God's love?' he was bursting to tell, and with either pleasure or grief.

'Great scandal in London. Great calamity. Great shame,' he cried, and drew a shuddering breath, loosing his news like vomit.

'Everyone has been arrested. All our chief allies—Sir Robert Clifford, Sir William Stanley, Sir Simon Mountford, Sir Thomas Thwates, Lord Fitzwalter, William Daubeney, Sir John Ratcliffe, Thomas Astwood. Tudor's had 'em all. The Tower's crammed with traitors to the realm. There's talk of execution—especially for Stanley. He's even taken the Dean of St Paul's, Dr William Worfley, and two Dominican friars, Rochford and Paines—all for upholding Warbeck—God's pardon, I'm losing my wits—I mean Duke Richard Plantagenet. Sweet Christ's hammer and nails, this is a dangerous game we're in, my friend.'

'Go up,' I said instantly, and directed him to the council

chamber. I sat down and thought about what he had told me. Stanley, that double-dealer from the womb, caught at last with a foot in the wrong camp. I thought of the ageless feud and the festering resentment ever since the battle; of Henry's long memory feeding on Stanley's tardiness that day; of how he had hung back until the last terrible moments when King Richard came blazing towards him . . . and Stanley's rancour when the titles and honours he had expected turned out to be a few paltry baubles. Now came the reckoning; Stanley would die.

And Thomas Astwood, who had returned lately to England to visit secret Yorkists, had also been taken. So much for Antoine's mistrust of him. I pondered gloomily on Astwood's future fate.

'No one wins against Tudor.' I spoke out loud, but the words seemed to come from some dark other place, and chilled my heart.

An hour later the prince sent for me. He was alone in his private chamber, wearing long black velvet, which made him tall and thin. His face was calm, but his bad eye, closed like a night-flower, rippled with hidden worry.

'Nicholas,'—his voice was quiet—'whom do I trust?'

'Me, my lord.'

'They will all betray me, when Tudor puts them to the iron' (and he shuddered). 'They will spill secrets, plans, as a drunkard wastes ale. All this will be a bad dream to them when they are back in favour, like Kildare.'

He walked away, looked through the casement, said almost absently: 'This is a bad blow.' Then he came back and said: 'Nicholas. Once you risked your skin without a thought, and for no gain. At this moment it is you I need. Ride to the Duchess Margaret for me. I want her counsel. I dare not move myself. The streets are hostile. Will you? I'll write to her . . . return in half an hour.'

'Yes, lord. Where do I ride? Tournai?'

'No.' He was already scratching with a quill. 'The Duchess lies at the Prinsenhof again. Ride to Bruges.'

I rode. That night. Sweet God, how I rode! I covered the journey in two days. Change, subtle yet visible, met me as I entered the town. Where once thirty-four kingdoms had been represented in the Staple of Christendom, there was apathy, bare streets and squares. The quays and basins that had once received a hundred vessels in a single day were emptying. There were a few traders still plying in the environs of the Cranenburg—orientals offering spices and shining stuffs, bright parrots and tragic little monkeys, but few folk were buying. Packs of men stood around long-faced and there seemed a lot of soldiers and special constables watching for any unrest.

To the Prinsenhof had also come change. Maximilian was in Rome, pursuing some scheme of power. Margaret of Burgundy, I was told, spent much of her time with her friend and adviser, the Bishop of Cambrai, and the reins of rule seemed to lie in the hands of the young Archduke Philip. A hundred or so new Yorkist partisans, frightened out of England by Henry's purge, had recently arrived at the court.

'There's nothing but trouble,' one of these, a gentleman from Kent, told me glumly. 'Riots in London—the trade embargo has hit us too. There were many killed outside the Steelyard the day before I took ship. The Hanse League is risen in arms. As for this place—' he pointed to a group of citizens silently waiting at the foot of the marble staircase—'see them? More folk petitioning Duke Philip to send Perkin Warbeck home.' He saw my expression. 'Well, yes. Everyone calls him that. You should hear the rumours. Some say he's the son of the Duchess Margaret and Henri, Bishop of Cambrai, and that's heresy, blasphemy and high treason in a bundle, a sure way to lose your head and your guts. But all the Flemings call him Warbeck now.'

With a dreadful anxiety that tempered for an instant my joy at being back in Bruges, I thought of the letter I had lost. To Vrouw Werbeque—who had been so kind to him, the prince had said. I resolved to tell no living soul. It was over, a mistake of the past, before Krista, and I now dug graves for the past.

'I wish by all the virgins in Heaven,' said the gentleman from Kent, 'that all were done with.'

'It will be, soon,' I said to cheer him. I had delivered the letter in which the prince asked for Margaret's aid, to her Chamberlain, and had been told to return next day for her reply. I tried not to hurry from the Prinsenhof, but soon my feet were flying. I

231

stopped once only, near the Markt, to buy, from the stall of an old and toothless Chinese, a gift for my heart.

'*Ach, mijn Got!*' Anneke cried. 'It's Nicholas, come home at last!'

She reached me first as I ran over the little bridge, she flung back the door with such force that it crashed against the lintel. Her hands were floured from baking, she smelled of warm wheat and woman's secrets as she caught me in her arms, drawing me tight against her breast, full and yielding as a bed of flowers. Over her shoulder I glimpsed Krista, pale, hair free, running across the room to reach me, then the close swooning sheen of Anneke's glass-grey eyes and the press of her warm mouth blotted out sight, until Krista came slipping under my arm to take her rightful share and the three of us clung in a frenzy of laughter, tears and kisses.

'Yes,' I said, when I could speak, tasting their tears and my own. 'I am most blessedly home. My dear ladies, my loves.' Krista's face shone up at me like a pale star. Anneke's strong hands led me to the settle. The two women began to cosset me. They exclaimed over the gifts I had brought—a long swathe of pure silk from some lost yellow land for Krista, a phial of ambergris for her mother. Then they noticed the black eye left by Wim Schenk's fist and Krista rushed to get comfrey leaves and they pleasured themselves doctoring me. I sat back in such a transport of felicity that could I have ordered the moment to hold fast for eternity I would . . . all the magic captured, the leaping stove-glow moving on the women's white hands, the feel of Krista's cheek on my thigh as she knelt lovingly beside me, the little pale road that ran on the crown of her hair and smelled of flax and flowers and weaving, strange scent, hers alone; a green log whistling in the stove, the click and jingle of Anneke's keys and rosary as she bent to bathe my eye . . . all this the essence of home and kindliness that I had never known and, in some other time, known always.

'Wine!' cried Anneke, rising quickly. 'We must feast. We'll have a revel. *Mijn Got*, what joy.' She hurled a fistful of worts into a gasping pot on the stove. 'Krista, go to the cellar, there are two good flagons left. I'll tend the stew. And bring another

232

bolster for his bed—you'll stay, Nicholas.' She swooped to ruffle my hair, laughing. 'This is a blessed, happy day.'

I unwound my arms from Krista's waist, so fragile, more slender than when we had last met, and she departed, looking back as if for fear I'd flee. As soon as the cellar door closed behind her, I stood up and faced Anneke.

'Mevrouw,' I said, 'I have not much time, for I have to return to Antwerp very soon. I beg to speak with you about my marriage to your daughter. I ask you now for her hand.'

She came close, searching my face with her lucent eyes.

'I give it gladly,' she answered. 'She has yearned for you. It would be an evil thing to hold you apart. Now, to her dowry . . .'

'I would take her without one,' I said instantly and Anneke stiffened, the barest inch.

'She will have a dowry,' she said evenly. 'I have money untouched over all the hard times, put by for the day. She will not disgrace you, the son of a gentleman.'

'Yes, of a knight.'

'So!' She smiled again. 'You are betrothed!' and she put her head against my shoulder and cried for an instant, the spring shower of mothers about to lose their young.

'Ah, but I do love you, Nicholas,' she said, drawing back refreshed by tears. 'Welcome, thrice welcome to my family, and may you give me many grandsons.'

We sat down on the settle. Faintly from below came the sound of Krista clashing bottles about in the dank, canal-cooled cellar. I wished she would return. Already a precious half-hour had passed, and much as I loved Anneke, I longed for Krista.

'When will the wedding be?' she asked. I looked down at my feet, sobered.

'Would to God it were tomorrow.' Then I explained, or tried to, the state of flux in which we all were with Plantagenet, the uncertainty of the immediate future. Wishing all the time that I had broached the matter of my marriage to him when I had the chance.

'I am bound,' I said. 'To him and the cause.'

'And when will the cause be fulfilled?' There was a deep and sombre look on her face. I recalled how many others had asked

233

this over the past few years. We were all suspended in ambition; nothing moved, and in some hope waxed stale.

'We have lately been set back a pace.' And, because I trusted Anneke with every vein of my heart, I told her about the arrests at home, in particular that of our most puissant ally, Sir William Stanley.

'And how you hate Sir William Stanley,' Anneke said, with a gleam in her waterwitch eyes.

'I hate all that family. Those Tudor creatures betrayed King Richard and brought about my father's shameful death. And once I had a beautiful horse . . .' I said, feeling dazed with memory, and she said gently: 'Yes?'

'Nothing.' That was delving back too far, where demons lived.

'So,' Anneke said. She went to the cellar door and called down to Krista, who seemed to be in trouble finding the wine. Then she came back with her stately swaying walk, long hands folded at her waist, and stood looking down at me.

'It's plain. You must fulfil your pledge, and follow the cause to its end.'

'That I know well,' I said. Suddenly dolour washed me. The black cat lying by the stove looked at me with a mean maggity glow. 'I swore it on the soul of my dead brother.'

'Then you do not need my counsel.' She took my hand—as always, sadness fled. 'When you crown your prince—then you shall claim what you desire, and marry Krista.'

'Yes. The prince will restore my estates, the inheritance taken by Tudor from my family. At this moment, I'm still an attainted rebel. But it may take months, years.'

'No matter. It is the law of chivalry. Just as in the romances—how I loved those old romances! You will wash your sword in the blood of your enemies and return for your white lady. Be loyal to your lord, Nicholas. Loyalty is one of the three clear threads in this flawed tapestry. The others of course are faith and charity.' She looked down, playing with her beads. 'Forgive my boldness. I must not presume to tell you what you already know.'

'I am privileged.' I kissed her hand. 'To have such counsel from a good woman.' She threw back her head, laughing. 'Ah, Nicholas! You honour me. Some would say I am not—I . . . how do you say it? . . . I make no bones. Some might say I have been a bad woman. You see, I love life. I love love. But here at last is my daughter with the wine.'

She could change in moments, this large, fine woman, roguishly patting my cheek and rising to flaunt over to where Krista came bearing two great dusty flagons.

'We thought you were drinking it down there.'

'It was well hidden.' Krista smiled at me, and again I thought of how little time there was until the morning, and took her hand, whispering: 'Don't leave me again,' while Anneke in a kind of joyous fury wrenched out the bung on the first flagon and poured copiously into three tall steins. She seized a dagger off the wall and thrust it into the stove-fire until the blade whitened, then plunged it into each vessel. There were three sharp hisses, and wisps of steam

'Old Jehan used to do that at the Herberghe Margaretha,' she said gaily. 'The wine drinks doubly strong. It filled the foreigners' heads until they were all mad. *Ach*! happy days. There I would go, and make much sport.'

'Mother,' said Krista, frowning.

I remembered the tavern; it was where we had had the encounter with Philip Proud.

'Bah!' cried Anneke. 'Nicholas and I understand one another. I drink to you both.' She raised her cup. 'To your long and happy life together, my dears.'

I turned to Krista. We linked arms to drink from one another's vessels. I kissed her, tasting the drops of sweet warm wine and the subtler sweetness of her lips. Her face was blurred. She was joyful, tearful. 'Now, my love, I plight you my troth,' I whispered, and Anneke came again to embrace us both, before rushing to see to the stew, in danger of singeing.

Later, after we had supped, Anneke took her lute and sang, songs by Gilles Binchois and bawdy sweet airs of England for my pleasure and her own. She danced, alone, her lamplit shadow undulating like a swan upon the walls. She drank deep, and glowed like a spring moon with the wine's radiance. And I drank too, wine, and the look from Krista's eyes. We sat a little apart on the settle so that we could gaze into one another. Sweet God! she looked so like Josina this night, with her fine cowslip-coloured hair and her pale star-face. But there was wisdom in her that Josina had lacked, and looking at her I could think of my sister without pain.

There came a moment when the wine turned enemy on Anneke and she sat down heavily at the table and stared into air, her chin on her hands.

'So you will be going to live in England, my daughter,' she said gloomily. 'In a fine house which Nicholas will build for you.'

'Yes,' I said. 'The prince has sworn that we shall all be rich.'

'Would that I could visit England.'

'You shall come and live with us,' I said.

Suddenly she began to weep, and we both jumped up to comfort her, but in the bat of an eye she was merry again.

'Tell me about the prince. I had but the briefest look, the day of the Holy Blood. Cursed Maxi blocked my view. Is he as handsome as his father? So big, so golden . . .'

'He has his father's lust for life.' I thought of all the eager women.

'And brave! The Plantagenets were lions. Has he their courage?'

And I answered absently, lost in Krista's shining skin and the curve of her cheek: 'He is the bravest of them all.'

'So! he has been tested and tried and has won his spurs,' said Anneke happily. I thought I should answer: No, not yet, but he must by nature be brave, but I was floating, spinning in a silent motionless dance of love for Krista. The pattern of her face, the lambency of her eyes, seemed part of my flesh, and the hard, hot jewel of desire crystallized and fragmented, spreading like grains of sweet poison through my veins, making me heavy and lost.

'And you, Nicholas,' Anneke said, filling the cups, 'you have a look of the Plantagenets yourself. So blond, so tall and elegant.'

I laughed. 'I was taken for the prince, once. I impersonated him for days, and none knew.' They listened then, captivated, to my tale.

'You played at royalty,' said Anneke, 'and I have seen princes play at merchants. Both Edward and Richard, when they were here in exile, dressed thus, the better to pleasure themselves.' Her face was flushed. 'I met Richard myself, and talked with him as I

236

do now with you, one night in the inn. I was with my dear friend, Alys, sweet Christ give her rest.'

Krista whispered to me: 'Alys died in childbed—before I was born. My mother still mourns her.'

'I remember Richard of Gloucester,' said Anneke. 'We both recognized him, for all he was plainly dressed. He had such a power about him. So quiet and still, like a deep mere. But when he smiled, it was worth waiting a month for.' She frowned. 'It made me laugh—it made me sad—when the tales of murder reached us, for many people knew the truth of it. Both those boys were shipped ashore—the sickly one died mid-ocean, so I'm told. Your prince was taken to Tournai and hidden with Catherine de Faro—Vrouw Werbecque as she became—to await his destiny.'

I said: 'I wish that Cardinal Morton could hear you say that.'

'Ach!' said Anneke, with a hearty swallow of wine. 'Who would listen? I am not a great prelate. The common folk have no voice.'

'They say that Vrouw Werbeque is my lord's mother.'

'They say what they have been taught to say,' Anneke answered. 'Hunger has made them cruel.' But her voice was absent, and she was staring sadly into her cup, her mouth drooping. 'So many are the vices of men—cruelty, pride, and greed, and wantonness. God forgive me! I have been so wanton.' Tears fell into her wine.

I went, deeply distressed, to take her hand. 'For the love of God! None will judge you, beloved Vrouw. Myself least of all. I am chief of sinners.' And as my hand lay over hers, I saw the gleam of Finch's ruby, like a bale-fire. 'You see that ring? It belonged to a man I loved above all other.'

Anneke quickly wiped her eyes. She and Krista listened intently. The night was right, the time was now for confession. I said:

'I loved him foolishly, and did wrong for his sake in many ways. So he brought about my brother's death and my sister's ruin. And I killed him, in cold blood. I am a murderer, Anneke.'

I felt as if my life hung by a thread. Then Anneke said quietly. 'You did what you thought to be right, no doubt. Will you be arrested? Are you in danger from this deed?'

I shook my head. 'Someone,' I said slowly, 'whom I know only

237

now to be almost a saint, took my sin upon himself, and lied for me. I am in no danger.'

'Then nothing is changed, Nicholas. We love you. You have our trust. Give that ring to Krista, as a token of our faith.'

I did as she bade me. On Krista's small work-sore hand some of the ruby's fire was dimmed; it seemed to glow less bloodily.

'A betrothal ring,' I said. My voice shook. For a moment I wanted to snatch it back. Was I giving ill-luck to Krista? Was the ring too evil for her hand? No; she herself would purify it. We all three smiled at one another. Absolved, we fed the stove and broached the second flagon, and Anneke talked, quite calm now, of her youth in Ghent, of times easy and hard, and of her dead husband, Krista's father, a master tailor who had taken her from the pit of her wild ways. And I listened with half my mind. For the night had taken on a different colour; whether it was Anneke's wild surges of mood, or the act of my own confession, or, more vitally, Krista's enchanting nearness, everything owned a shimmering urgency. The floor-tiles quivered beneath me, running into one another; the flames ran and leaped like dragons in the stove, while the form of Krista grew fluid and twining as if she had already crossed the little space between us and we were as close as man and woman can be, one flesh. Desire doubled in a fearful pang, and I knew she felt it too, as if we shared nerve and bone and blood. Anneke was asking me how many followers the prince had. I answered vaguely—fifteen hundred, neither sure, nor caring at this moment whether the figure were true.

'That is not a great army!' she said, raising her brows.

''There are many more in England, dormant, waiting for the ripening time.'

Krista swayed towards me the barest inch, as if her body were a candleflame, destined to bloom only for a night. A thought hammered at me: I would be gone in the morning, and I had never seen her nakedness. Out of the past came the pale body of the ravished red-haired girl in Paul's churchyard; a memory I had shunned in horror, and miraculously the vision was changed, I saw only beauty.

'Nicholas, be careful,' I heard Anneke say with a little laugh. 'Your prince must not attack his enemies until he has a great force behind him.'

238

'I cannot advise him,' I said. Krista's gown had a square border of little blue flowers at the neck; it mirrored the delicate veins of her crystal neck and breast. 'I am but his slave,' I said.

Sweet God! how I loved and lusted—on my soul, I had never thought such ardour lay in me. Worse than wine, more potent than hunger or fear, more vital even than the harbouring of life itself. I got up and walked into the shadows to find calm, but I felt Krista's eyes stroking my back, heard her heartbeat like a silent song, and there was no escape. I stared at the wall, remembering, with a hard appraising fearlessness, foreign to me, how Finch had used to sin—he would bed his fancy as carelessly as I would crush a louse . . . and I had kept myself from sin, these past years. But love—that was something other—how should I confess such all-prevailing love to some arid priest? As the sweet loving sin roared in my loins I prayed, to God knows what fierce pagan, that somehow Krista and I could be left alone together . . .

That was surely a powerful goddess. At the very birth of my prayer, there came a tremendous banging on the door. The dog leaped up, barking. Outside a man's gruff voice called Anneke's name. She rose quickly.

'Stay there,' she whispered. 'Away from the door. There have been riots tonight against the English. Don't let yourself be seen—you may be harmed. Sometimes they run demented.'

I leaned behind a tall jutting cupboard. Krista came across and stood as my shield and I knew that for me she would take an arrow in her without a moment's thought (as would I for her), and love, not alarm, made me tremble so that the pots rattled in the cabinet. They were speaking Flemish on the doorsill.

'It's the Guild chaplain,' Krista breathed.

We listened intently. They were speaking very fast, but I heard them mention Uncle Hannes. After a moment Anneke let the door fall to and came hurrying across the room. Seizing her cloak from a nail, she threw it about her, saying soberly:

'There has been a bad fight at the Speypoorte between members of the Guild and some English merchants. The military were called in, and Hannes is gravely wounded. He is making his will. As I am about his last living relative, I must go to him.'

'I'll come with you,' Krista and I said together.

'No!' She was at the door, holding up her hand. 'It's too

dangerous for you both. The chaplain has two of the Guild archers with him as escort. Nicholas, stay out of sight. It would be madness for you to be seen abroad tonight. I must brave Maxi's curfew as it is. Make fast the door. Keep my house, Nicholas. I may not return till morning.'

And the next moment she was gone, the timbers shuddering as she dragged the door closed, and there was a deep silence. Krista's eyes were fixed on the floor.

'Poor Uncle Hannes,' I said, and meant it, thinking of the thin weaver's kindly worried ways and the debt I owed him for leading me to Krista. Whatever deity I had prayed to had demanded a sacrifice; they always do. The cat stretched and hunched nearer the stove. The room seemed cold; I shivered.

'I fear for your mother,' I said. My words vanished into the silence like stones in still water.

'All will be well,' Krista said softly. 'She is strong and brave and clever. And Nicholas . . .' She looked up, her face full of sweet light. 'She is a good woman, despite what she says.'

'I know that,' I said. Still I stood as if wounded, half against the wall, my body on fire, my mind in a rage of duality. Keep my house, Nicholas, she had said, not dishonour it. Yet here was I and here was Krista, my heart's longing, and I should be gone in the morning. I felt her take my hands, and started, as if she had plunged them in deep flame.

'Come,' she whispered, and somehow we were sitting side by side on the deep mounded bed, and she was smiling, pure and wise—for a moment I felt no more than a child, or as if she were the man and I the maiden. She lifted her hand to look at the betrothal ring, the ruby.

'I will buy you better than that,' I said in shame.

'No, Nicholas. It is a fair token, that belonged to someone beloved by you . . .'

'In God's mercy, Krista!' I said in a shaking voice. 'That love was evil—noisome, almost against nature. The man was evil. May he be consumed in the pit.' And I bent my head against her slight, soft breast, and felt her hands in my hair and heard her voice, no louder than a sigh.

'Oh no, Nicholas,' she said. 'Forgive him. Forget, Nicholas . . . forget.' She was stroking my hair and I drew her close and felt our

240

galloping heartbeats. 'Forget . . .' she went on saying it, like a charm or a psalm. Images raced in me. Once more the sight of the red-haired girl's body, terrible again, the mocking press of Finch's lips on mine, Josina's screams, the blood pouring from the rent in her whiteness . . . Edmund's dead body stretched between candles on our dining table . . . 'Forget,' said Krista's voice, forget, said the caress of her hands, wilder now . . . Sin, breathed a dying voice within me, mortal sin, the blending of unchurched flesh that is destined for worms and the pangs of Purgatory . . . 'Forget,' said my love, and my heart chanted 'forget,' and all voices and visions died as I suddenly raised my head and met Krista's mouth in a kiss that will, I swear, stay with me for ever.

We became a tree from the same root, and the tree burst forth in flower. We were two streams flowing to form one sweet river and the truth was in us. Sin or no sin, I would have done no other than I did that night with my dear, my only love.

Anneke returned shortly before I left for the Prinsenhof. The Werc Clocke was sounding. She was unharmed, and told us that Uncle Hannes had died at dawn and that the streets were quiet. She looked weary beside Krista, who had a glow like sunshine on honey. For myself, I needed to leave quickly before the real pain began, when it would be impossible. As I held Krista close, I vowed, whispering, that this was the last time we would be parted. I embraced Anneke, and we clung for an instant. Strangely, none of us wept.

Trying to think of nothing, I went quickly through the town, carrying Krista's last smile in my mind like a banner, feeling still the clasp of her hands upon me, breathing her remembered scent, feeling joy and sadness and a strangely mingled sense of loss and rebirth. I shall remember for ever that walk through the early morning of Bruges with the rising sun a gold line on the dark walls and the fountains rushing and the windmills turning and the canal green and soapy where women were washing their clothes. People looked curiously at me as I passed; it was not until I reached the Prinsenhof that I found my cheeks and collar wet with tears.

We quit the town around noon—I, and an armed guard of Austrian mercenaries sent by the Archduke Philip. My pouch

241

was full of messages from the Duchess, and from Philip and Maximilian; gold weighed my packs, and the Duchess's counsel to Plantagenet rang sombrely in my mind.

'Right beloved nephew, it is time for you to invade England,' she had said in her privy chamber, while her clerk scribbled and I knelt in waiting. She looked strained, attentuated, with a sad unease that showed how Tudor's devious policies had found their mark, just as surely as he had conquered Charles of Amboise. The trade embargo had defeated even the great Duchess.

'Tell him that the Holy Roman Emperor is fitting fourteen warships for his purpose,' she said. 'And he will send as many troops as he can muster in the time allowed. Tell him to leave Flanders'—her voice wavered—'and claim his inheritance by the sword.'

Then she snatched the pen from the clerk, appended some loving postscript, kissed the seal and made the sign of the Holy Cross over it. She turned away, looking suddenly, irrevocably old, and left the room.

As the hoofs of our cavalcade hit the road to Antwerp, half of me sat straight in the saddle with masked and silent face. The other half lay in that warm chamber, laughing and kissing, with enchanted outpourings of body and soul and heart; a ghost-man rode stolidly away. There would be jubilation among our followers that we were at long last for England, and I must share their joy, for the sake of loyalty. Yet all the time, the rhythms of hoof and heartbeat cried out in protest: Krista, Krista, Krista. My love.

Part 3
1496-1499

'I have been all things and it availed nothing.'
Emperor Septimius Severus: *History of Augustus,* X, 18.

'A year of disaster,' said Maurice Fitzdesmond, for the twentieth time to my knowledge. He was another one incapable of leaving the past alone. 'Worm-shotten, God-cursed disaster.'

We sat lapped in stone in the Great Hall of Stirling Castle. Outside, an icy mist bathed the brown bare forest and the crag on which the fortress stood. A Scottish January, cold as a nun's kiss, gripped the plain of Forth and made the Bannock Burn a wandering vein of ice. Loch Coulter would be a barren beauty, frozen grey, and the thought of it made me shiver. Maurice grinned sourly.

'Give thanks you're not in the Highlands. The Wild Ones can send cold down here, cold borne by bogles, like a wet winding-sheet.' He rubbed his arm, the one I had maimed·at tennis four years earlier. The cold made it ache, for the bone had grown back misshapen, and I still felt sorry.

'I'll wager a year's pay,' he said softly, glancing up towards the high table where the nobles were gathered, 'that none of us dreamed we'd end here—by the grace of King James the Fourth of Scotland. By now we thought we'd be claiming our rewards—and cheering at a coronation in Westminster!'

John Atwater, Mayor of Cork, dipped a slice of roast partridge in pepper sauce and munched it thoughtfully. Wiping his beard, he said: 'But we haven't ended here, by God. Isn't this just a new beginning?' He was sitting across the board from us with his son. A few places along there were the old faithful faces: Antoine, John Heron, Ned Skelton, Nick Ashley. The hall was packed. Since our arrival before Christmas there had been feasts like this, lasting for hours.

'We could use a new beginning, by Jesus,' said Maurice fiercely. He swivelled to face me. 'What possessed our boy,' he demanded, whispering, 'to return to Ireland, of all places . . .'

It was on our latest ill-starred trip to Ireland five months previously that we had met Maurice again, attached to the Earl of Desmond's party. Until then, I hadn't seen him since Amboise.

'And why, by all of Ursula's virgins, did he pick Waterford? He knew that Tudor's lackey, Poynings, is overlord there, like a lion

245

in a sheepfold now that Kildare's out of office—and that Waterford's the stronghold of the Butlers, Lancastrian to a man!' He twisted his head and spat behind him—he could still spit far and bring a hiss from the fire. 'He must have taken leave of his senses.'

I drank some fine imported Clary and looked towards the dais. Foolish and irrational or not—and who was I to say?—he was there, apparently unscathed by past events, none of the sheen rubbed off him, sitting cheek by jowl with his newest mentor and friend, the brilliant, brave and beautiful young Lowland monarch, James Stewart. And I thought: He's lucky to be alive. We all are. How many of us, supping in splendour, realize it?

'Now,' said Maurice, 'you can tell me all that passed after you left Flanders.' He looked at me hard with his bright black eyes.

'Last July,' I said, and stopped. I traced a pattern in spilled wine on the table with my knife. 'It was as you say. A disaster.'

'You were equipped for the invasion.' Maurice sounded like an inquisitor. 'The Holy Roman Emperor provided ships, troops . . . what went amiss?'

I glanced again at the high table, where the prince was laughing at the antics of English John, King James's favourite fool. I was glad he could still laugh. No one likes to witness their leader's spirit broken. Yet . . . there were a lot of men whose laughter was forever silenced. Whether it had been the prince's fault, or the most damnable ill fortune, I had not yet decided, nor did it seem likely I would.

'For his attack, the Duke of York chose Deal in Kent.' I looked down at the little wine-pool. I drew a pattern of canals flowing outwards and placed a crust of bread for a bridge.

'Nicholas!' Maurice rapped on the table.

'. . . Deal, in Kent. We had a fair crossing, even the Hanse fleet left us alone . . . I suppose they were too glad at the prospect of trading again with Flanders to waste time harrying us with their piracy.'

'The *Magnus Intercursus*,' said Atwater solemnly. 'All's well again between Archduke Philip and Henry Tudor since they signed the new trade agreement. The embargo's been lifted. It's an ill wind . . .'

The prince had been in high fettle, striding the deck, giving

246

unsolicited advice to the ship's master, inspecting his Austrian troops and his personal guard, windblown, merry, with an ebullience that made me uneasy, for he seemed like a bubble about to fly and burst. A rainbow appeared in sea-mist as we approached the shore and he hailed it as a good omen, reminding his followers of the Three Suns which had appeared to King Edward over thirty years ago before the conquest of Lancaster at Mortimers Cross. The men of Kent, he swore, would rise in our favour, and, our troops thus augmented, we would move on London.

'Who were his advisers, for God's love?' asked Maurice, slack-jawed with wonder.

'I think, these days, he is his own adviser,' I said slowly.

Almost before we dropped anchor, the men of Kent rose, but not in our favour. Armed, they came out of Deal in force, loyal to King Henry, who had anticipated our arrival through his agents. Those of us on the prince's ship did not even have time to disembark. Three hundred of an advance party who went ashore were instantly captured by the townsfolk led by the Mayor of Sandwich. An élite force wearing the Red Rose laid irons on men whom I had known well or slightly. Within half an hour they were bundled ingloriously into carts and taken for summary trial by the King's justices. While we, bewildered, still rode the tide, a few of Tudor's fighting carracks rounded the headland and blew three of Maximilian's warships half way to heaven.

We had been expected off the coast of Kent, and with months of hindsight it was easy to finger the source of Henry's information. Men like Thomas Astwood, who had lived so close to the prince, privy to his plans, however nebulous. Like hidden mites working within an oak rafter, such men destroyed the fabric of our hopes. True, Astwood had been arrested during Henry's swoop upon our principal allies, but we had learned since that, after interrogation, Astwood had been richly pardoned. It was even said that Astwood now had a post as jailer in the Tower, and was openly the King's creature, as he had ever been.

'So then our prince took to the high seas,' said Maurice. He looked very hard at the dais. 'To besiege Waterford!'

'It was only sense that he should save himself,' I said crossly. Along the table I heard Antoine give a little whispering growl.

247

He disliked the tone of the conversation, and would still die or kill for our master without a second thought.

'And Tudor hanged the captives,' Maurice said.

'He was totally without clemency.' I had not seen, but could imagine from the tales that reached us in flight, the three hundred lolling heads. Tudor had executed them at Tyburn and Wapping, and then had them taken to the coasts of Kent, Norfolk, Essex and Suffolk, stringing up the bodies in the sea breeze. While terns feasted from their eye-sockets, they danced a warning. Did the prince weep for these ordinary men, I wondered?

At the time of this catastrophe I had seen him visibly diminished. Standing on deck as the stiff wind packed mainsail and topgallant with frightened blasts, he could not hide his consternation and a kind of amazed, almost childlike disappointment. Why he should have been so certain that Kent would rally to his standard was never clear. (My own father was of Kent and always spoke of them as a wary, watchful people, with their heritage of coastal threat.) They had said, we learned later: 'This feigned Duke is but a painted image!' That alone would have made me weep, had I been him, but he did not. He mourned inwardly, I am sure. His spirits did not improve when two of Maximilian's ships, bearing a garrison of men and guns, suddenly broke away and, catching the easterly wind that we were fighting, vanished on the homeward horizon. More Flemish vessels left us before we reached the coast of Munster, where the prince hoped to join the Earl of Desmond in besieging Waterford, and where the gulls, like a snowstorm against the dark cliffs, wept for us on the wing.

Waterford was a lamentable choice: A town that had once welcomed the wretch Simnel. There was no question of the people opening to us. Fitzgerald, Earl of Desmond, had made this clear in correspondence with the prince while we were in Flanders. Desmond had, however, confided that he would uphold any attempt to secure the town. It would give glory to all concerned, he wrote, if the traditional enemies of his House, the Butlers, Earls of Ormond, could be shaken down. (There would be no aid from Kildare, who was now in the Tower—having presumably overstepped the Tudor mark again.) And somehow we had reckoned without Sir Edward Poynings, Deputy

Lieutenant of Ireland, and his tough, experienced, well-provisioned garrison of King's men behind the town walls.

'Ten days,' I said, above a gale of laughter raised by English John. The dwarf was cavorting up and down the hall wearing a horned mask; a courtier had recently been cuckolded and he was about to indicate which one. 'Ten days we sat it out in that narrow harbour—the mountains to the west—at times I thought those mountains were creeping in to trap us . . .'

'Eleven days, it was,' said Maurice. 'Butler country all round us and straight ahead as far as Connaught. Worm-ridden Butlers. We should have blown them all to kingdom come. If,' he said, with another hard look towards the high table, 'we'd had the artillery.'

'No fault of the prince's,' I said, watching Antoine who was red with rage, 'if the Flemish gunners decided to go home. Your kinsman Desmond didn't make too good a showing.'

'No,' said Maurice glumly. 'Most of his men were killed, when they started loosing the fire-balls.'

I saw again the parabolas of light hurtling from the walls as the bursting missiles found their mark, and heard the roar of timber and the screams of scorching men as a ball landed amidships. It was then that a blazing spar had missed me by an ell just before the stricken ship, aflame from bow to stern, slid hissing beneath the ocean. I had returned to life, singed and waterlogged, on the deck of the prince's ship, babbling of swans and bridges and green canals.

'Did you know,' said Maurice, 'that Waterford, for holding out, has now been granted an elegant new device by Tudor? Her arms now read: *Waterfordia intacta*—like some devil-damned old virgin!'

The fool capered by, stopping in front of our table. He tugged off the goat-mask and waggled his tongue at me. I decided he was prettier with the mask. He was a malapert little fellow, and most of the time his face was screwed with hatred. The only other professional jester I had known well was old Patch, full of elegance and true wit in his time. I thought John was unlucky and was glad when he went on to torment some other. Maurice was beckoning for more wine.

'At any event,' he said, with a swallow and sigh, 'you should thank my lord of Desmond, Nicholas. Without him, we'd not be here.'

He was right. By the time we weighed anchor of our two battered remaining ships and sailed desperately away from the Munster bay, we knew of at least one safe harbour. Desmond had assured us that the King of Scotland would welcome his Plantagenet cousin with deepest joy. During a midnight council, when the firing was suspended though we were being watched from the coast, secret plans came to light, overtures made, through Desmond, by our master while we were at Antwerp.

'His majesty awaits you,' the Earl, looking haggard from sleeplack and furious at failure, had said. 'Never was there a nobler prince. His kingdom is more glorious than France, kindlier than Flanders and braver than England. Get you to Stirling, and safety.' So saying, he had departed in stealth for one of his strongholds, beset on all side by Butlers and the creeping mountains.

Thus after many fear-tossed days at sea we came to Stirling, and it was more than Desmond had said it would be. The prince received a welcome that beggared any that had gone before. Hope and brightness sat on him again, as on a sick child after a night of healing sleep. The first thing he did was swear to King James on a relic of the True Cross that he would restore the prize which all Scots held dear—that border bone for the dogs of war—the peerless stronghold of Berwick.

He was now no longer known as Duke of York. It was declared in full public assembly by King James, as if there were to be no more waiting, that his dearest cousin was indeed King Richard the Fourth of England, and that together they would do great things.

James was about five-and-twenty years old when I knew him, a little older than our prince, and the comeliest man, let alone king, that ever I saw. His features were wonderful, he was supple and straight, a dancer and a warrior with the health and grace of both. He enhanced his figure with a sumptuous wardrobe and jewels, pearls from the Scottish lochs and gold and gems, some of which, he admitted with pride, had been plundered by his forefathers from the English. His dark red hair he wore to his shoulders and his eyes were the colour of a winter loch without its coldness, full of fun and kindliness but with a spark that showed he was no one's fool. His spoken French was a joy; he knew the weird dialects of the Highland clans and many other tongues. He lived life with passion. The smallest details enthralled him, whether they concerned war, wood-carving, leechwork, boatbuilding, minstrelsy. I have seen him shirtless, helping the masons on the new gatehouse at Stirling. I saw him doctor a man crushed by a cart, searching the wounds for splinters so skilfully that the patient never even sighed.

Some of his passions were obsessive. The ambition to regain Berwick never left him, nor did his longing to conquer the English borderlands, held fast for centuries by the great Nevilles, Dacres, and Herons. Nor was he without the especial demon of guilt which haunts all men of sensibility, for under his fine robes he wore an iron band, a token of penitence for the death of his father. James the Third had been murdered—slain by treachery by a false priest on the field of Sauchieburn, where the rebel clans of Campbell and 'Bell-the-Cat' Douglas had fought against the Crown. The young prince James was held as hostage by the rebels at the time and was unable to prevent his father's death, although at Sauchieburn the King had worn the magic sword of Robert the Bruce.

To James, all men were equal and this premise by its very nature made him beloved as a king. He relished music and ladies, food and wine. His one regret was that he could not, like his ancestor James I, write poetry, but he kept in his house a gentle old bard from Dunfermline named Robert Henryson. This poet seemed to take a fancy to me—perhaps, as he said, because I seemed so sad. He was serious himself, and shabby. He could have afforded to dress grandly, for the King was generous to all his loved ones, but Henryson gave much of his pay to the poor. Yet there was no heaviness about his piety, and his wit was kind. I remember sitting with him not long after our arrival, on a winter day full of iced sunshine, behind the topmost ramparts. It made one dizzy to look down the soaring crag; the great bare trees grouped round its foot seemed like bunches of twigs and the steps cut into the sheer rockface, a staircase for insects.

Looking down, one could see where the Scots lords and ladies

251

promenaded and guards came up and down the spiral to patrol the battlements. Westward was the plain of Forth, dotted with oak and sycamore, visible to the Fintry and Gargunnock Hills, fragile with snow and sun. The burn wormed icily through dark rocks, and north, the Teith and Allan sparkled to their confluence at the bridge where, Henryson told me, the great Wallace had routed the English two hundred years ago. Loch Coulter was a cold star to the south-west, hiding trout and pike and white powan-fish. Eastward, beside the grey bulk of Cambuskenneth Abbey, ran the Forth, broadening on its course to the North Sea and the harbour that had welcomed us. Range upon range of mountains vanished into infinity in the north, water and rolling hills on all other sides, and somewhere far to the west was the wild beauty of Loch Lomond with its sacred isles. It was a good, safe world to be in, but it was not the one I craved.

'See, Master Nicholas'—Robert Henryson pointed west over the plain—'there's where the Bruce put the English king to flight. They call it Gillies' Hill. The Bruce's army was but a third o' King Edward's force, but they routed them down by the stream.'

He put a thin gentle hand on my shoulder.

'There's a deal o' dolour about ye, laddie. Ye carry a black corbie on your shoulder.'

We resumed our conversation in French; otherwise I could scarcely understand him.

'Is it your noble prince you're worrying about?'

I shook my head. I was less anxious about him now than for some time. Plans were going ahead. Ever since he had sworn to James that he would restore Berwick as a token of goodwill against the time when his father King Edward had won it from Scotland, there had been constant councils of war. Nobles from all over the realm had been summoned to the Castle's Parliament Hall. Almost every day saw the royal cousins planning their campaigns in the King's Presence Chamber, under the carved oak roundels called the Stirling Heads.

'I know now that he will soon be victorious,' I said.

Henryson sighed deeply. 'These battles! These wars! Since the birth of man. My only wish is to live without dread.' From his pocket he took a very small squirrel, and began feeding it with hazelnuts.

'I am over seventy years old,' he said. 'And I have seen dire things. I trust no harm will befall your young king. Or mine,' he added soberly, and fixed his eyes on the hard, glittering hills.

'But I did not bring you up here to sour your spirits,' he said. In the nest of his long, inky fingers the squirrel fed fearlessly.

'Or to show me the kingdoms of the world,' I said lightly.

Small birds were darting above the ramparts and he looked up at them, tender eyes glazed by sunlight.

'The kingdoms of the world are nothing. Men bleed for them, and shed blood to own them. Then they wear their splendours like a fine gown or a silk mantle that is useless to keep out the chill of further ambition. For such power men sin against the Holy Ghost and yet trim their battle-standards in Jesu's Name, binding the maker of peace to the service of war. And for what? So that men shall own them master. Upon their own death, be it in bed or on the bloody field, they who long to be master of all shall find themselves masterless. For I believe that God will forsake the seekers of power, and abandon those who would earn their own kingdom by the thrusts of strife rather than seek contentment in the kingdom eternal.'

Seagulls, flying in from rough weather in the firth, began to swoop among the little birds. One, tiny and bright-breasted, came for refuge to Henryson's shoulder. No bird feared him; his gown was sometimes specked with white, like a statue's.

'A dog,' said Robert Henryson, 'will follow his master through famine and foul weather to the other end of the world. Even though the master be ill-favoured, ragged, wretched, low-born, dirty, drunken and a coward. Through hardship and pain, through sticks and stones and thorns, he will follow with his last breath. And if at the end there is a place by the master's feet, and a little glow of warmth from the master's nearness, that is enough. That is a dog's poor kingdom, and the love he knows with his one true master outshines the pomp and empty glories sought by man. So much one can learn from these—and from watching the larks fly high above the carrion crows of war.'

He looked at me quickly, his eyes edged with laughter.

'You will be sick of my sermons.'

'No,' I answered, 'but I would rather hear a poem.' He had

written a ballad of Robin and Marian, less famous than 'The Preaching of the Swallow,' but my favourite.

'Later,' he said. The little bird flicked away into air. We moved to look over on to the green, which was full of people coming and going about their business.

'Ants,' said the poet, with a frail smile, 'though neither so brave nor so industrious.'

I could see one man, dark-habited, tall, and something about the lean way he strolled, his back towards me, lit a memory. He passed through the arch leading to the King's Presence Chamber, and was gone.

Henryson said: 'One of your enemies?'

'I do not know.' And I turned to face him, saying suddenly, 'In my faith, Master Robert, the day is come when I no longer know my enemy.'

He said soberly: 'The Lord Chamberlain of England. He was your enemy?'

'Sir William Stanley,' I answered, not without some satisfaction, 'is dead and chested. But I still do not know whether he was for us or against us at the end.'

I lifted my face to the wheeling bird-filled basin of the sky and thought of the manifold conditions of man. Of Sir Robert Clifford—who had once undoubtedly saved my skin in the snowy forest and who had protested his love for Plantagenet with enough devotion to have foxed a Solomon. How, I wondered, could any man dissemble as he had done, and keep his soul intact? For Clifford had been all along, Henry Tudor's creature. It had been Clifford who had seduced Sir William Stanley into joining our cause. Then through the agency of a dozen covert clerks, a myriad ears at the keyhole, Clifford had contrived to trap the hapless Earl. Every word written or whispered, every step and gesture, had been relayed over the months to the King. And Clifford had given evidence at Stanley's trial.

Clifford had gained a royal pardon. And Stanley? He had been beheaded; cleanly, with no obscene tortures, as befitted his noble rank, for his brother, as husband to the Lady Margaret Beaufort, was stepfather to the King. The other conspirators had been dealt with according to Henry's whim. The Dean of St Paul's and two of his priests were imprisoned, some said for life. Seven chaplains from the royal household, who had been acting as go-betweens for our prince and his foreign allies, were sentenced to death, later to be reprieved; likewise several members of the Calais garrison who had followed Clifford on his treacherous path. Some noblemen were executed with Stanley, and included Sir Humphrey Stafford and Sir Robert Ratcliffe. Others, equally guilty, were pardoned. Whatever else he might be, Henry Tudor was never predictable.

'Here comes my king,' said Henryson, gazing fondly down. Through the archway emerged James, the sun striking copper from his bare head. Beside him walked his Italian physician, Damian, and a youth to whose shoulders were strapped a pair of enormous leather wings. The King and Damian were laughing merrily, trying to bring a smile to the glum youth's whey face. They moved towards the spiral stair.

'So we are flying again today,' murmured the poet.

'Or hoping to,' I said. I didn't envy the youth, for all that he wore safety harness. James was always searching for volunteers, and it was a long way down from the ramparts of Stirling.

'One day,' said Henryson, 'man will conquer the sky. One day, Spain's questor, Cristóbal Colón will return with gold from the Western Ind, for all that that will profit mankind. And one day, my king will have Berwick, please God.'

'I wish him well. May he win Berwick from the usurper Tudor. May he be as successful in his quest as Charles of Amboise was over Italy.'

'Yes,' said Henryson soberly, 'King Charles is the master there. He has overridden Italy like a comet. He has turned her inside out and packaged her up. And now the Holy League is formed. Spain, the Emperor Maximilian, the Pope, Venice, Milan—all have ceased their quarrelling and cling together against the new might of France. You should not call King Henry usurper, Nicholas.'

'That he is. Always will be.'

'Not in the world's eyes,' the poet said gently. 'He is supreme enough for the Holy League to seek his alliance . . . ah!'—he saw me staring downwards—'you have found a face.'

The tall dark-clad man had reappeared and was looking up. I recognized him now. The Sieur de Concressault, one-time captain of our bodyguard in Amboise.

255

'I don't understand,' I said.

Henryson smiled. 'Why is he here? I will tell you. Charles of France has sent him with one hundred thousand crowns in his purse. He comes to try to buy your master from mine as a gift for Henry Tudor. You see how France woos Henry too? No, Nicholas. No longer a usurper.'

He touched my arm. 'Do not fear. James will not waver. For all that the Auld Alliance between France and Scotland still has teeth, he would never concede such an act, even for Charles. Now, look over there. The man in velvet. The Spaniard.'

I squinted against sunlight at a white, priestly face, many jewels, rich Segovian velvet, a hand fingering a sword hilt. Elegant. Chill.

'Don Pedro de Ayala,' said the poet. 'He comes from Ferdinand and Isabella to offer a Spanish princess to King James. There! Two brides in the offing for my king, for Henry Tudor has put forward his daughter Margaret. For the usual price.'

'The person of Richard Plantagenet.'

Henryson stroked his squirrel's head. 'Have no fear,' he repeated. 'James will not budge. Let them all come, with their presents and their pledges. My king is a good man, despite the burnings of war within him, and his word is unassailable. Even though all the powers of Europe cajole him. The Emperor Maximilian . . .'

'What? Has he betrayed . . .'

'No, he is more subtle. He wishes Henry and your Richard to live somehow in amity. Do not forget he is named as King Richard's heir. He has declared he will not desert him. But he has offered to be the arbiter of a ten-year truce between them. Henry will never agree.'

Ladies appeared below, bright-gowned like a swirl of flowers, the unmarried maids of the court, and their hair streamed loose—blonde, black as the doom-bird Henryson said I wore on my shoulder—and one had hair like an autumn tree. She was taller than the rest, with a pearly, high-boned face. She felt the frost and laughed, pulling a white fur about her throat. And the others laughed with her, pointing upward to where the luckless bird-man had got his wings stuck on the staircase.

'Are they not lovesome?' said Henryson, following my eyes.

'They are all free, save one. You are a knight's son, Nicholas. You should woo one of them.'

'I am already deep in love.'

'So that is why you look so sad.' And he sighed, almost satisfied, as if he had chased and caught the last line of a poem.

There was the slap of soft shoes behind us on the battlements. The squirrel bristled in fear and shot up Henryson's sleeve. The stunted form and leering face of English John stood squatly between us and the sun. He was wearing strange headgear—a crown fashioned of hedgehog skins.

'Ho, poet!' he began. 'I have been talking with Master William Dunbar. Inspired, he is. His verses would charm the bare shift off a nun. And so young! I swear he's the best bard this court has ever seen.'

Having delivered this shaft, he stood back, head askew like some poisonous bird, but Henryson merely gave his old, mild smile.

'True, John,' he said. 'As I wane, so must he wax. What have you on your head?'

The fool began to mince and caper. 'I'm a king!' he sang. 'A hedge-king. My realm is the briar, my court the marsh, and my subjects the foxes. Prince Perkin wants you,' he said to me. I felt my face begin to burn. I was so angry that I took a turn along the ramparts to cool down, and he followed close, mimicking my step, with an apple on his dagger to ape the royal sceptre. I turned and lunged to swat him but he danced out of the way.

'Hurry!' he cried. 'Prince Perkin wants a clean pair of breeches for his wedding-day! Your pardon! *King* Perkin!'

'Sweet God!' I said to Henryson. 'Can he speak treason as he likes?'

'I can,' said English John. 'Wit is not treason, but my shield. I am Lord of Misrule and master of the dark thought. Where other men mutter, so I sing. Touch me not,' he said, as I advanced on him. I had a blind desire to tip him over the battlements. I think I frightened him, for he ran, clasping his spiky crown gingerly with both hands, and disappeared down the stairs.

'I thought we had done with all that,' I said. 'This mal-mouthing of King Richard.'

'Pay no heed. Go down to your master. It seems that the new

257

wedding clothes are ready. Ah, did they not tell you? No matter. It will be announced tonight at assembly. The royal betrothal. Your King Richard and Lady Katherine Gordon.'

I felt the crippling prick of envy. And Henryson, his soul tuned to the music of man, read my melancholy.

'Be patient. Your day will come. But the prince's time is now. Katherine Gordon, Lord Huntly's daughter, is James's kins-woman. One of the most high born in the land. She descends from Sir Alexander Seton on one side and John Hay, the Laird of Tillibody, on the other. Her great-grandsire was Sir William Hay of Erroll, Constable of Scotland. And before that she comes from Archibald, Earl of Douglas, whose wife was a Moray of Bothwell. And through Henry, Earl of Orkney, and Egidia, daughter of Sir William Douglas, she is descended from King Robert the Second. She is a little older than your prince, but truly royal.'

He pointed with his veined, inky hand to the group of ladies. I saw now how they all tripped attendance on the tall, russet-haired maiden, holding her missal, arranging her fur, their gaiety tempered by deference.

'We call her the White Rose of Scotland,' said the poet. 'Very soon your White Rose and ours shall flower on one stem.'

She leaned against a pillar, one hand caressing a great dog that fawned by her. Her delicate face, raised to the frosty sun, was unflawed as if she had been kept silk-wrapped from her birth. One gold-lit tendril strayed against the pure coin of her cheek. Her small full mouth reminded me of Krista's, and for the first time in Scotland, my vision was fogged with pain.

'It is the greatest honour James can bestow at this time,' Henryson said. 'And the only price is Berwick, which your lord will help him win.'

The Wild Ones came riding over the westerly hill, a small company, dark against the harsh silver bulk of Ben Lomond. A party of us were flying hawks on the plain of Teith, its flat heathery belly starred by the navel of Loch Menteith and with the hills of Ochil and Fintry like encircling arms. We were away from the trees, the better to sport, but at the lakeside, fiercely leafless, they crowded: giant ash, oak and sycamore—elms too, full of sapwood for the longbow's making, and a spinney of rowans clustered with their devil-warning shiver at the lake's far end beside phalanxes of pine. Behind us stood the twin towers of Doune Castle and high on a bluff the haunted Priory of Inchamore, which always looked ghostly, however bright the sun.

King James shaded his sight against the white sky and studied the approaching horsemen. He called to his falconer, who whistled and whirled the lure. The royal gyrfalcon fell languidly through the air, her round eye a black carnelian, and pounced on the lure, digging in her talons. The King held out his buckskin fist and she flew to him. 'Ah, she loves me,' he said, expertly hooding her, closing the hoodbraces with his teeth and free hand. The hood was crested with a bright cock's hackle and sewn with pearls. The bird mantled gracefully with leg and wing, warbled her tail feathers in a cross on her back and sat, douce, on his glove. The riders came nearer, their hoofbeats taboring on the frost-rimed heather like the faint crackle of fire. Their beards were thick as the pelts of their half-wild horses. I had heard the saying *'fier comme un Ecossais'* and proud they were, kings in their own right, owning a fortune in huge, long-coated cattle and horned sheep and the horses which were broken within a day of capture in the mountains. They were quarrelsome, battle-scarred and mythical; today they wore saffron shirts and dark hunting plaids and were tooled with bows, knives and halberds, but the leader, who looked as big as a bearded oak, was grinning; they came in peace. James placed his hawk on the cadger's frame and spurred forward to meet them. The bearded man slid from his mount and, striding, roared a greeting.

'I see you, Jamie the Steward. Are we well come?'

James, likewise dismounted, walked swiftly forward, his red hair lifting on a small breeze.

'I see you, Chief of Clan Donald. Are you for the sport?'

'We heard there was to be a wedding!' Ben Lomond seemed to shiver from the booming voice. I stole a look at Don Pedro de Ayala, who sat on his horse nearby. He was trim and jewelled in velvet, and carried a fine passage-hawk on the right wrist in the Oriental manner. He was watching James, now having his forearm vigorously shaken by the MacDonald, and I thought his eyes would spring from his head at sight of this barbarian.

'They've all come,' I heard the falconer say to someone behind me. 'I spy a Campbell or two, and the Home chieftain. And there's Bell-the-Cat Douglas's son.'

'Murderer's son,' said his companion forcefully.

'Ay, but this one's a cleric. Did ye not know Gavin Douglas has sworn fealty to our Jamie? He swears to atone for his father's wrong. He'll be Bishop of Dunkeld, they say.'

Gradually riders from our party milled forward to talk with the Highlanders. James was speaking to the MacDonald in his own tortuous tongue; at one point they embraced. Close by stood the sober-faced William Elphinstone who had been instrumental in bringing some sort of peace between the warring clansmen and the High Steward of Scotland. There was laughter. It seemed as if the tragedy of Sauchieburn had been relegated to the bloody past. Eyes stared over curiously towards Plantagenet, face pink from the weather, gold hair bright under his brocade cap. He wore on his wrist a goshawk tercel, a small jewel of a bird, given him by the King. Not far away, sidesaddle on a white palfrey, was his betrothed, with a young boy who carried her sparrowhawk. I knew the boy's rich little face—he was Alexander, one of James's two beloved bastard sons.

While the incomprehensible courtesies went on and on, enough to make one believe that never more would the clans rebel, I surveyed the company. Near to the Lady Katherine Gordon was her father, the Earl of Huntly, stern and princely, threads of russet still in his grizzled beard, and the Earls of Atholl, Strathearn, Mar and Gordon. There was the genial Prior of Anselm, sporting a lively kestrel and gossiping with the Earl of Crawford. English John, astride a pony, gentling a merlin (the only creature he showed kindness to). And Patrick Hepburn, the arrogant young Earl of Bothwell, who, unlike many others, was showing little interest in the Highlanders. He was in close conversation with a newly arrived English envoy, a weasely man named Wyatt.

Gold gleamed on Bothwell's plaid, and few at court trusted him. Black brows met over his bright eyes, and his laugh rang harshly, while the envoy, who had come to press further the Tudor offer of a bride for King James, looked fidgety and anxious. Lady Katherine suddenly pricked her horse forward, nearly knocking Wyatt into the heather, but it was he who stammered an apology. The lady tossed her red hair and surged on, while Alexander trotted after with her sparrowhawk. Her fair face was set in boredom, on the edge of temper.

Antoine de la Force moved beside me.

'Those two,' he murmured. 'That Bothwell lord. I smell mischief. He's a proven traitor. And Wyatt—he's after our prince. De Concressault wants to buy him, but Wyatt wants to steal him away. Nicholas, we're still beset.'

'None can harm us here,' I comforted him, but I respected his fear; he had been proved right about Astwood. Maurice Fitz-desmond strolled up, looking carefree.

'I,' he said softly, 'have just stolen such a sweet kiss from one of Lady Katherine's women, may God forgive me. I got my eye on her eye and before she knew . . . there.' He pointed to the grove of rowans. 'By the Mass, these Scottish dames. They rouse my rod.'

'You think of little else,' I said.

'We're traitor-watching,' said Antoine.

'Oh! Bothwell. Yes, but that was last year he went against James, and the King pardoned him.' His eyes swivelled. 'Now *that* one'—he nodded towards English John, still stroking his merlin—'I'd trust him no further than you can draw a bowstring, Nicholas, and that's not far.'

'He's just a little tick,' said Antoine. 'He wishes harm to all, so he's harmless.'

'Is he though? Well, last night I heard him asking someone how large a bodyguard our prince was likely to carry when he goes on his honeymonth, and when, and where . . .' He spat, a token that he was serious.

The knot of Highlanders and courtiers began to disperse with noisy amiability. Campbells, Homes and MacDonalds dug big heels into their horses' woolly sides and the clansmen began to stream eastward along the lakeside, shouting and skirling like dangerous schoolboys. Lady Katherine and her father trotted away to fly their hawks in peace; the Earl of Atholl sent in half a dozen lean talbots to flush out partridge from the sparse cover. Soon there would be an end to hawking; it was already late for the game. King James mounted and wheeled back to us, teeth lit in a dancing smile.

'Well, my sweet cousin,' he cried to Plantagenet who stood

261

beside the Spanish ambassador. De Ayala was now stroking his crucifix, as if to thank God he had been unmolested by the Wild Ones.

'The chiefs wish to attend your wedding,' James continued. 'I bade them welcome. God knows, they should behave themselves after noble Elphinstone's work. And Gavin Douglas is man enough to keep them in order for a while. God's breath, but I can admire the MacDonald, for all his sinfulness. I swear there's almost love between us at times. They seemed much taken with you, my lord king,' and Plantagenet stiffened with pride. Today he was full of pomp, there on the moors in his fine clothes and jewelled bonnet. Even his stirrups were made of gold. When he replied it was almost a proclamation; he raised his voice so that many standing about could hear him.

'Gracious cousin, I am glad to hear it,' he said. 'The truth of my cause is so manifest that even your wild kinfolk must believe in it. Did it not move the most Christian King Charles of France lovingly to assist me?'

I glanced at de Concressault. His skull-face was impassive; God knows what thoughts he had.

'And my glorious Aunt the Duchess of Burgundy likewise,' he said. 'It seems'—he raised his face to the bird-littered sky—'that God above, for the good of this whole island and the knitting of these two kingdoms of England and Scotland in straight concord, has reserved the placing of me on the mighty throne of England for the arms and succour of your Grace.'

'Ay! it's a holy thing,' said James, and set to stroking his horse's sleek neck with a jewelled hand, as if to rub in the words for posterity. Plantagenet sat up straight and glowing. De Concressault fixed his hollow eye on a little wooded island in the lake. De Ayala polished his crucifix savagely, and, with a sudden crippling weariness that amazed me I thought: What a masquerade it is. Always words in place of deeds, and the chink of coin instead of the clash of steel, and the continual swearing on the right to a name, a title, a cause. Lord Huntly's falconer swung his lure and the trained bird stooped to clutch and rend a haunch of rabbit. On the hood of James's falcon the pearls glowed with just the same milky flowerlike sheen as Krista's breasts . . . small, perfect and lustrous against my hot face, again I felt her arms,

262

heard her broken love-cry as she received my life . . . Plantagenet was beckoning to me to bring him his wolfskin mantle. He turned, still proud, to face de Ayala and said:

'And, my good lord, I have no doubt that our dearest coz the King of Spain will aid us.'

The Christ on de Ayala's cross had ruby wounds. As if to look deep into them, the Spaniard's head bent low. James's lips twitched; he slid fingers over his mouth to hide a smile. The next moment he was sober.

'There's a fine heron over by the lake, my lord. That is a beautiful hawk of yours. Will you let her take the air?' He addressed de Ayala in lisping Castilian.

'Mine is a poor bird beside the *halcon girifalte* of your Grace,' said de Ayala politely. He rode away towards the water, striking open the falcon's hood and calling servants to bring up the dogs. James began softly to laugh, shaking his head. He moved close to Plantagenet and flung an arm about his shoulder.

'Sweet cousin, sweet Dickon!' he said, laughing all the time. 'Your bonny hopefulness gave him pause. May he cool his thoughts in the lake. Alas,' still smiling, 'I've seen a certain letter, received by him not a week ago from your dearest coz in Spain.' He sighed. 'It was not meant for our eyes, so I recall it well. It said: "We have no other purpose in our negotiations than to win over the King of Scots and make him friends with the King of England, so that he may no longer show favour to *him of York*"!'

He watched my lord, laughed again, and clapped his shoulder hard, so that the goshawk on Plantagenet's fist stirred and bated. 'Ah, pay no heed!' he cried. 'I love to watch this Spaniard. He's like an auld hen on a clutch of rolling eggs—knows not whither to shift. He's promised me a Spanish princess to wife, which is gey clever of him, as Catalina is already half-betrothed to Arthur Tudor, and Philip, the Archduke Maximilian's son, is to have Juana, who's so holy they say she's a little fey with it. Life's a great game. Come! let's sport and lose our long faces.' He looked at me. 'Master Archer!' (He knew my name; he knew everyone.) 'You've a pretty shortwing there. Let's see her fly.'

I looked round. A long way off was the burnished hair and white horse of Lady Katherine. De Ayala was plunging his mount about in the reeds looking for heron, while most of the Scottish

263

lords were on the far side of the lake, watching a herd of red running deer. Making towards the copse of rowans were three distant figures, the puniest English John. The field was clear, so I took my bird, Ela, from the falconer's cadge and she seized my glove with her razor pounces. She was an eyas goshawk; I scarcely found time to handle her and was afraid she would become lure-bound. I had been training her on the creance and she knew me, for I was careful always to wear the same clothes. I opened the hood and slipped her, then called her into the wind. She came to the lure as soon as I swung it, a free-falling jewel against the metal sky with the double discord of bells on her jesses singing her down. In the dead leaves near the spinney there was movement and the hoarse bark of pheasant. The dogs sped towards the spot, and I rode forward and slipped my bird again.

The pheasant burst upwards like a fire-ball and raced through the air, making straight for cover. My hawk rose and streamed after the quarry, flying fast to the thin music of bells and the clatter of wings. Small, delicate and deadly, she stretched her whole body in the chase as the pheasant gained on the trees. Soon they were two black smudges high above the spinney, then, as the prey dived, so did Ela, hitting the pheasant with a fierce ruff which left feathers floating. Both birds fell out of sight.

I set off to find her. Skirting the copse I listened hard, guessing that the undergrowth and Ela's mantling feathers as she crouched on her prey had silenced her bells. The hounds galloped off into a thicket. I sat listening, and heard the voice of English John, raised in a whine.

'Well, my lord, and what's it worth? I risk my king's love, well you know.'

'You'll have your blood money, you greedy little toad,' said Bothwell gruffly. 'If I plant my men on the edge of Falkland Forest, behind Meggie's Rock. Twenty-five to guard him, you say? Well, I can raise twice that number. Master Wyatt?'

'Twenty good men, loyal to King Henry,' said Wyatt, sounding nervous. 'I'll need to absent myself from the wedding feast if I'm to wait at Falkland to aid you.'

'They will depart round noon,' said English John. 'Och!' he mocked. 'A short honeymonth for that faker, I fear.' He followed this with a jest so foul that I felt my ears burn.

'His Grace will be pleased when we bring the pretender to London in chains,' said Wyatt.

'May we all be rewarded then,' said Bothwell, and laughed, as if he were in this only for the sport, which he probably was. Then a dog barked, and came crashing out of the thicket with the pheasant in its mouth. I backed my horse quietly on to the plain and called Ela; after a moment she came sweetly to my glove. She mantled and bated for balance as I rode as fast as I dared, back to King James and my master.

The nuptial day was pale with frost. I had risen at four, fraught with a thousand duties. Maurice, Antoine and I were assisting the royal bridegroom into his bath when a knock came at the chamber door. It opened on a panting boy in a plaid.

He handed me a note. 'King James requires his Grace's answer,' he said, and rolled up his eyes as if he too were beset by haste. I moved over to the cloud of scented steam wherein sat Plantagenet. 'Read it, Nicholas,' he said. The note was terse. 'Right beloved cousin, what shall we do with Lord Bothwell? Say the word, and he shall hang.'

Bothwell had been arrested within an hour of my overhearing the treason. I had had to give summary evidence, squirming and sweating before the peers in the King's Presence Chamber, but it was not so bad, for English John, like the craven little flea he was, broke into song almost before I had done, begging mercy and implicating the others. He, Bothwell and Wyatt were charged with attempting feloniously to abduct King Richard of England. For days following, Bothwell had lain in the dungeon below the fortress, and John had been locked into a little round tower within the walls. Wyatt was still at large but his servants had been stripped of their arms. The English envoy, white as a winter stoat, crept about, ostracized by the courtiers. What with the wedding preparations, I had almost forgotten about them all.

My lord said: 'Ah,' and squeezed a sponge of water over his head. Then he told me: 'Write,' and dictated a short message. 'Bear the answer yourself, Nicholas. I would hear his Grace's comment.' So I followed the boy, skimming down the cold twisting stair where torches were burning down to dawn embers. Chaos filled the courtyard, noise and odours and folk hurrying, brazier flames leaping. Men led ponies loaded with wedding gifts, fowls and dogs ran about. I almost tripped an old laundress carrying lacy linen for the marriage bed. Whole oxen and pigs were roasting in the kitchens. The hungry scent of new bread from the bakehouse was mixed with the smoky odour of dried flowers for the festive floor, the smell of dung and horses as the gates opened to admit a riding party. Robed friars and clerics got in everyone's way. Babies bawled, hoofs hit the cobbles, and in the armoury, steel hammered, as James's preparations for his war with England went on, wedding or no wedding.

The boy rushed me into the cavernous stables. From the corner where the grooms slept came an awful groaning, and King James's voice, soft as a nurse. Still in his nightshirt, he was bending over a man who lay on a pallet, leg-bone twisted hideously. James's young sons stood by, Alexander holding up a sconce of fir-candles and little James soaking a length of flax in a steaming pot.

'More light, Sandy,' said the king. 'Bring over the cruisie.' And as the child fetched a twittering oil-lamp: 'Hush, Tam. Be still.' He looked up as my shadow fell. 'Bonewort,' he said. 'A healing plant, mixed with white of egg, it will shape back the bone. Now, Tam.' The man gave one gasp. 'Wet the bandage well, my son.' As he worked the yellow light fell on his forearms, so slender, yet he lifted the man as if he were a baby. He wound the swaddling tight, poured on the hardening mixture. 'Rest now, man.' The groom looked up at him with dog-eyes.

'It was well done,' he told the boys. He looked at me. 'Ah! the sharp-eared one, you did good service, Nicholas.' He looked fondly at his sons. 'Are they not fine boys? Soon they shall go to Padua to be schooled as princes.'

I wondered who their mother was. She could be any of the fair ones who shared James's plate at the revels and his couch at night. I knew that de Ayala disapproved, finding James most holy in all other things.

'Have you sons, Nicholas?' he asked me idly. I shook my head. He said curiously: 'Do you like my country?' and I said with truth, 'Yes, your Majesty, almost as much as—'

'As France? Or as Flanders? Yes'—he peered acutely at me. 'I can tell you love Flanders. Your eyes changed when I spoke the name,' and he spoke in perfect Flemish, making me happy and sad.

'Now,' he said briskly. 'Your lord's answer,' and I put the message in his hands. He frowned. 'Set Bothwell free,' said the note. 'On this day, let all men be happy.'

He looked at me like a falcon at siege, his fine face suddenly armoured. 'This is mercy indeed,' he said.

I shuffled my feet. Suddenly he laughed. 'So be it,' he said. 'As for English John'—and he gave a great guffaw—'I'd skelp him myself, but he shall run the gauntlet of all the nobles he's offended in the past. That should blacken his arse for a month. But Master Wyatt . . .' Here he paused. The guest-law still obtained. 'I fancy he will soon be leaving for home.'

As I was departing he said: 'Tell me, is your lord always so merciful?' I just made a noise, having no answer. Then he said, very soberly: 'Mercy is of God and a thing of honour. Yet there are times . . .' and in the cruisie's baleful light his face was suddenly dread, implacable. 'There are times when mercy must be put to sleep for honour's sake. Your master should remember that.'

I did not tell him what the King had said. Neither time nor place seemed appropriate, and I had the feeling that James had been expressing thoughts unmeant for passage. It was such a day that I would not for the world have dispelled his joyful humour. The weather shone on bride and groom—it was almost like spring with the sun warming the shivering sky above the chapel of Holy Rood.

This is the day on which I would remember him best, and how my heart and mind *must* remember him, as if there were no more to come. Only the image of him in bridal rig, like one of the young kings in the Bible. How I wish that he could stay, spinning on so for ever in the eternity of my mind, in his tunic of purple cloth of Damascus. We clothed him in this (rather, James's treasury did, along with a yearly pension of £112), and over it went a robe of cloth of gold and ivory Milanese brocade. Jewels hung like tears from the brim of his velvet bonnet. We put on him buckhide slippers, silken hose. We brushed and curled his hair and held up the mirror. He stood tall, slender, for the sport of the Scottish moors had dispersed the paunch he earned at Margaret's court. In a face pink and gold as a child's, the blind eye was sleepily benign. As he studied his likeness he gave a long satisfied sigh, not of conceit, but saluting life's goodness. That is how I would, if I could, remember him.

I was alone with him for a moment before we descended to the chapel. He went to the coffer where he kept his privy purse, saying: 'Once more, your sharp wits have saved me. This time you cannot refuse a reward.'

I did not want his money; I was fairly well purveyed, for I had saved my wages and there were the legacies. He held out gold, and looked exasperated when I shook my head.

'Come, take it. I shall be late for my wedding.'

When he saw I was in earnest, he threw the coins back in the box and stared at me.

'There must be some favour. Tell me, Nicholas. Do not make me an ingrate.'

This was my chance to ask him for leave to marry Krista, and I almost took it, when in my mind came the bell-voice of Anneke. Sometimes I thought that Anneke lived within my head. *When you crown your prince, then you shall claim what you desire. Be loyal to your lord.* It was like an edict. So I would not ask—yet I would feel better if a little door were opened to me.

'Sire, one thing.'

'Name it.'

'May I have your Grace's word that, if and when the time should come, you will release me from your service?'

'You have my word,' he said at once. 'Aren't you happy here?'

'Yes. But there is a place I would rather be.'

'And I,' he said abruptly. 'Our rightful place. The Palace of Westminster.' Then, smiling: 'Come. Wish me joy.'

We started down the stairs. 'May heaven bless you, Sire,' I said. 'And your beautiful bride.'

He half turned, gleaming with pleasure. 'Ah, she is fair!' he whispered. 'Like a lily. She makes all others look like barnyard weeds. Her beauty frightens me.'

In the chapel of the Holy Rood, in a gown of silver and azure with her long red hair crowned by pearls, she was the haughtiest lady I had ever seen. Nearly as tall as her bridegroom, she towered over the genial Bishop of St Andrews who celebrated the Mass. Everything about her spoke of greatness. Watching from the back, I saw them kneel while the silvery Sanctus bell merged with the voices of James's great Italian choir like a skin-shivering wash of cold wine, and through the ecstasy I wondered whether Katherine had ever heard the rumours of her prince's base birth. And if so, would she defend him, as Margaret of Burgundy and all who loved him had?

The revel lasted all day and half the night. I tasted, for the first and last time, the *uisge beatha*, a terrible drink tasting of fire, malt and bog-water—brought as a contribution to the jollity by the Wild Ones. It was truly a war-weapon, for those who over-indulged fell as if poled into the hearth. The Highlanders behaved well. They were armed only with the black-and-silver *sgian dubh*, and left their broadswords at the gate. They looked like emperors in their intricately belted plaids, eagles' feathers in their headgear, silver buttons and buckles. James's nobles mingled with them in amity, but the King, wearing the red and green tartan of his House, maintained a watch on all, still managing to pleasure himself. We ate and drank and danced, and matched toasts in looted goblets of English gold, while the bride sat lily-proud, with high cheeks that lent her disdain whether she felt it or not.

A pack of courtiers bellowing bridal jests escorted the prince to bed, jesters banging bladders and someone playing a lusty little fife-tune. There Lady Katherine lay, sheets drawn up to her chin, in a bed smelling of heather-flowers and blessed by the Bishop. All her hauteur was gone; she looked small, soft, like a little girl.

We closed the door and took up our pallets outside. By now I was deathly tired, drunk, and a bit melancholy. Tomorrow we were to leave for the Forest of Falkland and the hunting lodge of French design. After that there was talk of golf at St Andrews, for the Bishop was enamoured of that unlawful game. It was all pleasure and play, I thought.

I was glad that the oak door was thick enough to drown their whispers, as I thought of my own wedding-night, the one un-hallowed by bishop or priest. Then I decided the only way to keep my spirits up was to think of war, as James did. The invasion of England would come soon; he could assemble 120,000 men at muster within thirty days, and he was building up a navy. I thought of King James until the cock chanted and the darkness greyed; of the grim way he spoke of putting mercy to sleep, and unease grew in me that was nothing to do with my own ache of envy on another's wedding-night.

> *To my little wife:*
> My dearest and best beloved, I write from Ladykirk, a few miles inside the border, the sixteenth of September in the eleventh year of King Henry's reign, to give you news of me, not least that my heart is still yours for ever.

I shivered, moving nearer to the camp fire. The red flames wavered suddenly and I blinked, blotting the letter with a tear, which like some arrogant guest, forced itself upwards from the deep longing within me. I wanted her so much that it was a torture, especially after a long, indolent, russet summer among the Scottish moors. I called her my little wife because it seemed her just and honourable title. Sweet God! I had not heard from her for months, nor had I been able to send word, until today.

> I write now through the kind offices of Master Henryson, a worthy master-poet. His cousin, a friar, is here in camp to pray for our enterprise. He will leave for Bruges on his own affairs before our battle is joined, so he can take my letter. Such kindness comes from God.

All round men were sleeping on the ground, rolled in plaid or snuggled into straw. Directly behind me was my lord's pavilion. Lamplight glowed through the tent's walls and I could hear his murmuring voice. King James was with him, discussing plans for this long-awaited assault on England. Lady Katherine had been left behind at Stirling. Whether my lord were glad or sorry I had no idea, for I could not judge how their marriage went. I had never spoken to her, for her gaze was too high to encompass any of the men and women who served her and her lord. All I knew was that her beauty besotted him, and he lay with her almost nightly. I dipped my quill again, balancing the inkhorn on my shield.

> We have been on the march for days gathering troops, some from Edinburgh, a great city with a castle built on a mountain. We marched east along the line of the firth and then down over the Lammermuir Hills to the castle of Duns.

The Lammermuirs—a sweeping beauty, the heather a tapestry of sunset flame, saffron and green, on the turn for winter, echoing the colours of the garment I held so dear.

And I still wear the cloak, heart's joy, a sorry substitute for being in your arms.

On the rising hills there had been sheep without number—'thick as lice on a harlot's bosom,' Maurice remarked rudely. And wild plum trees, and game abounding, pine-marten, red deer and mountain cat. As the thickening column of men marched, birds burst from the undergrowth; grouse, partridge and pheasant. Osprey clustered in trees and on mountain ledges, hares fled. Heron waded in the Blackadder river. But I had hacked Ela back into the wild a week earlier; the time for sport was over. When we had passed through thick forests to Haddington, the Lamp of Lothian shone like a funeral candle from St Mary's church, and that little glow had wakened my fancy. Would it soon be my time to die in battle? To fulfil the pledge I had made for Edmund, for Margetta? For a moment I felt Margetta's cold rageful spirit and dutifully I prayed for her. But I felt I would not die. For I bore two talismans—Krista's cloak, and my father's sword.

Henryson, dolorous at the thought of slaughter, had come to wish me Godspeed before we left Stirling. He looked sternly at the sword I was polishing with goosegrease and soft hide. I had cherished it over the years in exile and now I would carry it as one of the prince's household bodyguard.

'Soon, you'll be wiping some wretch's liver off that blade,' he said dourly.

'I've yet to use it.' It gleamed with dull mystery, the hilt was whorled with Milanese engraving. Henryson sat down on a chest and put his chin in his hands.

'I fear for my king,' he said. 'I fear for my Jamie. He is so rash. He should be called le Téméraire, like Charles of Burgundy. The Spaniard remarked the other day that James leads a charge before his army is ready, and it's the truth.' His eyes grew distant, as if, like many of his race, he scried the future: the bloody defeat at Flodden Field, when English troops under the Earl of Surrey would strike down the beloved king.

271

A little later he embraced me in farewell and told me about the friar bound for Flanders. My joy at this effaced the rest of the conversation. Only now did I recall his saying something that puzzled me.

'My king puts your Plantagenet to the test this month. That is why you march with such a small army. Only when your lord proves himself will James summon all the men he can muster. Meantime I pray God he does nothing foolish.'

Sitting with a cold wind blowing down from the firth and love-words poised on my drying pen, I knew that our army could number no more than two thousand. Of the fifteen Scottish earls and thirty-five barons who had attended the wedding there were but a handful. Many of them had come this way before—they were reivers, just as the English earls the other side of the border were reivers. Men said that the border was stained with the blood of generations, that the juice of the wild plum tree was like blood. On the outskirts of Ladykirk lay Upsettlington, the town where Edward I had extracted the promise of vassaldom from the Scots. And Ladykirk was named so by James, who had built the church there in thanks for a narrow escape from the English, when he had nearly been drowned at the ford nearby.

Our company included nobles such as Lords Huntly and Gordon, the Earl of Crawford. An undisciplined flank of borderers under Lord Home. Some experienced Flemish gunners sent by the Duchess Margaret, and sixty Austrian men at arms; Scotland's master gunner, Robert Borthwick. A few bonnet chieftains come down from the Highlands for the sport, fearsomely armed. Stewart of Lennox and Campbell of Argyll, each with a hundred men. Gavin Douglas had come with his priests, and the Bishop of St Andrews in full military rig. The remainder of the force was made up of men like myself, esquires and new-made knights, professional mercenaries and men from the Edinburgh garrison, together with any border yeomen who might join us as we neared the appointed time. There was a good arsenal—spears, axes, bills, French crossbows and guns—small serpentines, and a few trebuchets and mangonels. Sleeping on the other side of the fire I could see archers with quivers stacked full and longbows, and fire-arrows, their heads wrapped in pitch-soaked tow. The Wild Ones (who camped apart and could be

272

heard laughing raucously) favoured the *claidheamh mor*—five feet of two-handed steel which they waved as easily as if it were a needle.

The fire was sinking and I fed it so I could see to write more. Just then the pavilion flap parted and one of James's deerhounds padded through with a big bone in its mouth. Now I could hear the voices clearly. They were talking about the English border lords.

'So, cousin,' said King James, 'you are sure you can summon your kinsmen to our banner? You can initiate aid from the English lords to ride south with us against Henry Tudor?'

'Yes, I am sure,' said Plantagenet loudly. I heard James cough, and wine being swallowed, then the rasp of metal as if a gauntlet were being drawn thoughtfully across a breastplate.

'Much, if not all, depends on this,' said James.

'They will rise up and meet us,' said my prince firmly. 'They will ride with us into England. Your Majesty must know how gladly they would welcome riddance from Tudor. They will support me as their rightful king and you as my friend and ally. There will be peace in England, and peace between Scotland and England. Love and amity will rule and it is I who will bring it about.'

'You've sent your emissaries over the border?'

'Ay. All day they have ridden out to parley with the lords.'

James said: 'I trust your wisdom, Dickon. But don't forget. I've tangled with these English reivers, as did my father, God rest him. Jesus knows I'd like to see your dreams fleshed, and my own, but I've found the borderers stubborn. Bloody of mind and intent . . .'

'They'll aid me,' said Plantagenet. 'Scrope, Dacre, Heron . . .'

James said softly: 'They are all most powerful, cunning, many-coated men. More so perhaps than the Percys, the Nevilles . . .'

'They will come to our standard,' said Prince Richard. 'They have had my message, and tomorrow, all shall hear my proclamation.'

'I wish you good fortune then,' said James suddenly. 'And good night.' He came from the pavilion, whistling for his hound. I put my head down on my knees and feigned sleep until he passed. It was very late, and I had to finish my letter before the

273

little friar, waiting to ride back to the Firth of Forth, took ship for the loved land.

> I still wear the green willow round my hat, (I finished sadly). My friend the poet told me of this custom. It means true love for one far away. My heart aches for you, my soul craves you. May all the saints in heaven bless you. Sweet Christ bring me once more to your side some day.

I signed it lovingly and added: 'I pray you, commend me in love to your mother,' then I sealed it and went to find the friar. I slept little afterwards, lying by my sword on the hard ground, but neither did Plantagenet in his silk bed. For when I went to rouse him as the camp stirred he was on his knees, praying, and looked weary.

Shortly after dawn we crossed the Tweed westerly towards Coldstream in sight of the rushing confluence of the Till and the Tweed. Shoals of fish whirled in the water churned by our hoofs and wheels, and big flat stones in the riverbed gave us foothold. Water birds screamed and clattered upwards as our war engines rumbled across—carts carrying the guns, provisions and tents, wagons bearing the nobles' personal gear. As the silver salmon leaped in the shallows, dawn light caught the greaves and cuirasses of the armed knights, so that they looked like great silver-black fish who had mounted up to kill.

We had heard Mass at Stirling in the Holy Rood chapel where James and my prince had made offerings, beseeching God to bless our enterprise. Now, standing over the border, the Bishop of St Andrews said another solemn office, and those who were in fear of death this day made confession. They knelt on land that wept from underground streams, their steel feet crushed cinquefoil and purple heather. From a nearby hill a ribbon of white water fell to meet the river, its noise a rushing background to the prince's voice.

Regal, he sat on a white horse; he was mailed all over save for his golden head. On either side his standard-bearers held high the White Rose, the Falcon and the Fetterlock. There was little wind and the banners hung passively, but as he began to address the armies, mist, like a snowy sheet in invisible hands, lifted all at once, revealing dawn-clean grass on fire with dew.

'It hath pleased God, who putteth down the mighty from their seat, and exalteth the humble, and suffereth not the hopes of the just to perish in the end—to give us means to reveal ourselves armed unto our lieges and people of England. But far be it from us to intend their hurt or to make war otherwise than to deliver ourselves and them from tyranny and oppression.

'For our mortal enemy, Henry Tudor, usurper of the Crown of England which to us by natural right appertaineth—we being the very Richard Duke of York, heir male of the noble and victorious Edward the Fourth, our said enemy the usurper hath not only deprived us of our kingdom, but since his usurped reign hath put little into practice except tyranny and the results thereof.

'King Richard our uncle, although the desire to rule did blind him, yet in his other actions like a true Plantagenet was noble, and prized the honour of the realm. But this Henry, our mortal foe, according to the meanness of his birth hath trodden underfoot the honour of our nation, selling our best confederates for money, making merchandises of the estates and fortunes of peers and people by feigned wars and dishonourable peace, only to enrich his coffers. For he hath, to fortify his false quarrel, caused divers nobles of this our realm, whom he held suspect and of whom he stood in dread, to be most cruelly murdered—Sir William Stanley, Lord Chamberlain, Sir Robert Ratcliffe, Humphrey Stafford, and others of name . . . besides those such as have dearly bought their lives with intolerable ransoms.

'Also he hath long kept and yet keepeth in prison our well-beloved cousin Edward, son and heir to our uncle the Duke of Clarence, and others, withholding from them their rightful inheritance to the intent that they should never be of might to aid and assist us in our need . . .'

It was as if he spoke of ghosts. Young Edward of Warwick, attainted heir of the false Clarence who had drowned in wine. How many gave him a thought these days? He would be about Prince Richard's age, but he had been closely held in the Tower for years, a wittold. The last person to give aid, or hold sway.

The white horse shifted its feet. Armour creaked and jingled, shredded mist coiled above the heads of the listening mass as Plantagenet attacked, among others, Cardinal Morton.

'The usurper,' he cried firmly, 'has surrounded himself with

275

lowborn caitiffs and villains, who by oppression of the people and devision of dreadful taxes, have been a principal cause of the present miseries of England.'

I thought: It is six years since I set foot in England . . . The standards flickered in a breeze from the firth. Plantagenet was approaching his peroration.

'By grace and clemency we shall pardon any of our subjects who have transgressed in the past, and for such as shall come with the foremost to assist our righteous quarrel, we shall make them partakers of our princely favours and bounty . . .'

East and west were the rough roads to Berwick and Carlisle where the English lords lay. I could see the path winding over the hill eastwards. By now it should be filled with troops coming to our support. It was empty, likewise the road west, though as I looked, the figure of the last of Plantagenet's messengers, John Heron, came riding towards us through a grove of silver birch. He rode alone, without hope. Plantagenet's steady voice went on.

'And we swear to protect the liberties of Holy Church, to give royal contentment to all degrees and estates of our people— preserving the honours and privileges of our nobles . . .'

There was a glade of oaks southwards, broken by a clearing, and, dimly seen, the outlines of a fortified manor house, cottages, and the tiny figures of grazing beasts. A long way off someone had seen us, and was running with the news. There was movement too within the army. King James was deploying his captains, and lines began to form. I saw Sir Roderick de Lalaing, Duchess Margaret's captain, take his place at the head of the Austrian men-at-arms. Almost in silence two armies fell into formation under James's orders. Lords Home and Huntly would be our captains under Plantagenet; the Highlanders milled about on our flanks. James drew his own army tight about him, and my prince's final words were delivered across a little gap where sunlight shafted down from the cathedral of the oaks.

'May the Holy Virgin and St George most blessed, be with us all this day.'

'Amen.' I looked across at King James, mounted and cased in Nuremburg steel, the Scottish lion flaming on his banners. I saw him changed, his grey eyes suddenly large and black, shining like stones under water. The skin seemed to tighten over his facial

276

bones. War sat on him. The trumpets sounded advance. The man behind me jostled my horse with his mount as we moved forward, trotting, the household pressing close about Plantagenet, the mass of our army moving faster in its two segments, skirting on either side the grove of oaks, galloping, the sound of the trumpets shrilling in our brains, air thrumming through the tautening standards, and the wet music of hoofs beating the boggy land as we plunged fiercely down towards the first of the border demesnes of England. The manor, I learned later, belonged to a Dacre, something I doubt whether Plantagenet knew. James knew, certainly, but cared little by now. That day I saw him entranced by war, matching wild animal cries with those of the Highlanders, and recognized the rashness in him that Henryson had feared. But at this moment I was occupied with keeping close to Plantagenet, his fair face hidden beneath his visor, and with keeping my seat on an excited horse and my hands ready to grip sword and axe in my lord's defence.

It seemed as if the world were rushing past, suddenly earth and trees and banners flung about in a wild and wicked joy, everything too fast, like the romances in which a day becomes a year and the sleeper wakes from brief rest to find himself a dotard. Too fast we swept into the meadows scattering cattle who lumbered and lurched out of the army's path, adding their bellowing to the noise of the clarions and the rattle of steel. Our din was terrifying, our mail-clad rush and roar like a dragon's breath. We bore on across open fields and orchards where more animals plunged away in fear, and charged through a small village. On our way we left destruction, crops wisped and flattened, wounded fields that bled dew, pigs fattened for Martinmas shrieking as they fled our advance. A baby of about a year old was playing in mud outside a cottage. Its round eyes watched the metal dragon bearing down, then at the last moment its mother dived from her door and scooped it up, screaming curses from a white face that had seen these doings before and liked them less each time.

The fortified manor, turreted and walled, loomed before us. On our left flank James ordered his army to encircle the house. It was a moated manor and the drawbridge was up, for news had flown. On the far side of the moat the black noses of guns were already trained, while men ran crouching to take cover behind them. All

277

the dogs in the manor began to bark and howl behind the walls. Between the ramparts there were glimpses of people running—a man struggling into a mailed shirt, and several women in flight—the flash of a green gown, a ripple of long hair, a babe in arms. At several of the wall-slits arrow tips, each like a little winking eye, appeared.

No standard flew from the battlements. The lord was away from home. As we stood, jostling, armed, ringing the manor, a greybearded figure appeared at the wooden gallery above the drawbridge—a seneschal whose quavering voice demanded what, in the name of God's saints, we wanted. James's herald galloped forward. Not far behind him was James himself, smiling wildly with raised visor, terribly vulnerable on his dancing horse.

'We come in the name of King Richard the Fourth, rightful sovereign of England!' bawled the herald. 'Are ye with us or against us?'

Over the thousand little challenges, the shift of metal, creaking harness, the wet breaths and hoofs, the old knight cackled in mockery.

'Get ye gone! Scottish felons! We know no king but Henry Tudor. We are his people.'

Plantagenet sat very still, as if listening intently, his face veiled by steel.

The herald looked round at James, who nodded, drawing his sword.

'Then defend yourselves!' the herald yelled. 'For we come in King Richard's name against the usurper!'

He turned and rode back into the ranks. A palisade formed as if by some swift brutal magic. Men ran with baulks of timber, oak branches, overturned wagons, shields and pavises. Guns trundled forward, archers crouched, and, rolling on its wheeled platform from the woods, came a monstrous *beffroi* as high as the manor's battlements, shielded by cowhide and spiked with scaling ladders. The other weapons came, each pushed by a score of men, the trebuchets, scorpions, arblasts, all the deadly catapults, missiles of rock and flame. Had I been the old knight I would have surrendered instantly. They were brave, however, but unprepared despite their show of arms. It was not a long siege, but a matter of hours.

My mind never dwells on the day or the three days that followed. Yet little bloody images still come back to me. This was the first of six manors, often assaulted and rebuilt over the years, which we finally reduced to a hot shell, a kicked antheap, the moat clogged with dead, the drawbridge ashes, the corpses heaped in blood from great hall to solar and the stairs between jammed with slain, some of them crushed through panic flight. In each case our weapons were stronger, our attack more disciplined, our archers and gunners swifter and more deadly. On occasion, the English lords came out of their lair and fought back with fury. It was then that I saw James in hand-to-hand combat, shoulderside with the common man, or riding with lance outstretched or spiked mace whirling, or clipping the head from an English knight as easily as he might slice down a hanging apple. While I was in the thick, denting armour with all my power in the protection of my prince, such a head arched past my face and rolled at my feet. The mailed and mounted body, blood spurting from the neck, stayed in the saddle while the horse bolted back through the ranks. But the head, face up, bounced gently against my legs, eyes wide, two red runnels springing from the nose. And the lips spoke, words faint and clotted with death. Some name, unknown. The head frowned and twitched. On tired nights that comes to me again; that hopping, living, thinking head.

The women were ill-used, especially by the Highlanders and the Austrian mercenaries. The soft bodies, the lady limbs—these were good prizes, stripped white as corbies rip flesh from bone. I saw a girl—not yet a woman, very fair and too frightened to cry, with a giant Highlander, hairily half-naked, using his manhood on her like a sword. Three or four others followed him, thrusting and groaning as in some private agony. I think the Virgin, to whom she called once, showed mercy for I heard them cursing— no sport in a dead wench.

To me it seemed there was little discipline, and chivalry must have died the moment we fired the first shot. The passing hours found me dizzy from sleeplack and a blow to the head. I was unwounded and I recall killing an armed man by pushing him backwards into the moat while he was off balance aiming an axe at me; no great or admirable feat of arms on my part. All the time I strove for closeness with the prince—always in a mêlée—a turmoil of flailing weapons, deafening gunfire, war-crazy men howling in various tongues, the days and nights lit by gunflares, the crimson moats reflecting the damage done by this merry band in love with murder. We were all guilty. I saw a priest shielding three children with his robe and cross; him they impaled, like St Sebastian, with arrows against the chapel door . . . and the children . . . I looked away. All guilty. Austrians, Flemings, Scots borderers, some Irish. All the priests in the world cannot exorcize this mad canker of war.

In fairness I saw James commit no atrocities. I even saw him speed some women into the forest. But nonetheless he permitted things that can still bring me a great melancholy. Again, in fairness, he would have been hard put to it to quell the tide of murder, rape and looting. The men employed their best and bloodiest skill; a full-fledged border attack, the red game of the north.

It was on the third night that the armies camped about ten miles inside the English border. A thick pall of smoke from a burning village blotted out the stars. There was a heavy guard patrolling the wagonloads of plunder, their footsteps the only sound other than the gravediggers burying men who had died that day. Nearby in a rough compound stood more cattle and sheep than could be counted. The Highlanders would lay claim to a third of this booty; it was their chief reason for joining us on the foray. In the wagons were piles of gold and silver plate, vessels inlaid with emerald and ruby, pearls like fire in milk, brocade and damask tugged from blazing walls, chalices and patens from stricken altars. Somewhere a woman was weeping like Rachel, eternally comfortless, on and on.

The campfires bore a redder glow, the air was acrid and it seemed years since I had sat writing to my love outside the prince's tent, where I was now, but not writing, or thinking, bone-weary, stunned to find myself alive, a little deaf from the day and the hammer of death's anvil. I and the others had done our duty; Plantagenet was whole and quick, and again I could see his shadow limned against the pavilion's lighted wall. His banner, soiled and ripped at the corner, stood planted, retelling York's past glory. A group of men came out of the dark, picking their

280

way through the sleeping, huddled soldiers. I got up and crossed my pike across the prince's tent-flap.

'It is the Steward. Friend.' King James's voice was hoarse. He smiled directly at me in the glow of lantern. His neck bled from a shallow cut, sustained during the day's insanity. He dabbed at it with a balm-soaked wad.

'Is my sweet coz awake?'

'If your Majesty will attend.' I scratched on the tent-flap. Getting no answer, I pulled it aside a little.

'Your Grace. The King . . .'

Then I stopped short. Richard Plantagenet was standing naked, looking without much interest at a bruise on his upper arm. His hair was matted with sweat. His manhood hung small and frightened. He looked exactly as if he had just been born, a process which he would gladly reverse. Tears poured down his face, but he made no sound.

His left eye was closed; two long lids folded like a damp bruised lily. Alarmed, I entered swiftly and flung a robe about him. I felt like a child dressing a wooden mammet in a rag, for I had to force his arms into the sleeves, while he stood shaking like a thrashed horse. He looked at me but did not know me. My first thought was that he was sick with camp-fever, or unknown, had taken some inner wound. I was about to suggest the physician when he spoke, gasping croaked words.

'The children!'

Then sat suddenly, heavily on his couch. I poured wine, knelt and offered the cup, which he ignored. The sweat-rimmed eye rolled, stared over my head.

'Didn't you *see?*' he whispered to someone invisible. 'Infants . . . scarcely baptized . . . and the poor maidens, and the priests . . .'

Then I understood, I wanted to say, Yes, my lord, I feel your shock, your sickness, but it's the world, and I least of all have power to change the world. The Devil helps to shape the world these days. Ask Robert Henryson. Ask Piers of Eastchepe.

'We shall surely burn in Hell for this,' he said softly.

I drew a breath, to answer God knew what, but for the moment I had forgotten James, exultantly impatient outside the tent. 'Cousin,' I heard him shouting, 'why don't you open for the Steward's Majesty?'

Plantagenet sat staring ahead, still gripped by tremors. I moved uncertainly to the flap of the pavilion, just as James, with bright wild eyes, pushed in fast, almost knocking me aside.

'Sire,' I said in haste, 'your gracious pardon, I think my king is unwell.'

The fine brows shot up. James marched over to the couch. 'What's this, why wasn't I told? Where's the malady? Send doctors . . . nay, I'll physic you myself, sweet Dickon.'

'The wound is in my heart,' said Plantagenet quietly. 'My heart is . . . dirty.'

I watched King James, saw him begin to comprehend something outside his ken, dismiss it as fancy, then smile again, an itchy kind of smile. He thrust his hand into the breast of my master's robe, then withdrew it swiftly.

'Dear Christ, Dickon! Is it the sweating sickness?'

'No,' cried Plantagenet, and looked fully at him.

'Well, your heart's sound enough—beating like a stallion's. In God's name, what ails you, man?' And, curtly to me: 'Bring light.' I took a lantern closer. My master's face sprang into high relief. I saw that he had not bathed or washed, and the pattern of tears was like prison bars against the day's grime.

'Weeping . . .' James sucked in his breath. Then, merrily: 'Ah . . . you're weary. Drink your wine.' Before I could serve him, he poured a cup for himself and held it high. 'Drink to the start of a good foray. By God, we've shown them our strength. Tomorrow I'll send for reinforcements. I've told my captains we'll be marching south. Prepare your army likewise. Your throne's ten miles nearer, Dickon, and, by God's passion, my fancy sees the Scots Lion flying over Berwick town. Come, drink. Then get your man to gown you and we'll eat and revel a little. Your good father-in-law, Lord Huntly, and the others await us. Let's celebrate what's done and what's to come.'

Richard Plantagenet stood very still. I glanced to see James's fading smile, his crooked brow. It was like standing beneath an oak, with swords of lightning playing above.

'What's amiss, my lord?' he asked, frighteningly quiet.

Plantagenet rose, pulling his mantle tight. He moved close to James; his voice was quite strong.

'Today I knew great shame and anguish,' he said. 'Those *little* people. For the love of God, my lord, is there no mercy left? Those were *my* subjects we slew!' His voice rose, hoarse and high. 'The children! the church! My people! My church! All the vows I made to cherish and protect my people of England, and now we leave them in their blood! In Christ's blessed name, James of Scotland, how could you make me party to such vile acts? Would to God I were dead, or never born!' He turned away violently.

I must have made a sound for James wheeled, said 'Out!' and I blundered through the tent-flap and stood trembling under the smoke-filled stars. Then I heard the Lion of Scotland roar.

'God's Tongue!' he shouted, and men sleeping a long way down the line stirred. 'Do I hear you right? Are you mad, or am I! Christ's Passion! That was but a little border skirmish over which you're weeping like a girl! You'll see better or worse before we're done! What ails you, for God's love? Did you think we'd take England for you without spilling blood?'

I heard the reply come hard and distinct, with no tears in it.

'I shall go no further tomorrow,' he said. 'No more innocents shall lose their lives through my ambition. I intend to claim my throne peacefully, through the honour of my blood and birthright alone. And I have told my army we are turning back.'

I heard a crash as James threw his goblet at a suit of mail. Then he began to swear. Some of the oaths he must have learned from the Wild Ones. When he had control, his voice was very cold.

'So, cousin. You wish to break with us your contract sealed in love and honour, because of a few burned houses and a pickle of souls gone to glory before their time? You intend to tip Tudor from his throne with just a few soft words? Ah, I truly doubt it, my lord. There are many things, sir, that I begin to doubt!'

'Not my love for you, or my loyalty,' said Plantagenet. 'But I cannot—I will not—butcher my own people.'

'*My lord*,' said James, through his teeth. 'Richard. I remember the good fighting your father gave mine. I remember Edward, the scourge of the Scots and the warring English alike, my people and his own. The Rose of Rouen, tales of whose valour are still taught to children. I remember another King Richard, who burned Berwick to the ground before building it anew, and tamed my borderers when they fought for my father, who was powerless

283

against that skilled fury. Those royal men lived in the sight of blood, made such music with the axe that even the Wild Ones marvelled. Edward the Rose was sovereign of five great battles. Richard died a hero's death. And before that, Harry the Fifth slew, with but a handful of starving men, thirty thousand Frenchmen. All Plantagenets. I begin to doubt your courage, cousin. I even, this night, begin to doubt your name.'

There was a long silence. I thought: They will now duel to the death. But my master answered quite calmly.

'Doubt me as you will, your Majesty. But remember, all those great men were capable of mercy. It is by mercy and justice that I will go to Westminster. Those of my people who love me will follow when I claim only what is mine by birth.'

I heard merry, amiable, clever James, balked of his battles, spit and sneer.

'And how many, I ask,' he said cruelly, 'followed you on this campaign? Not one English lord, cousin, came to your standard. Despite all your proud boasts, *not one*.'

After a while Plantagenet said in a weary voice: 'Your Majesty will wish me to leave Scotland now. I will make ready in the morning,' and James made a disgusted noise.

'Cousin! I pity you. Where would you go?' and then, more kindly, 'Christ's bones! you can't help it, I suppose, if your belly shrinks from blood. No. I've sworn to protect you, and the Steward's word is inviolable. And, by God'—grimly—'you will need my protection. The English envoy Wyatt has been at Berwick these past three days, and will be back in London within the week with news of this foray. Tudor'll be hunting your head; you're no longer a May-game to him. God's death! Dickon, you've disappointed me sorely.'

'For that, pardon me.' The reply was very soft. 'I cannot change what I am.'

James loosed a huge sigh, then he came from the tent like a startled, angry bird, thunder still in his face but the lightning spent. He gave me a furious glance, snapped: 'Attend your lord,' and I dived through the flap. Plantagenet was seated, looking ghastly. He seemed to have aged a lot in the past hour. I wondered how to calm and heal him. Valerian—Maurice swore by its power. I rummaged in the medicine coffer and mixed him a dose, which he drank without argument. It could have been hemlock.

'Sire, will you couch? The draught will quickly take effect.' I turned down the bed. He lay, and I wrapped him warmly. He looked at me, and spoke my name.

'Nicholas. Stay with me. Stay wakeful if you can. The night is so dark.' And he studied me, squinting from his drained face. 'You are so strong,' he said. 'And calm, as if nothing can pain you. So wise. Would I could have your secret.'

I looked quickly at the ground, hardly believing what I heard.

'Oh, my lord,' I said sadly, 'I am neither calm nor strong. And certainly not wise.'

'You have that aspect,' he said drowsily. The quarrel and the medicine were doing their work.

I said: 'Things are never what they seem, Prince Richard,' and the truth of it came over me as never before.

The two armies parted at daybreak, James riding on to pillage a few more manors to the south-east until driven off by English forces from Berwick, and we back to Stirling, fording the river at Coldstream. We passed again through that first village where I had seen the mother snatch up her baby from our path. There was nothing left. Just a black circle of smoking thatch and one solitary cow, missed by the marauders, lowing in pain from her swollen udder. Even the little church stood scorched and empty. A man lay with an arrow in his back across the door. Plantagenet, at the head of the plodding army, dismounted. He knelt and prayed, and shed his last tears of the campaign. When he rose he said to those near him: 'One day, I will build them a shrine,' and we rode on.

I had known him now for some six years, and I knew that I loved him. Somehow this made me afraid. The fancy took me that all those I loved were doomed. Edmund dead, my sister locked away forever, Finch dead and damned. Even Krista—her maidenhead gone and still far from me . . . But I loved him, it was my heart's law. Yet I knew, as surely as if a soothsayer had told me, that one day I would leave him comfortless.

'Look!' said Antoine de la Force, his voice almost drowned by the

285

seabirds as they hung screaming above the bulwarks of the ship carrying us towards landfall.

'Look! Men say that is the land of Lyonesse!'

I stared over the side of the ship called *Cuckoo*, into the blinding silver-blue of air and sea, where the horizon shimmered and gave birth to sudden rocks, soft green earth and a fortress. The enchanted isle, the Mount of holy St Michael, lying like a stone kicked by England's foot. My heart lurched. Lyonesse, where Tristan, who loved Iseult, was born. Tristan, who loved and died of love, whose name of old romance was often on my little sister's lips. Clearly, Josina's face hung in the thick silvery air, changing only slightly to become Krista's.

'The last of the land of Arthur,' Antoine murmured. His small face, pale and stubbled with beard, was weary, still deathlessly loyal. 'The remainder lies beneath this ocean. You can hear the church bells ringing on stormy nights. My father told me.'

The isle receded as, with the painted bird's beak tossing at our prow and the ship suddenly asway on a drunken clash of currents, we drove towards Whitesands Bay. The coast of Cornwall stretched, toothed with inhospitable cliffs, but the bay was a strip of pearl in the sunshine of summer's end. A sudden gust bellied the sails. White waves lashed high, turning to spray mid-air. A downfall of diamonds poured off the painted sails and clung to the taut sheets. Roped to the masthead, a cluster of wine-casks shifted a little. They were empty, a counterfeit cargo. On our recent voyage from Cork, the latest of our wanderings, one of those barrels had served to hide the prince. In mid-crossing of the Irish Sea, we had suddenly been surrounded by a flock of Tudor's ships, and a party had come aboard looking for Plantagenet.

'In the name of his gracious Majesty, we seek one Pierrequin Werbeque,' they had said. Pierre-Jean Meno, to all appearance an innocent Breton vintner and master of the *Cuckoo*, had shrugged dourly. It had been a bad moment, with Antoine and I sitting on the lid of the barrel, looking gormless and wondering if the prince had enough air.

The pinnace *Cuckoo* belonged to the Spaniard, de Ayala, as did the two small Biscayan vessels sailing astern. They had been loaned to King James for his pleasure, that being our departure. Gone was Scotland, never to be revisited, and the court of James

Stewart, the loving cousin. Genuine regret had sealed the parting, but he had never forgiven Plantagenet for the spoiling of his sport, the breaking of the game, although a further nine months passed after the ill-starred border raid. And then, privily, to spare his cousin shame, James suggested that the time had come for him to seek his fortunes otherwhere. To our surprise, de Ayala had joined in, suggesting, most cordially, that Spain might now welcome the prince.

Plantagenet was wary of this. 'I will not be used as a bargaining counter,' he said to the Scottish king. 'Not as I was with Charles of France. I know how my Spanish cousins seek to woo Tudor. I would rather find my fate again in Ireland.'

At this, James screwed up his handsome face.

'You came to me for refuge, Dickon,' he said. 'And I have espoused you as a prince of my blood. But you have provoked Henry, my lord. He's a mighty and offensive monarch, with his kingdom now part of the Holy League. I wouldn't advise Ireland, but I'll get you shipping and provisions. Return quietly to Flanders. Safer there.'

Flanders. I went hot and cold waiting for his answer. I prayed, uselessly. Cork, he said firmly, where the Yorkist cause was ever loved. Where Desmond and Kildare (now released from the Tower) would aid him this time for sure. James sighed deeply at this.

'Kildare is Henry's mammet, well you know,' he said crossly. 'But you are the master of your destiny, and I now have a fight on my hands. I still lust for Berwick . . .' and a shadow of regret chased across his face as he dreamed of another Plantagenet, howling and bloody-handed, aiding his conquest. He motioned to his Treasurer. 'You must have funds,' he was saying, and at that moment a messenger came riding, red-spurred, with news of the Cornish rebellion against Tudor.

There had been a savage rising by the men of Cornwall, that mysterious, elf-shotten region whose fiefdom to the English crown was at best a tenuous thing. With splendid irony, the Scottish raid and the subsequent border affrays carried out by James had been the direct cause of the Cornish disaffection. The steel fist of Tudor's tax-gatherers, headed by Cardinal Morton and Sir Reynold Bray, had, to finance what was becoming outright war with Scotland, begun to squeeze the realm from end to end until the people howled in pain. The Cornishmen did more than howl.

The courier, a young man in the service of Lord Audley, had the news bubbling on his tongue-tip. He had worn out six horses riding from the toe of Cornwall to Stirling. He had Breton-black eyes and a touch of salt in his mouth.

'And they asked the tax-gatherers: where the devil is Scotland? What has war with Scotland to do with us, in the devil's name? We earn our own bread through the sea. We trade our smoked fish for a pittance with Spain and France and Brittany. We work our skins blue and our lungs ragged in the tin mines and the factors cheat us even then, so that we scrape and scrimmage for our livelihood. We are poor and proud, immortal Arthur's people, the scions of sacred St Kenna, who turned serpents to stone. Ours is a realm of penury and miracles, where we do not even speak the English tongue! What cause does the emmet Tudor have to wring our pockets for his fight with a land that is half our world away!'

'I like the sound of these Cornishmen,' said James, sitting forward to listen with an eager gleam.

'Ay, my lord, pirates, brave and wild, though the King outlawed their piracy and that's another grievance,' said the courier. 'They still make and break their own laws—cattle-thieving, brawling, stealing tin, refusing to pay tithes. The rioting started in St Keverne. The tax-collector there is Sir John Oby, provost of Gasney College by Penryn. He's hard, sparing not even the poorest. But Lord! he met his match. The village blacksmith, Michael Joseph—tall as a ship's mast and fat with it, bearded like a prophet. He called out the whole parish, then the county, bade them stand firm, sew up their purses, fight if need be. They began to follow him, gentry, yeomen, miners and fishermen. Even Thomas Flamank, one of the king's own tax-assessors, threw down his tallysticks and joined their cause. They marched to Taunton, where my master Lord Audley (he bears quite a grudge—Henry Tudor still owes him a fortune for services in France) joined them. Even the Wells cathedral chapter mustered arms—not that they've much in that line, scythes and billets of wood mostly, but Wat Tyler and Jack Cade fought for their rights with little more. When I left they were on their way to London in their thousands, and Henry's turmoiled enough to have sent his Queen and his children to the Tower for safety.'

'You could do worse, Dickon,' said James, looking hard at Plantagenet, 'than ride down and join these Cornish. There's a ready-made army for you to ride at its head!'

'No, my lord,' said the Duke. A look, hard and vacant as glass, touched his eyes. 'We shall sail for Cork. With your permission.'

He seemed obsessed with Cork. I wondered: Was it because it was there the adventure began? Did he remember parading the streets, golden and admired, with people touching the sleek merchandise he wore, and all the dangers and disappointments, the doubts and horrors, still unborn? A prince disguised, full as a wineskin with untapped glory? The Mayor of Cork, John Atwater, was, then as now, loyal to him, at his shoulder throughout our trials, like a symbol of the splendour once promised.

'As you will,' James said finally. 'I've good sea-captains for you. They sail just outside the law.' He laughed. 'A pair of pirate brothers, Andrew and Robert Barton. Many the Portuguese vessel they've plundered. Brave and canny rascals, fit for any renegade enterprise. Sail from Ayr—be sure that Tudor is having the coast watched, or will be shortly.' He frowned, his eyes grew sad. 'Ah, Dickon! we could have . . .' He said: 'You'll find no joy in Cork, laddie.'

He was of course right. We were there barely a month, during which we found Kildare and the other earls who dared to hold secret council with us more frightened and noncommittal than ever before. Munster and Leinster crawled with Tudor's loyalists. Everywhere, the sour flag of Tudor authority flew. Meetings were hasty, cloaked, and barren. There was a ransom of a thousand crowns on the Duke's head in Waterford. We sailed away, before a gale of bounty-seekers, for Cornwall, in hopes of catching the tail of the rebellion, as James had suggested, and we were too late. The rising had flamed and died, its leaders were hanged and quartered, their skulls grinning out from spiked city walls. By the time Antoine and I looked on lost Lyonesse, the Cornish rebels' zeal was all but fettered, and their captains dead.

No one wins against Tudor. I had heard it before; over the

289

dimness of years it came back to me, that unknown voice of dreadful certainty.

As *Cuckoo* and her two sister ships ploughed the sick currents towards Whitesands Bay, I realized how small our company now was. For example, Maurice Fitzdesmond had parted from us in Cork, saying simply: 'It is finished for me,' and sadly, I read his reasons and those of the many who had acted like him. Our captains had departed. Through fear, through *ennui*, through the foreknowledge of a cause lost beyond redemption, who knows? There were no powerful experienced councillors, no one to guide my lord. I counted no more than thirty of us as *Cuckoo*'s painted beak dipped to drink the lacy spray. Plantagenet's chief scions were now John Heron, Nick Ashley, Ned Skelton. A clerk and two poverty-ridden merchants. No lords, no great names to lend weight and solace. I myself was as well-placed in the hierarchy as anyone. The highest born in our company was, after the prince, his lady, Katherine Gordon.

She came up now on to the lurching deck, into the white assault of the seabirds' wings and a veil of fiercely flung spume that soaked her cloak and hood. Greenish-pale, she hung sickly on a rope-stay, the damp red hair curled on her forehead. The Irish Sea had been a torment to her, and when Tudor's agents came aboard we had had to hide her too. She was quite changed since her marriage, all her hauteur vanished, and I pitied her, homesick and seasick as she was. I also admired her; the prince had asked her if she would prefer to stay with her father in Scotland, but she would have none of it.

She came gingerly over the slick boards towards me. I stretched out my arm in support and she grasped it with a small icy hand.

'Thank you, Master Nicholas,' (she had changed, indeed). 'Where is my lord?' She gasped and bit her lips. I wondered if she were about to be sick again, all over Krista's cloak, and I pointed with my free arm, past the quivering whipstaff to where a mariner crouched in the prow taking soundings and the prince stood talking with Andrew Barton.

'There, my lady,' and to comfort her: 'Very soon we'll be on solid ground.'

'I need . . .' she said fraily, and the prince turned and saw her, leaning on my arm, her eyes large and frightened, the sea-wind whipping the damp red hair across her lips. He left Andrew Barton mid-word and quickly wove a path towards us between men running to haul down sail. Ahead, the pearly strip widened and waiting figures, insect-like against the giant blue rocks, were visible.

'Friend or foe?' Antoine said quietly, and I shook my head. Pierre-Jean Meno, leaning on a wine-tun, suddenly spoke.

'*Cuckoo!*' he said, and spat across the barrel. 'What halfwit named this ship? If those are Tudor's men, we shall be cuckoos all.'

I had an instant distrust of him. I knew he was with us for money. He had played his part well enough, denying, mid-ocean, all knowledge of the sought-after Pierrequin Werbecque, but I remembered Thomas Astwood's treachery. Doubtless Tudor had rewarded him, better than my prince could now. Plantagenet reached Katherine's side and she half fell against him as *Cuckoo* shuddered and furled her painted feathers, seeming to hang and totter for an instant on the head of a green wave. Katherine leaned her head against my lord's drenched doublet, and he held her tightly. While they stood framed in a nimbus of spray, with the savage water and land green and blue behind them, they looked like figures in a holy painting: saints in trouble. One could imagine a dragon's head suddenly rearing over the ship's side to devour them.

'Ah, my sweeting,' he said with immense tenderness. 'Are you still sick? Where are your women?' She had brought only two, plain, hardy Lowlanders, whom I had not seen since the voyage began.

'They're below, sicker than I,' said Katherine, trying to laugh. At that moment the captain weighed anchor, with a rattling splash.

'Land,' said Plantagenet, and tucked the wet red curls away under her hood, kissing her salty forehead.

'My lord,' she said softly, 'I am afraid.' She hung close upon him, as if to inherit his strength by the press of love. He smiled confidently at her with sea-wet eyes, the one eye bold and innocent, the other, as always, half closed as against some dread, forbidden sight. Andrew Barton stumped over the deck. *He* had one eye only, the other, socket shrunken like a navel, had been gouged out years earlier during a sea-fight.

291

'Well, master,' he said. He did not bow or bend the knee and Antoine glared at him. 'Am I to lower the boats?' He looked across at the group of men on shore. 'They're Cornish,' he said flatly. 'Come to welcome your lordship, no doubt.'

'You're sure?' John Atwater asked, and Barton shrugged, nodded, pointing. 'They're all in black. Mourning their leader, Michael Joseph the smith. A great man, so I heard.'

'Lower the boats,' said my master suddenly. Lady Katherine still held fast to his arm. There was a noise from the hatchway and two heads poked up on deck; the Scottish abigails, as miserable as wet hens.

'Where will your lordship be lodged?' Barton asked, and Plantagenet murmured the name of Tintagel Castle.

'It's a ruin.' Barton seemed sure. 'The roof leaks. Unfit for ladies.' He looked at Katherine with a practised eye. Men began to climb down into the boats, and the two Biscayan vessels had off-loaded their crew who were rowing towards the shore. But Pierre-Jean Meno sat down on a cask and the Barton brothers did likewise.

'We will stay here, my lord,' said Robert Barton. 'To man the ship should you need escape.'

We descended into the boats down a swaying ladder. The sea felt very cold as it washed my hands; the last gold of the September afternoon shone through the top of a little wave like bitter honey. Katherine shivered and Plantagenet wrapped her in a fur. I took up one of the pairs of oars and, as I rowed, feeling the tide bulking beneath us, I watched the royal pair, seeing how close they sat, their joint loneliness as transparent as the golden wave. Both exiled (she, particularly, for he was always landless), she in fear clutching him for her anchor; and he looking stronger by the moment, as if her weakness of necessity emboldened him. When we beached, I carried her ashore for him, darkening the hem of Krista's cloak in the wavelets. She smelled sour and sweet, of heather and vomit.

There was about a dozen Cornishmen waiting at the water's edge. Some of them were tin-miners, their faces and hands seamed with blue. But their leader was clerkly, in neat shabby gear. His eyes searched our faces anxiously, clearing when they reached Plantagenet. He went down on his knees in the moist sand.

292

'We learned you were coming,' he said, in a burring speech difficult to follow. 'Gracious lord. I am John Tresinney, at your Grace's service.' He gave a rough, unpractised kiss to my master's knuckle. The other black-clad men followed, moving slowly, murmuring: 'Lord', 'Duke', saluting him and his lady. One tangled his words, said to Katherine: 'God save York Duchess,' but it was near enough.

'You are the leader?' Plantagenet asked Tresinney, and he replied: 'I am now, my lord. Since the damned tyrant had Michael Joseph butchered . . . his head and his parts on distant pikes. May merciful Jesus comfort his hero's soul. So far we've not been granted leave to bury his poor flesh.'

As he spoke, the longboats were bringing ashore our personal effects and the armaments King James had provided. What weapons we had weighed down the boats, and Tresinney's eyes watched their coming longingly.

'We are naked,' he said, 'of arms and captains. But we are un-conquered.' A fierce little growl of assent came from the others. 'Your Grace, these are my friends.' They came forward to be named: John Nankivell of St Mawgan, Walter Tripcony of St Columb, Humphrey Calwodeley of Helland, Otis Philip of Polwhele, Wat Grigg, Nicholas Polkinghorne of St Gwinnear, Thomas Gosworthdogga of St Crowan, John Trehanneck, and from Devon, John Giles of Samford Spinney, Robert Sturridge of Ashburton, Tom Hart of Barnstaple. Outlandish names: blue or black eyes, an air about them as of leashed hounds.

Tresinney took us presently to his house. In a parlour crowded with the Cornishmen, he related the events which had so tur-moiled King Henry.

'We came closer to the overthrow of the government than men have done for decades.' He smiled sourly. 'Tom Flamank was a lawyer and full of tricks. He put it about that our rebellion grew out of good faith, to rescue the King from his evil councillors, Cardinal Morton and Reynold Bray, who advised him to oppress the people. Some believed this, especially the lords who joined us, though in our hearts we knew we marched solely for our own justice.'

He poured ale, clouded dark with honey, into the tankards.

'Lord Audley was our figurehead, but Michael Joseph was our

Samson,' he said. 'We marched through Taunton to Wells, and we hoped that Kentishmen would join us, but they were afraid. Henry Tudor lay at Richmond when the news reached him. He worked swiftly. There was no need for him to call together an army. He already had eight thousand men mustered under Lord Daubeney. The army assigned to ride against the Scots!'

Through the low window of Tresinney's house the day was declining. Melted sunshine ran down the casement. Princess Katherine sat quietly, gaze never leaving her husband. Now and then she smoothed her salt-caked gown.

'The King sent Lord Suffolk to hold the bridge at Staines so that we could not cross the Thames,' continued Tresinney. 'His own army guarded the Henley bridge. We camped south of London on Banstead Down. Lord Daubeney was in St George's Fields and it was there that Flamank played false. Cravenly, he went to Daubeney offering to surrender for a general pardon, promising Michael Joseph and Lord Audley as hostages. The offer was refused. Flamank is dead, may Satan have him.

'Tudor was at Lambeth with his army when we marched to Blackheath. The streets from London Bridge were lined with fighting men—all the craft guilds mustered troops, but Michael Joseph spurred us on. On Deptford Strand, where the Ravensbourne meets the Thames, he deployed our bowmen to hold the bridge, with the main force standing back on rising ground.' His voice lost its vigour; he bowed his head.

'They attacked us just on Prime. Sir Humphrey Stanley and a large party of spearmen. Our bowmen did well, but it availed nothing. Daubeney crossed the bridge and launched his force on our main body. We were placed too far back to aid the archers, neither could they help us. Lords Oxford and Essex blocked our retreat to the South. Audley and Flamank were captured; Michael Joseph fled to the Observant Friars at Greenwich, but he was taken before he could reach Sanctuary.'

The rest he told briefly: how Henry Tudor rode back armed and triumphant that June day to be greeted as a victor by the aldermen of London. He knighted the Mayor for provisioning the army, and gave thanks in St Paul's.

'He took up lodging then at the Tower with the Queen. And there, Flamank, Audley and Joseph were put to the question.

They have monstrous means these days. Some new Gascons skilled in torture—they vie with one another who can extract the longest confession, albeit from half a man. Who can winch and burn and mutilate to the nearest point of death and still preserve full feeling in the victim . . . your Grace?'

The evening had come down. Greyness, with a lonely chill breath of sea-mist, filled the room. I followed Tresinney's eyes and then looked swiftly away, at the dusky shape of a seabird roosting on the window-sill. Anywhere, so as to avoid the naked terror on my master's face.

It lasted but a moment. He squeezed his bad eye tight and said calmly: 'Pray continue, Master Tresinney. But let candles be brought.' And soon the room leaped with light, and the sea-fog with its smell of drowned men no longer seemed so strong.

'Audley was beheaded after trial,' said the Cornishman. 'The King had him wear armour made of torn paper to mock him on the scaffold. The other two were hanged and their living entrails drawn. Flamank died badly. But Michael Joseph—dragged on a hurdle through the streets—even then, that great man kept faith, roaring that he would be remembered for ever and that only God would judge him.'

'And yet, Master Tresinney,' said Plantagenet slowly, 'when we first met, you said you were unconquered.'

Tresinney gave him a deep look of mingled pleading and defiance.

'We are wounded. Depleted. We have had to pay the cruel taxes after all, and above that, we have been fined for our protest. But we are the elect of royal Lyonesse. There are still enough to march again, this time to victory.'

Plantagenet, silent, turned his tankard round and round. A boy kindled logs in the hearth and Katherine moved nearer to the flames.

Said Tresinney: 'The King is our true enemy now. Whatever loyalty we may have had is dead. While your Grace was lately in Ireland, we sent word to the Scottish king, telling him our intent so that he might move against Tudor over the border. If, in our thousands, and thousands we still are, we were to rise again we could crush Tudor between north and south. All we need is more arms. And a leader.'

The Duke wound his tankard round and round. I was suddenly reminded of the way his uncle King Richard used to turn his finger rings, in indecision, or grief, or profound thought. None really knew, or ever would now.

'Does Tudor know I planned to land here?' he said, without looking up.

'Yes, lord. His steward, Lord Brooke, had your ships watched round the coast. Already there is a proclamation in Exeter against your coming. And he has promised to come himself to subdue you.'

The seagull sat on motionless in the window. Katherine, at the fireside, shook off her hood so that one of her women could comb her hair. Her hair was the colour of the fire, and on her cheek I saw one tear, a small crystal of foreknowledge.

'I am your King, Master Tresinney.'

All at once the Cornishmen slid to their knees, like a flock of proud black birds homaging the dead. Chill fog drifted against the windows, but in the room, warm light burned steadily.

'God save King Richard the Fourth,' they said.

'King of England and Ireland.'

'And of Cornwall,' someone said zealously, and Tresinney smiled a little.

'Redresser of wrongs.'

'Defender of the poor.'

'Lead us,' they said, 'and we will follow unto death.'

He stood up and drank his ale. He looked very tired, as if the curious fog outside was sucking at his life.

'I will lead you, my people.' His voice wavered but both that, and Katherine's sob, were drowned in the grim cheering.

Never have I heard woman weep so, as when the next day the Princess was parted from her husband. (Perhaps I did, though, once; Margetta faced with her darling's dead body.) It was a dire sound; a piteous low keening from which, in Tresinney's cramped lodging, there was no escape. Poor lady! she had been cherished all her years. Now in this new wild world, with her pride left in distant summer moorland, she suffered.

'My lord, for God's love, don't abandon me!' she cried, clinging. Her small hot hands left dull marks like breath, on his shining cuirass as she strove to hold him. It is not easy to embrace a man in armour and I had readied him for the ride, first to Bodmin and then Exeter. He looked at her with rueful love. Antoine and I, hastily packing his travelling chest, tried not to watch them.

'Abandon you? My heart's blood?' He kissed her mouth and I saw how his skill in love had tamed and bound her. Her tear-streaked face became like a rapt white rose under rain.

'It is safer,' he said. 'You shall be lodged on St Michael's Mount while I ride to join my loyal subjects. The Mount is a good place, under a holy spell. Eh, my friends?'

Shining and fair in his bright harness, he smiled at us. Last night, when the tide was almost out in the bay, he had sent men to capture the Mount. With cunning inspiration, he had bidden them wear white shirts, and as they crept across the mist-hung bay they looked like sea-waves. Not a drop of blood was shed, and the crumbling fortress was given up almost gladly, for though the men there looking out towards Marazion were royal guard, they were also Cornishmen.

'The spirits of Arthur's knights will protect you until we meet again,' he said, and raised her chin, trying vainly to make her smile, for she had been raised on legends of great Wallace and the Bruce her ancestor, not Bors, Galahad or Gawain.

Tresinney came, to say that the Cornishmen who had gathered and were still gathering in eager dozens, were ready to march to Bodmin, the county town. News had jumped like lightning over the cliffbound moors. A new leader was come, who outshone even the hero Michael Joseph, a nobleman destined to sweep the Welsh usurper off his fragile perch. A Plantagenet prince whose hands were shaped for the showering of largesse, not the squeezing of taxes. Tresinney wore armour which had seen better times; one pauldron had a broken rivet where a lance had pierced it, and the vambrace on one arm was shorter than the other. The men were lined up in untidy segments on the moor. Here and there the morning sun lit a twinkle of steel harness, but most wore the archers' boiled leather and the rest only their rough work clothes. Their weapons were equally rude; pitchforks and billhooks and pieces of planking, but one miner had a mace and chain (surely his grandfather's) which he was whirling delightedly to the hazard

297

of his neighbours. They were in noisy, indefatigable mood.

Tresinney had a matchless team of spies who could move fast and were acquainted with the untenanted moor. They ran like ghosts over a desperate, haunted region of healing wells, near Dozmary Pool where Excalibur lies drowned, awaiting Arthur's return.

He said: 'My lord, if you wish to enter Exeter, we must move quickly. Sir Piers Edgecumbe has been sent to block our march to the east. But, praise God, most of his force deserted and are joining with us. Sir Piers has gone to take refuge in the city and warn the garrison there. Exeter itself is well defended under Courtenay, Earl of Devon. Lord Daubeney is coming west from London on the King's orders. And he has bidden Lord Brooke . . .'

'The same,' said Prince Richard thoughtfully, 'who was once sent to seize my wretched cousin Warwick and immure him in the Tower these many years ago. Tudor . . .'

'Tudor shall answer for that, my·lord,' said Tresinney hastily, glancing at the restless mass in the meadow. 'As I said, Lord Brooke has put to sea on guard against our escape. It's forward, now, your Grace.'

'Yes,' he said, and glanced wistfully towards the west, where lately the weeping Princess had been escorted back to the Mount. Tresinney stood on tiptoe, surveying the heads of the ragtag army.

'Sire,' he said diffidently, 'have we no more arms than these?' And Plantagenet shook his head, as if dream-bewitched.

'The quartermaster will tell you the numbers,' he said after a moment. 'Five hundred lances, as many bows and quivers, or some such.'

'Scaling ladders?' Tresinney said unquietly. The prince smiled that dreaming smile. Uneasy, I was put in mind of the days before love healed me, when I was elfshotten at Amboise. Love, I thought, can also sicken the wits, for Richard was still staring westward. Tresinney gazed grimly at the comely face, perhaps remembering the fear he had seen on it last night. Then the good eye blinked, unmisted, and the Prince said:

'Yes, there·are ladders. Few horses, though. Our ships were small. Can the men march fast?'

'They will run there, if need commands.'

I sidled close, saying: 'I'll march, my lord, if there are so few horses,' and he turned, looking for a moment as if he had forgotten who I was, then said: 'No, Nicholas. You must ride, my loyal one,' and then his own mount, a white destrier fit for kings, hung with a jewelled bridle given him by Margaret of Burgundy, was brought up by Nick Ashley. Behind me I heard John Atwater say to Ned Skelton in a voice made testy by anxiety: 'Ladders, yes, but where's the artillery? In St Jude's blessed name, where are the guns, the mangonels, the . . .'

'I pray constantly to St Jude,' said Skelton, low and clear. 'Only he can salvage a lost hope. There aren't enough guns to kill a treeful of blackbirds.'

I wondered whether they were planning to desert, as so many others had done before them, and turned to glare. The armoured prince, being heaved aboard his horse, must have heard them. He turned with a brilliant smile.

'We shall need no guns, my friends,' he said. 'Exeter is already mine, for I shall make it another London, a royal city. I shall tell the people so, and they will rejoice. They will open to me without gunshot or blood-letting. Let us now ride to Bodmin.'

At Bodmin they had laid the street from gate to Guildhall with smooth white sand in our honour. Thin broken pearls of scattered shells gleamed in the softness, sand from the enchanted beaches of Arthur's lost land and the banks of sacred rivers. Tawny-faced women leaned to rain white roses from their windows, children clung in glee to gables as the prince passed, tabors and fifes banged and squealed. Clerics blessed us from the porch of St Thomas à Becket's little shrine. Our clothes grew damp with water from the dozen holy wells of Bodmin, each flung drop a benison. As we passed through to the Guildhall the cheering grew and so did our company. Scores of townsmen and some women joined the march. The streets grew blocked and the tail of our army stretched out into the meadows around the town. A brisk wind arose, shaking the scarlet robes of the welcoming Mayor and aldermen, the banners of their guilds, and the standards of York and Plantagenet. The device of the Falcon spread and folded its great wings within the fetterlock, and the lean-jawed wolf with the red rose rippled faster in his endless chase of the boy fleeing the tomb.

299

On the afternoon of the following Sunday, we came to the walled and silent city of Exeter. I rode behind the mailed figure on the white horse. Around us were the captains, such as they were. Skelton, Heron and Ashley, although no veterans of battle, seemed to bear the captaincy among them. I had the notion that anyone, even I, could have given commands. The prince sat very straight, his raised visor revealing a distant, glacial calm. Down a grassy hill we rode, cattle lumbering away at our advance. Autumn sunshine gleamed on the easterly river, showing it empty of boats, a sure sign that we were expected. The west gate was impregnable by reason of the water, and as we came near the city, we saw the other gates were sealed against us.

He had chosen Exeter because it was the most important city in the West, and there he planned to make a fortified base from where he could organise the final claiming of his kingdom. Yet on the garrison tower the standards of Courtenay, Earl of Devon, and Sir Piers Edgecumbe flew, and the figures of armed men manning the ramparts could be seen. Behind us, the broad ribbon of marchers toiled, briefly sunlit over the hill-brow, then spilling down, a vast undisciplined mass, black against the summer-bleached grasses. They must have numbered six thousand, sailors, marching splay-legged, farmers, miners, and women too, many dressed like men, even children. All of them with their rustic weapons following the prince as if he were a sorcerer who had stolen their will. A few hundred archers marched at the flanks of the column, and in the middle, horses pulled wagons carrying our small artillery. 'There must be no blood shed,' he had said, and then, realizing this impossibility: 'There must be as little blood shed as possible. But God will favour us. I will parley with the city fathers, and they will welcome King Richard of England and Ireland.' At Bodmin, he had once more given out his formal proclamation, and been received with faith and joy.

As we moved under the city walls he looked round, saw the rolling serpent of Cornish following in its eager coil and frowned, biting his lip. I could almost guess his thought: This army had no aversion to the shedding of blood. It would take strong men to command them to hold back. A force of landless peasants, almost naked of arms, led by men naked of experience; a bankrupt merchant, two clerks, an exiled Irish mayor . . . my eye was caught by a band of horsemen riding fast over the hill north of the city. John Atwater rode up beside me.

'Did his Grace see?' he said worriedly. 'They're going for reinforcements. My scout came back a few minutes ago. He's Tresinney's man and knows the moor. He's heard that the Duke of Buckingham is within a few days' ride, likewise the Earl of . . .'

The bursting silver bray of several clarions wiped out his words. The prince's musicians had moved to the fore. Silk flags swaying from their instruments, they were announcing our presence. John Tresinney had donned a herald's tabard with a giant White Rose. Following the line of the city wall, he began to walk ahead of the prince's horse. In his raw-knuckled hand he held high a gold, gem-studded rod, which I recognized as a gift to Prince Richard from the Emperor Maximilian.

'Forward! To the north gate!'

North gate, north gate, the words taken up like a talisman by the buzzing, shuffling mass behind. Antoine de la Force had his hand on my stirrup and clung, being jostled by John Heron's horse. In his other hand he grasped a rusty lance.

'The north gate is undefended,' he gasped above the din. 'They keep their great guns at the west gate, to guard against invasion from the river.'

Drums were being struck, an impatient rub of sound. Between each rub-a-dub came the faint dark burden of a psalm; in our company were priests and monks from the holy houses of Cornwall. Fierce sunlight shafted down from behind a cloud and blazed on the prince's mail and the steel chamfron and bardings that protected the head and body of his horse. Reflected light silvered his white face and for a moment he seemed on fire. He urged his armoured mount into a fast walk up to the gate, halting suddenly as he saw the deep trench that had been dug in the city's defence. He raised himself against the cantle of his saddle and made a cage of hands about his mouth. The drums crackled, a fanfare sounded. The crowd fell quiet. High up on the walls men watched and listened, while beside them weapons pricked the shining air.

'I come in peace,' he cried, a long, far-reaching call. Tresinney, voice booming like a tin mine, took up the cry.

301

'For King Richard! Open, in the name of King Richard the Fourth!'

Silence, from above and within, although the guard moved between the crenellations of the walls, and the weapon-tips seemed to grow in number. A wind blew off the moors, stretching tight the lords' standards. A new one had been hoisted, a small replica of the largest, being three roundels on a gold ground with a label of three azure points. The Earl of Devon's son was within the walls; Tudor's brother-in-law. I looked down into the trench. It was filled with rubbish; iron spikes, stinking latrine-debris, boulders, beams, iron hawsers. Faintly from behind the gate came hammering as the citizens built reinforcements to keep us out. Plantagenet heard it; he turned, showing his visor-framed face whiter still, as if at last he had woken from his dream. Tresinney stood stolidly beside him, hand on the destrier's bridle, still grasping the golden herald's wand.

'Hear ye! citizens of Exeter! I am your lawful, rightful sovereign, son of King Edward the Fourth!'

Clouds raced to dim the sun. Behind me was the restless buzzing of the Cornishmen. The bowmen, contrary to orders (if, indeed, they had received any), were notching their arrows, taking a squint at the sentries on the walls. Beside me came a strange clicking sound: Antoine, grinding his teeth in anguish.

'Jesu, Jesu,' he muttered. 'He must make his proclamation. Then they will open. They must open. He promised they would open. Jesu, God.'

Richard stood tall in the saddle again, and addressed the hidden city.

'Good people. I come to free you from the tyrannies of the usurper Tudor.' From somewhere within the walls came a gross, mocking laugh.

Three hours we stood there, the threadbare army fidgeting a little, some resting on the grass, children playing or asleep, our archers with bows raised but strings slack, and the sun began to decline, amber and orange like the leaves of trees near the silent, barricaded gate. And suddenly there was a commotion, movement on the walls as if a giant was waking. A boulder, which must have needed a score of men to move, was suddenly propelled over and out from the top of the walls, bounding over the trench and burying itself deep in the ground near the prince. Had it been an ell to the right it would have crushed him. I felt my heart jump into my jawbone. The destrier tried to rear, but its armour weighed it down. Tresinney snatched the bridle and led horse and rider back into our midst.

The mob behind us was in an uproar, pressing closer. The archers fitted barbs and bent their elbows. John Atwater said: 'My lord, we must attack. We shall be trapped like mice; Henry's armies converge on us from all points,' and his urgent voice was taken up by Skelton, Heron, and many others.

'We must besiege them,' the prince said faintly, and turned to give an order. Only I, and perhaps Antoine, caught his whisper. 'Little bloodshed, sweetest Lord Jesu, I pray . . .'

Someone was yelling for the scaling-ladders to be brought. The small party of armed horse-soldiers around us fought to control their mounts as the siege-carts were dragged through the ranks. Wheels bounced over tussocks. A ramshackle wagon collapsed, shooting its load, a small serpentine and several precious cannon-balls into the stinking trench. A flash from the ramparts caught the eye as the red sun glowed on the tips of drawn arrows.

'My lord,' I yelled. He was battling with his excited horse, turning it in lumbering circles. 'My lord, close your visor.' I saw his face vanish behind steel and snapped my own headpiece shut. Stifling, I felt it moisten instantly with my own acrid breath. Even then I heard the sound of the loosed arrows like a thousand geese in flight from the walls. The sky darkened briefly with their rain. One impaled itself at my horse's feet. Another struck the prince's mount and skidded harmlessly off the plate-armour, but from behind came cries of agony from Cornishmen. Unprotected, they fell spitted like fowls on a fire. It was then that the women and children began to leave the scene, scrambling away over the hill. On the ramparts, the piked noses of three ballistas appeared, the kind that can fire off a dozen rocks at once, spraying them far and wide. I saw one coming towards me, it seemed to float, it was smooth and round. Some mad fancy told me it was soft, and I held out my arms to catch it.

Late afternoon sun was on the tent-flap where I lay. I woke speaking Flemish. I had been talking to Anneke, and her ageing

303

beauty smiled and swirled away. I was naked, and the surgeon was prodding my ribs. 'You should be dead,' he told me crossly. I sat up gently, through surges of pain. Antoine crouched beside me, holding my sword as if it were an infant. I looked down. One side of my body was black, and there was a big lump under my chin.

'His Grace feared you were killed,' whispered Antoine.

'I will live.' I strove upright, groaning. Dying men with blue faces lay near me, and a priest knelt, giving absolution. 'Sweet God,' I said. 'The prince. I must guard him. Are they still firing upon us?' There was a tremendous dent in my breast-plate. In agony, I helped Antoine harness me again, then, sick and reeling, I left the tent. After a moment my head cleared and I realized that we had moved round to the east gate, where swarms of men were filling up the trench with boulders and broken wagons. There were no defenders on the walls that I could see. More men were frenziedly chopping and gouging at the gate with bills and axes, while a battery of seamen and miners ran at it with half a tree. Then I saw Plantagenet. Dismounted, he was beckoning to others who carried armfuls of timber which they threw against the gate. Men ran to kneel beside it with tinder-boxes. John Tresinney staggered up with a case of black powder.

'This is all we could find, my lord,' he gasped. The workers seized the powder and heaped it on top of the timber. I shouldered my way to the prince's side, sword in hand.

'Your Grace, 'ware,' I cried, for his head was bare. A Cornish boy was holding his helm for him, and I distrusted the quietness on the ramparts. 'Guard yourself, Sire.'

He turned to me. 'Nicholas! Praises, you're whole. I give thanks to the Holy Virgin. When all is over, you shall be dubbed knight, I swear . . .' His face was lit by a sudden surge of flame. The timber stacked against the gate had begun to blaze. There was a small yelp of triumph from the men as they leaped back from the fire. Dragon's tongues of red and amber crawled, then flared, up the gate, and rolls of pitchy smoke masked the ramparts above it. There was a bang as the first sprinkling of gunpowder erupted. The gate shook, and men with blackened faces crawled from the trench, holding their ears.

'We'll smoke 'em out,' growled Ned Skelton at my shoulder. 'Damn their hides. The Earl of Devon is wounded,' he told me. 'One of our bowmen winged him through the arm. Fine shooting, by the Mass . . .'

'Where are their defences?' Another shattering explosion rang along the walls.

'They're busy fetching the great guns from the West gate,' John Heron said, wiping away grimy sweat. 'Look! God's robe! One more blast and we're through. My horse!' he yelled, and the Cornish boy came running with his mount. I found my own nervous nag, and the prince's destrier, its gold ornaments still bright, and helped the Duke to mount. The sky became blotted by black smoke. By now the fiery gate was roaring like a sea, its frame crumbling. It collapsed inwards just as the muzzles of the big guns appeared through the crenellations. Sparks and billows of ashy flame shot up as the seared timber crashed down. Planks had been laid across the trench, and we rode in through an arch of flame. Our charge went almost at a walking pace, so heavily armoured was the prince's horse, and we shielded him left and right in the fierce heat.

I thought: This is Hell Mouth, as in the Guild Plays. We are riding through the gate of Hell. Although since then I know that Hell can take other forms than fire—the breaking of hearts and vows, being cast out . . . The streets were clear of townsfolk. No thrown roses here, but from high on either side, where the gables leaned close, came a growing babble of animal anger as the people of Exeter jeered and cursed us at their windows. Women, grey-beards and little boys hung taunting us viciously, banging pot lids together. Multicoloured ill-wishing, foulness like dirty rain, mounted to a storm as we pressed on up the narrow street between the shaking walls, hearing the great guns boom behind us. Poor Cornishmen, packed tight and clawing through the gate in our rear, were being maimed and killed in scores, and the trench outside was filling with dead.

So cramped that it was an effort to move, so close that stirrups locked and spurs tangled, we pushed our mounts, no more than four abreast, in the narrow way. None of us knew the city save that this street led to the Castle, with God's grace, to be captured and held. There was a shout of 'Forward!' and from somewhere back in the muddled ranks the cracked whinny of trumpets relayed the command over the hideous noise from the windows.

There were missiles now as well as maledictions. Hurtling upon us came iron bars, dead cats, table legs, ladles, knives and cookpots. Two hags at one house threw down a blazing canopy, setting mens' hair and clothes alight and cackling at their screams. Among the torrent of flung rocks, piss and ordure from hurled chamberpots, came arrows, as archers deployed along the rooftops fired on our progress. The man riding next to me raised his arm against the hail and a barb thrummed inches deep into his oxter. He grunted and died; as he fell his horse whirled and tried to plunge back along the way, blocked by confusion.

We ploughed blindly on and at times men rushed from their houses, leaping to strike daggers at our legs and the naked faces of the footsoldiers and trying to slash the horses' hamstrings. We neared the top of the street; a rain of nails and bolts rattled down and bowls of boiling fat sheeted on to the heads of the desperate, lurching column. Blinded, flayed, blistered, men shrieked and fell. A further flight of arrows dented our harness and hellish noise bounced off the house walls. Hoofs went lame on a carpet of ironware. Our mail streamed and stank from the filth and seething oil. A turdpot aimed at the prince hit my visored face; spray stung my eyes through the slits. Defilement hung about me. This was Exeter, and this its welcome to the rightful king, Richard.

I did not blame him; throughout our time together I think I never blamed him. From an inn a man darted to swing at him with an axe, and I sent him to Hell unhouselled, to save Plantagenet the guilt of shedding blood. Then suddenly, knifing through the din of steel-muffled cries, slithering hoofs, the thunk of thrown pots and hum of arrow-fire, came the sound of trumpets sounding a charge up the hidden alleys, in our rear and ahead of us. Lords Courtenay and Sir Piers Edgecumbe were attacking— through the stifling dust and the deadly metal song we heard the rearguard of ill-armed Cornishmen falling to their forces. Trapped in our armour, packed between walls that rang with the clash of wildly wielded pikes and billhooks, we swore and sweated and wept, forcing our stumbling way towards the Castle against foes which now erupted from every side street, our every plunge forward mangled by a wild press of steel. The prince's destrier flared scarlet nostrils and cried in fury, thrusting and butting with

306

chest and legs splashed with blood. It was like pressing forward through a dream, where a giant's hand effortlessly held back our squirming advance. And all at once we were confronted with Courtenay's forces. They came from the street of the Blackfriars smashing into our left flank, a powerful cross-current of mailed men and weapons that ran through our ranks with heart-stopping shock. The clarions yelped, and their noise, like us, was trapped and beat back from wall to wall. Steel shapes came to attack, in a mêlée so close that it was difficult for either force to swing with sword or shortened lance. Above, the standards dipped and lunged, shaft rubbing against shaft, embroidered blazons crossing and tangling like sheets on a wild washday. I saw the blood running greasily along the edge of my father's sword, as I pressed my mount and body closely alongside Plantagenet. Whether he struck a mortal blow I knew not—I fail to see how he could avoid so doing and live; I know I slew four men and felt nothing but a great thankfulness. In this seething trap, full of shrieks and steel-slither and the suck of metal in flesh, there was no place for words of peace such as Henryson had given me. We locked with Courtenay's forces; I saw him, a tough veteran soldier, fighting one-handed, his arm cased in a bandage, his face grimed under a rashly raised visor. We—Heron, Skelton, Ashley, Atwater, Antoine and the score of other mounted men—forced ourselves at them, gasping our cries of loyalty: 'Plantagenet! à Richard! Jesus, Mary and St George!' against the roaring rival bellows of Courtenay's trained and disciplined force. The waves of steel lurched back and forth, smashing and buffeting. Stones and pots still showered down from the citizens' windows, as they screamed for the rebels to be routed. They cared nothing for the plight of the Cornishmen, and as for the man who had broken down and burned their city gate, well, they had been taught of him—by Tudor heralds—these past few weeks.

'Beggar!' they howled, voices cutting through even the roar of battle. 'Mountebank! Bloody ape-face! Pigs-ballocks! False villain! Kill! Kill! Die, jackanapes Warbeck!' Like a litany of hate: 'Warbeck, Warbeck! Piss-a-bed Perkin! False Pieter Warbeck! Foreign traitor!' Most of the shrieks were female, but one man with the voice of Stentor, called from a church roof: 'Go back to Flanders, you bastard cur! Go sleep in the canal, you buggering barge-dog!'

We had attacked Exeter without forethought or strategy. With our planless, abortive rush, we had run ourselves into the heart of an unknown city, our formations broken and our troops disseminated; part of our army being slaughtered a street away, our rearguard fighting for survival, and our vanguard itself as frenzied as a hunted fox who finds its lair stopped with stones. With our cavalry engaged with Courtenay's troops a few yards away, there was a moment for brief counsel in the precinct of a little churchyard.

'My lord,' cried Ashley, 'it's hopeless, they're swatting us like wasps.' As he spoke a Cornishman's body, piked through the entrails, crashed at his feet. The citizens were using nets to haul up the enemy, killing them and throwing the corpses down on top of us.

'Sire,' I whispered, voice gone from shouting, 'we must retreat. Sound the retreat.' A trumpeter stood by, face and banners red-dappled.

'We can't go back,' said the prince, looking round wildly at the carnage. 'We cannot breast that fighting. It will swallow us. Mary have mercy.'

'Then, for Christ's blessed passion, let us flee where we can!' Atwater screamed. 'To the nearest gate—the north gate. I know the way. Follow!' And he spurred his mount, its forefeet flailing, through a gap in the mêlée. The prince stood undecided, his face anguished, and I knew in another moment we would be lost. I dealt the destrier a blow under its tail with my sword-flat and it lurched after Heron and Atwater and the others, over cobbles thick with blood and dying men while the yells from the rearguard grew fainter. We moved down side alleys quite fast, protected by our flanks of archers, loading and loosing in answer to shots from the walls. Like a miracle the way showed clear. The great destrier broke into a heavy run. Courtenay's face and that of Sir Piers Edgecumbe flashed before my reeling eyes, skull-like with weariness, for Exeter had not seen such an engagement for years. No one followed us. I hauled the prince's bridle along and we surged up towards the north gate, our foot soldiers running to force it open. Some Cornishmen had already weakened its structure and it fell outwards, forming a bridge over the trench. We breasted some small barricades in a dream of freedom, taking in great gulps of sweet moorland wind, and from the smouldering gatehouse a woman with long black hair appeared.

'I curse you, Perkin Warbeck!' she cried. She threw a bowl of hot cinders into his face; had his visor been open it would have blinded him. 'Curse Warbeck, false mammet! Your vanity brings war again to peaceful England!'

Skelton drew his axe and went towards her. The prince shouted: 'No! Let her be!' Then in a choking breath scarcely audible over the sounds of Hell that we were quitting, 'In God's holy honour, she may speak truth,' and in that moment I knew the cause was lost.

They kept the great fires burning in the gates that night, and all the next day and night to keep us out of the city. A kind of unspoken truce prevailed, and there were no missiles fired on either side. Long afterwards we learned that Courtenay's garrison was near exhaustion and not sorry to see us retreat. Courtenay himself was very ill with the arm wound, and the Cornish were burying their dead.

We made camp in the lee of a little hill lit by the flame-red sky east of us. We washed our wounds in a tributary of the Exe. Hourly came the low note of confession and absolution and a deeper sound, the Cornish conducting their rites in a tongue older than the claypits or the sea from which they sprang. And where once the endless train had wound over the moor, there was only about fifty of the army gathered from the West Country. Tresinney was one. He stood still for long periods, apart, his face greyed with thought, his body humped like a fine bow cracked by a clumsy archer.

In his tent the prince himself anointed my side with witch hazel. I was black and scarlet from the stone's strike.

'Are you in pain, Nicholas?'

'It hurts when I draw breath, your Grace.'

And then he said: 'Christ's passion! Call me Richard from this time on. I have been lorded and graced through the world to no avail, and I have been given dog-names to spit upon. Neither

309

fortuned me. My world is upside down, so call me Richard and see if that will right it.'

He dropped cloth and ointment and shuddered.

'Is there wine?'

We drank together. 'It's like water.' He drained another cup. 'What hour is it?'

I had heard the cathedral chimes beside the river. 'Matins, my lord—Richard. Take heart. Antoine can ride fast, you know.'

He bowed his head, whispering. 'God help him. God help her.' He had sent Antoine on the best mount we owned down to the coast to glean what he could about the Princess Katherine's welfare. Messengers had been arriving all night—with frightening news. Lord Daubeney was levying the men of South Wales, Gloucester, Wiltshire, Hampshire, Somerset and Dorset. The latest rumoured number was 20,000, and it was said that the King himself was journeying west with more men, to subdue 'the French lad'—his latest appellation of my master.

Antoine had been told to try to reach Michael's Mount and if needs be, bring Katherine by the *Cuckoo* to Southampton Water, should escape by sea be necessary.

'Well, sir,' Tresinney stood before us, thin and tense, against the bleeding sky. 'We have failed. We cannot stay here. Our nation has suffered much, yet again. It might be wise, Master Warbeck, if you took another road away from their great displeasure.'

I jumped up, ready to call him disrespectful, but Richard waved his hand, a kindly, down-dog, it matters not, gesture. He said: 'Truly my heart is sad for your good brave kinsmen, Master Tresinney. Would to God I could undo their deaths.' And at no time did he cringe or cry: '*Not my fault!*' while I glared at Tresinney, who shrugged.

'Word comes in hourly that you are ringed by great forces.'

'Yes,' Richard said gently. 'So you must disperse the men. Go home while there's time.' Then he stretched out his arm. 'Forgive me, if you can.'

Silently Tresinney grasped his elbow.

'The great Michael Joseph also failed,' he murmured. 'Tudor holds England by the entrails. She dances when he jerks. Farewell then, and good fortune—Perkin Warbeck.'

When he had gone quietly away, we lay down on our straw pallets (the silk cushions had been looted while we fought) and tried to sleep for a few hours before cocklight. He slept at once, exhausted. I raised up to look at him in the fiery night. Tresinney had challenged him with the name of Warbeck, and he had uttered no denial. My mind shaped my tongue into a question of pain, something I had never, should never ask:

'Richard,' I whispered. 'Richard, who are you, truly?'

We left Exeter still Tudor's city. Its watch-fires out, and its surrounding moat filled with the corpses of young men who had once fought in and for a dream. Hourly messengers came saying that royal forces were converging upon us from all points but south—the crack troops of the Duke of Buckingham, Daubeney's great levies, and the terrible Welsh warriors of Rhys ap Thomas, not to mention what skilled men Tudor himself had mustered, although none expected to see the King in combat—it was not his way. He lay at Woodstock, and he was gambling to pass the time.

Why then, instead of riding for the coast, did we take the road over the Blackdown Hills to Cullompton and make for Taunton? Six of us were in agreement among the leaders—Heron, Skelton, Ashley, John Atwater, myself, and the prince. It was as if we could not bear the once blazing hope to shrink to a spark and die. Disgrace and ridicule were dark bedfellows. Taunton, it was said, was a neutral town, there might be men there still willing to reap redress for past injustices, by a new show of force. Our number was small. About sixty horse-soldiers, little baggage or armaments (we hoped to augment these within the town), a few Austrian and Irish mercenaries, and a handful of Cornishmen left over from the débâcle. They had their own reasons for wanting to enter Taunton, and these were nothing to do with loyalty to the prince.

Scouts, stationed at relay posts along the road, were reaching us with news that grew daily more alarming. Buckingham's force was little more than a day's ride away. Rhys ap Thomas was coming fast. And there was no word from Antoine de la Force, who should by now be with the Princess on the Mount. Richard and I looked at one another with the same thought, and dared not voice it.

'Now I know how the bloody stag feels,' muttered Atwater, as news came of Daubeney's troops being sighted on Salisbury Plain. 'Can you hear those dogs baying? Sohow, boys, avant, sohay, sohow!' And he laughed, bitterly, calling on holy St Brigid. We were all badgering our private patrons. I wore my cloak tight about me against the autumn chill, and I spoke its maker's name more often than that of God.

We rode into Taunton on 21 September. The streets were quiet, with neither cheering nor cursing. People looked out—not at an army—but rather as at a band who had wandered far in search of a land more lost than Lyonesse. I swear I saw some mystified pity before the window-shutters closed, softly, as against a funeral riding by below; not wishing to attract some black and sleeping death.

One moment stays with me. We had entered the market-place, the Cornishmen looking delicately about, with knives unsheathed. There was a tavern called the Limer, and outside, lounging on a bench, a fat man in doublet and fringed hood, beringed, a plump purse at his hip. One of the Cornishmen said softly: 'That is Sir John Oby, tax-collector. Under sentence of death.'

They moved forward in a pack. An alepot rolled on the ground. Perhaps in the bloodsoaked moments that followed, Oby knew why they had come for him. They tore him limb from limb, their knives butchering him piecemeal. The tankard rolled and his blood dripped into it, so where he had come in with ale he went out with wine . . .

Otis Philip of Polwhele wrenched off the head with an axe and held it by the hair. 'For Michael Joseph!' he cried. 'Go tax the Devil, John Oby!'

Then calm, red-spattered, they quit Taunton for their homes. A potboy swilled down the street, wearing a satisfied little smile, as one of our scouts rode towards us, face beaded, white as milk.

'My lord,' he told the prince. 'You must fly from here. Lord Daubeney is now at Glastonbury. He knows your whereabouts and will arrive by nightfall with six thousand men.'

The prince said quite calmly: 'Have you met Antoine de la Force upon the road? Is there news of my wife?' The courier shook his head, dismounting stiffly.

312

'Go, refresh yourself,' said Richard, and as the scout entered the tavern, he put his hands together, not caring who heard his prayer. 'God keep her, sweet Jesus and St Jude; holy St Katherine, keep her. Most blessed Virgin, be at her side. Send her safe to me. Watch over my wife, my Kate, my life's white flower . . .'

'Amen, amen,' I said. Krista.

There was no returning to the West. Already King's men were on the road to Cornwall. The scout had seen them. They were royal commissioners riding to exact a further terrible justice of the rebels from the Tamar down to Helston. Years later I learned just how dire the penalties had been; every monastery and borough fined, then each of Cornwall's nine hundreds, and then every parish. The county was bled white.

Night was coming as we saddled our horses and put together our meagre baggage. We had with us now only a score of mounted men. No farriers, grooms, chaplains, and no fresh horses for the ride to Southampton. With darkness came the rain, a storm like Noah's Flood. The cold black rain slashed down as if a great bowl had been overturned, and I heard the men muttering about God's vengeance. As we moved from the inn, the teeming water washed away the last of John Oby's blood, struck down the red leaves from the trees, running in torrents across our path. Our faces were battered, rain spat on our tongues if we tried to speak. Thunder roared like a judge. The horses laboured and steamed against the frail swinging glow of our lanterns, until rain extinguished their light, and, with Daubeney's levies somewhere hard on our heels, we rode blindly towards the New Forest at a splashing gallop in the open pit of night.

Strangely, I was not afraid. Only tired, sick, stale, and sad for that which had gone so wrong. With the beat of the rain came the knowledge that this was the adventure's only true end. The thread of the years, the gaudy days of being lauded by great rulers in the courts of illusion, were all frayed down to this, the race against time and death, the bloody running of the stag. Someone had begun to weave this tapestry long ago, taking the flowers of hemlock and rue for its colours, and now sat unseen, working the loom to the finish, busy, dispassionate, slamming home the shuttle with the sound of a scaffold building. Someone with a skull-face was weaving the colours of the years into a shroud for us all.

Our soldiers abandoned us before journey's end, some coming to Richard with a sorry smile and a farewell, others just vanishing like cutpurses into the forest, afraid in their rusting armour. Six of us rode into Southampton one morning. The sea was boiling over the grey quay and the moored vessels pitched queasily in the harbour. They were Tudor's ships, and there were also a great many sharp-eyed men and royal forces about the town. The rain beat on the cobbles like urgent hands. Prince Richard stared in anguish at the heavy sea, searching in vain for a sight of *Cuckoo*. Then Antoine came running along the quay, half drowned, stubble on his exhausted face. He fell to his knee and kissed the prince's hand and I jerked him up quickly before a knot of King's men who were questioning some people about to go aboard a vessel could turn their heads.

'My liege lord,' he gasped. Quickly we moved beneath the stone arches of a warehouse before the Tudor soldiers, rain glinting on their helmets, started to patrol along the quayside.

'Tell me quickly.' Richard shut his eyes as if to bear the news better. 'What of the Princess?'

Antoine made a strange sound; I thought he was about to fall in a fit. Then he whispered: 'Tudor's men have her.'

'Speak up,' said John Atwater crossly.

'Tudor's men have recaptured the Mount,' wailed Antoine. 'The Red Dragon flies there. I could not get near. The coast is blockaded by Lord Brooke's fleet. Tudor sent a force of five hundred to take the Princess. They are bringing her to face the King at Taunton. He rides there now.' He clutched my arm as if he were drowning.

Prince Richard bit his own lip, so hard that a line of blood appeared. He licked it, cleared his throat. Finally words came out of him.

'Is my wife . . . has she been harmed, Antoine de la Force?'

'No.' Shivering with rain and tears. 'She did not resist capture. Her women are with her. It's said she is to be placed in the care of the Queen's sister. I heard no wrong had been done her.'

314

'Sweet holy Jesu,' said Richard painfully. 'What of our ships? Our captains?'

'The Barton brothers sailed away, they managed to evade the fleet. I don't know where they went. Pierre-Jean Meno . . .'

'Yes?'

'He was in Tudor's pocket all the time,' said Antoine miserably. 'The *Cuckoo* is his payment for betraying you. Don de Ayala blessed the plan. Spain would never jeopardize the love between them and Henry. The marriage of the prince Arthur and the Infanta must come about as a bond within the Holy League. The Spanish King thinks to please Tudor by engineering your capture, my lord.'

The sea hissed, steaming on the grey quayside, the masts swung in harbour. Rain poured as we stood in our doomed circle. The prince stared down at the cobbles, his harsh breath mingling with Antoine's chattering teeth and the tramp of the royal patrol who came searching along the dock, arms lit by the sheeting rain. I looked at Heron, Skelton and Ashley. Their faces were full of terror. Soon they will bolt for safety, I thought, but where is safety now?

John Heron had his hand on his mount's saddle-horn. His eyes darted like fish in the white pool of his face. He said in a rasp: 'We cannot stay here, your Grace.'

There was no answer. Nick Ashley, his gaze reeling in and out of the shadows, from the group of soldiers to the prince, burst out: 'For Christ's mercy, lord, let's ride,' and swung up on to his tired, dripping horse.

'Ride where, for God's love?' Atwater put a foot in his stirrup. I bent and cupped hands for Richard to mount his own horse, its white coat now darkly mired. In the saddle he sat still silent. Over the sounds of the sea came the stamp and jingle of armed riders approaching. Richard, for all our sakes, I said—I may not even have spoken aloud. With great sadness he looked down at me, and said.

'My Katherine—at Taunton. God knows what the King will do out of his great rage. I must . . . should I throw myself on his mercy?'

I looked at him in horror. There was an outcry from the others. Atwater leaned across and seized the white horse's bridle, dragging mount and rider forward. 'Madness,' he said through his teeth. The noise of the approaching horsemen grew.

'God help us all,' said Heron wildly. In an untidy flurry we wheeled, hoofs striking meagre fire from the ground, and down the road, hell-bent, the prince being carried away by Atwater still tugging the bridle.

'Where?' they cried, as we rode, dodging carters, wagons laden with wool for the docks, merchants who cursed our wayward flight, through the dour streets of Southampton and out of the gates, expecting at any moment a challenge, or arrow-fire.

'Into the Forest,' Atwater gasped, hauling up the prince's hood so that Richard's face was half hidden, like a nurse roughly putting a child to rights.

'We can't live in the Forest!' Antoine cried from the rear. Atwater turned in the saddle. 'We'll ride to Beaulieu Abbey!' he roared. 'They'll give us sanctuary there—it's under royal charter. There's nothing else . . . forty days' grace, until the hunt dies down.'

Richard nodded at this, and almost smiled, peering from the hood. As we rode he seemed to grow younger; his mud-splashed face took on a strange, witched youthfulness that had its roots in age, as if his life were rounding to full circle, a mystery enhanced by the rhythm of the desperate hoofs which beat out sanctuary, sanctuary.

With a sharp flint, I made my little mark on the wall. I had never missed a day.

'Thirty-nine,' I whispered. Through the night, the monks began Matins. Their chant wound into our cell on a trail of freezing mist. I heard Richard stir behind me. John Atwater snored softly and in the far corner, Antoine lay in sleep, lax as a dead dog.

'Then it's tomorrow,' Richard said. He got up from the straw and came over to me. Standing on tiptoe, he touched the window-bars. 'Tomorrow, Nicholas, we shall come face to face with his Divine Majesty, Henry Tudor. At last.'

Beaulieu was a prison. Perhaps we had known it from the beginning when, dripping and weary, we cried: 'Sanctuary, for the love of God and the King!' The door had swung open as if handled by ghosts. Word had gone forward of our coming, and had we looked into the forest shadows we would even then have spied Daubeney's levies moving in to surround the Abbey. They had stood guard during the days of our imprisonment. Beaulieu was a web for us, with the Abbot, primed with gold and royal promises, sitting spiderlike at its heart.

Richard laid his arm across my shoulder.

'Would to Jesus I had some clean clothing,' he said, and shivered from the lice that ran on us all. We reeked of sweat and dirt, and the cell, although a sour-faced lay brother came to sweep it occasionally, was noisome as a midden. We had been able to buy food, but no fresh gear. For some reason it pleased the Abbot to keep us dirty. Perhaps he imagined it doubled our shame.

We had been taken to his parlour on our arrival, walking through the chill cloister with keys turning behind us. He sat, cowl pushed back from his shaven head, his grey wattled neck emerging like a dragon's from the folds of his habit. He was warming himself before a fire-basket, and looked up from the flames, smiling dreadfully with long yellow teeth. His eyes were like small wounds in his skull and I thought instantly: If this is a man of God, I will settle for Satan.

With the hellish light on his bones he addressed Richard.

'So! traitor Warbeck! You come bearing weapons in the House of God!' And very quickly, clerks came and took our swords and knives and we stood stripped of arms before the terrible old man.

'We claim sanctuary,' Richard said, and we all nodded, while Atwater let out a little Irish oath as he surrendered his sword.

'You treacherous dog,' said the Abbot softly. 'You have risen against God's anointed king. You have the smell of death about you already. To your knees, traitors, and pray for pardon. Pray for the leniency of King Henry, whom you have so grievously offended. By your crimes against his divinity, you are judged. Kneel, carrion, and crave pardon, for it is heresy to rise against one anointed with the Chrism. Grovel, though I doubt you can save your vile bodies from his wrath, or your souls from everlasting Hell. Why should I harbour you? God's house is not shaped to shield treason.'

Richard said quietly: 'It is canonical law, my lord Abbot, that

317

you give us shelter for forty days. And I am no traitor, but the rightful king of England.'

'You base worm,' hissed the Abbot. 'You sign your death warrant with your boasting tongue. Wretches! King's men are all around you, and the King's justice will be terrible . . .'

That was the moment when Skelton's nerve broke and he thumped to his knees, followed instantly by John Heron and Nick Ashley, all of them crying: 'Mercy! Mercy!' with Atwater looking down at them in disgusted amazement and Antoine standing firm and pale, and the prince looking at me with a rueful little smile, which the old Abbot saw.

'You laugh, you whelp!' he cried, even the fire flaming and sparking to mimic his rage, and the awful chorus of Mercy, Mercy! continued. Skelton had his face pressed to the flagstones, and was howling: 'We beg mercy: send us to the King! We crave his forgiveness! We abjure our past works, we renounce this false captain . . . mercy!' and I heard Atwater whisper something to Antoine about 'before the cock crows thrice.'

I think the Abbot was pleased with this betrayal; no doubt he imagined Henry could make use of the three frightened men. They had ridden with us loyally for years, and, watching them shepherded away by the clerks, I felt angry sadness yet an understanding that this was one more colour in the pattern that someone, unseen, was weaving.

So now there were four of us, kept in this cell, and I scratched off the days on the damp grey wall and of nights I talked with Richard, and we comforted one another. One monk, a sharp, stunted creature who oversaw the lay brother's cleaning, had a particular enmity for Richard. He also had a brother in Exeter who wrote to him. The King was at Exeter now, and so was the Princess Katherine.

'He saw King Henry riding through the cheering streets,' he said, smiling with rat's teeth. 'And your lady wife too.' He cocked his rat's head to watch Richard. 'Very pale that lady looked, and there were bruises on her wrists as if she'd been tied. Guards all about her litter, and swords at her back. My brother said her gown was torn, I think.'

I got up and pushed the monk in the chest, and he sat gasping in the straw. Antoine came and stood astride him. He cringed, covering his face.

'Get out, you little turdpot,' I said, 'before we slit your lying tongue.' That tongue was why Richard was wakeful tonight, standing with his arm across my shoulder.

'If he should harm her, Nicholas,' he said, 'I do not know what I shall do. Would I have a chance to kill him? With my bare hands?' He sighed. 'I'm glad our time here ends tomorrow. Then we shall know our fate.'

'They'll probably hang me tomorrow,' I said. The words seemed to mean little. 'And I shall never get to marry Krista.'

'Is she your lady?' He did not wait for an answer, but buried his face in his palms. Anguished and muffled, he said: 'Oh, holy Mother of Christ! protect her—if her blood should be shed because of me . . . that whiteness torn . . .'

I rubbed his back. There was a real pain in my side, legacy of the Exeter siege where the bombard's ball had hit me. It came and went. Tonight it was bad, and I had to breathe carefully.

'Tudor would not put a woman to the torture,' I said. 'And certainly not the coz of King James. James would set fire to the border as far as Nottingham.'

'James is a world away,' he answered faintly. 'It's Spain which is of paramount importance to Tudor. If Spain thinks that he cannot hold his throne and his place within the Holy League— because of my claims—the alliance will be sunk between them. No, Tudor may stop at nothing to break me down . . .' Then he began to tremble, like a hare in a snare, and I held him close to my aching side.

'They call me Werbecque,' he said. 'You remember them— Catherine de Werbecque was kind to me when I first came to Tournai, like a mother. You took a letter for them once, to Osbeck, in Bruges . . .'

'I lost it, my lord.' There, it was out. It had been a boil in my brain for years. Now it burst, I waited for his wrath.

'But you gave Osbeck the money? It was a repayment for the clothes, the victuals and my schooling . . . Say you did that, Nicholas.'

'Yes. But I lost the letter, somewhere in Bruges.'

He was silent, then said with a little sigh. 'Ay, well. A pity.

Someone, somewhere, has a letter to Vrouw Werbecque with my signet and in my hand. What's done is done. I don't suppose it makes much difference. Werbecque is as good a name as any to hang me with. It sings sweeter in Henry's ears than does Plantagenet.'

The night was one for talking, all the unanswered riddles posed. I found a candle end and struck flint until a spark gleamed.

'So, Nicholas.' In the masked light his left eye was open wider than I had ever seen it. There was, I was sure, no sight in it. 'You are the loyalest servant I ever owned. Do you love me, after all we have come through? In face of all we may endure?'

'You are my liege lord,' I said. 'My true sovereign.'

'But'—and in the tiny light I saw him smile—'once you asked me who I was, truly. I heard you through a dream. Who am I, Nicholas? King Richard the Fourth of England, scion of the great houses of York and Plantagenet? Or Pierrequin Werbecque? Perkin Warbeck, son of a Flemish bargemaster? Have I played false? Or am I the son of the Duchess Margaret by her paramour, the Bishop of Cambrai? Or am I a royal bastard of the great dead ones—Edward the Fourth, Richard the Third, George of Clarence, who ever craved kingship. Do not think I haven't heard all the wild tales. Who am I, Nicholas?'

The pain in my side burgeoned. Every word of his seemed to rub the sickness into fresh vigour.

'I do not know, my lord,' I said. 'Tell me.'

'Are you a good judge of men, Nicholas?'

I had not wept in a long time. Now I felt tears falling, and was glad of the gloom. The pain in my side was like the twisting of devils.

'I think I am,' I said. 'Seven years ago I put myself to school as a judge of men. Before that, it cost me dear.'

'Will you judge me tomorrow?'

I bowed my head, lost. Then he said, so softly that Atwater's snoring almost effaced his voice:

'I am in mortal terror, Nicholas. Henry Tudor and his Gascon torturers—the thought of them wrings my spirit. I feel my bones on the rack. I fear for my wife, but I feel not only her torment, but my own. They rack the bones until the skin is a mere bag holding splinters. Fire is used with great skill. And did you know that

320

they can take the living heart from out of a man so that he still feels—so that he is still a screaming shipwreck of a man? Did you know that they can gouge his manhood and then burn his parts before his face?'

In the dark night, a darker night remembered me. My father, in Leicester market-place.

'Yes,' I said. 'I know all this.'

'I am in perfect dread,' he said. 'You ask me who I am. I speak now of the man within.' Through the shadows I saw him press his breast urgently. 'Me! that thing that loves and strives and thinks and feels . . . tomorrow . . . will you still keep faith? Or will you count me craven, as James of Scotland did in the field of battle?'

The monks had finished Matins. It was the hour between dog and wolf. I said: 'I will keep faith.'

'I wonder,' he said, and very sadly: 'All those lives lost, lives ruined, through my weakness. Nicholas, tomorrow. Fear will show you who I really am.'

I had one more question. My pain had left me suddenly, and I could breathe.

'Richard. My dear lord. How did you hurt your eye?'

He made a little noise of surprise. Atwater snored on, and Antoine gave in his sleep a twisted cry.

'At Barnard Castle,' he said after a moment. 'Where Brampton took me and my brother before the battle. Some keen young archer drew his bow. I was kneeling by, too close. The fletch went in my eye and wounded it. His name—the archer's—was Edmund. I wonder what became of him?'

It was tomorrow. I lifted the light and made another scratch on the wall. Very soon it would be All Souls once again. The Day of the Dead.

The scaffold was built to hang twelve at a time, with a trestle that could be wheeled from under our feet. I stood next to Antoine, the hemp hard beneath my ear. We had been hastily confessed and shriven by a very young priest, one of Cardinal Morton's. With difficulty I twisted my head to look at Antoine who, eyes shut tight, was praying. I tried to pray too, to the Virgin, and to St Jude, patron of lost causes. But if I closed my eyes all I could see was the small brown mole on Krista's left breast like a freckle

321

on a white hen's egg, and clearly I heard Anneke singing one of her fractured English songs, laughing on each note, and I was glad that my dear ones shone so sharp in the moment of my death.

The Sheriff's executioner watched the King's herald closely for the signal. Next to Antoine stood John Atwater, likewise haltered, then a man who had been master farrier in Henry's household and had deserted to come with us to Ireland; then Skelton. Somewhere down the line with others were Heron and Ashley, and Atwater's son.

The scaffold stood outside the house of the Exeter Cathedral Treasurer, where the King was lodged. Earlier they had chopped down eight of the sixteen great trees in the close so that the King, from a raised platform, could survey the mass of rebels who had been hunted down by Daubeney, Sir Piers Edgecumbe, young Courtenay, Rhys ap Thomas and the Duke of Buckingham. In their scores they knelt on the ground, ropes round their necks, some weeping, many prostrate, and the muted cry for pardon and mercy was like a sour litany. Even brave Cornishmen, including Tresinney, were singing for their lives. I asked for neither pardon nor mercy, and that is no conceit. Truth to tell, I did not want Tudor's mercy. For I remembered that my father had not cried for it, and neither would I.

A great assembly of courtiers watched from the platform opposite. In the middle, the King sat on a golden throne. Behind him, looking gross, old and rather ill, the bloated red shape of the Chancellor, Cardinal Morton, leaned on a silver staff. There was Sir Reynold Bray, the Queen Mother's clerk, who had risen to great heights in recent years. Above the bright tabards of the King's lords of office, the Red Dragon flamed and ramped on a green ground.

And near these nobles, yet apart, flanked by two Yeomen of the Guard with pikes, stood the man who had led us to this time. Known to me as Richard Plantagenet, he stood, eyes fixed on the ground, as if counting his sorrows in the soil. Still in his filthy clothes, his hair matted, his face like chalk, a self-confessed impostor. 'Stay close to us, foolish fellow!' I had heard Reynold Bray say, 'or these Cornishmen will tear you in pieces! You are their ruination!' I wanted him to look up and meet my eyes for the last time, so that I could show I forgave him, I understood him. Fear will show you who I am, he had told me in the Abbey, and I knew. But he stood like marble, and I saw the parchment on which had been written his confession fall from his lax hand. One of the Yeomen picked it up. It was precious, the most costly thing in all our lives.

We had been taken from Beaulieu to Exeter to face the King in Guildhall, and on the road we passed the rebels, being herded like cattle towards the city. The four of us had been pushed by pikemen into the big chamber with its pillars supported by gilt bears and the raised dais at the far end. To one side of the dais was a closed antechamber, and above it a minstrels' gallery. I recall what a long walk it seemed to the dais, how my side pained me when I breathed, and how a sudden ardent curiosity to see, at last, the King, cast out any fear. He was so clustered about with nobles that it was hard to pick him out. Morton loomed largest in his cardinal's red, and the Yeomen, like flamboyant red-and-gold roses, all but diminished the sovereign. But as we closed with the dais and went on our knees before the guard could fling us there, his presence swam darkly out to meet us, and the chamber could have been empty save for him.

In York, soon after Bosworth, a saying sprang up whereby mothers would frighten their children. 'Be still!' they'd say, 'or Henry Tydder will come and get you!' Yet he did not look such an ogre. He sat there, slightly bowed, frailly formed, wearing purple velvet whose richness sicklied his skin and mimicked the shadows round his long dark eyes. Thin greyish hair hung under a close black cap pinned with a diamond and a priceless pearl. He did not, at first sight, look majestic, a force courted by the heads of Europe. He looked too careworn for that, the veteran of many invisible battles. And yet all about him was an air. Such power, such certainty radiated from him that it seemed to imbue even the wood of his chair and the stuff of his clothes with a might which made them shrink and fold. As I raised my head slightly, I felt his mind stretch out and touch us, and it was like being licked by a cold sharp flame. I felt my head grow icy, as if it had been shorn of hair.

Antoine, Atwater and I were manacled together. Richard's hands were free. We knelt there for minutes, while Henry's lips

323

opened, not to speak but to cough fretfully, and a page brought napkins so that he could spit. I remembered hearing that he was plagued by tertian fever, and the November day was raw. When he had done coughing, he spoke, a hoarse voice, querulous rather than unkind.

'Oh, strike off those chains!' he told the escort, and smiled at us.

Something happened when he smiled. The skin stretched tight over his nose and the knobs where cheekbone met jaw. His teeth were completely black in a mouth with lips so thin that it was hard to imagine that they had ever kissed, or drunk too deep, or cried out in war or pleasure. Blackness within the smiling mouth, blackness in the tired eyes, like two grave-pits. For in that smiling moment he had become Death, the invincible, arbiter of all truth, the maker of skulls.

'Rise,' he said, with the same slight impatience. The black smile vanished. Delicate ringed hands, blotched with the pigments of age, stirred the air upward as if testing its weight.

'Come, let us see you clearly,' he said. We moved forward in a line. His eyes flicked over Antoine and me dismissively, then rested on Atwater.

'My lord mayor of Cork!' A note of pain. 'How sad we are to see you in these straits. Why were you never content to give me fealty in exchange for pardon like your compatriots Kildare and Desmond? Ireland is very dear to our heart!'

Atwater bowed, and did not reply. The feeling of cold numbed my chest and shoulders. I felt a terrible urge to piss, as if all my will were dissolving. The King looked at Plantagenet, deeply.

'I have long dreamed of this meeting,' he said, so softly that the courtiers craned to hear. 'I was curious to know the face of the foreign lad who has brought such evil into our realm. You have plagued us long. Are these your servants, Master Warbeck?' He smiled again at us, and I looked quickly at the floor. 'Rogues, if ever I saw them. Do you rule them well?'

Richard answered, his voice bold, too bold, and too high. 'You mistake me, my lord. I am not Warbeck. I am your cousin, sir. The throne where you sit and the sceptre you hold are filched from me. By birthright and blood they are mine, as is the kingdom. I am Richard, second son of Edward Plantagenet of blessed memory.'

The King leaned back slightly in his chair and waited, folding his hands. Love and fear and pride mingled in me. I let my sleeve brush Richard's, hoping that I could perhaps feed him a breath of strength, though I was still icy cold.

'Yes, these are my servants,' Richard said into the silence. 'Honest men, bound to me by livery and maintenance. No blame attaches to them, for they only obey my will. The one is very young, and the other somewhat lackwit.' A further wave of love for him pierced through my fear, together with a mad lust to laugh. Yes, I thought: I would play the wittold, not to save myself, but him.

'It is you who lack wit, Master Warbeck,' said the King. 'Faugh! how foully you stink.' He drew a pomander from his gown and wearily held it to his nose. This made me want to weep, as I remembered the perfumed baths, the glorious elegance of the courts of Charles and Margaret and James. I felt Richard's sleeve quiver against mine, and hoped it were with rage, but his voice trembled too.

'You still address me wrongly, my lord,' he said. 'I am Richard the Fourth of England.'

Another little hush. Henry looked thoughtfully over the top of the gleaming pomander.

'God have mercy,' he said in a kind of wonder. Cardinal Morton leaned and whispered in his ear. The other courtiers behind him were silent, breathless and intent. The only sound came from outside, where workmen hammered at the new scaffold.

Suddenly Richard shouted, a harsh cry that bounced off the beamed roof and stunned itself against the velvet of the peers.

'I *am* Richard Plantagenet!' he cried. 'I have come over miles of striving, through years of waiting, to claim what is mine alone! Great rulers have upheld me, and the people of England . . . the peers of the realm . . . they will do likewise . . . my claim is good . . .' The shouting tailed off miserably. His own bravado had outmatched him and he was lost. Henry's silence, coupled with the two keen darknesses peeping out over the pomander, became unbearable. At last he spoke.

'This cannot be, foolish one,' he said. 'The youth whose name you counterfeit was murdered years ago by the tyrant Gloucester in London Tower. But, merciful God! what dreams you've had, wretch! To steal my throne? To cast me and my Queen into the wilderness and set yourself and your lady in our place!' Quick as a cat, he tossed the pomander to a page. 'Your lady, Master. You do not ask of her welfare. Alas. Shame.'

The sleeve against my arm began to ripple with waves of trembling. Richard said faintly: 'Yes. My lady. I am greatly concerned for her.'

'Jesu, mercy,' said the King, and bowed his head as in requiem. On the periphery of the crowd of nobles stood two men; clad top to toe in black boiled leather with only their eyes visible, and their waists girded with great keys. At a signal from the Cardinal, they moved down from the dais and stood at the antechamber door.

'We must find her for you then, if we can,' said Henry Tudor. 'Before you confess that you are no prince. You will speak out before these peers admitting you are but a feigned youth, led sadly astray by the vanities of foreign powers who lust to bring us down.'

'No, my lord,' said Richard. 'Never.' But I felt his arm in its sleeve jerk, like that of one with falling sickness whose limbs betray him. Henry rose and the courtiers bowed in a wave. The Yeomen flanked him as he moved from the dais. Suddenly I could smell him and his clothes. He smelled of gold, and like a clerk, of ink. Fatigue, and a vague sweat of sickness, were overlaid by the last breath of orange from the pomander.

'You prate, poor wittold, of being England's heir,' he said, close and soft. 'But kings are divine. You are a mean man. A man of flesh and blood. With a tender wife. Let us seek her.'

He moved through into the antechamber. The Yeomen came and took Richard from my side and they followed. After them went the two black-clad figures. I suddenly knew that these were two of the Gascon torturers, and the cold feeling reached my heart.

We waited for two hours, tolled by the cathedral bell. Long before the end the King returned, not to the dais, but in the gallery above, coughing as he seated himself. There were ladies with him, dim in the shadows behind him, their faces blurred by distance. At the same time a clerk hurried with parchments and pens into the antechamber, closing the door behind him sharply. Little conversations fluttered in the crowd, and some soft laughter. The hammering outside stopped. There was another strange, tiny sound, a silvery jingling. I searched the assembly for its source. One of the royal jesters was sitting cross-legged on the floor, nodding in sleep and waking with a jingling jerk of his belled tricorne. It was Patch.

I stared, amazed. I had long imagined him dead, or pensioned off in a monastery. His sight seemed as bad and groping as ever, he would not recognize me, yet I was oddly cheered to see him even in this dreadful moment. Then the door opened and Plantagenet reappeared, under escort, with a parchment in his hand. What had been said in that secret room I do not know to this day, but he was broken. Not a mark was on him, but he was touched by death.

Cardinal Morton came heavily forward, leaning on his staff. He beckoned Richard up on to the dais, and motioned he should turn about, his back to the gallery. The courtiers pressed quietly about him.

'Begin,' said Henry from the gallery. Richard lifted the parchment as if it were lead, and began to read aloud. I would never have recognized his voice. It was hollow and flat and tripped continually on the words he held close to his eyes. I was to know the text very well in time. It was a garbled farrago of contradictions, with names that neither I, nor he, had ever heard before this day.

'Be it known to all men that I was born in the town of Tournai in Flanders, my father John Osbeck, Comptroller of the said town, my mother Catherine Haro, and my grandfather Dirick Osbeck, after whose decease my grandmother married Peter Flamine, receiver of Tournai and Dean of the Boatmen over the Scheldt. My mother's father was Peter de Faro, who kept the keys of St Thomas's Gate within the town. I had an uncle John Statime of St Pia's parish, with whom I dwelled very young, he married my Aunt Jane and brought me up very well, yet my mother, being very fond of me, had me sent to Antwerp to learn Flemish, more exactly to a kinsman of my father's, John Steinbeck, with whom I remained half a year. By reason of the wars I returned to

Tournai where I was placed with Mr Barlo at Antwerp where I fell sick, and so was boarded in a skinner's house, whereby I learned the English tongue as you see.'

He raised a ghastly face and looked full at us. Forgive me, the look said. I tried to smile at him and failed.

'I went to Barrow Mart, and lodged at the Old Man, and afterwards with John Straw, a merchant, who first made me believe I was better than I was. From Antwerp I sailed into Portugal with my lady Brampton in the Queen's Ship, and served a knight in Lichborne, called Don Peter las de Cogna, who had but one eye, but the order of his household made me tarry there a year. Then Pierre-Jean Meno, a Breton, called me into Ireland, and either commanded so by my Lady Margaret who, as she said, was my aunt, or projecting something for his own private interest, persuaded me that I was a Plantagenet of the House of York.'

The time-server, Meno, I thought. May *Cuckoo* founder!

'When I arrived in Cork, because I was handsomely apparelled, they bestowed on me the title of the Earl of Warwick, son to George Duke of Clarence, and this John le Wellin the Mayor, maintained. And forasmuch as my denial was contrary to their expectations, they brought me to the Cross and made me swear, which I did, disclaiming him, until Stephen Poitron, with John Atwater'—he looked sorrowfully at the mayor—'came to me, as resolved I was King Richard's bastard son (then in the hands of the king of England) persuading me not to be afraid at any time.'

King Richard's bastard—John of Gloucester? A strange choice for any man to counterfeit. Tudor had executed John years ago, seeing a focus for discontent in his noble birth. The charge had been that of treasonable correspondence with Ireland. Richard swallowed hard, croaking out the final paragraph.

'For they would aid me even to the obtaining of the Crown of England. They knew the Earls of Desmond and Kildare were ready to venture their lives and estates for my sake. After this they carried me to Flanders to Lady Margaret, Regent of Burgundy, who prevailed upon me so far that I took upon me the person of Richard Duke of York, and so I returned back to Ireland, where John Taylor, the foresaid Earls and others entered with me into a dangerous rebellion, and I was proclaimed by them

328

Richard the Fourth. From hence the King of France sent for me by Stephen Frion, but, making peace with England left me to my fate. Then I sailed into Flanders where my supposed aunt made more of me, so I attempted England but was driven back again into Flanders, whence I went into Scotland and from thence again into Ireland and so into England . . . and this is my true confession.'

The parchment drooped. He wept silently, so did Antoine and I. John Atwater looked shocked and angry. But the faces of the court were bored, as at an old story. I wondered wearily why Warbeck was now called Osbeck, and if there were, somewhere in the world, a young fair man called Osbeck or Warbeck. Henry appeared again, coming from the antechamber. His voice too was tired and halting, as after a long journey. He mounted the dais.

'It was well done, foolish boy,' he said. 'I promise you shall have practice in this penance, for your soul's good. You shall read your confession throughout London. And now, you may see your lady wife.'

Richard, his eye caught by movement in the gallery, looked upwards. From the shadowy knot of ladies there a veiled figure stepped forward and held the rail hard with both hands.

'Behold her!' said Henry almost merrily.

Two maids drew back the veil from Katherine's face. She had never looked lovelier, wearing rose pink velvet and cloth of gold. Her red hair hung to her waist like a virgin bride's. Her colour was high, her chin raised. I heard Richard mutter to himself: 'Ah, God be praised, ah God . . .'

Henry cried: 'Madame! We greet you. Now, lady, do you see this man? He says he is husband to you, and was sorely troubled for your health.'

Katherine leaned slightly over the gallery and fixed her eyes on Richard. The hiss of her drawn breath was as sharp as steel.

'I do not see my husband,' she said clearly. 'I see a false deluding slave who masqueraded into my cousin James's favour and into my bed. I see a peasant wretch who dares to rise against his betters. I see a tricky Flemish knave whose confession shames my honour. I see no husband. From this day, I am unwed.'

She jerked the veil over her face and swung back into the dark

329

recesses of the gallery. I think she wept; women were cosseting her in their arms.

'So be it,' said Henry Tudor soberly.

The Sheriff's executioner passed down the line. 'The King has shown mercy,' he said. He was slipping nooses off necks. 'He will make an example only of some of you.' He freed Heron, Skelton and Ashley. He tightened the rope about Antoine's neck, and that of the master farrier.

'He has decreed that only one in three shall hang,' he said. 'He shows great mercy.'

I felt the hemp slide from off my head, and rubbed my neck in bewilderment. 'One in three,' he said again. 'Get down.' He pushed me from the trestle. He freed Atwater. My feet hit the ground as the trestle rolled back. Antoine's jerking feet struck my head. He gasped, and began to strangle.

Richard and I were taken under close guard to the Palace of Westminster. Atwater went to the Tower. I never saw Skelton, Heron and Ashley again. But I had seen Antoine die, in anguish, for he was my friend, and so loyal to our cause that I fancy he would have chosen no other way.

I know that St Jude, blessed patron of lost hopes, made Henry Tudor spare my life. Yet had I then known the thing that was to follow, I might well have wished it otherwise.

The ship luffed and came up to the wind, and, mainsail hoisted, sprang forward briskly over the grey North Sea with its little frill of white. She had been becalmed for a space and now rode free. And I had been becalmed for the best part of a year and I was going home. Home to Flanders. She was a big ship, to me the dearest ship in the world, and as I clutched part of the standing rigging to steady myself on the dancing deck, I loved her from her topgallant to her belaying pins. I listened to her master's flat Norfolk voice calling to the bosun. The crew brought the ship in line with the main course, half lowering the main yard and securing the weather end to the deck. The leeward end rode high, leaving part of the sail set like a lateen.

The waves' white frill lessened. Spring sun warmed the fair

wind. The master gave a final order and turned, his big ruddy face calm and fresh.

'Set fair now,' he said. 'This is a good voyage. That's lucky to have someone with St Nicholas's blessed name aboard. Come below.'

He wanted to talk with me again. He was curious, and I trusted him completely. I followed him past the stacked cargo, the barrels of Colchester oysters and dried herring, the sarplers of wool from Braintree, the casks of malt and packs of samphire, and, with his rosy bald head like a beacon before me, climbed down into the belly of the ship.

'Tell me'—he splashed ale into tankards, and seated himself—'how long were you in the Welsh dog's custody?'

He was Yorkist to the marrow. His humour warmed me. I even forgot the pain in my side.

'Near eight months at Westminster,' I answered. 'Until we escaped.'

'*You* escaped.' He spoke soberly, looking at me under his eyebrows, his bald head a great judicial sun. 'His Grace was taken again.' It was always 'his Grace'. All the forced confessions in the world would not have turned his tongue to 'Perkin Warbeck' or 'Osbeck'. 'May God's grace be with him, blessed boy.' He shook his head. 'The east wind blows off the river there. It's a bad place, the Tower of London. I had friends inside.'

I sat on a barrel of fish in brine and told him all from the beginning, for I owed him more than gold. Over months of searching he was the only man who had helped me obtain passage from England. I spoke of the terrible months from November to June, when Richard and I shared one small apartment in the Wardrobe wing of Westminster, my one-time home and the very place from where he had once dreamed of reigning.

Before that, however, was the slow ride through the City, where his confession had already been displayed in Paul's churchyard and on the London Stone in St Swithin's parish, and in Petty Wales near the Tower. Bound, we rode into the City over London Bridge with its frieze of spiked felon's heads circled by ravenous crows. Along Fish Street, Vintry, Poultry, into Chepeside and down to Paul's, finally entering the river meadows of Westminster. The whole of London was out, their eyes on us in our filthy clothes. If Richard sagged on his horse, they screamed in jeering pity. If he sat straight and proud, they tore off their hats and mocked him with courtesies: 'Prince Perkin!' they cried. I heard a child say curiously: 'Be he a monster?'

Our chamber had heavy bolts and chains on the outside. There was a tall arched window, with leaded mullion panes, overlooking the river. Boats were tied up at a small jetty. On the further bank a huge bare forest of oaks stood. The cold green water flowed on day by day, marking out our life's passing on its way to the eternal sea. That inexorable river drove me half mad. I thought how it moved on without hindrance past Greenwich and Gravesend, to curl about the Isle of Sheppey and then lose itself in the ocean bearing craft to France—to Flanders. I cursed and envied the river its freedom.

Almost at once we had our clean clothes, sent by his Majesty. Richard's gown was very good and cost eleven shillings. Each item had to be signed for in the prince's hand. Doubtless these bills were later studied by the clerk in charge of forgeries. There was even a bill 'to Robert Jones for 5d a day for Perkin's horse's fodder.' But when I tried to help dress him, tie his points and put on his shoes, he pushed me roughly away, and shouted: 'It is not fit!' turning to gaze from the window. He spent much time there, or sleeping. For the first month he slept all day and tossed most of the night. Sometimes he wept in his pillow. Good victuals were sent in but he ate little and grew gaunt. In daylight he could not meet my eye. Shame hung about him like a dark habit and blackened our conversation.

But at Christmas, when we could see merry lighted barges going down the river, the pain in my side suddenly grew new teeth and put me on my bed. Our guards, whose names were Bull and Barnesfield, came in with a roast capon for our supper, and took up their accustomed stance against the door, faces bland as eggs.

'Perhaps his Majesty could send a doctor,' said Richard, rising from my side. 'My servant is sick.'

Bull nodded at Barnesfield. Very soon one of the royal physicians came with an astrolabe and leeches. Bending his skull-capped head, he stroked and poked, drew off blood and studied the pisspot's yield. 'The heart would seem to be bruised,' he pronounced. 'The ribs were broken at some time and have grown aslant so they obstruct the lung. This in turn sets up evil humours in the heart.' He handed me a phial. 'This will bring sleep. And remember: never become distressed or overset. It will exacerbate the humour.'

After he and the warders had gone, Richard came to sit by me again. 'I am so sorry, Nicholas,' he said, and I knew he wasn't speaking of my sickness. 'God's blessed Lady! how sorry I am.'

I smiled at him, blissful from the mandragora. 'There is no need,' I said. 'My place is with you. I'm content.'

'Ah, my dear lying friend!' He blew a great sigh. 'You and I both know how hard we strive to keep our souls steady.' He ran his thumbnail down the side of the tightly leaded windowpane. 'Had we only a knife,' he murmured. We were of course allowed nothing sharp; our eating irons were gathered up as soon as we had finished. They had even torn the buckle from Krista's cloak, to my anger. We had no belts or scarves lest we should hang ourselves. No little flints lay around; I could not even mark off our days on the wall. We could only watch the seasons, the dark flakes of ice floating downriver, the frigid moon, the rimed branches like black forked lightning on the far bank, the thin birds who came to the sill. Then the sudden, imperceptible lengthening of the days, and the first leaves like tender green fur, just visible on the starved oaks.

'Don't suffer when I shout at you,' he told me. 'Do your duty to me carelessly, with a sloven's hand. Upset water, tear my hose. They must think you witless.'

I stared at him.

'It's better,' he said. 'If anything happens to me, you may escape punishment.'

'My lord,' I said, alarmed, 'what do you mean?' For all I foresaw was a lifetime in this place, until they carried out two cadavers. I groaned aloud, so thinking.

'Any day now,' he said grimly, 'I am going to retract that foul, feigned confession, that paper penned in Hell.'

His courage was returning, his shame lessening. Soon they knew it, for Bull and Barnesfield often had red eyes from leaning on the spyhole. It must have been early June; the cuckoo had been calling for weeks, and the dawn birdsong was enough to

333

break your heart. Below the river freshened and gleamed, reflecting the grassy wharf and the little boats bobbing at anchor. We had a visit from one of Reynold Bray's clerks, and the chaplain who came in for Mass on Fridays. They brought a new parchment, very fresh, and spread it for Richard's eyes. It was a letter from him to his mother, allegedly intercepted on the road, and in effect, a more intimate reiteration of the confession.

> *Ma mère*, as humbly as I can, I commend myself to you. And may it please you to know that by chance, under the excuse of an invented story, certain Englishmen made me take it upon me that I should be the son of King Edward of England . . . now the King has me in his hands. I have told him the truth of the matter and very humbly begged that it may be his pleasure to pardon the wrong I have done him . . . I am very sad. *Ma mère*, I pray you to have pity on me and procure my freedom.

He read it briefly, then flushed with anger or grief, said: 'And, holy sirs, what shall be the name of *ma mère* today? Warbeck? or Osbeck? What Fleming would address his mother in hated French? But your scribe is an artist, he has my hand to the life. You forget, sirs, that were I to write to my mother it would be in heaven, where, by God's grace, Queen Elizabeth Woodville now is.'

'You have only to ask his Majesty's pardon in public assembly,' said Reynold Bray's clerk.

I began to giggle and roll my eyes, and Richard swung round to smack my face, which gladdened me, as it eased his pain. Then the holy men gathered up the letter and took it away, telling us it was to be displayed with the other evidence on Paul's Cross. I went to the sealed window and looked at the water dappled by the oak's foliage and on its way to the North Sea and the harbour of Sluys or Damme, then the painful ooze up the silted mouth of the Zwyn, flowing thence past the weaver's shop and the tavern to the glass-green pool of the Minnewater. There, Krista stood on the bridge alone, older, her mortal hands clasping the stone, waiting. Sweet God! did she still wait for me? Anguish sprang; the pain in my side acknowledged it.

'Do you remember,' I said aloud, 'the Festival of the Holy Blood?'

He came to stand by me. 'I remember. It was beautiful.'

I told him about Krista, who was my beginning and end, her form and name woven into my soul for ever. I brought her into the room like a white candle, a burning beatitude, burning down and out with another dawn in the prison-house.

'We must get out of here,' he said. 'I swear, Nicholas, I'll find a way. Tudor will not keep me for the rest of my life till I am old and mad. Like he keeps Warwick, my wretched cousin, in the Tower.'

The next day two Yeomen came for him. He was gone until supper-time, when he returned with a tight mouth and feverish face. He hushed me roughly as Bull and Barnesfield brought in our food and left. Then, speaking soft and quick:

'The Bishop of Cambrai is here! My aunt must have sent him to see if it were truly I. Jesu, the shame of it! Also, I learned that Charles of France is dead these last two months. An accident on the tennis court at Amboise. His cousin, Louis *Duc d'Orléans* is to succeed him and will marry the widow, Anne. I prayed they would not make me read the confession again and they didn't. There were quite a few foreign nobles there, de Ayala, and an Andalusian, Don Rodrigo Gonzales de Puebla, a doctor of common law—a vulgar little man, King Ferdinand's envoy. He never stopped eating while I was there. They say he only stays at court to eat.'

I laughed, but his face was sickly.

'That traitor Clifford was there. And the envoy to Scotland, Wyatt, remember! And I heard someone say that Pierre-Jean Meno has been given a pension for life—for services to the Crown.'

'What happened to you?'

'Henry made me stand on the dais for them to see how well treated I am. He made me turn about so they could admire my gear and poke my belly to see if I were fat or thin. Then the usurper said in that raven's croak: "Well, gentlemen! This one has deceived Pope Alexander Borgia, the Holy Roman Emperor, the King of France, the Archduke Philip, the King of Scotland, and almost all princes in Christendom! Take warning, lords. This pretty face and mountebank's tongue once nearly set England and Europe on their head! Be chary of such . . ." Then he waved me down, calling me his loving dupe, while they laughed and laughed. Henry called to his old jester to brush up his wits or he would be out of a job . . .'

'Did you answer?' He was very red in the face, telling it.

'Only as I was leaving. I said: "I am Richard." It made me warm all over. This time I was not afraid.'

I said suddenly: 'Was the Queen there?' and he looked at me as if with pity.

'Do you think they would let me see the Queen my sister? Or would let her see me? Even if she flung herself on my bosom it would be the worse for us both. For she is Tudor's chattel, schooled in the belief that I died long ago. Anyway she keeps her chamber. She is with child again.'

'And your lady?' I ventured. 'Was there news? . . .'

He swung round, his look sad with rage. 'Do not speak of her. Ever. Already she seeks annulment of our marriage and talks of new husbands. If you love me, never speak of her.'

The next day the King sent him a summer doublet—blue broadcloth with a belt. The belt had a diamond-shaped buckle and was sharp enough to mark the wall. Whenever the guard were away we took turns to pick at the mortar round the window-frame, hiding the debris in a rat's hole. Within days we could lift the window free. It was so easy. I leaned against it to keep it in place when Bull and Barnesfield came in for a last look at us, one night when the full moon blazed white in sky and river. We waited for the quiet to be broken by a distant watchman calling that all was well at eleven o'clock.

He climbed out first, and dropped on to the little green. I followed. It was just far enough to knock the wind out of us for a moment. The loudest sound was the splash of an otter diving from the bank. 'Sweet God! how bright it is!' I whispered. We crawled, hugging the palace wall. The river looked as deserted as if man had never been borne upon it. There was a boat, oars waiting, as if moored for our pleasure. We slid like snails down to the wharf; on the far bank a willow splintered the white light on the river with its delicate leaves. As we crept into the boat and pushed off I saw Richard's moonlit smile against the night and heard him whisper: 'Free!'

The creak and splash of the oars sounded like cannon exploding. I was sweating with fear, more frightened by the unreality of this escape than I had been in battle or even on the scaffold. Once free of the midstream currents I rowed close to the shadowed bank and the boat moved like silk through the water. Westward from the city towards the forests of Sheen where lately, the ancient palace had caught fire and burned to the ground. There was the drifting scent of meadowsweet and clover. King-cups bloomed along the bank. Fish rose, sending dark discs into the darker shallows. I had been rowing hard for some time, and pain was lancing my side, when to my alarm I heard him begin to sing, a jolly air of Burgundy.

'My lord. Please hush.'

'Why? No one hears. I doubt if Henry would care that I'm free. He's had his way. He can be done with me now, having displayed me as a charlatan. But next year . . .' his voice broke, oddly, 'let him beware me. When I have gathered another army . . . Ireland will help me again . . . it will be Tudor's turn to make confession.' He began to sing louder. He sounded drunken, dangerous. I rowed harder, dismayed. The pain caught my lungs, and I shipped the oars.

'Richard,' I said. 'I must rest.'

'Address me fittingly,' he snapped. 'I am your king.' I was in too much pain to be surprised.

'Your Grace,' I said. 'Have mercy.'

'Pull in to the bank,' he commanded. The night seemed almost daylit. The moon, limning the dense forest of Sheen, was suddenly rosy, with a pink glow round the curve of the river. He jumped out of the boat, stretching his hand to help me. His grip felt strong, almost frenzied.

'Now we shall walk,' he said.

Even from a distance I could smell the old fires that had consumed Sheen. A black smell of ruin, of charred timbers and roasted stone, borne by a chilly pre-dawn breeze. He plunged up the bank and on through swathes of meadow grass where the silvery moon ran like a tide. I stumbled after him. 'For the love of

God, my lord, where are we bound?' Distant, across our path was a long, dim building.

'The Carthusian Abbey.' He tossed back the words. 'Sanctuary, if only for a day.'

'No!' I cried. 'For God's love. They'll sell us again. My lord, remember Beaulieu.'

'Not these.' I knew he had convinced himself; there was nothing I could say to change him. 'Come. A day's rest, then horses and away from England . . .' He stopped and faced me, silver lit. 'You shall be my chief lieutenant, Nicholas. We'll travel . . . we'll raise the world to my standard.'

You, I thought, who abhor fighting and carnage. What sorry dreams! And while he talked with a doomed, desperate gaiety, I saw, over his shoulder, the Abbey suddenly outlined clear in the glow of approaching torches, then, faint but sure, heard the sound of hoofs, steel, the relentless riding of armed men.

'Jesu. We're trapped.'

And the thought of the past months, the dying by inches with the summer world outside, coupled with the threat of years of the same, seized and shook me to the core. As he clutched my arm I heard myself say: 'It was planned for a purpose. This flight was all too easy.'

'Quick,' he said. 'We can reach Sanctuary if we run low and wide. Keep to the trees.'

'No, my lord.' I heard my own cold voice. Not prison again. No Flanders, No Krista, ever. It was finished for me, the cause, the posturing, the tears, the lies, the truth. No more for me, the courts of illusion.

If I doubled back into the forest I would seek the scent of the burned palace, dig myself in there like a beast. Die there if I must, but die a free man.

'You promised, Richard,' I said steadily. 'If ever I wished to be released from your service, you would agree. The time is now.'

'I have broken all my promises,' he answered. 'The deaths of many are on my head. I have failed you all.'

Lights showed below the river bank, and there was shouting. They had found the boat. More lanterns, swinging like corpse-candles, came from east and west.

'Warbeck!' someone roared. 'Surrender, in the name of the

King! Warbeck! All roads are closed to you. Show yourself!'

He stood before me, etched in flamelight and moon. I couldn't see his face.

'Don't leave me, Nicholas,' he said quietly. 'Not you. Not now.'

So alone he looked, my charge and my cause, my master and good lord. My heart hurt, as Judas's probably did. I said nothing.

'Farewell, then,' he said. He flung his arms about me, kissed each cheek. The voices roared 'Warbeck!' louder. 'God keep you safe. Get you gone.'

He turned and ran towards a belt of darkness where trees girdled the Abbey and I, heart pounding with fear, ran back into the forest's depths. I was within reach of the blackened palace when I heard the shouting swell, an almost jocular sound, and knew they had him.

For two days I lay in the broken black bones of Sheen with owls and mice for company and the smell of destruction all around. My thoughts were heavy. By night, when I deemed it safe, I crawled out and found our boat still anchored near the river bend. I rowed east, keeping to the south bank past sleeping wharves and barges, and came ashore at Southwark, safe harbour for all criminals.

By the time I had finished telling we were on deck again, driven by a fresh south-easterly wind, and landfall was being cried from the rigging. I searched the horizon for the first faint line of the beloved country. I was light with love, as if the breeze had crept beneath my skin.

'I'm to be married soon,' I told the captain, but he was looking at me sadly.

'So you left him,' he said in a flat tone. 'He would miss your comfort.'

Inside my head, unbidden, echoed some old, lost words. *A dog will follow his owner through famine and foul weather to the other end of the world. Through hardship and pain, he will follow with his last breath. And if at the end there is a place by the master's feet, that is enough . . . the love he knows with his one true master outshines the pomp and empty glories sought by man . . .*

339

And then, still older words: *Nicholas, have you ever heard of the Hooks of God?*

'Sweet Christ!' I cried over the flutter of the sails. 'Would you not have done the same?'

The master frowned. 'Likely,' he answered. Then: 'How was he, the last you heard?'

'Very close confined in the Tower.' My rapture at sight of the coast faded a little. 'They say he shares the same wing as the Earl of Warwick.'

'And he,' said the master, 'is so crazed he can't tell a goose from a capon.'

'Port of Damme ahead!' cried the lookout, and my heart was borne up again on the breeze. The crew was furling topsail and mainsail. The ship swam on gracefully towards that flat grey finger of land forked by the estuary. She seemed to dance a saltarello on the waves; my blood skipped with her. Cranes and the topgallants of craft anchored in the estuary became visible. My father, with his enchanted sight would by now have been able to pick out the ships' figureheads. For a wild moment I wondered whether Krista, primed by some mystic knowledge, was waiting on the quay. I thought of Iseult and Tristan and the journey on the White Ship.

She could not know I was coming. I had had no means of sending a letter during the past months, when I was laired like an animal on the wild side of London. In my lust to lose myself I must have picked the worst inn in Southwark; the filthiest, its denizens the most evil, with a price on every head. It was so dreadful I never remembered its name. I shared a corner of hell with two known murderers, a runty pickpurse named Dickon Meadows, and several foul-smelling and ancient whores.

I purchased a sharp dagger and kept it in my night-straw; what money I had I put in my boots and slept in them. Every movement of the constables who walked the streets in pairs for fear of murder, set me shaking. I was sure they looked for me. It was weeks before I dared show myself north of the river, when I ventured once near the Tower. Mystery rose from the river to fog its contours. Although during my father's time I had been inside it and found no more than another royal palace, it now looked final, a stone judgement. While I was gazing at it from the shadow of a wall, a man, a stranger, casually spoke to me of Richard. That was when I learned of his imprisonment there.

'What a roundelay the French lad led our king!' said my companion. I had the feeling he was connected with the Tower. 'The last time he was so angry was when a pet ape ate his privy account book!' Then he began to look at me rather closely and I left in haste. It was weeks again before I ventured from the Southwark hovel, and this time I went uneasily to an address on London Bridge where lived the Lombard notary who had been keeping my legacies from Finch and Margetta.

There was rather a lot of gold, and some of Finch's neckchains, which the notary bought from me at, I suspect, a pittance. I almost expected to see Nemo waiting for me there, but he would have died long ago, either in blood and honour in the pit, or crowing his lusty last, having sired champions. I felt so heavy and sad at it all that this outweighed my nervousness at having to identify myself. In any event, the notary made no comment, neither did his scrivener, brought in as witness. Then I crept back down the ways of youth to the seamstress's house, where I had bought Josina's dress before the Fair. There I asked them if they would sew the money into the lining of Krista's cloak. They seemed old, faded women. I wondered if I looked old to them. I thought: I must get to Krista, if I have to swim the North Sea.

I went to ask about a ship. At every wharf the captains were wary, and there were many royal agents asking who went aboard and who came ashore. I was asked name and business and when I declined to give them eyes probed me until even the pain in my side awoke to see what was amiss. Guilt went with me like a dog. By early spring I was no nearer Flanders than when I had run from the prince's side.

The cutpurse Dickon Meadows could smell my money. One night in cold spring I felt him edging near me in the straw where I dozed, one eye open like a hound. I had him down, my knife at his throat, before he could speak.

'Let me up, lord,' he gasped. 'Share your troubles. I might help you. There's a price for everything. Even the moon pays her dues monthly. What does my lord need?'

'A ship. It seems the ports are being watched.'

He was full of knowledge. 'That's because of the new impostor.

Ralph Wilford, a cordwainer's son, posing as the Earl of Warwick, the silly oaf. Some villain of a friar put him up to it . . . they're out to catch them. Don't go to Southampton. Go to Colchester, then Harwich. Ask for the master of the *Bluebird*. Will you pay me now, lord?'

I left the hell-hole and bought a horse on which I quit London. Living there had been a kind of penance. I could have gone to Piers at the cookshop, or Master John at the Greyfriars, but I had decided that I had brought them sorrow enough. I found the stern, bald sea-captain in a Colchester tavern. At first he was wary of me, and my gold. Then, suddenly unafraid, I told my story, and everything changed. The thief Meadows could not have known that this man's father, like mine, had fought for the vanquished at Bosworth, nor that he had, in his time, sent money to further Plantagenet's cause. It was simply fortune, smiling at last.

I dropped down and kissed the quayside when we landed, and a group of Flemish boys laughed at me without malice. I think they were pleased to see someone who loved their land so much. The shipmaster covered his baldness with velvet and shook my forearm.

'Good fortune, then,' he said gravely. 'Do you wish to return to England, Master Nicholas, you know where to find me. I sail on the first tide every month, God willing.'

'No,' I shook my head. 'My thanks. I shall never return. Here is my home. Here I shall bring up my children.'

I had sold the horse in Harwich so I set off to walk to Bruges, greeting people, the Flemish easy in my mouth. My heart beat fast, hurting me a little, and I tried to be calm. Soon I heard the bells of Bruges and scented the canal and the flowers of spring. I had long decided where I should meet her—a place dear and sacred to us both. I walked round the town, savouring the homecoming. The streets were tranquil, with no sign of the rioting of the past. All the old landmarks rose up lovingly; the Cranenburg, the Guild House of the Archers of St Sebastian, the Houtmark palace of the Lords of Cleves with its moat and four turrets, the Waterhalle sprawling astride the Rey, the Church of St Donatian. I walked up der Nieuw Straat and saw the Paradise Porch of Our Lady, and I came at last to the chapel of the Holy Blood.

There was a boy standing there. I knew he was meant for my

purpose, I said: 'Do you know the weaver's shop? Meneer Hannes . . .'

'Hannes is dead,' he said quickly. The tarnished scent of spring rose from the green canals. The bells rang for Hannes's soul, and my new rejoicing.

'Vrouw van Sluys owns the weaver's now,' said the boy.

'She has a daughter. Will you take her a message?'

I asked her to meet me on the bridge over the Minnewater. I did not give my name, only said I would wait for ever, or until my life's end. I went slowly, full of savour, all past dues and failings forgotten, and soon I stood on the bridge. The coloured stones of the Begijnhof doubled themselves in the lovers' lake, and a pair of Lanchal's swans, black as the devil, sailed through the shadows of the bridge. Little candles, coloured by the windows, began to shine like silent Aves on a thread of blue and gold and green, and the nuns sang Vespers. It was almost dusk when she came. The last light touched her hair beneath the white cap, drew a gleam from her eyes and hands and her white stockings where she held up her skirts, the quicker to come to me.

'You are bold, lady,' I said in English, 'to risk an assignation with one unknown.'

The jest failed. She knew me. It was four years since I had held her in my arms. Now, I was whole again.

Now I was in the house of my beloved, in that room whereof I had dreamed. In all that beset me in real life I had escaped there, through some warm harbour of my mind. During the Scots campaign and the hell of Exeter, during flight, foreboding, prison and near-death, that room had been more real than the events I suffered. And now a strange, contrary thing happened. As I stood by the chuckling stove on the dazzling chequered tiles where lay the black cat and the little brachet bitch, her muzzle greyed by years, it seemed that this was a dream where, in my mind, it had been reality. I stumbled, lost in place and time.

Spring had come to Bruges. Lines of sweet clumsy cygnets sailed behind their parents on the green canal. Small creatures were in constant liquid activity in the reeds and dunes. There was a rising moon like a great pearl over the windmills, and young men played drenching games around the Waterhuis. Everywhere

343

the plangent bells sounded and the trees prospered with leaf. Anneke had prospered too, as owner of the weaver's shop. There was silver on the dresser and silk hangings for the great feather bed. I had not yet lain again in that bed. My nights were spent in the Hertsberghe Godshuis, with the retired, impoverished nobles, my days learning the weaver's trade, for, as Krista's husband, I could be so employed within the family. These had been weeks of dreaming, and the awakening would, I knew, be to rapture, but it was still unreal.

To the black cat I said: 'In two days' time, cat, I shall be married to my lady love.'

Anneke stood in the doorway against the clear evening, wearing a gown of fine black silk with a silver crucifix. Her cap was like a béguine's, with great starched wings. I went to her, touching, as I passed, the two spinning-wheels, just to establish their truth. Anneke took me to her and kissed me.

'And, sweetest Vrouw,' I said, leaning on her breast, 'were it not for your fairest daughter, I would gladly wed you.' I meant it. Her large loveliness filled me with strength. She moved away so she could look at me, her grey-green eyes clear as the Minne-water.

'How are you? The pain has not returned?'

She always knew when the pain was on me. The first moment of my homecoming, when, as I had dreamed, we all clung weeping together again, she had said: 'You are sick, Nicholas!' and had gone straight to pound woodsage and horehound in honeyed ale, a drink so bitter-sweet it seemed to encompass this moment and all the moments that had gone before. Truth to tell, the pain visited me at times, enough to discomfort, but not enough to mar my contentment, and I doubted it would prevent me from loving Krista in two days' time, when we would renew the bliss of our one encounter in that deep bed. As to that matter, I had a notion that Anneke knew all about it. One of her cures for my pain had been a bath from a sacred well near the Waterhuis. The water had to be drawn by a virgin, and she had not sent Krista, but one of the young spinsters from the shop. I also felt that Anneke did not judge me. She had not changed; she was still in love with love.

'I have been to see the priest.' She closed the door, and,

removing her cap, sat down beside the stove. I went to kneel at her feet. The stove's glow bathed her cheeks and ironed away her age. 'He will come at noon to perform the ceremony.' I was filled with utter relief. Even at this late hour I had feared she would withhold her consent. For in a way I had failed her.

Soon after my arrival she had taken me aside for a talk, on just such a green spring evening as this. The pain round my heart had been very keen, as I sought to give her explanation. She had said sadly:

'Is it really over, Nicholas?'

'Yes, dearest Vrouw, it is over. The cause is dead.'

'And the prince? You said he was a brave man. Did he not bear himself bravely, then? Was that why he failed?'

I looked deeply to where the fire played like sunset in her eyes.

'He was a brave man,' I answered. 'I do not speak of battles. Not all who do battle are brave. He feared pain greatly, but what man does not? He hated blood and the slaughter of innocents. He cared for the suffering of others. He was no match for the usurper. No one wins against Tudor. This I learned.'

'Is there no last hope? Truly?'

I shrugged, my side aching abominably. 'What hope? England has abandoned him. The Cornish will never forgive him. Charles of France is dead. James of Scotland has signed a seven-year peace with Tudor, and it's said he will marry Tudor's daughter Margaret. And the Duchess of Burgundy . . .'

'The Duchess, God preserve her, is old and tired,' Anneke said. 'And yet . . . Nicholas, could he not escape again from prison, and raise a new army? What of this boy . . . what was his name . . . could they not combine forces and try again?'

'Ralph Wilford,' I said with disgust, 'was a common impostor. He thought it the fashion to play at princes. He has been caught and hanged, and the friar who lit his longings imprisoned for life. I heard so today, in the English Inn.'

And then I spoke more sharply than I had ever done, to this beloved woman.

'There *are* no new armies, Vrouw! And no one ever escapes from the Tower of London.'

'I would have rejoiced to see him crowned King Richard the Fourth of England,' she said in a soft, sad voice. 'I have prayed for

345

Plantagenet. I have prayed for the souls of his father Edward and his uncle, Richard of Gloucester, with whom I once drank and sang in the Herberghe Margaretha. Many years ago, yet unforgotten.'

Sweet God! I thought, shaking. Let her hold me no longer to the pledge. I said: 'Sweetest Anneke, I know that in chivalry I swore not to claim Krista until my lord was in his rightful place. But I can do no more. All we laboured for is gone. Hope is dust. On my soul, I did what I could . . .' And all the while a voice nagged and niggled from the pit of my life: You abandoned him. When he needed you to the end you bereaved him of your miserable company. Steadily I put the voice away.

'So I cannot take Krista to live with me in England now,' I said roughly. 'But live with her I must. She is my life. She has been like my patron saint. I burn to marry her. You cannot, you will not, deny us.' And I knelt then, as I was kneeling now, and kissed the lambsoft wool of Anneke's gown.

And she said: 'No. I cannot deny you. Make your home with us here. You've suffered. It is right. We are none of us as young as we were, and I wish to see my grandchildren.'

Now she was smiling, stroking my hair. Our conversation had never been referred to again, and she was talking gaily, with the thrust of promised pleasure in her voice, of a small revel she planned for the three of us on the eve of the wedding.

'But you must be gone before sunset,' she said, and dropped a kiss on top of my head. 'It's bad luck for groom to see bride on the wedding morning.'

I heard Krista's footfall outside, echoed by the tranquil water. She came in from the greenish sunset, her loosened hair angelic in the light. I rose and embraced her with tenderness and lust, uncaring of her mother, feeling the fragile ardour of her body, her lips' hot promise. Two days seemed a long time to wait.

'We'll roast a suckling pig,' Anneke was saying. 'And we'll have a lot of wine, and singing. You are right, Nicholas. This is our happy time. We have all suffered. Now the past shall die.'

Demons dwell in wine. Some are benevolent. Wine can sweeten bad water and brighten the eye. It can quell melancholy, and summon it. Wine can be invaded by the essence of Christ. There was once some heretic talk that the Holy Blood was nothing but wine, sparkling for the people. And James of Scotland, once seeking remedy for a flux that was crippling his army, tried an experiment; he soaked a hog's liver in wine and saw it eaten away within hours. The men watered their wine and the sickness subsided. Women in childbed are fortified with wine, and smiles grow in a flagon. But it can sway the steps, and change, as witches do, the blood in a man's heart.

And above all, wine is the tongue's lord and suzerain of the soul. It bores holes in the mind, through which leak words buried for years, and secret longings not shaped for the daylight.

I often wonder . . . I *know*, that if we had not drunk so deep at that little celebration on my wedding eve, certain words would have been sealed and surely remained so. And now I must remember it. I must taste again the gall of that last drink.

I see so clearly. Just as I remember the sun shining through the window on the morning I went to meet the bad angel who was to destroy my family, or the blur of wings in the cockpit at Bart's Fair, and the small straight figure of my brother between candles on the table. As I remember the little Brecher wife, twitching on the bloodstained ground at Leicester, and the shining figure of Plantagenet, gowned for his wedding. And the dark-eyed look of Bedesman as the Stanleys led him away. These are the things of pain. There is no need for torture chambers; the soul has its own.

So I remember how the evening sky was rose and amethyst over the westerly windmills, and how I looked down at the silver buckles on my shoes bearing me across the bridge to my beloved's house, and glanced up to see the silver fall of a shooting star, an angel cast from heaven. My cloak was still heavy with the gold in the lining which Krista was going to unpick for me. She was waiting for me in the doorway, wearing white, her hair in a thick, lint-blonde braid. My heart began to beat so hard that the pain awoke for a moment. I kissed her hand, just above the finger where Finch's ruby glowered, and called her by the pet-name of one who was lost to me.

'Iseult,' I said, and took her close. 'My Iseult.'

She leaned back in my arms, frowning, smiling. She did not know the story. Her face was pale. A pulse beat just above her square white collar. I hungered for her.

347

'Come,' she whispered. 'My mother is waiting.'

Perhaps I should have known then that that falling star was mine.

Anneke's eyes were full of mischief and joy, grey-green as the black cat's. Her gown was the purest saffron wool, and she stood proudly by the table which was strewn with green branches, dishes of sweets and bowls of frumenty. The suckling pig was glazed brown with honey, jaws gaping round a yellow fruit. I stood there, admiring, and a jest, brutal and strange as if from another's tongue, popped out of my mouth.

'A lovely pig,' I said. 'They could have let him finish his apple before killing him.'

Anneke laughed. Krista leaned her cheek softly against my arm. Then Anneke beckoned me. Her embrace was almost desperate, her bright eyes glittered, and I knew this was a night for laughter and probably tears, and none the worse for that.

'Tomorrow!' she said, soft, like a conspirator.

'You are my family,' I said as I had said before, 'Today, tomorrow, and always.'

Flagons of red Clary, dark with unholiness, were lined up on the chest. Anneke had her dagger heating in the stove, she whipped it out and plunged it, like the leap of a white-glowing fish, into a flagon, stabbing the wine to the heart. The deep demons hissed in pleasure and pain. I did carver's duty, slicing great gobbets of the salt-tingling pork seethed in thyme and rosemary. I sat close by Krista on the settle, my foot round hers, and Anneke sat opposite. The dog and cat fawned below for bits, and the stove belched comfort. We drank the fire-shot Clary from tall Venetian glasses brought out for the celebration. I could not keep pace with Anneke. Enthralled, I watched her long throat tip and stretch like a swan's. Krista smiled her wise little smile, as if she were the parent and her mother a child up past bedtime. We ate the comfits, too cloying for my sore teeth, and Anneke ripped the bungs from flagons and kept turning each glass into a ruby.

She could not sit still, constantly leaving her food like a court minstrel to seize her lute and sing, voice hoarse and rich with wine. *Filles à marier*, laughing at the silly words warning maids against marriage, and then, unexpectedly, a song so sad it stuck in the gullet.

'Allez regretz, vuidies de ma presence;
'Allez ailleurs quérir vostre acointance
'Assez avez tourmenté mon las cœur . . .'

a song of hopeless love, in hated French.

'Pray eat your supper, Mother,' Krista said, and Anneke was frolicsome again. We talked of the weaver's shop.

'How were the little spinsters today?'

'Ah, they work well. Good girls.' Krista was now their overseer, the ogreish lady having been dismissed.

'Because they're happy.' I pressed her leg with mine. *'I* would work well under you, my love,' and breathed in her ear something else to make her blush.

'No whispering!' Anneke cried. 'Nicholas, I drink a toast to you, a debt of joy.' I rose and bowed. 'And I will toast my lovely bride,' I said, and so we did, then Anneke called for a drink to the soul of Uncle Hannes, whose legacy had made us rich. Krista rose and made a half-attempt to clear the dishes, then fetched my cloak to unpick the lining so I could have my gold.

'There's something else here,' she said. 'Paper.'

'Your letters, my dove,' I said. 'And one from Piers. They can go in my pouch for safekeeping.'

'Let's drink to Piers,' said Anneke, neither knowing nor caring who he was. And I said yes, for Piers is the best person I ever knew. I wondered where he was, if his life went well? My eyes skimmed the letter, saw the name of Master John at the Greyfriars, and I put it quickly away. Anneke's gaze was on me, almost too ardent; it singed and drained. I stroked Krista's little round knee and thought of the morrow.

'Ah, Nicholas,' said Anneke, 'would that your family could be here in this glad time.'

I answered lightly; there was already moisture round her eyes.

'Beloved Vrouw, you know I have no family.'

'Let us drink to the dead,' said Anneke with mourning. We downed this bitter toast to please her. I glanced at the window. It would soon be dusk, time to leave. In the ceiling corner was a giant web with a dozing spider. The last light shimmered in a crystal splash on the ceiling from the reflection of waterfowl passing down the canal.

'I think,' said Anneke, 'I would like a grandson first. Promise . . .'

'We will do our best,' I said.

'A boy babe, strong and fair.' She dropped her face in her hands.

'Mother, be happy,' Krista pleaded.

'Sing to us again,' I said. I looked away from the tear-stained face now raised. Too much Clary, I mouthed to Krista. In the corner, the spider had woken and was jigging in its web.

'Not even you knew,' said Anneke. 'Not even you, my daughter. The burden of my sin and shame.'

I knew she was about to voice an echo of her youth's wild ways, something that always plagued her in her cups. Her saffron sleeve was dabbled with wine. Let her talk, I thought. She said: 'It was so long ago. Richard of Gloucester, when he was exiled, came to the inn with his handsome friend. His esquire, so merry yet so innocent. I played wanton. My dear friend Alys, God rest her, she was no better. We were Eve's daughters. Alys died, bearing noble Gloucester a child. Most holy Jesus! I see him now.'

'Yes. I too remember the king.' And so I did. At long last, his ghost, gleaming, dark, shrouded always with anxious doom, peeped with clarity from the mist of my childhood. In a blink of my mind, it was gone.

'I bore his child,' said Anneke. Beside me Krista drew a sharp breath. We both stared in wonder.

'You too? A royal child?' I said.

Down on the table crashed her knife, making us jump. 'No, no!' she cried. 'Not Gloucester's. Nicholas . . . my daughter. Let me confess.'

Krista leaned across to her mother, stroking her sleeve.

'It's not fitting,' she whispered.' Nicholas is not a priest, and it is not right for my ears. Be still, Mother.'

'You must know.' Anneke's eyes were clear, the wine-flush was fading. 'I want no secrets now between us three. Tomorrow I shall welcome Nicholas as I would the babe I lost. So fair and smiling. Not a day has passed but I have thought of him. He would be about your age, Nicholas. That is why I love you so.'

'He died,' I said, for her face was tragic.

'For all I know. I was unwed, and in great shame. For one night I loved his father, though'—with a twisted smile—'the rogue never told me his proper name. We were all a little mad those dangerous days, all the princes in exile and playing games to ease their dolour. Gloucester called himself "Dickon Broome" and King Edward was "Ned of Rouen". As for my paramour, his nickname boasted of his great talent. He told me his services would be sought before a battle, to survey the enemy colours from afar. He had very long sight.'

The spider was running up and down its web in an unknown frenzy.

'We called him Sir Mark Eye,' she said. 'I never knew him as other. I gave my son to be cared for by a good woman at the Herberghe Margaretha. I sent one letter, addressing it only to the keen-sighted man in Gloucester's service. Then, when King Edward was victorious at the battles of Barnet and Tewkesbury, word came. My lord had married. He wanted his dear bastard son to live with him in England. So I clothed him warmly and blessed him and put him aboard ship. A gift of money came later, which I used as my dowry. I had always been poor.'

As she spoke I had a vision of the inn, the familiar doorway carved with margeurites and a young child's fingers tracing them. My heart leaped like the spider; for an instant the room went black. Then the sound of my voice—it seemed to come from the spider's web.

'What did you call your son, Anneke?'

Brooding and soft she answered, as she poured more wine. 'Joachin. My Joachin, sweet as honey.'

Krista cried out softly. Looking down, I saw that I was gripping her hand as if to break the bones. She wrenched it away. My betrothal ring, Finch's ruby, slid off and lay in my palm. In my mouth was a strange taste, as if I had been sucking a knife, and beneath my ribs something swelled to bursting. The spider said, in my voice:

'His father wore a scar on his hand. A new wound, done that night.'

'Christ have mercy,' whispered Anneke. 'How did you know?'

'A scar,' said my voice, 'shaped like an arrow, from a burn inflicted by Gloucester over a flame. Some arm-wrestling game that started gentle and waxed rough. He carried that scar with pride. He bore the memory in his blood, for Edmund was born

351

marked likewise, and with the same keen sight. But Edmund's dead, and so is Mark, our father. I loved him sorely, and watched him die.'

I tasted blood, as something broke and wasted in me. The settle shook, the dishes on the table rattled. All from Krista's trembling. The spider hung still in its web. Everything stilled, save for Krista's trembling, and I wished she would stop, for it was like a thousand knives round my heart, as the pain grew and grew.

'Ah, Mary, Mother of Christ,' said Anneke. 'You are my son.'

I coughed, and a little spray of blood, like pinpricks, stained the tablecloth. My voice went on, very steady, and through my agony I marvelled at it.

'You are my mother, Anneke,' I said, through a film of blood. 'My father's wife spoke of you the last time I saw her. She hated you most powerfully, and called you whore. She's dead, too. I thought you were dead, but you are alive. And you are my mother.' With pain I turned to look at Krista. She had stopped trembling and was leaning back against the settle, white as milk, her eyes closed.

'And this girl is my sister,' I said. 'Tomorrow is our wedding-day. Already I have pricked her maidenhead.'

Anneke flung herself away from the table. Two of the beautiful glasses flew to bounce in bright shards on the tiles. She rushed towards the door and back again. The cat, fleeing, tripped her, she half-fell against the wall where she remained, hands and face flat against the stone. Krista got up too, like an old woman, picking her way to a gloomy corner where she stood, her white gown a candle.

'Say you are mistaken,' said Anneke, face to the wall.

'My name is Joachin,' I said. 'My father was Mark, of the keen sight. I was born in Bruges. I remember the inn, and the ship. I am in mortal sin.'

'So are we all,' said Krista from the corner.

And then I knew I must leave before the crippling pain round my heart laid me dead on the floor. A voice which came from where the pain was and ordered all my actions, bade me to my feet and out into the air where, on the canal, swans paddled to bed in the reeds and the sun bled to death behind the windmills. The pain was supreme. I spat a gob of blood over the little bridge. Behind, faint and far, came the voice of Anneke calling my name—Joachin!—pleading, for the son she had loved had come and gone like a false spring, had been hers for a moment and was lost for ever.

Of the rest I remember little. I sought the sea, which alone could wash away this grief. That is all—that, and one other certain knowledge. Margetta's curse had followed me.

Outside the window of my cell was a belfry. House martins had nested there in spring, and during the summer had taught their young to fly. Now as the days shortened they had departed, all but two of them who had lingered late. They were my friends, those little birds, this cell my little womb. For months I had not left it. I did not think I could ever leave it.

For a long time I had not known where I was or how I came there. I had only a shell. I was drained of thought. A pall of unknowing lay over the whole summer. Time moved only with the passage of the little birds. Now there was no pain in me. It was as if I had been extinguished. All desires and regrets were blackened and still as the wick of a snuffed candle. During the height of my sickness, when black-clad men had come and gone with softness, blood-irons and herbs, there had been one small flicker from that dead candle: this is the death denied me by Henry Tudor at Exeter. This is the final knotting of the thread; the tapestry is finished. But I did not die; my heart healed, taking as hostage my memories. Maurice once told me of a place called Tir-na-nOg, where there is no weeping and no laughter, a landscape of timeless grey. I know it.

I was in the Greyfriars on Newgate under the care of Master John and the brothers, though summer was almost done before the knowledge came to me. Before, I had dreamed I was in prison, awaiting execution, with Plantagenet. A pile of my gold stood on the chest near my bed, like a little brown tower. There had once been a many-coloured cloak woven by a woman in Flanders whose name I could not remember, but that was gone now. In high summer I had reared in the bed crying for them to burn it. One of the brothers protested gently—some poor man would be glad of it—but I had raved so fiercely that in the end they took it

353

away. Later through the window wafted a foul scent, as if a sheep were on the fire.

It would soon be November, month of the dead, day of the ghosts. By a strange and bitter paradox, as the hearts of youth and lovers quicken in spring, my being took strength from the mists that fell. Feeble as an old man's steps, my mind tottered carefully into the light, avoiding, like holes in the road, the things of pain.

Round and round went the house martins outside the window. Stretched on the pallet under a bleeding effigy of Christ, I saw them rehearse their long journey. I turned my head at the flicker of a page from the lectern where the lay brother stood reading, faceless in his cowl. He had stood there day in, day out, silent, pausing in his study only to attend me if I suffered grief. He had been standing there all my life. Without him, I was nothing.

He closed the book and came to me, pushing back his cowl. He put his cold small hand on my brow to feel if I had fever. His spectacles travelled down his nose and he tightened the rivet, frowning, to pin them in place.

'You look rested,' he said. 'Nicholas, I think you should be out and about a little soon.'

'Leave here?' I said. 'No, Piers. No.'

Piers smiled, that earthly lighting of his unearthly face. He was unchanged in all ways, save that he looked even younger than in the days at the cookshop.

'Stretch your legs,' he said, and helped me up, and, his arm linked in mine, we walked round and round the small grey cell. 'How goes it with you?' he asked gently, and I said:

'I remembered today how I came here. I remember that wharf and the constables shouting at me in Flemish because I was drunken and running into walls and people. And the bald-headed captain, about to go aboard . . .'

'The *Bluebird*. Yes,' said Piers. 'What then?'

I said: 'Nothing much. There was a storm. They lashed me to a post below decks, like when I was a child.'

'The letter,' said Piers. 'You carried my letter. That's how they knew your friends. It was the captain who brought you here.'

'I remember.'

'The Hooks of God,' Piers said. 'The divine and omnipotent plan. He fished you, Nicholas. He pulled you in, and brought you here. Some would say it was fortune. But it was the Hooks of God.'

His skin was dun with fatigue, his robe grubby and threadless. There was dirt between his toes and I suspected he scourged himself or wore a hair shirt, for often a shiver chased over his thin body. This, then, was what he had meant when he wrote: 'You have chosen your road and I mine.' About him he carried perfect peace, a kind of restrained joy, as if the end of the road was gained already, in secret.

'I had a vision just now,' I said. 'A man's hand, striking up out of snow. But I can't remember where.'

'You must come out into the city,' he said, still walking me round. 'It's time. Confinement breeds melancholy in you. It is not useful. Come, before it's too late.'

Too late for what? I wondered.

'I will come with you,' he said, his grip iron on my arm.

Through the poor quarters we went together, I with stumbling, trembling gait, looking nervously about me at the folk muffled against November. They all seemed faceless, and after a time I knew they wished me no harm, but still I clung to Piers, whose cowled head came only to my shoulder but whose presence was a tower. People greeted him; the good monk cherishing the madman. He went inexorably on his way, softly, with little blessing gestures. Ragged children played in hovel doorways, threadbare women shuffled by carrying bales of firewood. Every other person seemed a beggar.

'I know them all,' he said. 'They are most beloved to me. I bring them medicines and prayer. I try to bring them hope.'

'What if there is no hope?' At this he glanced up, his smile like a flame within his hood.

'Wait for the Hook!' he said. 'All that God inflicts a man can take cheerfully. He will be caught up into blessing, and the more he is caught the more he is set free.'

'My life is blasted.' The streets closed round me in agony. 'There was a tempest at sea. The wind was too strong.'

Beside me he moved like a rock. 'Ah, Nicholas,' he said, and laughed. 'If the wind fells your favourite tree, plant a new seed.'

We were approaching Eastchepe, and I stopped. 'No,' I said. 'Not this way. There's dread here too, Piers.'

355

'Come.' He was irresistible. 'Let us go and see my father. He's at home today. Don't you want to know what passes with your late lord?'

Chaos had left the cookshop. The boys were scrubbed and serene. There was no terror in the kitchen, and in the parlour there might never have been murder done. An orderly fire burned, and in the inglenook, nodding, sat Patch.

'Sit,' said Piers. 'I shall go down the street and visit Mistress Seward. She's old, sick, and very poor.'

Mistress Seward, who had once given me a pie because my thinness grieved her. I sat. 'Well, young master,' said Patch. His eyes rolled to survey me. They were clear. Red, but clear.

'The pearl has gone from your eyes,' I said in wonder.

'Betony,' he answered proudly. 'Poultice of betony. The Italians have a saying—sell your coat and buy betony. Matchless herb. You look old and sick, Master Nicholas. The last time I saw you, you had a rope necklace. His Majesty spared you, you caitiff. You villain. You sinner.'

I felt comforted by his abuse. 'Do you still entertain at court?' I asked him.

'The King has been very good to me,' he said, quirking his wrinkled mouth. 'He could have given me a pension but still employs me. The King loves fools. I shall stay at court until I die'—his smirk faded—'to watch over one I love. My little maid of York.'

'The Queen. How is she?'

'Poorly,' he said flatly. 'She should have stayed in the nunnery,' and his look grew lost, and I remembered how he mixed up the Queen with his old love. 'And his Majesty?' I said. I had to know.

'Jesu!' he answered, 'this month he's aged twenty years.' He spat in the fire. 'Your Master Perkin has aged him. Petronus, the astrologer, warned that the King's life would be in danger all this year, and spoke of a strong enemy. The King fears for the future of his son, for the alliance with Spain. Only when Perkin's dead and chested, and young Warwick too—for he's a good name for impostors to wear—will Henry be at peace.'

I waited for pain, but my heart continued its dead, untroubled taboring.

356

'Such fear,' I said slowly, 'of one Flemish impostor,' and looked hard at Patch, who I deemed knew all, living close by the King, and invisible in cap and bells.

'Is he so?' he squinnied at me. 'What mummery then, what counterfeiting! to sketch those lines on my sovereign's face! You lived with him. He lorded you, this Perkin Osbeck-Warbeck. You tell me, young master.'

There was pain here, not the agony of the past, for that had welded itself into my soul and become one with me so that I felt it no more than I felt the stretch of my skin. There was sadness that kept me silent.

'And the Earl of Warwick,' I said. 'He would have young Warwick dead. That simpleton, who has lived out his days in the Tower. He led no uprising. He has committed no treason. How can he have young Warwick?'

Patch laid a jovial finger against his nose.

'Warwick is a Plantagenet,' he riddled, 'and in the Tower, there is a cell above a cell and a hole in the floor between the two and merry messages pass. "Good morrow, Perkin, and how goes it today?" "Good morrow, Edward Warwick my cousin, be of good cheer." And there is a jailer called Astwood.'

'Traitor.'

'—and another called Cleymound, and one called Blowet, and if you would see the future go into any inn in Tower Street and draw a pot of ale and the future will come to your eye. And in a month or so from now you and I will take a little outing to Tyburn. Then we shall see if Perkin Plantagenet was an impostor or no.'

I looked at him. Something within me furled and sighed like the cloak of a mourner.

'For what most becomes a nobleman's life is the manner of his leaving it,' said Patch, and bowed towards the fire.

November caught us up in its swirling fist of fog, but Patch's words had wakened a spark in my dying will, and so I went to the Talbot near the fortress on Tower Street, an inn used by the jailers in their hours off duty. Patch told me that John Taylor was now imprisoned in the Tower, with Atwater. He had been arrested by the new government in France during the summer, and had been shipped back to England for Tudor to decide his fate. The capture of Taylor, prime initiator of our cause, had impressed the Holy League. The arm of Tudor vengeance against his rebels is long, they declared, 'none can flee from his presence.'

In the dim low tavern I sat before a tankard of ale, without tasting it. It looked clouded, full of poison and malice. I watched the drinkers. There was a veil of glass between them and myself; their lips moved without sound, and when intermittent words reached me, they lacked meaning. After a while a group of prentices came in. Among them was a dark, rollicking little man with food stains down his velvet. He clung, whinnying at their jests, while the prentices suffered him, buying him food and ale. Soon he hopped away from them, and tucked himself, uninvited, into my booth. Like all others, he seemed unreal. He eyed my untouched tankard.

'Don Rodrigo Gonzales de Puebla,' he said proudly. 'Doctor of civil and common laws. You do not drink, my friend.'

I pushed the tankard towards him with a bow. He quaffed it with one greedy swallow, then began to demolish a wedge of cheese. So this was the new ambassador from Spain—the one Richard had seen at Westminster.

'I love your English taverns,' he confided. 'The people—so generous. And you—you are employed at the Tower?'

I shook my head. He made me feel sick and sad, as if I had presaged his next words.

'I have just come from the Tower,' he said. '*Ay de mi*! That French lad—Warbeck! he is not long for this world. I shall write to my lords in Spain telling them how he has altered. It will please them to think he has not long to live, for they are weary of these impostors. Any more of them, and the royal match between our beloved Infanta and the Prince Arthur Tudor would have to be reconsidered.' He leaned, confidentially. 'They have Warbeck in a dark cell now, you know. He sees neither sun nor moon. He has been ill for weeks—so starved and dirty he is like a bone. *Ay, ay*! but he must pay for the evil he has done.'

I left him quickly, moving to another booth. At that moment the door opened and Thomas Astwood entered. I saw him cloudily against the smoke from the fire-basket. His skinny form looked sleek, but his face was harassed. I was not wearing arms, but I thought: my duty is to rise and kill him now for his treachery. But the strange veil between me and the world made him a figure of dreams. Deep within I felt the unseen weaver at the loom begin work on the final patterns of our fate.

He peered at me, unsure, and came over. He leaned quite close to the table, though his face seemed far.

'Is it,' he whispered, 'Nicholas Archer?'

'No,' I said. 'Joachin van Sluys.'

'Ah!' he said. A look of relief crossed his face and he sat down, glancing hurriedly round. 'No need to hide from me, Nick. This is fortune that I found you. We need good men for this enterprise. Men unknown in the Tower, who can move freely in London . . .'

'You betrayed him, Astwood,' I said, through the veil of glass. 'He was our lord. You are Tudor's creature.'

He glanced round again, and clapped his hand to his forehead. 'No, no!' he breathed. 'Lies. Listen. There is a plot.' He jerked his head over to where a great-bellied man was pouring wine from a flagon. 'That is Cleymound. And over there'—a weary-looking man in forest green—'is Thomas Mashborough, one-time bowyer to King Edward. These, and Blowet, my partner and I, are to engineer our lord's escape. Not only that'—and he leaned so close that his breath seemed to mist the invisible wall between us—'but we will have young Warwick out as well. Two kings to choose from, free as air. Already Cleymound has arranged letters between them, there's a hole in the ceiling joining their cells, and Earl Warwick and Warbeck pass messages daily. Digby's the Lieutenant of the Tower, but he's Tudor's man. Cleymound's the one with the power, he holds the key. This time, we'll bring down Tudor, well and truly, like we always dreamed.'

I looked slowly away from him and across at Cleymound. In his fat, wine-ruddled face his eyes were like little flints. Suddenly the veil about me seemed to explode. I saw, smelled, knew. The roar of the tavern rocked me. The stink of treason and double-dealing wrapped me like a miasma.

'You are a traitor, Astwood,' I said, loud and clear. 'Still a traitor, and you will end on the gallows.'

His face blazed. 'I could arrest you,' he growled. 'As a past rebel, I could hand you over to the King's officers here and now.'

'Do it, then.' We both stood up. 'I've little to live for.'

359

I saw his eyes change as if he knew he had nothing to fear. I was broken by life. Yet with a last, half-hearted appeal, he said: 'Join us, won't you? You were always the prince's favourite. There were times'—he laughed sourly—'when I was jealous. You could be of infinite service, passing word to men like Philip Proud. He's in the plan too, trying to raise an army.'

Philip Proud, with his songs of death. The last man on earth to trust. A tiny flicker of the old pain rose round my heart.

'Astwood'—and something in my voice made him flinch as if a leper approached—'you will hang for this. I do not know whether you are the dupe, or whether you hope to dupe others and bring about the certain death of my lord Richard and the Earl of Warwick. I know that you will hang. You were born to it. You have embroiled yourself in a net of *provocateurs* . . .' I looked at Cleymound, the red, wine-flushed jowls, the rich clothes, unsuitable for a jailer. 'For my part, I do not care if you hang. But with my heart I care that you seek, through your folly or your greed, the death of my one and only lord.'

The thin invisible barrier came down between us again. It was only faintly I heard him say, as he shoved himself away from the table:

'You're mad. You ever were. Get you to the madhouse, and die there.'

November was nearly out, and the house martins had flown. Their brown bee-swarm of a nest looked worn and patched but it clung firm beneath the belfry. Only a flare of white splashes down the wall bore evidence that once they had played so merrily in their little court. Winter was coming; its cold breath filled me as I came back to the Greyfriars. I had taken a walk down Eastchepe, alone and in sadness, for the veil between me and the world had thinned almost to nothing and my spirit was naked.

Piers was cleaning out my cell. He had given up reading, for his soul's good; he said it gave him too much pleasure. As he knelt scrubbing the floor, I could see every knob of his spine through the threadbare habit, and the sight choked me. I knew he would never be an old man.

I bent and took pail and cloth away from him. He looked up cheerfully, shaking with cold.

'Piers,' I said, 'for the love of God.'

'Yes, for the love of God, Nicholas.' He knew my fear. We had grown so close that there was between us some alchemy of the heart. 'Do not fear. You will go on without me.'

'Never. I would be lost, ended.'

He rose. 'You will stand alone,' he said. 'You are not without courage. And I shall always be with you. I can pray better for you after this life. If God allows.'

'Weeks ago, I should have let Astwood arrest me,' I said miserably. 'Now Astwood is himself under sentence of death. It is nine years since I set out in quest of atonement. I achieved only further guilt. And I even led you into sin, when you lied for me over the murder.'

He laughed, shook his head. 'No, Nicholas. I could not let them take you for that. There is a higher court than that of men. I doubt whether the Lord Christ would have let you hang.'

The last word dropped like the sound of a heavy bell, its implications all round us.

'The date is fixed for your lord's execution,' he said softly.

'Tomorrow.' I sat heavily on my hard little bed. 'The last of those I have loved. And now you talk of death. There will be no one to love me.'

'Someone will be sent,' he said, so firm and sure that surprise cut through my misery. 'And be sure that your sister loves you.'

I did not ask which sister he spoke of. There were things shut away, not to be thought of or named. At least, not yet.

'Josina is happy at Leicester,' Piers said. 'I made enquiry years ago. In her safe retreat from the world she has found joy and comfort of which she never dreamed. And she is cared for by an especial person. My father's nun, the one he always loved. A little nun, both mad and wise. Once, long before she entered cloister, she was King Richard's leman.'

'I saw her,' I whispered. 'She followed his corpse.' Somewhere, the unseen weaver at the loom twitched the dark tapestry, lighting a corner of its strange, sad pattern of years.

'Your sister prays for you,' he said.

'Prayer is no substitute!' I cried. Sorrow ringed me, buttressed by dread of tomorrow. Leicester had been bad enough. This would be insupportable.

361

'No, it is no substitute,' his even voice echoed me. 'It is love itself. There are many kinds of love, but love cannot endure anything anywhere that is not God. With love there is no time or distance. And love is strongest when there is a valley between you and the beloved. For then it must grow wings and fly.'

Out of the years came Robert Henryson's tale of the birds soaring high above ambition and strife, gentle and free. Piers was looking out at the house martins' empty nest. I moved to join him.

'Broken and battered,' he murmured, 'yet still a safe lodging, awaiting their return.'

'My father used to tell us—' I stopped, began anew. 'My father had a very old tale. About a seer who told his king: "Lo, while we sit in the Hall in fireglow and brightness, there enters a small bird from the storm. He flies the length of the Hall and is gone, through the window. Who shall say that our span of life is not like this small bird's flight? For none knows from what dark bourne he came, neither do they know whither he departs".'

'A man is born,' said Piers. 'He gets children, he dies. The worms eat his flesh. But prayer is eternal, a body composed of thought and dreams and love, in this world and the next. Meantime, we do what we can to assuage the pangs, not of ourselves, but others.'

On the chest still stood my money, untouched over the months. I started to divide it, pushing it into half a dozen piles. The largest I laid before Piers.

'For Master John, and this house,' I said. He gave a little bow.

'It is more than enough,' he said. 'But this is your home, this portion will keep you here, as long as you wish.'

'I wish to be like you,' I said. 'To wear your habit, to walk in your ways.'

Again he bowed, acquiescent. Then he said: 'Now there should be true atonement. Then penitence.' He turned to look at me. 'What saw you in Eastchepe today?'

'I saw Mistress Seward,' I said, and he nodded, like a patient tutor hearing some fumbling lesson.

'So ill she looked, so poor.' Then in a rush: 'And I recalled how she gave me food when I was hungry. It is time I made good my debts.'

'Ah!' he said, in a kind of ecstasy. 'The divine Fisher. You are on the Hook!'

'And I saw beggars,' I continued more surely, seeing with my inner eye more of the sad-coloured tapestry. 'I have never seen so many starving children.'

He sighed. 'Yes. They trouble me. We have room for a poor boy in our house; we could pay for an apprenticeship. But I can never get near them. They are little wild things. They run at a word.'

I went on putting the money into piles.

'I will repay,' I said. 'That is atonement. But the other—the penitence. I cannot go, Piers. I cannot witness that execution. I myself would die.'

'You must.' I knew that note in his voice. It was steel—it put a yoke on me. 'This will be the last torment for him and for you. It will be a final act of love, the last of all your debts.'

As soon as it was light I went out into the City, wrapped against a winter-fanged wind, with the purse a drag of wealth at my side under my mantle, and lead within my heart. Walking into Eastchepe, I became part of a throng hurrying to the place of execution. From the streets around Tower Hill people waited to see Plantagenet begin his long journey to Tyburn, hauled on a hurdle behind two horses. Then they would follow, like folk pursuing an enchanter. The din of their excitement began to bubble up. It was a holiday; they were avid to witness this royal judgement. In their hearts they knew Perkin Warbeck like a villainous son; his confessions and disclosures had lit their dull days, his treason was meat for their gossip, and for a short season he had rocked their world.

All through the City the crowd doubled and trebled, halted and massed, as they swarmed towards Ludgate Hill and St Paul's, and out through Newgate into the meadows of death. They came from Thames Street, from Billingsgate and Petty Wales, from Fleet and the Inns of Court, from the parishes of St Mary-le-Strand and St Bride. And from Westminster, the lords and sheriffs, horsed and arrayed in velvet grandeur to see justice. The constables of the Watch moved among the people arresting pickpockets. Adding to the fierce gaiety were troupes of

363

mountebanks, stiltwalkers, women with trays of pippins and hot Spanish chestnuts for sale. As I neared Mistress Seward's shop, a man with a dancing bear, chained and muzzled, opened a way before me as the people lurched and scattered and laughed. Beggars moaned round them for alms.

Mistress Seward was in her back room, nursing herself by a smoky fire. She looked up startled at first, then with a small recognition. I took her hand, twisted with rheumatism, and made it into a funnel, then poured in a chinking stream. I closed her fist tight. She started to cry, and so did I.

'Buy medicines,' I said. 'Buy fuel. Buy comfort.'

'Why, master?' she said, and quickly dried her eyes.

'I was hungry once,' I said. I left her then. There had been no satisfaction in it. I was still hungry.

As quickly as I could I went to all the shops and stalls from which I had collected Frays' dues, and as quickly as I could put money in their hands or in their coffers. Some laughed in a kind of fear, some pocketed the money and looked eagerly for more, and one man fell to his knees before me, saying I had come from God as he was on the brink of ruin. And some shook me off as a madman, eager to close shutters and be away to the hanging. But word spread none the less, and a skein of cripples and beggars began to follow me. The children came from their alley lairs, bone-meagre, with eyes like holes in snow. I scattered little coins among them, and they began bloodily to fight on the cobbles, tearing mercilessly at one another, and, fearful that I did more harm than good, I put the remainder of my money away. And there was no joy in any of it—no righteousness. It was like bringing a doctor to a dead man.

When I reached the cookshop where Patch's horse was saddled and waiting outside, my sleeves were torn and my heartbeat ragged. I was twitching with a palsy of grief past and to come. The old man was standing before the fireplace, frowning.

'At last,' he said when he saw me. 'You and I had an appointment, Master Nicholas. Now we shall have a poor view of the hanging.'

He had a little monkey on his shoulder, a living penance of a thing, bristling with fleas. It clung to his ear, and wrapped its tail round his throat.

'You like my pet? His Majesty gave it to me. It's the same one that ate his privy account book.'

He seemed calm yet jocular, so dispassionate that he fed my despair. The noise of people passing outside buzzed against the window.

'We might as well wait now until the crowd has passed,' he said. 'Soon, they'll be bringing the feigned boy through town, riding on his hurdle.'

Sure enough, from the direction of Tower Hill, the noise soared, not so much in volume as to a new pitch of intent, a glory of jeering.

Patch sat down in the inglenook. 'They're hanging Atwater with him today,' he said. 'His Majesty thought it time Ireland had a sharp lesson.' He squinted at me. 'Sit down, Master Nicholas, or you'll fall down. I'll tell you about the trials in Westminster Hall. Nobody could agree on the charge, but they settled in the end on conspiracy. They charged the Earl of Warwick, along with Thomas Astwood and his partner Blowet, and Cleymound—fat beer-belly—with conspiring with Perkin Warbeck. First the messages were passed through a hole in the floor and then by the jailers. Then there were guilty men on the outside—old Tom Mashborough, Philip Proud and a few others . . . are you listening, Master?'

I hunched near the fire. The monkey leaped on to my shoulder. Like me, it was shivering, and scratched me with its little paw.

'Conspiracy of what?' I whispered.

'The Earl of Warwick plotted to seize the Tower, the Crown Jewels, and to set fire to all the gunpowder stored within the Tower,' chanted Patch. 'And to set Master Warbeck on the throne of England.'

He opened and closed an eye.

'Astwood and Blowet are to be hanged next week. Thomas Mashborough is imprisoned for life, but he's a poor old man. Proud was reprieved for reason of his youth. And bigbelly Cleymound was never brought to trial. He was the *provocateur*, you see, Master Nicholas.'

'Earl Warwick is witless—imbecile,' I said. 'He is incapable of such machinations.'

'His will be a private beheading on Tower Green, in five days' time.' Patch gave a sigh; it vanished as the wild sounds from the street grew. 'And now, Master Nicholas, King Henry will be able to sleep of nights again. England will sleep too, in peace. There will be no more risings. No more feigned boys. There will be no more Plantagenets.' He patted his shoulder, and the monkey leaped. 'I trust his Majesty,' he said. 'He rules England wisely and well. He is passing clever in his ways. He governs without mercy, as a king must.'

He got up. 'Time to go. You can hold my stirrup.'

The noise outside changed from a babble into a wild yell, and somewhere in the noise's core were the sound of hoofs and the drag of wood on the cobbles. A child screamed, clearly a woman burst out sobbing, there was cheering and a smack of fists and oaths as a fight broke out. Patch's horse was nervous and shied as I held it for him to mount. Ahead the crowd was a mass of backs, following the focus of their excitement. I could see only the swaying rumps of the horses, and then the crowd parted. I saw, strapped to the hurdles, their heads bumping the ground at every step, John Atwater and my prince, Richard.

So we followed them to Newgate and into the meadows of Tyburn—I kept my hand on the horse's stirrup and my eyes on the ground, and one prayer throbbed on and on in my heart. Let him not be tortured. This, sweet God, is all I ask. His fate is fixed. But let him not suffer or scream. Divine Fisher of men, show mercy.

There was a good view for Patch after all. A steward had kept it for the royal jester. Fine day for it, he remarked to us pleasantly. And an orderly crowd, Christ be praised.

O Christ be praised for ever and ever if somehow he escapes the disembowelling. I looked wildly about. There was a family of jugglers entertaining the people and a puppet show. A giant youth was allowing himself to be punched in the face for three-pence a time. The drawn hurdles came into the space before the scaffold. Atwater was almost unconscious from the rough journey, but my lord stared at the sky, and his hands moved as they unbound him. He stood up of his own will, and mounted to the gallows with steps far steadier than mine. They haltered him. Nearby a butcher sharpened his knives, and fire burned in a brazier.

So, for the last of all my debts, I made my head steady and did not look away. I saw that in the recent past he had been racked; his one shoulder was out of joint and his fingers broken. There was dried blood on his mouth and he was streaked from head to foot with the dung of the streets. I thought of him garbed for his wedding-day, but did not weep, for my eyes must be clear for this final act.

The herald finished reading out the charges. Some ermined lord put the confession into my master's hand, but his broken fingers could not hold it. They stretched it in front of his eyes, and he began in a hoarse, faint voice, for the last time: *Be it known to all men* . . .

After it was done, he stepped forward at the rope's end, as if to be closer to the people. I looked lovingly at him—the mired, once-golden hair—his shirt, I recognized a hole I had mended in it long ago—the weary, wounded eye, the tall grace. The majesty, even now, of his stance. I saw his torn lips move. He whispered to the air *Pray for me*, and then, unmistakably, soundlessly: I AM RICHARD. Then the executioner began his work.

Something went amiss with the hangman's rope. It was meant to strangle him slowly, but as the trestle leaped away from under his feet he dropped like a falling falcon. I had seen death, and I knew he was dead. Even as they began to butcher his body, I knew they could not touch him. He was beyond them all, and he had shown no fear.

'I am going home now,' said Patch crossly in my ear. The monkey, terrified by the frenzy of the crowd, was half-choking him with its tail. 'Death to all the King's enemies!' he called loudly, his voice drowned by the hubbub. Then he said, close to my face: 'Well, master? Who was he, this Perkin of yours?'

'It is of no matter who he was,' I said. 'He bore himself like a prince. He was my lord. I loved him.'

'So be it,' said Patch, struggling up on to his horse. He looked at me very hard, and said very soft: 'My Queen will weep tonight.'

When he had gone, I wandered for an hour, my heart numbed in grief, yet with a tiny glow, like kindled embers, token of my answered prayer. When Atwater was dead, in equal mercy, his head and that of Richard were struck off to be displayed on

London Bridge, while their bodies were taken to the House of the Augustine Friars for burial. Almost devoid of thought, I stood unseeing before the booth of an entertainer. From empty air he produced a growing apple tree, complete with fruit, and made it disappear the next instant. Illusion, he told the few awed watchers. Illusion. The people were fast dispersing. I stood alone. Then suddenly I felt a hand slip under the side of my mantle and remove my purse. A very small hand, not much bigger than the monkey's paw, and icy cold as I gripped it in its secret flight.

He looked up at me. He was about nine years old, the winter breeze played among his rags, his bare feet were crusted with the mud of months. His nose was running and his face filthy. But his eyes were beautiful, so blue they were almost violet, and black curls, matted and verminous, fell to his shoulders. As I held his wrist, he stared deep into my eyes, defiant and pleading.

'You villain,' I said softly.

He smiled enchantingly, and began to praise me with lordly names: 'Please, great sir.' Then gave a sharp tug to free himself, but I held him fast. So he swore at me, vile maledictions, then burst into tears, imploring, his nose a fountain, that I should not turn him over to the Watch. He wouldn't do it again, he vowed it on his life. It was just this devil-damned hunger.

'Come with me,' I said. I led him over to a now deserted ale-stall and sat with him on a bench. I took my handkerchief and tried to clean his face.

'So you're hungry? We must do something about that. Where do you live?'

'Nowhere. I used to live in Kent. My mother died last month and I ran away. My mother used to live in London, at the tavern.'

'Which tavern? Have you no family? Where's your father?'

He shrugged. 'Dead. Years ago. I was with my grand-dad in Kent. It was him I ran from.' He shivered as the wind blew his shirt up. Someone had beaten him badly not long ago; there were marks on his thin body.

'What's your name?' I still held his wrist, but he had stopped resisting.

'I sleep with the dog,' he said. 'In the yard at the tavern. They don't know I'm there. They put out food, you see, for the dog.'

'Sweet God,' I said. 'Which tavern?' Then, as this seemed a lost cause: 'What is your name? Don't you have a name?'

'Nicholas Finch,' he said. 'The Eagle tavern. My mother once worked there. Agnes, they called her.'

There was a red rush to my eyes and my ears for an instant. The boy was looking up at me curiously. I no longer held his wrist, but he moved closer.

'Sir?' he whispered. I had the purse in my hand. I said:

'Then this is your money, Nicholas Finch. Much of it is your father's. You were right to take it.' He was frowning, wary of my flights of fancy. He was still shivering, and he seemed thinner by the minute. I looked into his eyes. They were all there—the three beasts: the leopard of lust, the lion of pride, the wolf of avarice. But they were unawakened, and he was mine. Mine to guard, to love, to teach. Mine. Piers had said it: *Someone will be sent.* I began to think that Piers was not just a near-saint, he was a prophet.

'Nicholas,' I said, 'will you come back with me? To the Greyfriars?'

'To the monks?' he said doubtfully. Then, brighter: 'Will there be food?'

'Much food,' I said. 'And a fire. Safety, warm clothes. And you have an uncle there. And you will have me.'

I could also have said: And your father's grave. I had seen it—a strip of stone in a green garth; it held no terrors.

He thought about it for no more than a moment. Then he stood up and took my hand, and, leaning on the bitter wind, we led one another back along the old ways made new.

Piers was waiting anxiously: I could see him peering through the little door by the belfry, but still we entered slowly, as if the journey had been from the world's end. Illumination filled me—thoughts from the past: the weaver's law—how God will sort our crimes, the long from the short fleeces. How, when the weaver's work is turned about, the knots are hidden, the colours clear, a perfect piece of cloth, most pleasing to God. And Henryson's lessons—of the loyal dog and the birds. I could say now that the dog had been at his master's side to the last, his prayer answered.

As for the birds: they would return to their battered brown

369

home, a safe lodging. But now they were flying far, above the striving wind. Buffeted and blown, yet like the souls of the beloved dead, nearer and nearer to heaven.